Praise f~~ ᵀᴬᵗ~ ···

D.K. Maylor and his bud‹   f
spiritual meaning—deconst   ;
as the sacrificial scapegoat v
with his crucifixion. And, ‹   ...,..₃ ...a..es great sense AND
offers a much better interpretation of 'salvation.' . . . The message of this real
meaning of Christianity rings true . . . and his explication of spirituality is
logical, appealing and inspiring . . . and it results in a rich spiritual teaching
appropriate to the 21st Century. It stirred up so many wonderful feelings and
insights for me. This is a *marvelous* book. I loved it and want to recommend it.

—Toby Johnson, author of *The Myth of the Great Secret:*
An Appreciation of Joseph Campbell

Though Maylor's book will probably captivate anyone of faith—or even
of no religious interest at all—it is a *must-read* for every serious Christian,
and especially for those who consider themselves to be "fundamentalists."
The book is cleverly and provocatively written, in both cadence and content,
making it a simple, humorous and delightful read and easy to turn the page.
Much of what is covered in this engaging dialogue will certainly cause the
open-minded to reconsider the outrageous claims of religion over the years.
Perhaps more importantly, the interview not only takes a critical look at
Christianity, using verifiable facts and intelligent discussion, but also leads
the reader to a nicely laid out explanation of spiritual unity. In short, this
book should be at the TOP of every Christian's reading list and could really
serve to change lives, and maybe religion itself, very quickly—the book is
that powerful and compelling. Until it's read, you don't understand your faith.

—Reader M.G., London, UK

Frankly, I've never given Christianity or religion much thought, so when a
friend recommended reading *Wrestling with Jesus*, I wasn't enthusiastic—
but finally I yielded because he praised it so highly. I'm glad I did because
"*Wrestling*" is a truly extraordinary book and is exceptionally well written,
extensively researched, loaded with fascinating facts, and often surprisingly
entertaining. This wonderful book has been a real eye-opener and probably
will be for almost anyone, from the skeptical to the ultra-pious. D.K. Maylor
deserves to be lauded for having the courage to write this controversial,
but valuable and powerfully enlightening book. Bravo, Mr. Maylor, Bravo!!

—Caleb Spalding Atwood, Author of *Quip Factory*

A monumental work! I read the first 12 Chapters and did not want to stop. Excellent research, humor, history, and mind-altering views of a political church. As a person raised as a Christian, I consider this a real gift to put spirituality back into life. D.K. Maylor has done a fantastic job of bringing clarity to a very sensitive, vital part of existence. A must-read, long-overdue book about spirituality. Great writing on the level of great literature. One caveat: if you become emotionally triggered, keep reading. It's worth it.

—Amazon Reviewer P. Huffington, M.D.

I am an 83-year-old Emeritus Professor of Philosophy who also has a Ph.D. from the Divinity school of the University of Chicago. Though primarily a philosophy prof (Kierkegaard, Heidegger, existentialism, phenomenology), I usually taught one course in either Old or New Testament each year for about 40 years—and I am most impressed with your remarkable book! You certainly put a great deal of both research and thought into it. And you have a number of highly quotable, relevant one-line comments. I wish I had thought to write these down as I came across them.

—George Guthrie, Ph.D.

Mr. Maylor, you write masterfully!!! I know I have an instant worldwide Classic in my hands!!!! Masterful! You've written a classic! In fact, THE classic!!!!!!!!!!!!! I believe you received "grace" from the Holy Spirit to do this work. I could NOT give you higher praise.

—Brother Tony Hearn, contemplative ecumenical anchorite, Community of the Blessed Mother; former university professor and theology student at Oblate seminary

Maylor nailed it all; the confusion of the 'church' teachings, the offensive historical behavior of 'Jesus's Church,' the disaster of human delusion when it comes to simple TRUTH . . . This book brings light to dark understandings of Jesus and allows some fresh revelations and 'expansions' of consciousness to grow and take root . . . Maylor did a great service to humanity and to future generations by writing this book. I recommend it to everyone.

—Amazon Reviewer 'Bobby'

This book liberated me from the doctrine of the church and helped me to embrace the real meaning of Christianity. It has opened my heart and my mind, which allows me to continue my spiritual growth. *Wrestling with Jesus* is inspirational. I highly recommend it.

—Amazon Reviewer 'Sharon'

In a humorous and at times irreverent discourse with our great Master, Jesus, D.K. Maylor has articulated the profound confusion that many of us feel when trying to grasp the underlying "facts" of the Bible. Maylor identifies the inconsistent, and often times contradictory, statements of the "Good Book," and questions the portrait of an angry God that is painted throughout much of the Bible. Through a probing dialogue with Jesus, we are given new clarity in the Christian message, and a spiritual viewpoint that is refreshing, uplifting and potentially life changing. This is a must read for Christians *and* non-Christians who want to better understand the underlying spiritual message as given to us by Jesus."

—Amazon Reviewer Susan M., M.D.

An insightful, entertaining, thought-provoking, multi-faceted *tete-a-tete* with Christology. Made me reverse course to my parochial teachings and lit a fire for me to examine such teachings from a different and challenging angle. From the prologue to the last page, a refreshing examination of dogma and the written word. Recommended!!

—Mark Matthiessen, international magazine writer
and author of the *Shelby's Creek* novel series

After reading this book, my relationship with Jesus has changed dramatically. He is now my best friend. I laughed and cried. It touched me. Now my 15-year-old is reading it. Thank You, Mr. Maylor—your book lifted me back up again.

—Amazon Reviewer Jeanette DiPasquale

Supported with an abundance of historical facts, this comprehensive work will make any free-thinking individual look inward and reassess their spirituality, regardless of their faith—or lack of it. The book is page after page after page of stimulating, thought-provoking stuff. Highly, highly recommended must-read. And be sure to bring your sense of humor; the book can be super funny at times. This is no dry, tedious read—it's fun!!

—Amazon Reviewer 'Mountain Chick'

As a Hindu, I found a lot in common between what 'Jesus' says in the book and what I have studied in Hinduism . . . The beauty of this book is that it reflects complex ideas in an engaging and understandable prose. It's a book to be re-read many times because it is dense and full of wonderful information and insights.

—Amazon Reviewer Ranjani V.

WRESTLING
with JESUS

A global gift of love and liberation

Third (revised) edition

D. K. MAYLOR

CONTENTS

All truth passes through three stages. First, it is ridiculed. Second, it is violently opposed. Third, it is accepted as being self-evident.

The discovery of truth is prevented more effectively, not by the false appearance things present and which mislead into error, not directly by weakness of the reasoning powers, but by preconceived opinion, by prejudice.

—German philosopher Arthur Schopenhauer (1788–1860)

People often claim to hunger for truth, but seldom like the taste when it's served up.

—George R. R. Martin

And the Spirit shall teach you all things and shall bring all things to your remembrance.

—John 14:26

PROLOGUE

Looking back now, I see that his plan made sense. The tantalizing mix of secrecy and symbol, the lighthearted intrigue—the gradual outwitting of my resistance. It must have been clear that I wasn't yet ready for a spiritual head-on collision. The spirit was quite *willing*, I assure you, but vision was far too weak.

So, even as the life-changing moment drew near, I never could have envisioned the astonishing events that awaited nor the serious danger they would pose to the empires of faith. Luckily the hours ahead were still wrapped in mystery as I pulled off the interstate and drove toward country just after dawn.

A beautifully clear spring morning was spreading across the Old South, and the rising sun thawed the lingering chill as I drove to a secluded area near a quiet river, not far from a lush section of foothills. With first rays of light sneaking over the summits, I was struck by the resulting silhouette: a near-perfect rendering of a dove in flight. While Mother Nature's timely shadow art was unexpected, the overall setting was not . . . this was most surely the place I'd been seeing in my dreams.

The dreams weren't prophetic, though. I wasn't having visions of some mystical, unknown locale. I had traveled this part of the country thirty years earlier while taking a break from college. Not sure of my life's direction after squeaking past my sophomore year, I decided to drift awhile and search for some sign of my purpose—my reason for being on the planet. And even though that trip of my youth had been routine and uneventful, somehow this particular place stuck with me.

Driving along in the dim early morning light, I hadn't seen another car for at least ten minutes. Nearing the destination, I pulled off the road and maneuvered my old GMC truck through an opening in the dense forest. I drove maybe two hundred yards, weaved my way back to sunlight and parked in a clearing just past the trees.

Alone amidst the woods, I had entered my own paradise—luxuriant spreads of exploding electric greenness spanning about two hundred acres along both sides of the river. The forest was much taller and thicker than I had remembered from when I came vision-questing through it those many years ago, but I knew it instantly as the place I once visited and recently had seen again in my dreams.

The area was deserted excepting a few deer across the river and the birds chirping and squawking in the trees. Seeing no man-made structures or any sign of a landowner—surely I was trespassing again—I climbed from the truck, popped the rear hatch, grabbed two folding wooden chairs and positioned them beneath some majestic oaks with their dewy wind-flapped leaves fluttering life-green and vibrant from recent springtime rains. Twenty feet away, an unruffled river flowed through from the nearby hills, and thriving clusters of water lilies nestled in a few small inlets along the banks.

Here, near the water's edge, I began arranging my bare-bones 'field office.' Between the two chairs with their seat cushions, I sat a small, round patio table—about two feet high—and cluttered it with some pens, a clipboard, bottled water and a new 500-sheet box of my favorite writing paper. Beside one chair, I placed a large leather satchel containing a few personal items and some books, including several versions of the Bible and a dictionary. The scene now looked almost exactly the way it did in those strange, recurrent dreams.

℘

The morning breeze was cold and brisk, but the sun was brilliant, warm, and comforting—even healing. The fresh country air was clean and crisp and seemed to mirror my own budding sense of *inner* clarity. I grew philosophical. Have we missed something? Have we spent our lives reaching and straining, hurrying hither and yonder, bartering away our limited breaths and heartbeats while we scrape tooth-and-nail for baskets of junk, and all with the precious gems of creation strewn at our feet?

I had known for many years that, by American standards, I basically missed the boat. I owned very little and had never even mortgaged a house. Divorced many years and still without a life companion, I had no family of my own and made my way through freelance journalism and occasional odd jobs on the side. Apart from college days, I had lived more than thirty years in my south Texas homeland just three hours from the Mexican state of Tamaulipas.

Admittedly, my unconventional lifestyle—and that's putting it kindly— had taken its toll on the psyche over the years. But on this magical day I was free of all neediness or lack, flowing in a joyfully uplifting awareness of timeless existence. I felt no need to peer into the future nor any want to swim reminiscently in the proverbial water under the bridge. My world felt suddenly complete, though every piece that's said to bring us 'happiness' was missing. Blissful in a way I had forgotten was possible, I suddenly thought that I couldn't be happier if God himself walked in.

℘

In the dreams that brought me here, I was seated in one of the chairs on this very spot near the river under the oaks. I didn't know why, but the second chair had always remained empty. Now, I've never assigned much meaning to dreams and I rarely even remember them. I've certainly felt no need to analyze them. But this dream was different, and I recalled it every morning when I awoke. Aside from its mystery and persistence, however, it was quite unremarkable and plain. Except for one odd thing . . .

In each dream, as I calmly sit in my chair next to the river, enjoying the view and not thinking of anything in particular, there on the ground around me lay several brightly colored Easter eggs.

A few weeks later, the dreams stopped just as suddenly as they began. But even if short on content, they got my attention. I *had* to re-visit the place—a two-day drive eastward near one of the huge forest preserves on the far side of the great Mississippi River. (In respect of its residents I won't disclose the location, so let us call it 'somewhere in Dixie.')

Heeding the apparent dream message of the eggs, I planned my arrival for the Christian holy day of Easter. I felt that something big could happen, but even this limited intuition was nothing specific and no hint was given of the freight train barreling toward me.

Several weeks before the dreams, I considered writing a book based on some powerful spiritual lessons I'd been learning. It seemed that, subconsciously, this might explain the reason for the dreams. Were they a sign that a concept for the book would finally crystallize, there in the serenity of the isolated river valley? Pen and paper at hand, I was ready for inspiration. Now all I needed was the Muse.

With everything in place and still wearing a light nylon jacket, I sat in the chair on the left and drew a few long, deep breaths as the waking sun cradled me like a baby in the warmth of its primeval womb. I melted into its fiery, ancient nurture and thought how many wayfaring souls throughout history must surely have gained solace from the sweet, profound glory of a simple sunrise. For a few sacred minutes I sat, eyes closed, soaking up Brother Sun's radiance into every cell. It was indeed a glorious Easter morning, and soon I would be resurrected.

☙

What happened next I still cannot explain. The strain of unconventional life had taken its price, I confess, and some within my orbit have suggested I only *imagined* it, suffering as I had from those years of financial distress. Or maybe I simply fell into a sort of half-sleep and had what's known as a lucid dream, when one plays director of his own slumber time wanderings from somewhere in consciousness limbo.

But never mind technicalities. After all, what does it matter how a man like Jesus shows up? No one's going to believe it anyway. In hindsight, the strangest part of the confab wasn't that I was meeting with one of the most prominent figures in history, or even that the man had emerged from spending two full millennia stone dead.

No, the most peculiar thing about my day with Jesus was I felt no sense of marvel at the time. I was *energized* in a way I had never experienced but had no feelings of awe because of *him*—and not until later did any strange feelings arise. Not once on that momentous day did I question its bizarre reality.

But that is precisely the thing: I did not *perceive* it as bizarre. Conversing with Jesus felt as natural as meeting a friend for some coffee or talking with the guys at the gym.

I should mention, though, that when the gathering ended I did sense a weird warping of time and was somewhat confused, unsure of the typically clear boundary between experience and fancy. The feeling reminded me of creepy testimonials I had read about alien abductions. I couldn't tell whether I had temporarily *entered* reality—or temporarily *left*. Either way, what happened in those remarkable hours remains seared in my memory and was, for me, as real as a rainstorm . . . solid as a woodman's axe.

☙

Due to the far-fetched nature of this account, the reader may wonder of my background. Reared in various conservative Protestant churches from early childhood and having once considered entering the ministry, I abandoned Christianity at age thirty-six and have now gone more than a decade with no desire to revisit those roots. To me, the church had become irrelevant. I wanted neither its cloudy, futuristic comforts nor its pressing, uneasy demands. Jesus became—in my world, at least—hardly more than a name. Not just *any* name, of course, for his is one charged with passion, perplexity and mystique. A name with exceptional historical impact . . . and even after centuries of his absence.

Jesus Christ. Powerful. But utterly vulnerable, too. Indeed, what strange or freakish thing has not been claimed, performed or attempted in this man's name? And all the while, silence. Not one public response from this allegedly risen savior since his cruel, sordid death long ago. Still, his influence remains undiluted; and for many, the mere mention of the man evokes deep and visceral response.

Jesus: the most loaded word of God.

☙

Suddenly the word became flesh. With no announcement or fanfare, one of history's most commanding figures—the man known as Jesus of Nazareth, two thousand years deceased—had coolly appeared from the forest like a laid-back camper on a hike. He walked from the woods to my right and strolled easily into the clearing toward my humble workplace by the water.

And yes, it all happened just that fast. Jesus had come as he once warned he might—quietly, like a thief in the dark. Without speaking, he gave a friendly, acknowledging nod as he took in the view, clearly appreciating the invigorating backcountry beauty. I was so comfortable in his presence, I barely gave it a second thought. And though Jesus was very attentive, he too was quite informal and relaxed.

I recognized Jesus immediately—but to this day I cannot say why. Too long suckered by the arts, I had always seen him as the sweet-looking fellow in Da Vinci's or Bassano's depictions of The Last Supper. Aside from his clothes, however, Jesus looked nothing like his Western stereotype. No classic Hollywood jaw line, hazel eyes, or long, flowing chestnut hair.

So, how did I realize it was Jesus? I honestly don't know. I can say for sure that even though his *features* were unexpected, his identity—his *presence*—was as dear as that of a brother.

He was, I would say, a somewhat handsome man, though probably not a candidate for the covers of celebrity magazines. Fit and slightly muscular, he appeared to be in his mid- to late-forties. About five-ten, he weighed maybe a hundred and sixty pounds and was dressed in a long, off-white toga covering all but the bare right arm, just as in movies about the period. Old leather sandals were strapped to his feet and—except for the biblical garb—for the most part he was average Mideastern. His skin was very much darker than usually imagined and his hair thick and curly, black with a few woven strands of gray. His eyes were dark and piercing and a short, scruffy black beard covered most of his face. Even at a small backyard cookout, no one going by the usual pictures would know him.

When our eyes finally locked, his gaze was compelling and I could hardly look away. His smiles were kindly but mischievous, and he acted so familiar it was almost like we roomed awhile in college. Without shaking hands (I realized the following day that we never actually touched) he sat in the chair on my right. Hiding embarrassment for my interest, I glanced at his hands and feet. But I would quickly learn that thoughts, for Jesus, were freshly hung laundry on a line for all neighbors to see.

"No scars," he said. "That was never the point."

We both knew why we were there. I had long yearned for answers, and Jesus was obliging me with an interview.

With this brief recounting of events, I will now let the following dialogue speak for itself. Here, then, is the talk that unfolded on that marvelous day by the river . . .

☙

CHAPTER ONE

DK: Well, I should've known. Just when a fella's found a refuge from the storm, in walks some hippie to break the peace.

J: Show a little gratitude, pilgrim, that Milky Way traffic's a nightmare.

DK: *Heh heh.* Sorta figured this trip might hold a surprise or two. Clever how you laid the groundwork, what with the dreams and all. You do this kind of thing often?

J: Just when it's fitting. I work best in realms of the spirit . . . I find that it's safer that way.

DK: Yes, I would imagine so. Your biblical life was no summer in the alps.

J: No, I meant that it's safer for *you*. When word gets out that I popped in on someone, they're vilified, worshiped or hauled off to an asylum.

DK: Prob'ly not an issue with me. Some *already* think I'm nuts and my pedigrees aren't that impressive—so I've got no rep to defend. And really, I don't much care anymore what people *think*.

J: Seems you've attained quite a level of spiritual detachment.

DK: The blessing of the underachiever. But what I lack in ambition I gain in more sleep.

J: I see straight off the bat I've found the right guy . . .

[Jesus had a sharp sense of humor and it surprised me. Wanting to get a better feel before getting *too* cavalier, I wasn't quite sure how to proceed— he's been so long revered that I didn't want to seem too casual or presuming. I gathered pen and paper to start taking notes in shorthand, but He picked right up on my reluctance to really let loose and be myself.]

J: Hey, do me a favor. Take me down from the crucifix and talk like you'd talk to a friend. I don't want this discussion coming off like a rehash of the King James Bible. Real discourse must always take place among *equals*— so making me something special poisons the pond.

DK: Alright, what do you suggest?

1

J: Talking like two buddies over a friendly glass of beer. No pretension, no formality—no holding back or playing it safe. Just honest, everyday chat.

DK: Okay, you got it . . .
    So here I am, face-to-face with history's most famous carpenter. I guess I should start by saying thank you. By the way—why *me*?

J: Network guys were booked.

DK: Serves me right, fishing for some praise.

J: And just for the record, I wasn't a carpenter. Wouldn't know a sawhorse from an old cow pony.

DK: But the sixth chapter of Mark's gospel says th—

J: I know, it says I was a carpenter. It's hard getting past a couple thousand years of tradition. You may not know it, but that passage from Mark is the only New Testament verse calling me a carpenter. The story says people were astonished by my teachings and the miracles happening around me. They asked, "Is not this the carpenter, the son of Mary?"

DK: Yeah, seems pretty clear.

J: But there's a problem. Although the word was translated "carpenter," it's also used to describe a very scholarly person or teacher, even a great builder—someone who's a master of his trade. In the gospels, at least seven different groups called me Rabbi, which means teacher, and various passages have people referring to my "authority" and to my "teachings." Carpenters didn't have authority, they weren't called "teacher," and they weren't commonly known for their teachings. So, considering there's not another scrap of evidence I was a woodworker, which meaning makes more sense?

DK: Okay, let's go with teacher. But wherefore the longtime confusion, Rabbi?

J: Translators blew it, that's all. Probably just an honest mistake. It happens a lot. To convey just a hint of the challenges in Bible translation, consider the beautiful prologue to the gospel of John. The passage famously opens, "In the beginning was the Word . . ." The original *Greek* text, though, says that in the beginning was the LOGOS—a concept so crucial to the ancient Greek world, it would merit a talk of its own. To make a point, however, the term LOGOS has more than half a dozen different and deeply interwoven meanings, not *one* of which would ever be translated "Word."

2

DK: So, like the LOGOS translation, Mark's "carpenter" bit was just an unfortunate scholarly screw-up.

J: Or possibly an intended one. The story is also recorded in the thirteenth chapter of Matthew. In that account the people asked, "Is not this the carpenter's *son*?" Now they've got my *father* doing the hammering. The Bible has loads of discrepancies like that. Some Christians justify this one by concluding that Joseph and I *both* must have been carpenters.

DK: Doesn't seem likely if you really did come from royal blood.

J: That 'throne of David' stuff is only dramatic New Testament spin. I mean how can Christians state with certainty my Hebraic lineage, when Jewish scripture experts still know nothing about it? My family and I were never members of the ruling class or the dynastic hierarchy, but neither were we the common laborers people envision. I didn't mean to start with a lecture, though—I just wanna set things straight on a few fundamentals. It could be a while before I get back this way.

DK: And that begs a critical point. Humanity's waited *twenty centuries* for this. What took you so long?

J: Once martyred, twice shy.

DK: Seriously . . . after you disappeared, you made no further statements or appearances. What happened?

J: Oh, I still talk with anyone who's willing—but some need more *substance* than others. Talk between bodies is the only kind of dialogue they know.

DK: People like *me*, you mean.

J: Right. So that's why I'm here. You believe that having a body is the one way to exist and communicate and that death instantly breaks the connection. This common belief that conveyance with the 'dead' is impossible is what makes it, in fact, nearly impossible. This is why, when someone leaves the planet, the crowd loses interest pretty quick.

DK: Well, they didn't lose interest in *you*.

J: No, in my case they heard all the miracle stories and made me another earth god, casting me as 'savior' in those lofty, reverent tones you hear in church . . . like the phony way people talk of a guy at his funeral. I'm idolized and deified—turned into a kind of superhero.

3

DK: Apparently you *are* a superhero.

J: In what way?

DK: Just as you implied: hundreds of millions still see you as 'God's only son.' Been like that twenty centuries now.

J: Sure, the claim is that this energy we call 'God' has only one true cosmic child—the kid had to be male, of course—mystically conceived within Mary's womb, and with no other human involved. I'm surprised more people haven't asked why this surrogate mother process wasn't used when creating Adam. For *him* God needed only mud and a minute for sculpting.

DK: What's that got to do with you?

J: Well, if God had really wanted to make an impression and prove my divinity to the world, why mess with the murky, drawn-out drama connected with a controversial pregnancy? Why not get everyone down to the beach and have me descend from the sky, right before their disbelieving eyes. Wouldn't that lend a lot more credibility?

DK: The church says your humanity was a crucial part of the gig— so skydiving wouldn't do the trick. Anyhow, it's not just the story of your birth that makes you different. Scripture makes *many* claims of your specially divine nature. At your baptism in the river, a voice from heaven declares, "This is my beloved son, in whom I am well pleased."

J: But the voiceover bit wasn't new. Two thousand years before my birth, the Pyramid Texts reported the coronation ceremony of a pharaoh in which God proclaims, "He is my beloved son, in whom I am well pleased." So the magical heavenly blessing story was a rip-off from the beginning. And the vaporous voice doesn't say or imply that I'm the *only* "beloved son."

DK: Well, I think we just assume that yo—

J: Not so fast with your assumptions. I never claimed specialness or favor, nor did I call myself the only child of God. And what a thing to say in the first place!

DK: What about your declaration, "I and my Father are one"?

J: I was merely stating a fact. The Father and I are one, and the Father and *you* are one as well. I was simply *aware* of my unity with everything, while most people just didn't get it. If I were the one man gifted with

4

potential for Christ-consciousness, I never would've taught my disciples to "be perfect as your heavenly Father is perfect." I urged them to follow my example and become shining mirrors of Source. How could they do this if their nature was unlike my own? It would've been asking the impossible. So I viewed everyone as equals. I knew their full potential and I often referred to God as *their* heavenly Father, too. Even my best-known prayer starts with salutation to "*Our* Father."

DK: What about this one: following your capture in the gospel of Mark, the high priest asks you pointedly, "Are you the Christ, the Son of the Blesséd?" Your answer is, "I am."

J: That story's told in each of the New Testament gospels—and all four tell it differently. Matthew says that Caiaphas demanded, "tell us if you are the Christ, the Son of God." In that version my quoted response is only, "*You* have said so."

The gospel of Luke has another variation: "and they said, 'If you are the Christ, tell us.'" There I'm said to have replied, "If I tell you, you will not believe; and if I ask you, you will not answer." Which sounds more like double-talk from an indicted politician.

In the gospel of John, there's no mention of Caiaphas even *asking* of my divinity. As for that quote from Mark, I'm not answering Caiaphas' question in the affirmative or I would just say "Yes." I'm merely stating an obvious existential reality: *I am*. This simple assertion has been used by mystical teachers for thousands of years and shows a knowing of Self as part of the timeless, spaceless, nameless Absolute— the One, the All, that which has no traits or limitations. Most people just call it God.

DK: Not exactly a *Christian* idea.

J: Not for *present*-day Christians, perhaps. Yet, one of the most respected church patriarchs, Clement of Alexandria, talked of this very idea when discussing God, or what Greek cosmology calls "First Cause"—the mystery from which all things in Universe arise. For Saint Clement, God was beyond space, time, name, or even conception, and has no definable attributes.

DK: But that's not a *biblical* thing.

J: Are you sure? In Exodus 3, Moses tells Yahweh that the Israelites are pressing him to determine God's name. But Yahweh tells Moses only this: "I AM THAT I AM." Moses then returns to his people and announces, "I AM hath sent me unto you." In John 8:58, I explain that the eternal I AM existed even long before Abraham.

DK: Yes, and they almost killed you for saying it.

J: They didn't get the gist of my teaching. But even when I'm quoted in the gospels making an "I am" statement, it's often followed by a metaphor.

DK: "I am the vine; you are the branches."

J: Yeah, symbolic stuff like that. Anything after the words "I am" is fleeting—another false impression of yourself. Masters know that only the eternal is real, so that's where they place their attention. Whenever they say "I am," they teach a reality far beyond surface labels.

DK: And I thought my college *philosophy* tests were tricky. But getting back to that meeting with Caiaphas . . . the gospel writer says you informed Caiaphas that he would see you return and then watch you assume world leadership at what you described as "the right hand" of God.

J: It would've been condescending, to say the least. And Caiaphas didn't live to see anything like it.

DK: Okay, here's another twist in the story: in answering Caiaphas' question on your divinity, the scripture writer has you calling yourself not the "Son of God," but the "Son of *man*." And this wasn't the only time you referenced yourself that way.

J: Scripture writers took creative license. "Son of man" was an ancient designation for someone representing all humanity. You think I went preaching my way through Palestine as "the Son of man"? *That's* a little weird, don't you think?

DK: So, others were given that same prestigious title?

J: Oh, lots of 'em—even in pre-Christian writings. One work from the Dead Sea Scrolls, Book of Enoch, predates Christianity by a hundred and fifty years and has Enoch as a kind of messiah character who ascends to heaven and is welcomed as the "Son of man." A divine "messenger of God" known as "the Christ," he's even called "a light unto the Gentiles." Any of this sounding familiar?

DK: Sure, but why all the squabbling over *you* as God's sole child of choice? Two thousand years of disaster's been the result.

J: Don't be too hard on my disciples. It's not uncommon for students to venerate the teacher. As Book of Enoch makes clear, I wasn't the first one ever called savior—that's been going on for millenniums. Even today, various people on earth are seen as full incarnations of God.

DK: True, but the church does sell you as a one-and-only, the real McCoy—a one-of-a-kind blend of God and man. I've never really understood it, but that's how you're generally packaged.

J: This claim that the cosmic Mega-Force has but one true sentient child is a crock. God's offspring—or his 'son,' to use the obvious earthly analogy—is his *creation*. A metaphor. Even a public school graduate oughtta see *that*.

DK: Well, I can tell you one thing: the *church* doesn't view it that way.

J: I'm not responsible for myths—and once they gain status as 'facts,' they're tough to bring down.

DK: Even myths can have *some* factual foundation.

J: The 'son of God' idea took root in astro-theology. Like some of its ancient forerunners, the Christian religion is chock-full of links to sun worship.

DK: Now, *this* part I gotta hear . . .

J: Well, it's no secret that earliest man revered the sun as the giver and sustainer of life. The prominent thing in the sky, the sun was held sacred for bringing the earth light, warmth, and a feeling of safety among people. Nighttime, conversely, was ominous, cold and frightening—exposing man's fear of the dark and its unknown threats. Some said that night was ruled by an invisible 'Prince of Darkness,' and Christians later gave the name to their devil.

DK: Connecting light with goodness and life was only natural, then, while darkness held uncertainty, danger and death.

J: Right, so the sun was seen as the source of all goodness and it got a lot of notice from religions. As centuries passed, humans turned their gaze from the sky to the earth and began ascribing godhood to *people*. At first these characters were only mythological—but later they included historical figures who, some believed, were sons or daughters of God. Like me, they were seen as a mystical mix of divinity and flesh. But all of it began with the daily birth of 'God's sun' which, in English, turned out to be an excellent play on words.

DK: Apparently, then, some cultures thought the sun *itself* was God.

J: Yes, and even the Bible has remnants of that. In the King James Version, the books of Deuteronomy and Hebrews both refer directly to God as "a consuming fire." Now you know why.

DK: So the sun played a pretty big role in forming religions.

J: Oh, for sure. Even some Christian metaphors about me can be traced to the humanized sun. I come 'walking on clouds,' 'illuminate the darkness,' and of course I 'bring life to the world.' The sun was aptly viewed as a 'savior from heaven' and is literally 'the light that shines in darkness.' In John 8:12, the writer has me claiming an exalted title: "I am the light of the world." Christians think this originates with *me*—but first it was a popular name for the Greek god Helios, a divine embodiment of the sun.

DK: *Good heavens*, you might say.

J: A few more facts . . .

Early Egyptians knew the sun was at its highest point, or nearest its daily zenith, when little or no shadow was cast by the pyramid. That's when they offered their prayers to the 'most high God' in his 'heavenly temple' . . . words you might still hear inside a church. I'd easily keep going but you probably get the idea. The oldest religions and their various gods—including ol' Sandal Straps here—have several close connections to your neighboring star.

DK: I think I hear thunder rolling in . . .

CHAPTER TWO

J: Well, it's good that you've learned to chuckle at the typical rendering of God as a cranky old judge. For millions of others, though, it's no joking thing. Religion's got them imagining some humorless, irritable old coot who's dangerously unforgiving of backtalk, challenge or debate— but they never really *examine* this God of their faith. They may not be so childish as to see Him with a long, white beard and sitting on a giant throne in heaven, but they do generally perceive Him to be just a larger, more powerful version of *themselves*.

DK: That's roughly how a lot of folks see it. The Bible says that man was made in the image and likeness of God—but it's said that man has generously returned the favor by creating God in *his* own image instead.

J: Too many people go from cradle to grave without ever questioning their faith. As products of their environment, they seldom arrive at their convictions through any kind of soul-wrenching search for meaning or passionate quest for truth. The reason devotees believe their holy book is straight-from-the-horse's-mouth 'word of God' is usually because people they loved and trusted *told* them it is. They mostly lock on to ideas they inherited from others and tuck 'em away conveniently out of sight— sort of like the letter you've got stashed there in your satchel.

DK: Hey, how the heck did you kn— Oh . . . right. Sorry, I'm not used to dealing with omniscience. But yeah, right at the last second I decided to bring that letter along and I wasn't even sure why. I certainly didn't expect to be *sharing* it with anyone—and least of all with *you*.

J: Well, who better to hear it than its intended recipient?

DK: Maybe, but under the circumsta—

J: C'mon, you were brave enough composing it in the safety of your home. Show a little confidence and lay down your cards.

DK: Right . . . absolutely. Of course. Uhmm . . . well, as you know, many years ago I grew pretty cynical of religion and began having more questions than answers. But I wasn't just starting to have *doubts*—I was wondering if I ever had cause for *faith*. And I saw so much hypocrisy, including within *myself*, I was forced to question the practical good of Christianity, or even of religion at large. I also had big problems with the Bible. But instead of

9

simply *ignoring* those passages that were conflicting, irrelevant or bizarre —as I'd done for many years—I quit repressing and denying my doubts and started *voicing* my concerns to friends and clergy.

J: But you didn't find them too helpful.

DK: Oh, they generally meant well, I'm sure. But usually they just talked around the core issues and didn't seem too willing to explore—they didn't want much meaningful, uncomfortable dissent. They always began with the assumption that the Bible is beyond dispute and that my questions were very likely based on 'gaps' in my knowledge—even though they themselves could never seem to fill in the gaps.

So I finally called it quits on the church and scratched my name from the rolls. But I knew that some of the old programming wouldn't be so easily deleted, and a few days after walking out on religion, I sat down one evening and started the letter—a letter meant specifically for you. I worked on it night after night, and once it was finished several weeks later, it just got tossed in a drawer. I mean there wasn't much else I could do. Mailing to heaven is hell.

J: Well, here's a chance to take your best shot.

DK: Sure, okay . . . here you go. I'll walk the river while you check it out and I'll hope we're still friends when you're done.

J: You don't understand, comrade. I don't wanna *read* the letter. I'd like *you* to read it *to* me.

DK: *What!??* Look, I know I'm responsible for my actions and all, but I never imagined that I'd someday be conversing wi—

J: Hey, no waffling. If you're gonna talk tough and make challenges, you gotta see it through to the end.

[Jesus was just playfully prodding here—but *I* was growing a bit tense. The letter was fairly lighthearted but was terribly forward and blunt, as he surely knew, and he was cleverly calling me out on my bravado. Awkward silence followed while I stalled and fidgeted in my seat.]

J: You look worried.

DK: Guess I'm a little embarrassed. After all, this thing is punishing— I was pretty darned angry when I wrote it. By the time I cracked, I wondered if I'd wasted a lot of good time on bad religion. Anyhow, what's the point of me reading it? You already know what it says.

J: Humor me and prime the pump—it'll give us things to discuss.

DK: Are you sure? You already know I hit way below the belt with this thing.

J: Don't worry, I never take anything personally. And you've been dying to get it off your chest . . . so consider it cheap therapy.

DK: Well, alright, if you insist. I guess there's no time like the present.

J: Actually, there's no time *but* the present.

DK: No, I s'pose not . . .   Well, okay then, here we go. But don't forget when I'm reading that you're hearkening to a mere mortal—in fact, one of the *merest*. Also, it's kinda long, so you'd better settle in awhile. And I'll have to read it straight from the paper, so it might sound a little bit stiff.

J: Whatever's comfortable, old chap . . .

[Not sure how this is going to be received, I nervously clear my throat and begin reading.]

DK: **Dear Jesus,**

> I am writing today to announce that I have reached a critical juncture in my longtime spiritual quest. Having now been many years an avid follower of the Christian religion, I regret I can no more stay committed and compliant in my faith, nor can I continue accepting the accounts of your life as presented in the four New Testament gospels. Naturally I am forced to question as well your widely held status as God.
> I fear I have reached the limits of my trust in this matter and —unless you are willing to *address* my concerns—I will no more bow to the authority of the Holy Bible or any organization that supports it.
> While it is not my goal to be unkind, I must convey my growing uncertainty of Christianity and my increasing discomfort with its sacred foundational texts. In so doing, I rely on your purportedly benevolent nature should I overstep the bounds of good manners. As a member of the omniscient Holy Trinity, however, you surely must have seen this letter coming, and nothing I say going forward should surprise you.

J: Pretty ceremonial so far . . . like a dispatch from the House of Lords.

DK: I prefer an air of courteous formality when corresponding with God's immediate family. You never know who might be listening in . . .

Speaking of the Trinity, allow me to begin my inquiry with this notion of a 3-part God, one of the great mysteries in all religion. According to the Christian church, you are the second component of the sacred Trinity—the Father being the first, of course, and the Holy Spirit the third. As I understand it, all three of you are God, each indiscernible and inseparable from the others.

Is it possible that Christendom is demanding of its followers somewhat more faith than it should? For it has given us a holy triad comprised of an eternal Father who is without beginning or end; a Son who was with his Father from the start; and a ghostly spirit (also referred to exclusively in the masculine) who sprang somehow from the previous two but is, like them, devoid of any temporal beginnings. Certainly this is all quite astounding. Just as impressively, the creation of this all-male deity trio was wholly accomplished with never a female involved!

Now, I think most would view me as a man of at least average intelligence. I do confess challenge, though, in grasping the reality of three distinct beings who are likewise separate and connected, different but identical, and partial yet complete. This baffling arrangement strains every shred of normal human discernment, but the church asks that we nonetheless regard the Holy Trinity as a single unit. "After all," your clergy is quick to remind us, "there is but the one true triune God." (How they determined it has not yet been revealed.)

Although this thorny proposition of three-gods-in-one has apparently not been a problem for most believers, I did want to mention the peculiar and sometimes distressing concepts advanced by your church to its members.

Another confusing Christian teaching is that you were with your father from the beginning. Yet the Trinity was not a part of ancient Judaism, which is, of course, Christianity's 'mother' religion, nor are you ever mentioned in Jewish scripture. Biblically, the term "Trinity" is never used, nor is the concept explained. Perhaps the boys found it too much to manage in the space of just sixty-six books.

But now let us turn to more serious affairs . . .

As you must certainly know, there exist gaping holes and critical discrepancies in the many records scribed by your followers after your death. Not least of these is the glaring division in the gospels of Matthew and Luke on your family tree. Both writers claim you descended from the throne of King David, but Matthew records only twenty-eight generations involved while Luke lists a full forty-three. This biblical 'generation gap' means time differentials of three or four hundred years at the least—and facts like this should no more go ignored.

To cite but one incongruity, Matthew's author says that your paternal grandfather was Jacob. The writer of Luke, however, swears the fellow's name was Heli. Given the claimed precision of Christian scripture (coming as it does from God himself) striking conflicts like this must be addressed. Scholars and laymen alike have found it quite troublesome that, apart from establishing your father as Joseph, the authors of Luke and Matthew cannot agree on a single name in the entire messianic lineage!!

Still more confusing is why these gentlemen even *bothered* with Joseph's prestigious royal ancestry, when both writers go great lengths to explain, in each of their virgin birth accounts, that Joseph played no part in your creation, you had no familial ties to the man, and he was not your father in the first place.

In theory, all Christian scripture was inspired by the Holy Spirit (who via the mystical Trinity is also you). Apparently you engaged in a kind of virtual dictation to the authors of these holy works. I would suggest that you might gain more traction amongst the growing number of modern-day skeptics by giving the world substantially more history of your life. We know so little of your infancy, your childhood, your growth as a young adult.

Of greatest interest, naturally, is a thorough explanation of events surrounding your unusual conception and your birth. Was your mother truly a virgin impregnated by God—inseminated, as it were, by the Holy Spirit? Why were we given so little to learn of this truly historic event?

You doubtless realize that, aside from grocery store tabloids, tales of such strange affairs are quite rare, and, if we're honest, always are suspect from the start. As skeptics will quickly point out, the virgin birth hangs by a thread on an unconfirmed dream by your father. (Or did you consider Joseph your stepfather?)

Further weakening credibility, the content of the dream is, suspiciously, given us by a third-hand party, still unknown, who claims no witness to these events and clearly has no links to the story or to any key players involved!!

Frankly, dear sir, this would seem touchy stuff on which to build a major religion. One is awed by the widespread zealous faith in that story, well into the age of modern science. For if a woman nowadays were to claim she got pregnant 'by Spirit,' she likely would not meet with many believers, regardless of all revelatory dreams by her betrothed.

Can we in the scientific era still safely rest our faith upon these stories? Is it possible some of your passionate supporters slightly 'garnished' the facts in their zeal to advance the Christian cause?

I wonder if any unbiased townsfolk knew the 'inside' details of your mother's scandalous state. Did they know it was all based on claims that could never be verified, things such as personal dreams and closed-door meetings with angels?

I do not mean to—excuse the pun—belabor the virgin birth. But certainly the topic should be broached, as it holds implications for all *subsequent* claims of your life.

Also regarding your earthly arrival, we are told that a guiding star led several wise men (though seemingly no wise *women*) to your birthplace. This could mean, as some have proposed, that the "wise" ones who first found you were actually astrologers, since few others paid such close attention to the stars. It is well known, of course, that the Bible holds many important astrological and numerological allusions, and other symbology as well. Why, then, does it also carry so many stark warnings and injunctions on the *practice* of these long-reverenced arts?

Here is another great puzzle: The church says you have been always with your Father—and even before *history* began. Did you therefore know God-consciousness from the start of your human existence? Did you, as a young boy, realize you were ruler of the universe and Lord of all creation?

CHAPTER THREE

J: Well, you're certainly not holding much back. There's more sugar coating on cold pills.

DK: I grant it freely that *tact* was never my strength—and prepare to suffer *more* abuse pretty fast . . .

I'm afraid you must forgive me, dear friend, if my words are sharp. But who could read the astonishing content of Christian scripture and fail to raise an eyebrow of suspicion? It seems only fair, I think, to seek explanation for that which, from this end, appears both impractical and unconvincing. For instance, if born into this world fully divine, did you have to study in school— or did you know all from the start? Were other kids curious you finished your homework so fast? Did anyone know you were God?

And what of your romantic life? Most Christians think you lived a celibate, monk-like existence to your death. Is this accurate? Did you never kiss a woman, spend time with the ladies or feel like you were falling in love? Much speculation over the centuries has focused on your seemingly special relations with Mary of Magdala— yet barely is there a biblical hint you had any of the usual desires for the gentler sex.

If you were in fact amorous with women, however, I believe your religion would be much better off in knowing it. Have you seen the unnatural and puritanical sexual freakishness that has long plagued 'developed' earthly societies? Personally, I feel that religion is largely responsible for the centuries-long, ongoing pandemic of obsession, shame, fear and inhibition that so many people have experienced with the body and sex.

Even today, the Catholic Church proudly insists that your mother remained virgin to her death, as if celibacy in marriage were somehow commendable and deserving of distinction and renown. This dogma's maintained, by the way, despite scriptural verses— Matthew 13:55, for example—which clearly indicate you had several brothers and sisters (or half-siblings, depending on how you view it).

Defending the doctrine of your mother's unbroken virginity, the church implies that sex is somehow unclean and perhaps even spiritually weak. It hints that Mary's image would in some way be tarnished had she ever indulged sexually with her husband . . . even had she done so long *after* her initial, divine impregnation.

Are we to believe that your parents had a lifelong marriage and never had sex? If so, would this not indicate that all of your siblings were divine too? Should they not each be honored as God, just as you have been? And should not your father be held one of the greatest, most disciplined and certainly most trusting saints ever born?

More to the point, why would belief in your mother's perpetual chastity be crucial to our faith or salvation? And speaking of human sexuality, why has religion been so long preoccupied with this? Is it truly any business of the rabbi, the minister, the priest or imam what consenting people do behind doors?

Judging by history and headlines, it would seem that any sexual monitoring or moralizing would best be performed by parishioners upon their clergy. Why does religion so casually claim right to lecture on even the most personal areas of humanity's life? Its bothersome meddling spills over into every part of existence, including seeking *political* advantage in attempts to make its moral codes *legally compulsive*—even upon those who reject its authority outright!!

But is religion's *own* house in order? What about the Christian church in particular? Certainly you are aware of the sordid, shameful and often shocking sexual misconduct frequently proven of various priests, ministers and other 'representatives' of the faith. The long, criminal record of clerical hypocrisy is disgraceful, and one must wonder if your church —instead of poking its nose into the bedrooms of its parishioners— might be far better served watching activities within its own rectories, convents, monasteries, vestries and sacristies.

As with society at large, sexual abuse by church officials takes place with increasing frequency and it now seems clear that such appalling misbehavior among clergy arises from the same basic confusion, anxiety, guilt and frustration that organized religion has long created in the laity. A case in point: the church signals that sex is somehow impure and perhaps even morally degrading—but then says to *save* it for someone we *love*!!

Presumably, your religion views sex as only an animal instinct, included in God's plan just to thoroughly propagate the species. The great Saint Paul himself explains that even sex within marriage is nothing but a kind of workable compromise with sin. Official church pronouncements on the subject are at best contradicting and always perplexing at least—including, in the case of Roman Catholicism, advocating against birth control by a bunch of guys who claim to never have sex. Is it truly any surprise that so much of our societal dysfunction revolves around this largely taboo topic of sexuality?

And what of *your* teachings, sir? Unless you meant something far different from what is recorded, I take serious issue with some of your instructions to your followers. As one example, you declare in Luke 6 that if someone steals my cloak, he then must be given my undercoat as well. One would think that such *rewarding* of criminal behavior would only be more likely to further encourage it.

As for some of your stricter teachings, in Matthew 18 you instruct us to cut off our hands and pluck out our eyes should they ever enable us to sin. These draconian measures will certainly ensure that the left hand will not know what the right one is doing and *could* be rendered uncertain of even its general GPS *location*.

Since so many Christians relax your rigorous rules and commandments, few of your followers, if any, fully obey them. Realistically, the task appears impossible and your faithless flock must likely keep you sleepless 24/7.

With this much occasion for members to misbehave, it is surely no shock that the church has so strongly enforced confession. In this regard, it would seem that Roman Catholics are especially to be pitied since they are encouraged to visit their clergy *routinely* and set out even their shallowest shortcomings to these fellows . . . *in person*. The Church of Rome now boasts more than a billion members and one marvels that a single parish priest is ever able to set foot outside his confessional.

CHAPTER FOUR

J: On second thought, you might save time in strapping me to a post for flogging.

DK: Hey, I told you this wouldn't be pleasant. You should've dropped in years ago, before I lost *all* reverence. But back to the drive-by mugging . . .

Here is yet another of your messianic mandates long a point of concern. In Luke 14 you insist that your followers must *hate* their parents, spouses, siblings—and even their own children—before you take them as students. Could such a statement possibly emanate from God? How would encouraging intra-family hatred help further your cause of brotherhood, harmony and peace? Did you hate everyone in *your* family? Does not this warped decree conflict with your instruction that we should "love one another"? And does it jibe with the Ten Commandments, which forcefully state that we are to *honor* our fathers and mothers?

Somewhat coldly, you even kept your twelve chosen disciples from honoring *their* parents when, in the ninth chapter of Luke, you wouldn't let them say goodbye to their kin. Surely this desire was not excessive, as they meant to cast off everything—security, possessions, even livelihoods and fortunes—for you. It seems you dishonored your *own* mother too when you asked her most strangely, in Matthew, "Who is my mother?"

Following is more scriptural mud: in the gospel of Mark you assure your disciples that "he who is not *against* us is *for* us." Yet somehow you shift views in Matthew, where you take a less merciful stance: "He who is not *with* me is *against* me." These words are quite clearly contradicting, both in spirit and within simple logic. Were you torn in your view on this point—or did you, for reasons not *told* us, change course?

Next, did you in fact tell your followers, "I come not to bring peace, but a sword"? If you did make this ominous threat, you deviated completely from your assurance to Apostles James and John, in Luke 9, that you came not to *destroy* men's lives, but to *save* them. According to Isaiah—if in fact you were the target of his words—you would someday be called "Wonderful," "Counselor," and even the "Prince of Peace." Did the Old Testament prophet have it wrong, or shall we be expecting a more enlightened, less violent Messiah?

Ironically, history is awash with the blood of religious intolerance, and Christians must own their part. Under church supervision, millions of innocents over the ages have been smugly shunned, harassed and humiliated—even tortured, brutalized and murdered in the name of Christ. It seems then, sir, that your famous threat was spoken quite in earnest and you truly did *not* come to bring peace—and God knows your followers give plenty of time to the sword! In truth, your warning of the fast-coming Christian violence would seem to be, so far, one of the few New Testament prophecies to transpire.

[Now I was *really* feeling uneasy and looked up from my reading to address Jesus directly.]

Maybe we'd better quit right here. The rest can just wait for another time.

J: No, no . . . I'm loving every second. Just the right mix of indignant anger, cutting humor and healthy disbelief. Anyhow, it's nice hearing a little heartfelt candor now and then—I'm shocked how much patronizing I get. You willing to forge ahead?

DK: Are you kidding? I have not yet *begun* to bitch . . .

Moving along, I feel I would be seriously remiss not to inquire about the great Fall-and-Redemption theme that colors so many Christian texts. It is, after all, the very backbone of the faith.

To begin, it seems demonstrably absurd that God created humans then complained they were not up to par. If anyone's at fault in this, it is surely the Creator himself. Strange as it seems, however, his fury is forever aimed toward *us*—as though we had begged him for our creation and He, only grudgingly, complied.

But the failure of the human experiment must fall squarely on the shoulders of the Lord since we mortals were made and molded with no smallest clue or consent. Nevertheless, when bemoaning the sins of the world, you and your heavenly Father seem ever inclined to point the accusing fingers earthward as you keep subjecting countless billions of your brothers and sisters to potential sufferings of damnation—a practice over-reactive by any gauge. We cannot all be liable just because our Edenian ancestors could not follow simple instructions.

Having now gathered twenty centuries of data by which to analyze this harshly bizarre, believe-or-be-damned foreign policy, have you and your Father found reason to wonder if truly any wisdom's in the scheme? How are you doing, statistically speaking, in your soul redemption work? Is your sinner-to-convert ratio satisfactory? Are you happy with the results of this hit-or-miss, sink-or-swim strategy? I see no wisdom in exposing all your brethren to an afterlife of eternal vexation, simply because some of them cannot believe things they honestly find unbelievable. Is it realistic, wise or fair to ask acceptance of unconfirmed theologies and theories whether sure of their truth or not?

And what of the billions of believers from *other* religions? Do you care not for *their* cherished ways? Do you ask them to drop years of ingrained social programming—or centuries of cultural tradition—and instantly take up practicing Christianity? Is this even vaguely judicious, coming as it does from a channel of cosmic intelligence?

Why, in your omniscience, did you and your Father let other religions develop? Why permit them to blossom for centuries, and always without interference, if Christianity was coming and you knew all non-believers would be damned? If truly you wanted all people turning Christian in life, why did you not descend to earth when Adam and Eve first rebelled? And just incidentally, which god was responsible for *inspiring* pre-biblical religions?

Next, you surely must know that those most fixed on Christian proselytizing are often seen by non-believers as presuming, close-minded, judgmental, intellectually dishonest in the extreme—and sometimes even hostile and aggressive. Having once roamed their ranks myself, I tell you first-hand that many of these zealots are frequently quite stubborn or demanding . . . and sometimes even cruel in their 'witness.'

Is it wise to use such people to spread your message of forgiveness, non-judgment and love? Do you know that many of them are, in your behalf, issuing low-minded literature aimed at frightening non-believers into professing you as the Christ? These embarrassing tracts contain laughable, childish cartoons depicting ridiculous end-of-the-world dramas and wildly concocted scenarios of the 'Rapture.'

Tell me, sir: do you feel your movement is well served by this kind of ignorance and outright folly? And is a man truly 'saved,' having turned Christian through nothing but fear of postmortem reprisal? Might it be better to employ in your expansion efforts those who exemplify light, love, wisdom, gentleness, reason, tolerance and compassion? To be candid, dear sir, given those disturbing Bible accounts of your *own* coarse words and behavior, I now question if it is realistic even to think of *you* as having lived out these noble pursuits.

J: *Ouch*, a direct hit.

DK: Oh yeah, brother, and I'm just now finding my rhythm . . .

Pushing on, you no doubt realize that vast sums of money are raised throughout the world each day in the name of "the Lord Jesus Christ." Sprawling infrastructures and massively funded organizations and hierarchies have arisen to wield both promise and power in your name. And I am sorry to report that our radio and television airwaves are now *cluttered* with programming by so-called 'Christian' ministries, hosted by some of the cockiest personalities on the planet.

Are you comfortable with these disingenuous hucksters bilking millions of credulous believers by promising healing, wealth, good fortune or other special blessings in return for sending a check? Some of these swindlers enjoy luxury and scandalous indulgence, while many of their gullible donors have almost nothing.

I have no doubt this excess and profiteering is not what you strove to establish, and all this pomp and circumstance has surely proved your statement that we cannot serve both God and money too.

Sadly, your religion has become a thriving industry—and I cannot believe this was your goal. Am I right to think you would find it all a perversion of your message of simplicity and humble devotion to God? Would not the displays of piety you found so despicable during your lifetime be just as abhorrent to you now?

By and large, it is my personal view that religion's overall impact on the world has not been good. Admittedly, various faiths do occasionally spawn true models of wisdom and beacons of spiritual light. Generally, though, the limited good arising from religion has rarely offset the disastrous, far-flung effects of its publicized harm, and I do not back the notion any longer that religions make the world a better place.

Religions in general—and yours in particular—bear long and shameful histories of intolerance, divisiveness, judgment, arrogance, hypocrisy, persecution and violence. Indeed, one could argue, perhaps, that religion has clearly delivered impressive evidence for the fact of a wicked devil, but hardly has it shown much convincing verification of a loving or compassionate God . . .

CHAPTER FIVE

J: Feeling any better?

DK: Turns out it's *fun* unloading like this. You said "nothing personal," right?

J: Not at all—we messiahs specialize in catering to the ignorant. Please go right on dumping.

DK: Alright, but remember this was *your* idea . . .

As for your *personal* character, we are told in the gospels that you once exploded with anger down at the Temple, throwing around furniture and smacking Temple businessmen with a whip. No matter how justified you felt in this righteous rampage, did you not firmly instruct your disciples that they should be "wise as serpents and harmless as doves," that they should "resist not evil," and when confronting wickedness they always must "turn the other cheek"? As far as I can tell from the church's gospels, you didn't much practice what you preached.

Also, did you later think that your hand had "offended" you through those moments of rage at the Temple? Can this clear case of assault and battery be seen as anything less than *sin*? And why did you not quickly *sever* the hand that enabled this violent act? Perhaps the whipping incident made you re-examine your official requirement of limb-lopping. Why, then, were *we* not informed of this crucial post-doctrinal revision?

Pressing ahead, I must ask of another scriptural austerity long intellectually taxing. In the fifth chapter of Matthew, you sternly warn that whoever insults a man by calling him a fool shall be subject to the torments of hell. Would not these particular quarters be far better-suited for those with sins more destructive, inhuman, and profane? Candidly, I am saddened that the loving Lord of the ages cannot overlook this relatively minor offense, and even stands ready to cast 'victims of the dictum' to his fires of everlasting regret!!

Given this shockingly harsh penalty for a brief moment's slip, you clearly considered this beastly misconduct *unbearable*, this risky business of calling someone a fool. If that is truly the case, however, I find it most strange that you felt no hypocrisy —nor any seeming regard for the safety of your *own* eternal soul— in meanly calling all of the Pharisees fools! You did this not once, in fact, but twice: first in Matthew 23 and again in Luke 11. The *latter* case is *truly* troubling since one of the Pharisees you berated had kindly invited you to join him and his friends for dinner. On arrival, instead of showing thanks for hospitality, you quickly slandered every soul in the room, again calling the Pharisees outright "fools."

Poor table manners not considered, what became of your unbending warning about calling someone a fool? Did you forget the dire consequence of it? Furthermore, should we not find it confusing that, in Luke chapter 12, God himself calls the rich landowner a fool? What are we to make of these stories? Are they simply faulty translations . . . or do you and your Father stay safely exempt from the rules you impose upon others?

Also, what of the story that you once cursed a fig tree solely for holding no fruit? Is it right for a spiritual leader to go scolding perfectly innocent vegetation? The strange act of cursing inanimate objects sets a very poor model of detachment. Did you ever curse any cows for carrying no milk? Were you equally peeved as well when happening upon honeyless beehives and eggless hens?

Next, please explain your words in Matthew 24 that your disciples' generation would not pass away before you returned to earth. How strange to foretell the precise historical timing of your great Second Coming while declaring immediately after, "Of that day and hour no one knows, not even the angels of heaven, *nor the Son*, but the Father only."

You further predicted that, within your disciples' generation, the sun would be darkened and the moon would cease giving light—sounding, in my opinion, very much like a total solar eclipse. You prophesied too that the stars would then fall from the sky, the powers of the heavens would be shaken, and you would return in billowing clouds of glory.

These words were said with convincing degree of authority, and rational readers are roped into a single, inescapable conclusion: you believed the end of the world was *close*.

How curious that you next issued The Great Commission, instructing your followers to commence roaming the earth and establishing your new fledgling church. But what was the *purpose* of this directive? For if a man believes that the world is quickly nearing destruction, why would he start a long-term project to *build* something?

As two thousand years have elapsed since your predictions of cosmic apocalypse, modern observers must wonder if perchance you were mistaken in your prophecies of the world's conclusion.

Is it possible you miscalculated by centuries the general timing of these depressing events? On another somber note, would you mind clarifying the exact nature of your execution? Was it death by crucifixion, as described in the New Testament gospels— or were you hanged in a tree as claimed in Acts 5 and again later on in Acts 10? No one I can think of would confuse any cross for a tree, and never have I seen the two words interchangeable outside of the Christian religion. While handling this point, you might expound as well upon the death of your disciple Judas Iscariot. The book of Matthew says that after Judas betrayed you, he "went and hanged himself." But Acts 1:18 says that Judas died from a serious fall in which his stomach split open and his intestines spilled out—truly a messy path is this path of betrayal.

Lastly, the Apostles' Creed states that when you died, you went straight to the fiery depths of Hades, seemingly to pass the following forty-eight hours. Yet you are said to have told one of the criminals with whom you were crucified, "Today you will be with me in paradise." Was your executed partner disheartened and shocked on his entrance instead to the hot, smoldering fires of hell? And was he not profoundly bewildered at your curious conception of bliss?

The Christian church still firmly maintains that its scripture is divinely inspired and without any meaningful flaws. As shown in the examples above, however, the Bible contains *numerous* disparities, contradictions and provable factual misstatements. That so, what shall we make of the idea that its God is infallible? And where does this leave the poor Pope!!?

[Once more, I paused to test the waters.]

DK: How we doin' there? Any temptation to run?

J: I'm not sure whether to keep laughing or call in for help.

DK: We can stop here if you'd like.

J: No way, I've not been this tickled since Jim and Tammy Faye went national . . .

CHAPTER SIX

DK: I gotta give you credit . . . so far, you've been a good sport.

J: Don't get too cocky, though—I'm just biding my time. Better get your licks in while you can.

DK: Okay then, on with the mutinous drubbing . . .

And now, good sir, I fear I must become still more demanding for additional insight regarding the Christian faith. This next part is so vastly important, so theologically tied to our existence —so crucial to everything for which your religion stands—avoiding it would be unforgivable. I warn you now that I will be as passioned in my critique of this long-held doctrine as your church has been in its confident pronouncements about it. I speak, of course, to the issue of Christian redemption and its theology of damnation.

To begin, we are told in the Holy Scriptures that before you began your ministry, you ventured out to the desert where you then prayed and fasted forty days and forty nights. I have known of Christians and other believers to achieve this impressive feat and I make no complaint of the claim— beyond that, however, I begin to have serious misgivings. Let me explain . . .

Scripture states that when your forty-day fast had ended, you were hungry. Now, please be assured that, regarding this *particular* assertion, I have no doubt whatever of its truth. Suspicion is piqued, on the other hand, by what is said to come about next: you then are visited by the devil, Satan himself.

Is this claim true in its *literal* sense, and did you know the devil was coming? Why does your deadliest foe feel so safe and secure in your presence—and how could this casually take place? Was this the kind of God-and-devil comradery that occurred centuries earlier involving the Old Testament character Job? Did you ask Satan—as God does more than once in that story— where he had just come from and what on earth he was doing?

Are we to understand that, in a given moment, the God of creation knows neither the devil's location nor a thing of his daily pursuits? Can you see how divine unawareness in this area might give us some genuine concern? When even God himself is unsure if his devil lurks just 'round the corner, how can simple *mortals* hope to know it?

An obvious question arises: why is Satan allowed to roam freely around Earth, when other sworn enemies of God are said to be strictly confined to his hell and its immediate campus? If I may, allow me to examine in detail that day's reported sequence of events and explain why I believe them to be strongly relevant to the Christian presentation of redemption.

The first occurrence in the story, according to Matthew's gospel, is that Satan, who seemingly knows you haven't eaten in several weeks, tries coaxing you to make bread from surrounding stones. What *he* hoped to gain by having you change rocks into carbohydrates is never explained, so let me assume that he too was getting a bit hungry out there in the desert but didn't have the same conjuring skills. Nevertheless, this is where faith starts to fade . . . for it is here, says scripture, that upon confronting the red-tailed Tempter, you quickly start spouting philosophy.

Unless this strange recounting is unreliable—and one can only hope that it *is*—you who are the Light of the World are given occasion in that selfsame moment to *slay* the demented Prince of Darkness on the spot. Doing so would free the world at once and forever from the onslaughts of corruption, guilt, sin, suffering and death. And wasn't this your mission from the start?

Instead of *killing* the devil, though, you oddly chose to engage the Lord of Destruction by quoting him an old Hebrew scripture. What were you hoping to accomplish by this approach? I cannot sufficiently share my confusion at this Spirit-inspired reporting of your behavior. In this singular, pregnant historical moment —one of enormous theological importance—the long-loathed Enemy strolls right into your deep-desert camp, unrestrained, and boldly starts challenging the omnipotent Master of Creation!!

Now, it is clear in scripture that you knew this obnoxious fellow was your old archenemy Satan. As one who commands the unbridled power of God, you easily could have ended the devil's ruinous reign by rigorously kicking his diabolical ass. Yet, what goodness came from a weak war of words with the man? Seriously, sir . . . what, in even a semblance of sanity, were you thinking?

If, as the church has said, you are in fact an ever-loving God, why did you not finish off the celestial maverick then and there? Would not an ever-loving deity do everything He could to "save us all from Satan's power"? Is it possible you are not ever-loving after all? Or were you, perhaps due to extreme malnourishment, simply out of your ever-loving mind?

It is said you once told your disciples, "All power is given unto me in heaven and in earth." Why, then, did you not choose to *engage* this godly power by stopping the devil in his tracks? Did you not realize that doing so would render all suffering —your own, as well as ours—forevermore obsolete? And since you did say that you came to bring not peace to the earth, but a sword, why in God's name did you not gird your loins that day and *use* it!??

Whatever the reason, your choice not to stamp out Satan while standing there beside him seems madness. It was, in my view, the most calamitous show of poor judgment in the history of this suffering world. It is past comprehension that you've allowed the Grand Villain to slip through your fingers for two thousand years when you once could have finished him for good. Failing to resolve these burdensome heaven-and-hell dramatics remains, in my assessment, indefensible and forever beyond absolution.

J: Well, at least you're not bitter.

DK: Hey, I warned you this would be brutal . . . but why the big grin?

J: Good cynics are a pleasure to behold.

DK: Well, I'm glad you're enjoying the show, 'cause there's still a few surprises 'fore the end.

J: By all means, push right ahead with your gripping little melodrama. Wouldn't have some popcorn, I suppose?

DK: No, but there's plenty of stones about if you care to make the conversion.

J: Really works best for bread. Oh well, no matter—back to the frontal assault.

DK: Right . . . where was I?

J: Zorro of Nazareth meets Lucifer of Southern Hades.

DK: Ah yes, here we are . . .

Without question, the world has paid a dear price for your failure to stop Satan that day in the desert. Certainly you must realize —and please suffer the pun—the grave implications of that choice. As you know, your refusal to slay the Great Adversary has resulted in countless billions falling victim both to him and his numberless aides. As I shall quickly demonstrate, most human

27

beings will suffer deathless tribulations of damnation, directly because of you and your short-sighted dealings with the devil. Let me be clear on this point: your decision to let Satan resume his crusade of temptation was a stark, hypocritical denial of all you preached, defying not only your *own* recorded teachings, but all obvious logic, compassion . . . and plain, old-fashioned common sense.

J: Boy, when you start shooting, you really empty the clip.

DK: You shoulda heard the parts I cut out . . .

Moving forward, the writer of Matthew next avers that after your first sharing of scripture with Satan, he took you to the holy city of Jerusalem. Do you often take outings with the devil? Did you go willingly that day—or were you coerced? Did you and he walk together, and did you swap stories of the good times in heaven when the two of you were still best of friends?

Here again will I err on the side of lenience. Perhaps you and Satan did not actually journey together but agreed to meet up later at the great city's Temple. Travel arrangements removed, either you complied with the devil's suggestion or you balked. If you *did* go along happily, would this not constitute another serious hypocrisy? Your actions do clearly oppose New Testament cautions to avoid temptation, and they dangerously defy the Book of James' advice to "resist the devil and he will flee from you."

Why, pray tell, would you ever travel *anywhere* with *Satan?!?* Do you often meet his demands this way, or was this your greatest lesson on your directive to "resist not evil"?

I hope you will see now why your critics—and even many Christians, truth told—have been so skeptical of the biblical chronicling of your life. Might it be wise in these critical times to issue some re-do or explication of these narratives?

Further straining the limits of credibility, the gospel writer next relates that, upon your entry to Jerusalem, the devil took you immediately to the pinnacle of the great Temple. But, again, does Satan wield such power over God that he whisks Him about in this fashion? Scripture doesn't clarify the devil's need to meet atop the Temple—but did *you* not think to ask the reason for it?

Given my present poor cash flow, would you object to my earning a few dollars by honoring this tale with a play? Which title better suits the scene: *Savior on the Roof,* or *Devil on a Hot Tin Turret?*

CHAPTER SEVEN

J: Well, I'll give ya this: you sure don't let *decorum* stifle your style.

DK: Okay, so I took a few cheap shots. Unfortunately, things get even cheaper pretty fast . . .

> Once you and Satan reached altitude at the Temple's apex, the devil tried using your strategy against you by prodding you with scripture of his own. Like a five-year-old badgering a playmate who has just climbed onto a high tree branch, the devil—quoting Psalm 91 like a priest—challenged you to the ultimate leap of faith by cynically daring you to jump from the building and trust angelic guardians to save you.
> Instead of *chiding* the devil for this foolishness, you strangely decided, again, to reel off another holy passage. But as you verbally jousted with the malefic Stealer of Souls atop the Temple, did the larger picture of salvation cross your mind? Did it seem that you had been given still another opportunity to end all future suffering at once? Think of all you might have accomplished on the rooftop that day by simply giving the bastard a little shove!!
> Pressing on, the gospel writer tells us that, after your romp with the devil in Jerusalem, he took you to "a very high mountain" and showed you "all the kingdoms of the world." Did Satan really sweep you to the top of a mountain, and could you see all places from its peak? Even on a spherical planet!? Which mountain was it? Did you get a good view of Rhode Island?

J: Skeptic, skeptic, why do you persecute me?

DK: Sorry, I couldn't resist. That last jab was someone else's—I know a good line when I steal it.

J: Your plagiarisms are pardoned, Sir Maylor. Trample on.

DK: With scornful pleasure, m'lord . . .

> I realize, of course, that many people in Palestine seemingly thought the world was flat. When gospel writers scribed these scriptural stories of your stunts with Satan, did they know the true shape of the planet? Or were they, more likely, still thinking the earth was level?

The next thing we are told of your mountain trip with the devil is that he promised to give you all you surveyed if you briefly bowed down to revere him. Now, normally this would be an inviting bargain. A brief show of counterfeit worship in exchange for possession of all goods and real estate on a planet is generally thought by shrewd negotiants to be the kind of deal worth making. Fortunately, though, you rejected the devil's offer, apparently realizing that, in *making* this wild proposal, Satan was only bluffing. After all, none of the world's kingdoms has ever belonged to him and not one foot of property or structure is his to trade.

By this time, mere practicality would seem to have shown the futility of quoting any further scriptures, since Satan was quite familiar with the writings himself. Nevertheless, you decided to share with your evil opponent one final verse, from Deuteronomy.

Following this concluding citation, you ceased your battle of banter with your old celestial friend and ordered him to leave, thus squandering your final—and perhaps easiest—opportunity to take the devil by the horns and slay him. For it was then that you might have ended Satan's ongoing enticements by doing what a thinking man would: quickly push him hard over the high mountain ledge and send him soaring to his demoniacal death. Tragically, however, *you* merely told him to scram.

At this literally unbelievable turn of events, I remain both disheartened and stunned. Was it wiser, do you think, to suffer a torturing crucifixion than to solve the scourge of sin at its source? Why did you not *kill* the wicked Ruler of Ruin on the spot? It would have been humanity's greatest gift, and *your* greatest gift as well. In the span of a single hour, your Father's objectives would be wholly accomplished, with human suffering forevermore unneeded and all earthbound drama made moot . . . no nails or crosses required.

So, the question remains: why did you not *do* it? Did your own suffering and death soothe your Father's need for justice better than the death of Satan would have done? How did your violent demise harm the devil? And why was he allowed to go free when you knew fully well of his reckless, bloodthirsty resolve?

And why, in Revelation 20, is it prophesied that Satan will be freed *yet again*, when already caught and bound a thousand years!!? Does it show any wisdom to have him secured—the scamp at the very *top* of the most-wanted criminals list—and then send him off for one final round of destruction? When reading such things, do not people far and wide have right to ask if you have taken leave of your senses???

If, as you claim, all power belongs to *you*, why keep lending so much of it to the devil? If you do in fact have sway over Satan, why is he allowed to continue unmonitored casting his evil spell? Are you unconcerned he is gathering billions of souls into his demon-filled dungeon, even as you and your Father sit idly aside and allow it? Truthfully, do you not find all this salvation/damnation business devilishly strange from the start?

J: Hang on . . . I'll be right back.

DK: Where you goin'?

J: I thought I'd check the truck for a mattress.

DK: Hold your camels, we're comin' to the dagger in the heart . . .

My dear sir, *lengthy volumes* could be written listing endless questions on the vagaries, contradictions, riddles, doubts, and extreme logical challenges presented by Christian scripture. For instance, where did you and your Father come *from*— where did the two of you live before He created the cosmos and nothing existed? And how did the first three days of creation involve both evenings and mornings? Genesis states that the sun, moon and stars were not made until sometime on day number four.

Also, if there is no predestination, how is the book of Revelation able to assert that only 144,000 souls will be saved when time meets it close? This sum of exactly twelve thousand dozens seems too perfectly round to be random. And permit me, if you will, to put this frightfully small number into perspective . . .

Since Christianity's formation, many billions of people have heard the gospel message proclaimed. Barring your quick return, several billions more will likely hear it. Figures like this are quite staggering, are they not? Sadly, however, 144,000 salvaged spirits is a tiny, insignificant fraction of all those given occasion through history to accept you as their personal Lord and savior. By almost any measure, sir, this clearly is no meaningful achievement. Given the kinds of numbers we are discussing, you'd easily have been more successful finding folks who believed in elves.

But let us for the moment ignore non-believers entirely and focus on your historical supporters. By your own accounting in the book of Revelation, the number of souls saved by Christianity remains trivial even when computed as a percentage of those eagerly embracing it. A few simple stats should prove the point . . .

Of countless seekers claiming to accept the Christian gospel since your death, let us say that only two billion have ever committed sincerely to its practice. (For means of comparison, the world has more than two billion Christians this very moment, and relatively few seem very much committed to its practice.) This figure of two billion is quite low, I imagine, as the number of true Christians over the centuries would surely be far higher. But, relative to the following point regarding those ultimately 'saved' within literalist Christian theology, my guess is quite conservative in your favor.

Even so, given just 144,000 of your devotees at last permitted past the Pearly Gates—and even supposing just two billion Christian faithful across the years—your 'success rate' computes to a trifling .000072%. Stated differently, of all those earnestly adopting your message of redemption, the number actually *redeemed*, according to Revelation, is barely more than seven-thousandths of one percent.

So it cannot be denied that, even for deeply devoted Christians, heavenly prospects are bleak. Accounting for everyone in history, however, makes a grim situation still worse. It is scientifically estimated that 100 billion humans, give or take, have walked the earth to date. Dividing this number into Saint John's divinely revealed counting of 144,000 refurbished souls, your deliverance rate plunges to a paltry .00000144%. Stunningly, this amounts to one rescued spirit for every 695,000 people who ever lived.

J: How could a guy this good with numbers so badly fail first-year math?

DK: Hey, no teenage boy with a *pulse* could focus sitting right next to Donna Mackenzie. The girl's whole wardrobe was sheer, skimpy skirts and tight-fitting, low-cut tops. I got repetitive motion injuries that year and I didn't even own a computer. But don't trip me up, brother J, I'm just about nearing full boil . . .

It should be here noted that many Christian apologists will argue that Saint John's reference to the 144,000 is merely *symbolic* and does not reflect the actual number of the saved. While this view presents big problems for Bible literalists, let us disregard John's mysterious prediction and suppose that your inglorious death does finally ransom a full 25% of all those ever born to earth. Even using this generous but historically untenable figure, there remain roughly 75 billion—*seventy-five thousand million*—of God's children who will yet suffer everlasting misery amidst the fadeless fires of their heavenly Father's hell.

The numerical models above are just theory, of course, since John makes clear in his writing that the small group of God's elect shall include only members of the twelve tribes of Israel. This is the more puzzling by the many New Testament reports that heaven's inhabitants are those who claim Jesus as savior—something not a single member of the original twelve tribes could have done. Adding to the mystifying nature of the issue is Revelation 14, which states that heaven's redeemed will be only "truthful male virgins." In other words, to be crudely frank, if female, or ever you've told a lie or been screwed ... you're *screwed*.

But let us leave these peripheral concerns and strike hammer to anvil now. Has not the devil been far more proficient in his soul-collection campaign than the Holy Trinity can ever hope to be? Are the three of you not terribly embarrassed by this exceptionally poor showing? Indeed, the inspired facts above indicate of your plan for 'salvation' a failure so colossal as to be nothing short of pathetic.

Given the contradictions, the enigmas, and its deeply mystical nature, should anyone depend on John's revelatory accounting of Last Judgment? Can the record of his unusual vision be trusted as emphatic words of the Lord? If so, you have strangely decided to condemn even Yahweh's own specially 'chosen' people. From its origin among the ancient tribes of Israel to the many modern-day Jews, this group alone must now total tens of millions at the least. Apart from the lucky remnant gaining salvation through your religion (honest male virgins every one, I assume), most will be left wondering why you chose them at all.

I put it to you directly, sir: do you expect us to worship a God so inflexible, so cruel—so entrepreneurially inept? Does He merit adoration or devotion while persisting on a course that has proven so consistently and appallingly vain? Should we love Him for your own senseless murder and for blaming every human on its need?

To be short, dear Jesus, I fear your try to *save* us all has failed. Aside from profiting the fortunate few, the pain you suffered in our behalf was sadly borne in vain. One thing is sure past dispute: if the 'truth' of Revelation holds fast, mathematically your efforts are wasted. Merely speculating, perhaps the blame for your gospel's failure to save us from a postlife perdition in hell lies chiefly with those who purvey it. Judging by the facts of Revelation, your large corps of evangelists through the years has basically been worthless. Their poor ability to effectively 'close the sale' shows that most Christian ministers would probably struggle selling ten-dollar pardons on Death row. If they can't talk people out of burning forever in fire, their sales skills are exceedingly lacking, no?

Despite your discouraging salvation debacle, there is one small facet of the Bible's Last Judgment that may bring a slight bit of solace. You predicted in Matthew 7 that, come Judgment Day, you personally will lecture the hundred billion souls standing shell-shocked near God's mighty throne (a multitude which, by my calculations, needs space about the size of West Virginia).

Just before casting the pitiable hordes into hell, you will face them and coldly declare, "I never knew you." It is small comfort, I suppose, but have you realized that when you deliver this brief announcement you will lecture the largest crowd ever?

In closing, renowned sir, I offer these questions and remarks hoping you will find it both wise and compassionate to respond. Naturally, given my poor prayer results in the past, I will not wait by the mailbox for reply. Please be assured, however, I will bear no resentment if an answer is not forthcoming. And though I may indeed be disappointed, I certainly shall *not* be surprised.

Yours most humbly & sincerely,
D.K. Maylor

DK: Well, there you have it. So whaddaya think?

J: I think I'm the first one in history crucified *twice* . . .

CHAPTER EIGHT

J: Actually, truth be told, it was quite an effort. That thing would pass for a lousy scripture critique, a character assassination—*and* a cure for insomnia.

DK: Well, perhaps I owe an apology . . . it *was* a bit harsh, I confess. But never did I think I'd be raking you over in person.

J: No, it was great. Intelligent, provocative, honest. And *funny*. Genuine top-notch stuff.

DK: Thanks, that really means a lot, 'cause it took about two solid mont—

J: But of course it just proves how *deluded* you've been.

DK: *What!?* Listen, I must've suffered through *two thousand hours* of those soul-scaring, mind-numbing sermons and tedious New Testament study group sessions to soak up all the knowle—

J: Whoa, calm down there, pilgrim . . . don't take offense. In a way, your letter speaks for billions of skeptics through the years. Even many Christians have the same kinds of doubts but they don't have the nerve to admit it. So let's spend a minute on the notion of scripture, since all of this claptrap hangs upon ancient, third-party reports.

DK: Well, that's about all we've got. As far as I know, you didn't leave a signed autobiography.

J: Let's be practical, then, and review how scripture evolves . . .

First, someone of faith writes down events or opinions he considers important and then shares his thoughts with some of his fellow believers. Over the years these letters turn 'sacred' in some circles, especially if they came from any early stalwarts of the faith. At some point, select groups —usually men, it would seem—decide that some of these writings should be canonized and henceforth deemed 'holy.' And they make sure that everyone knows it: "We've compiled a pile of paper piles," they explain, "and we're pretty sure we figured out which ones issued from God!" So, who's being 'saved' in this chaos? And what are they being saved *from*?

DK: Nonetheless, believers start treating these works as though almost legally binding.

J: Oh, and forcing their entire lives—and even their views about the structure, function and purpose of the bloody *universe*—to match the crazy paradigms and parameters of conflictive ancient-day texts. And the story is always the same. Formal corporations are formed around the faith's sacred "scriptures," and pretty soon the devotees are snapping up property, hiring a preacher and checking out building codes.

DK: Cynical, for sure . . . but going from what I saw when actually *living* the circus, a reasonable summary, I'd say.

J: Alright, so stick with me here and see how these things really progress. Initially, when one of these 'sacred' works is written, its audience doesn't give it much thought—to them it's just a well-intended letter. It's not like the guy walked downstairs one morning and told the wife, "Looks like rain comin', hun. Can't be out plowin' in weather like this. Think I'll stay inside this mornin' and knock out a few lines of scripture."

DK: Of course not.

J: No, it's more like a friend of yours writing down some thoughts he wants to share. He sends you the letter and you read it—and his words may well be impressive and even inspiring. But would you conclude that ol' Fred has sent a transmit from heaven or that everyone on earth should take it immediately as watertight words of the Lord? Yet believers around the world do this every single day and with documents written by people they never met—and in many cases can't even name—and whose personal lives they know little or nothing about. Now, *that's* what I call *faith*!!

DK: So, to the author's peers, a document we now hold sacred could well have been just another letter of interest from Fred.

J: Right, but then the letter starts circulating and with time it takes on a very different glow—especially if the writer is now a member of the dearly departed.

DK: Strange how a guy's work gathers so much more weight when he's *dead*.

J: But here's the horse's hitch: unless it's revealed to each and every believer that a letter in question was in fact an inspiration from God, how could they know for certain that it was? A passage that inspires one reader might well leave many others unimpressed—it's always a very *personal* thing. And lots of crazy stuff has come forth from Bible personalities who claimed to be hearing from God, as we'll discuss later on.

DK: But once a text has been used as a guiding light for a while, some of the faithful start insisting it was inspired, when only the author himself would know for sure.

J: Well, even if you were sitting in the room with someone who had just finished penning one of these works, you *still* couldn't be sure what inspired him. Even so, most religious faithful start their journey with the premise that the founders and custodians of their faith are to be entirely trusted on exactly what comprises 'God's word.'

DK: I'd guess that's mostly how it works . . . it certainly was true in my case.

J: Okay, so *now* what've we got? With the Christian New Testament, we've letters and narratives in ancient tongues that are hard to interpret and translate and whose words are often mundane. There's John bemoaning his tiff with a guy named Diotrephes; Paul handling ongoing admin matters; the writer of Timothy urging wine for stomach complaints.

DK: So, a lot of stuff that's pretty routine.

J: Right. And no one who hadn't been *told* this writing was 'sacred' would likely perceive it as such. Still, the authors of these 'holy' works are said to have received a kind of direct download from heaven, each line holding profound theological weight. Some believers think these special words *must* be inspired or the church wouldn't put them in the Bible.

DK: I doubt very many have thought it out. Most Christians believe God was *in charge* of the process—even if He didn't do the writing.

J: By *that* thinking, though, He's far less focused on the sufferings of his children than He is on his publishing biz. He's willing to watch wartime massacres unfold but He just can't bear the thought of spurious scriptures. "Genocide's no problem," He says, "but let's be sure we've quality books on the shelves."

DK: Why so facetious?

J: Well, I'm staggered that believers throughout history have so blindly accepted their religions' opinions on what constitutes 'God's word.' You know so little of the writers and their background, so little of their motives and superstitions, the truth of their data, surrounding political and social environs—or the long, murky course of transcription. It all happened hundreds or thousands of years back and yet the faithful soak it in like a sea sponge and without ever raising a hand.

DK: So, we quote the Bible chapter-and-verse but never explore how we *got* it.

J: Yeah, you quiz the average Christian on the Bible's evolution and you'll likely get a blank-eyed stare. He may know scripture's *content* but seldom knows its *history*—and doesn't really care to. So he grimaces, drinks it down quick and calls it faith. I'm telling you, a fella might be a bloody genius, but bring up politics or religion and his perfectly good brain turns to Jell-O.

DK: I s'pose the proof's in the pudding . . .

J: It's ironic, but the average guy nowadays is pretty suspicious of wild, unproven claims. Yet religion puts forth all these fantasy-like tales of his spiritual forefathers and he's instantly on-board. Walking on water and raising the dead he'll accept without even the slightest proof while ignoring all experience that denies it. But then his next-door neighbor offers him a sweetheart deal on a car, and right away he's phoning his mechanic: he's *certain* there must be a catch.

DK: An unexpected view from the Christian leader himself.

J: Well, obviously I wasn't a Christian, and I certainly never intended to start a religion. I came to lead you *beyond* religion—to "fulfill the law" by restoring your awareness of your wired-in connection to that force which most believers call 'God.'

DK: Doesn't that require being Christian?

J: Why should it? Parroting dogmas and labeling yourself doesn't change your eternal reality as an undying spark of Infinity.

DK: The church says that God wants everyone speaking the name Jesus.

J: That's not what I hear from the Hindus, Buddhists, Muslims and Jews. Do you realize that all it takes to be a Christian is the simple declaration that you *are* one? I mean who could tell whether you qualify? What are the criteria? History shows aplenty: not all who claim religion are sincere. Who would know if you're honestly, inwardly devoted?

DK: Certainly *God* would know.

J: Perhaps He would, but are you sure that God is a Christian?

DK: Well, the church teaches that God's view toward man is basically, "Christianity: My way or the highway—to *hell*."

J: So the church views Christianity as God's indicated 'religion of preference.'

DK: Of course. Philippians chapter two says, "at the name of Jesus every knee should bow . . . and every tongue confess that Jesus Christ is Lord." According to the New Testament, God wants an all-Christian planet.

J: "Christian" means "Christlike," and most people are Christlike at core, but few of them actually express it. The Christ energy is cosmic, *universal*, and it isn't controlled or confined by any religion—it's as present for the atheist as it is for the priest. Despite its confident claims to the world, Christianity owns no monopoly on the Christ.

DK: You're saying everyone has the latent potential of Christ? With so many rotten apples in the world, it doesn't seem too realistic.

J: The Bible parable of the prodigal child shows that even if the son of the wealthy man *believed* himself to be poor, unloved and disowned, never in truth was it so. His status as the rich man's heir was never lost, but his ignorance of it led him to a sad, demeaning life attending pigs— a veritable vision of hell to a faithful Jew. The father knew the son had every right to his inheritance, and not for a blink was it withheld . . . all it took was the knowledge and willingness to *claim* it. I told this story because I never viewed others as anything less than divine. The Christ can rise up in anyone, and ignorance won't alter the facts.

DK: But the Bible also says tha—

J: Before we start bantering with scripture, let's not use religious books to argue things that are nuts. That's led to lots of suffering through the centuries . . . and I, of all people, should know. I defied the barbaric ideas of my ancestors and quickly got myself killed. Like many cultures do, mine gave way too much power to contentious old papers.

DK: Are you saying that scripture is useless?

J: I'm suggesting that you test its validity in the same ways you would test anything else. You tend to use reason and discretion in most *other* aspects of your life—well, maybe excepting politics— so why would you not do that with your faith? Is it wise to quash critical thinking because someone tells you a particular thing is 'holy'? What if they're wrong? God gave you the ability to reason and so must've expected you to *use* it. Why should He worry you'd apply some intelligence to anything connected with Him? Think what kind of god *that* would be.

DK: Oh, believe me, I've definitely got my doubts—it's just I'd rather not *burn* because I *had* 'em. It is true, though, that my faith finally crumbled like a piece of old peanut brittle.

J: Take heart, O ye of brittle faith. The simple-minded thought that God will punish you for doubting a scripture brings a quick intellectual pickle. If Christianity's God created both the Bible *and* your logical, reasoning mind, whose fault is it if those two things conflict?

DK: Some claim you shouldn't *base* your faith on using only reason and logic.

J: Convince me of that without using reason or logic.

DK: Hmmm . . . well, some Christians say that God's words take *priority* over reason. Preachers sometimes use the term 'transcendence.' They say God's ways can 'transcend' all reason or sense—and in religion, at least, they frequently damned sure do.

J: That's like saying that God's ways are sometimes not reasonable. If true, why would any thinking people *respect* them? An ideology is senseless that can't be shown to make sense, and the rule of Occam's razor alone will slice most religions to shreds.

DK: Okay, but how do we solve the problem? Every faith has its book of sacred writings, and most contain pretty wild stuff. The Islamic Quran, for example, has about forty passages of Allah commanding Muslims to *persecute and kill non-believers*. Are any 'holy' works really of use?

J: Of course. Some of the world's scriptures are worthy, love-based writings with deep levels of—yes, we can say it—inspired knowledge and wisdom. Many of the Psalms, for example, are beautifully uplifting hymns of praise and encouragement. Others are only selfish calls for vengeance, though, and a goodly number of the world's religious texts are just stories of divine partiality—stories of God choosing sides. And some of these scriptures make 'God' as often devilish as divine.

Take the famous Passover story from Exodus: no hint of godliness in the mix. Scripture says that Yahweh brought his tenth and final plague upon the Pharaoh and his people by instructing the captive Israelites to smear lamb's blood around their front doors. That night the Lord would move eerily across Egypt, murdering all first-born Egyptian children —and even all the first-born *animals*—of those who hadn't complied. Exodus says that not a household in all of Egypt was spared from this heavenly terror. I mean, who *is* this Yahweh bloke, and from whom did I inherit my loving nature!?

DK: Pretty spooky stuff, without a doubt.

J: So, tell me: what about this legend is uplifting or worthy of remembrance? Yahweh hates the Egyptian parents and kills their first-born children. Personally, I never saw the point. In effect we were celebrating our people's deliverance from Yahweh's deadly storming through Egypt. If Passover is a grateful remembrance of Israel's alleged liberation from slavery, it's also a grim reminder of a homicidal 'deity' at his worst.

DK: Didn't Yahweh give Pharaoh several warnings?

J: Sure, but so what? If only one God exists, He was also God of the Egyptians. But why does Yahweh never claim parenthood over anyone but ancient Israelites? Who was responsible for *creating* all the others!? The book of Genesis says that everyone descended from Adam and Eve. Anyhow, couldn't an all-knowing deity solve the crisis in ways peaceful for all concerned? There's no point punishing an entire society by killing thousands of innocent people—including even infants and kids—when it would be a whole lot smarter and easier to install a more agreeable Pharaoh.

DK: I never understood it, either. Killing blameless animals and children doesn't seem like the politically imaginative solution you'd expect from the great universal creator. And this was the very same deity who sternly warned his people not to kill.

J: Perhaps He was thinking that was *his* job.

DK: Could it be that we mortals just don't grasp the deeper significance of Yahweh's behavior? You gotta think He had a good *reason* for that Passover kill.

J: Actually, there's no convincing evidence that it happened and every cause to think it never did. But even if it had, the Passover is just one among many biblical stories of divine malevolence. The Old Testament *oozes* with gory accounts of Yahweh not just allowing but often *ordering* Israel's leaders to kill their enemies—hundreds, thousands, even tens of thousands at once. And the *New* Testament carries its *own* special strains of madness, the most obvious being the Crucifixion itself.

DK: *Mother of Judas!* I can't believe what I'm hearing! I already see the headline: "Jesus Returns for Interview, Miffs Jews and Christians Alike."

J: But no one can deny that the Abrahamic God of the desert is quite often just a deified thug. In the Old Testament, He's chastising, punishing,

41

and killing practically everyone in sight—including the Israelites themselves. In the New Testament, He's pushed off to the sidelines but is still letting guilty men go free while watching over the needless murder of his heretofore unmentioned 'only son.' *Honestly,* now . . . who could really warm to a God like this and why would his theologies be appealing?

DK: I didn't like Him from the moment He asked Abraham to murder his son on the altar—as a kid, it scared me to death and I never forgot it. And if it had *me* worried, can you think of the emotional trauma this must've caused both Abraham and his son? As I recall, Isaac was at least a young boy by that time, and some say possibly an adult. That alone is enough to freak someone out. And despite Yahweh's merciful last-minute save, I honestly couldn't embrace a God who would do that. If one little trace of discernible love lies lurking in that story, I'm just not pickin' it up.

J: Well, as you suggest, what kind of God would even *ask* such a thing? Anyway, all of it was needless commotion. Any God with predictive talent would've known that faithful Abe would answer the call.

DK: Maybe the Lord's not the all-knowing fellow we've thought.

J: Possibly not. In Genesis 22, just before Abe drives the knife into his terrified son's quivering chest, God's angel conveniently intervenes. Speaking for the Lord, as made clear in verse sixteen, the angel says, "Lay not thine hand upon the lad . . . for now I know thou fearest God . . ."
Now, certainly Yahweh didn't mentally torture Abraham and Isaac on behalf of a curious angel, nor would a mere angel be *conducting* this extreme test of mindless compliance minus God's prior written consent. So it's safe to assume that it was Yahweh himself wanting insight to Abraham's faith. This means the God of the Bible doesn't really understand his own children . . . which doesn't argue well for his omniscience.

DK: I once heard a preacher say that Yahweh did it not for his *own* sake, but for Abraham—so Abe would know the strength of his conviction.

J: What!? God asked a man who had already proven quite faithful to kill his one child with Sarah as a pure-hearted show of *good faith*!?? As a way to reinforce his own devotion!?? *Get serious!* You might expect that sort of hazing ritual from a street gang or a major crime syndicate, perhaps— but not from a deity of love. And what kind of parent would even *think* of complying with this thing? If a modern-day father laid his child on an altar in preparing for some bat-crazy sacrifice to God, the man would be locked up faster than you can say, "Grab the narcotics and needles."

DK: Well, depending on culture, I'd say . . .

J: Frankly, this God of the Bible talks a righteous game of his endless mercy and his ever-abiding love—but if He's *cranky*, they may not last the night! He's clearly a god of death, doom and destruction. He scares the hell out of people.

DK: And that's what the literalists are hoping—they *like* living in that frightening God-versus-man Bible paradigm. An elderly fundamentalist friend used to love quoting a line from Exodus. "The Lord is a man of war!" he would bellow. He said it was a victory song to God by the Israelites.

J: Well, they certainly gave Him the right title. Although, given his people's routine calls for mutiny and their insatiable thirst for new leadership, I'll bet He was caught by surprise at the spontaneous outpouring of praise. But then, why *wouldn't* they be living on edge? How could they be faithful to a God so dangerously disloyal? The one who claims to 'love' his earthly children will sometimes kill off thousands in a blink, often acting as little more than a celestial enforcer. You couldn't love even an *earthly* parent so vile, unforgiving and cruel.

DK: I think a lot of folks view their religion's God as like a stern stepfather in the sky. Or maybe a kind of cosmic cop who's got us under constant surveillance.

J: Yet, what does it say about the nature of your character if someone must be constantly policing it? And what does it say of the *policeman*? Most religious disciples would claim that the force they refer to as 'God' is omnipresent—everywhere all the time. And they're right. But they're missing the logical conclusion. If the force they're talking about is everywhere, it can't be separate from anything, and least of all from themselves. Judgment, and therefore guilt, is based entirely on the belief in separation, and a world of mistaken perception's the sad result.

DK: But even if God doesn't judge us, He must get angry at *something*.

J: Angry at *what*? Why would He be angry at his brilliant creation and always stressing about it? One of the dumbest, most poorly considered concepts ever advanced about God is that He gets angry. Even modern psychology can tell you that anger, at its center, is usually based on fear, either obvious or covert—and God does not experience any fear. The Consciousness backing creation is a constantly purring kitten. As pure love, *and nothing else*, Life extends only love and only lovingly creates . . .

CHAPTER NINE

DK: I see I won't be loved by the Christian right. I publish *this* stuff and they'll be calling me the devil's little helper.

J: Don't lose sleep over *that*. Every age has its 'moral majority.' Rarely are they very moral and *never* the actual majority.

DK: Strong talk from a man whose philosophy was based on a platform of forgiveness and non-judgment.

J: What, I'm not allowed to have my perspectives? Compassion doesn't mean being blind to what's really happening. Even the gospels don't always depict me as the charitable, mild-mannered guy that children learn about on Sundays. Now, I never condemned anyone, because I saw the illusory nature of the world. But that didn't keep me from pointing out wickedness, hypocrisy . . . or even outright stupidity. You've got to call out dysfunctional behavior sometimes, but always remember the spiritual truth at its core: you and the 'other' are one.

DK: Then what of your instruction not to judge?

J: It doesn't imply denying what *is*. Non-judgment, which is very much connected with compassion, is refusing to see yourself as separate from or better than anyone else. You look upon everyone as a full child of God and realize their fundamental interests are really no different from yours— you stop judging the inner based on the outer. I've always felt that two people can call each other an ass and still *love* each other.

DK: Well, I dunno . . . some people's hearts seem black as coal. And not too very lovable, I'd add.

J: But don't let it blind you to reality. Acknowledge the *effects* of darkness in the world—but learn to respond with light. If you love only those who love *you* . . . well, you're just another narcissist, right?

DK: So, where does all this Christian theology-trashing leave us? What are we now to do with the Christ of the Bible? After all, you've mostly demolished that 'inerrant scripture' thing. So, *are* you God . . . or not?

J: Instead of feeding old delusions, I'll make a startling statement that every devotee of every religion must face: *Belief in God is a meaningless idea.*

DK: Illumination, please.

J: Look at it like this: the cosmic power called 'God,' if it exists, is either known and experienced or it isn't. Beliefs are just opinions that can't be proven—barren desert where nothing new can grow. A lazy, stale comfort zone of gray.

DK: Then beliefs are just poor substitutes for *knowledge*.

J: Right, because believing, by implication, obviously means *not knowing*. Scripture says that freedom comes only from *knowing* the truth— not meekly believing in things you've been *told* it might be.

DK: So either we know this thing we call 'God' as our own reality, or we don't.

J: Sure, because everything else is guesswork. Would God want his children to *believe*—or would He, more likely, want them to *know*? God isn't hiding something from you, and nothing of himself remains unshared. Does it make sense He'd create you and then sit around hoping that you'd one day come to *believe* in Him? That is absolutely ridiculous. True joy requires knowing, and anyone serious about spirituality wants some kind of personal experience— otherwise, it's nothin' but secondhand news. I never sought or encouraged blind faith, and any opinions about me or God, or frolicking fairies in forests, are never more than fanciful *ideas* if you haven't got proof to back 'em up.

DK: Okay, but still . . . I'd like to come to grips with who you are.

J: And how would you know if what I tell you is true? You're right back where you started by depending on beliefs. You're far wiser asking who *you* are. 'Who *am* I?' This is the question of the ages. Many resist asking it—they worry that they may not know the answer. It's easier to think that I'll do the heavy lifting *for* them. "I'll stay tight with Jesus," they say, "and surely I'm good to go."

DK: Not realistic, eh?

J: Well, to live a lifetime and never learn much about the nature of the Self is to have wasted the precious chance, wouldn't you say? I've been referred to as 'savior'—but for all the wrong reasons. I didn't come to prove how powerful I am and how weak and inferior you must therefore be. The two of us are *one*, and you have the same divine nature as anyone else. Why choose to see yourself as spiritually defective? That's not doing God, or yourself, any favors.

45

DK: You talk about our equality, but I'm thinking you have some advantage.

J: Only this: I'm in full awareness of our true spiritual reality, and some, temporarily, are not. But even this single difference can't last, since most people's self-images are false, and the false has no chance in the end— illusions won't forever mask the real. How can something that doesn't exist keep you back from the one thing that does? So truth will triumph simply because it's true . . . and even the gates of hell shall not prevail.

DK: Ah, so you're *not* above resorting to scripture.

J: Like I said, a few of 'em can be useful. I'll have to beg your forgiveness.

DK: A paradoxical plea if ever there was. And what *is* forgiveness, exactly? Must we constantly beg heaven for mercy? Is God angry one day and pacified the next, just because we offer up a prayer? How can He handle billions of them each day? Does God experience every emotion at once? The whole shootin' match seems slobberin'-mad-dog nuts.

J: To believe that God is separate from his creations leads only to preposterous conclusions. In your divided thinking, you perceive God as separate and judgmental. You think He's got to be appeased through sacrifice or flooded with prayer before He'll look past your mistakes or fill your requests. Projecting this guilt-based thinking onto God, you believe that judgment and forgiveness coexist.

DK: Well, of course . . . that's the basic message of the cross. The church says there's a price to be paid—or at least some action required—before our 'redeemer' will finally accept us and grant the full scope of his love.

J: I'm afraid you can't have it both ways. You can't say that God created you in love and then argue He expects you to *deserve* it. You wouldn't even succeed in convincing me that He wants you grateful. This kind of separation thinking is senseless and contradicts the *meaning* of grace.

DK: I was taught that God's grace was having you killed upon the holy cross of Calvary, to atone for the sins of the world. You did die willingly, it seems—but there were a few strings attached. We're told to confess our sins, both to God and to each other, to accept you and you only as our savior, and profess that your death was God's atoning gift to us all.

J: It's a pretty sick deity who makes a 'gift' of death. But even if you claim to believe it, you never let down your guard—deep inside, you're not near as sure as you say. You gush of God's wonderful grace but then spend the rest of your life trying to earn it, deserve it, or keep it. With *that* kind of pressure, how bloody grateful could you be!?

DK: You're trampling where angels and associate pastors fear to tread.

J: Look . . . when gauging any concept of the great Universal Intelligence, you've got to ask first if it's *reasonable*. Does it ring true in heart, mind, and what you call 'spirit' or 'soul'? If something you're told about God seems absurd, you should figure it probably is.

DK: With all the conflicting theology we're given, who'd blame us for being confused? First the New Testament claims that only your grace can save— and the saving centers solely on faith. You said so yourself several times in the gospel of John.

J: He who believes in me shall not perish and all that.

DK: Right. Unfortunately, that contradicts your statement in Matthew 19, where you tell a man that all he must do for eternal life is steadfastly "keep the commandments." You never even mention the aspect of faith or believing in you as God's savior. Furthermore, in the book of James we're cautioned repeatedly that even if we *do* have faith, it's useless if not backed up by good works.

J: That's true. James' notion of what he calls "pure religion" centers less on faith and belief than on *behavior*.

DK: But that thoroughly challenges the views of Saint Paul in Romans 3, where he basically declares that our works aren't all that important. However, just one chapter prior—in Romans 2:6—Paul states clearly that God will reward us *according to our works*!! And if *that* swamp of muddy theology doesn't keep us in therapy, the New Testament adds the entangling factors of spiritual rebirth—the 'born again' thing—and baptism. Some New Testament writers say these things are essential, while others don't give 'em a thought. And just so that no one's caught napping, we're also warned that works without faith are as worthless as faith without works. So all your sermons of love and forgiveness are moot without proper *beliefs*. And finally—to ensure there's no sane man or woman left standing— Paul says in 1 Corinthians that faith *and* works, when offered without love, are fruitless.

J: An exasperating maze of conceptual goulash. Theological sludge.

DK: Hell, it's one big, boiling, chaotic mess . . . the kind of stuff that compelled me to write you that letter. Salvation is only a blurry smear, with no clear boundaries or basics. And what about predestination? Revelation 13 says the names of the saved were written in the Book of Life *before the foundation of the world*. Apparently our fortunes were *fated* before anything was even *created*! This would mean that all of God's meddling with people is pointless and that *nothing*—internal, external or otherwise—can save *anyone* . . . not faith, love, works, nor keen sense of fashion.

J: Good grief. If that's what they're offering in church these days, you might as well stay home and watch the game . . .

CHAPTER TEN

DK: Well, now you see what we're fighting. Religion will drag us from pillar to post with its riddles and austerities, its mysteries, contradictions, and grossly implausible claims. Where does one turn to find the truth?

J: I told my disciples, "The kingdom of God is *within* you." It peacefully rests in the heart.

DK: Hold on, now. One of the few Old Testament quotes I can remember is that "the heart is deceitful above all things, and desperately corrupt." It's right there in the Bible, straight from the book of Jeremiah.

J: The Bible also says, "I will put my law *within* them, and I will write it upon their *hearts*." That too, by the way, is straight from the book of Jeremiah.

DK: Touché.

J: You see? This is the problem with scriptures—they're as common as corrupt civil servants. And you can use these religious writings to 'prove' almost anything you want.

DK: So, which ones can we trust?

J: First of all, if a scripture causes fear and separation, it cannot be a love-inspired thing. Even on earth, love does not inspire fear, does not set people fighting, nor could it be mistaken for a threat. Take what you read or hear and weigh it on the truth of your spirit. Does it vibrate with the energy of love and feel harmonious in the knowing of the heart? Is it sensible from a viewpoint of oneness? Listen to your instincts and learn to have faith in *yourself*. Your body's natural intuition is your failsafe portal to knowing, so always examine ideas or opinions to see if they 'feel' correct. Even the sincerest of saints can sometimes be wrong.

DK: It seems there's no end to ideologies, philosophies, or the infinite spewing of words.

J: Every seeker should know from the start that words are primarily symbols and are several degrees removed from reality. Words represent *ideas*, which again point to something else entirely. They're signposts—

they may lead you *toward* the truth but are not themselves the truth. And the difference *between* the two, once you get it, makes all the difference in the world. A simple example should clear up this point for good. Recall one of the most exciting days of your life.

DK: Okay, got it firmly in mind . . . an incredible, life-expanding, never-forget-it moment frozen in time. Still brings me joy just to think of it.

J: Great. But now, imagine being denied the actual experience of that glorious day and being forced to settle for reading just a vague *description* of it instead.

DK: Well, the two things aren't even related. The words have no meaningful tie to the experience, and neither one equates to the other. The longest, most detailed description wouldn't even be a poor proxy for the moment itself. For any *practical* purpose, it'd be worthless—I'd be giving up *everything* for *nothing*. No words could ever come close to the reality.

J: So all this talk of words being 'truth' is rubbish. Words can barely *begin* to express the truth—the heart and soul of what the words are describing. Trying to convey reality through words is like explaining the taste of mangoes to people who've never had fruit. You could ramble for hours and they would still have no experience of the actual taste and the absolute knowing that comes with it. Words and the reality they point toward are as different as experiencing your priceless, never-forget-it moment . . . and merely reading a summarized *story* about it. One is only a rough description, the other the thing itself.

DK: It's obvious, then, that truth is not the words we use to discuss it.

J: And in John 5:39 I warn of this very mistake: "You study the Scriptures diligently because you think that in them you have eternal life."

But there is no life in the scriptures . . . they're *words*. The life is in what the scriptures *describe*. You've got to look beyond the words to what they represent because they're two different things from the start.

DK: It seems that we took *your* reported words and built up a new religion.

J: This is what misguided souls will do. Once they're sure of 'the truth,' they carve the words in stone and make them doctrine. Truth becomes a prison of ideas for the mind to live within and help it make some 'sense' of its 'reality.' That's what happened in my case. To use the old Buddhist analogy, I was pointing to the moon and everyone fixed on my finger.

DK: From another view, beliefs *can* bring us spiritual comfort.

J: Yes, but that's not *truth*—and it's often intellectual anesthesia.

DK: Pontius Pilate is said to have asked you, "What *is* truth?" There's no sign you ever explained.

J: Speaking your 'truth' to those unwilling to hear it is feeding caviar to the dog. My mother would say there's no use selling perfume in a barn.

DK: I'll let that one slide . . .

J: So truth isn't just a bunch of concepts and beliefs. It can't be memorized, described—or even explained. Truth is far beyond all words, ideas, or symbols, and you need not even understand it. You need only to *know* it. To *be* it.

DK: And yet John 8:32 has you declaring, "You shall know the truth and the truth shall set you free." It sounds like something specific.

J: The truth *does* set you free. And what is truth? The only thing it *could* be: reality. You shall come to know reality, which will show you clearly that you *already are* free. While it's accurate to say that truth is simply what *is*, you sometimes don't *recognize* what is because—admit it—your emotional and intellectual filters are skewing all you perceive. They can keep you from knowing yourself as an extension of 'God,' a living expression of Truth.

DK: It's tough accepting 'oneness' with God when, honestly, I'm not really all that saintly.

J: Not saintly compared to who? Comparing yourself with biblical descriptions of *me*, you've got a role model no one could match . . . raising corpses, water to wine 'n that. Then you're fed diets of guilt and those post-world threats of abuse. Christian theology centers firstly upon human shortfalls, sacrifice and sin—there's nothing uplifting about it.

DK: Don't we all need saving from our sin?

J: People think of sin as something splitting them off from their Source. In this sense, there *is* no sin . . . which also means there's no one out there tracking it. Man's 'original sin'—a purely *Christian* concept, by the way— was falling into forgetfulness and fear. He lost awareness of his holy, or his "whole I," nature. In truth, no one is guilty of anything very much more than ignorance and being out of alignment with love.

51

DK: You must not be reading the papers.

J: I won't deny the obvious evil, but you don't understand what you see. The world as you presently perceive it is indeed undeniably tragic— a perpetual flow of fatalities. But God creates only the whole and perfect, so the world you presently experience is not the real world. The real is eternal and the eternal has no end, whereas the dualistic world, with all of its pain and disaster, is bound to rise and set with your awareness.

DK: Nice theory, perhaps . . . but not too biblical, I'd say.

J: Don't be so sure. Luke 6 teaches that a good tree doesn't yield bad fruit. This means that light can never birth darkness nor does goodness give rise to the base. Creations of God aren't defective or sinful, and the children of this Divine Brilliance must also be one with the Light.

DK: I'm sorry to be kicking dead horses, my friend, but you know very well that many will call this stuff blasphemy.

J: George Bernard Shaw famously said that nearly all great truths start out as blasphemy—a label used by ideologists to guard what cannot survive on its own. "Blasphemy!" is the curse that superstition, fear and ignorance will lay upon the mind that dares to *think*. In every culture, 'blasphemy' is whatever threatens current beliefs. A few hundred years ago the Polish astronomer Copernicus declared that the sun does not revolve around Earth.

DK: Yeah, they said the dude was crazy and his theory was blasphemous.

J: Soon after, however, a guy named Galileo comes along and *proves* it. Doesn't matter, though—he's quickly labeled 'heretic' by the church. And even though he'd hit upon one of the greatest discoveries of his day, the church gave him nothing but imprisonment and sorrow for his trouble. He knew he could prove his position but was forced to deny it under threats from the Inquisition. As usual, religion led the revolt against knowledge, and dogma once more triumphed over reason. Boy, does *that* bring back a few mem'ries.

DK: Still, the fact that a thing's controversial doesn't always mean it's true.

J: Nor does the fact that it's widely believed.

DK: Granted. But again, how do we know what's true and what's not? Christians say that's why we have a Bible. They say it has all the right guidance.

J: The Bible's 'guidance' is cloudy, though, brimming as it does with contradictions, violence, and suspicious, implausible claims. In whole the Bible is relevant only for Christians, and no two Christians on earth interpret it the same. Each new reader brings years of deep conditioning to its passages, and every sentence meets *layers* of programs and blocks— there's little objectivity involved. Christians across the world are constantly fighting, and even *killing* each other, over what these 'holy words' mean. And as they say, if you have to explain against opposing evidence how your faith is a religion of peace . . . it *ain't*.

DK: In non-Christian cultures, the Bible is largely irrelevant. Hinduism has its Bhagavad Gita, Islam has its Quran, and so it goes.

J: And who should determine which, if any, is the 'inspired word of the Lord' . . . and how would they go about doing it? Almost every time, the one *making* this claim is a follower of the very religion whose rabid partisan line he's feverishly selling.

DK: So assessor and advocate are the same person.

J: Right. But how would you like it, in a court of law, if the one working to jail you were also the judge in the case? Or what if the ref in your ballgame is a coach for the other team? See what I mean? You favor the conclusions you prefer.

DK: It seems that nearly every faith claims sole possession of truth.

J: But everyone has different *perception* of truth: one man's devil is another man's god. *I'm* the top dog for the Christians, of course, but for Hindus the main man is Krishna. For tribes along the Amazon, it could be a special sun god, or even a particular animal. With so many people on the planet and with so many different perspectives, how would God best convey 'truth'?

DK: I was told that God considers Christians the modern-day 'chosen' —the new standard-bearers—just as He once favored Israel long ago. In church, I was raised to believe that Christians are special . . . that *they're* the ones who have the story straight. The church insists that the world received the ultimate truth in *you*, and that anyone who buys this concept is saved. We're asked to spread the good news of the New Testament gospel through 'witness.'

J: And what's this 'good news' the church would have you out witnessing?

DK: C'mon, you're setting me up. You already know the Christian spiel.

J: Play along here. Sometimes it helps to say this stuff aloud.

DK: Okay, which Christianity shall we cover—the literal or the liberal?

J: I don't see there's really any choice. In mainstream Christianity, non-literal reading of scripture isn't allowed. The staunch portrayal of me as the exclusive redeemer of sin means that New Testament writers have carved a narrow, well-defined path to an unavoidable, cast-iron conclusion: "Baby, you're no darned good, and God had to kill poor Jesus *because* of it."

DK: That may be too restrictive. The moderate churches don't usually emphasize sin. They focus instead on God's love and forgiveness and help us become better people. It's true they snub certain *parts* of the Bible, but they still consider themselves Christian.

J: How do they justify that? Rejecting various scriptures means you also spurn the conclusion that each little word is inspired. And if some Bible passages can't be trusted, on what grounds should I be viewed as the Christ?

DK: I just feel you've got to allow for compromise . . . *middle* ground, let's say.

J: Sorry, but scripture is quite explicit on humanity's breach of covenant with a God who demands compensation—and oftentimes in blood. The overriding theme of the Bible, including my own role as savior, is clearly one of guilt and atonement, and no one reading the scriptures can deny it: you're either headed to heaven or burning in hell. Softer views are capricious and biblically unsupported. Using the New Testament only to become a 'better person' is to slight its solemn warnings on the "wages of sin" and the jeopardized state of the soul. Arguing that Christianity is merely meant to spread some brotherly love around the place would entirely skirt the gospel's urgent call for repentance and profession of faith . . . it's forming one's religion to one's taste. To examine Christianity properly, we have to weigh what scripture actually describes. The *details* may contradict—and boy, do they ever—but the *point* is unmistakably clear.

DK: Convert to Christ *now*—or burn.

J: Yes, and churches that *dodge* this primary principle of the faith are being dishonest—they're cherry-picking their 'truth.' If genuine Christianity's what they're practicing, they aren't preaching pleasantries from the pulpit.

DK: It's true. A southern pastor once told me, "We ain't here just to make these people behave."

J: And from his perspective he was right. There's no defending a softball Christianity that sweetly teaches people to play nice.

DK: Well, in that case, the most literal interpretation of the gospel is we all inherit a sinful nature from initial transgressions in the Garden. The good news, from the New Testament bearing, is that your atoning death can *absolve* us of our sinning and forestall any post-world pain. It's not automatic, though. We're told to accept your lordship as the 'Son of God' and the sole viable path to redemption.

J: Okay, but for some people this wild story of God's self-incarnating suicide mission is a pretty tough sell. What if potential converts aren't interested? What if they don't *accept* this glorious news?

DK: Literalists say that those who reject the message will soon be wailing forever down in hell. Their God doesn't tolerate dissent.

J: Another way of saying, "See it *my* way now, or buddy you'll be burnin' quick enough."

DK: I know it ain't pretty, but that's how the church lays it out. The *good* news is, we save ourselves from hell and spend the rest of our days in heaven if we comply.

J: Well, then, I gotta be really honest. Suffering an infinity of horror in retaliation for refusing to be horse-collared into submission by a shockingly cruel and unforgiving parent doesn't sound like very good news at all.

DK: Helluva non-performance clause, for sure.

J: So the *real* reward of accepting me as redeemer—apart from gaining entrance to that gated community of Yahweh's—is that it saves you from his never-ending torture in unquenchable fires of perdition.

DK: I'm sure there's a prettier way to say it . . . but that's the bone and marrow of it all.

J: And that's what the church calls *good news!*? What in the world is 'good' about a God who carries long-term grudges against his children and won't forgive them 'til an innocent man is killed? What's good in a theology asking slave-like obedience to a fearful and controlling master? And I can't see what good comes of learning that no matter how loving, compassionate or forgiving you are, you're headed for a world of hurt if you don't raise the flag and salute the church's scary plan of 'redemption.'

No, from my view there's not a small shred of goodness in Christianity's gospel of 'good news.' But even if there's no sign of virtue in this theology, there might be something to the part about the news. If God had someone killed because of other people's behavior it would certainly be news to me.

DK: All I know is that the story of your death and its impact on man's destiny is central to the Christian faith—rejecting it is not a viable option. Besides, we're told we shouldn't *want* to reject it since God is all-loving and wants but the best for his brood.

J: Really? Was that his view, do ya think, just before He killed nearly *all* of 'em in his legendary flood? Will He still wish only 'the best for his brood' when He rains down hell's fury in his upcoming Great Tribulation?

DK: I'm boxing an opponent who isn't wearing gloves . . .

J: So the core message of Christianity is that, in the beginning, God created all things pretty much perfect. Adam and Eve then fell quickly from grace in eating some government-banned produce—therefore your *own* perfection was lost because God considers *you* their criminal accomplice thousands of years past the crime.

DK: Yeah, which is really stretching the statute of limitations, I'd say.

J: Even so, the church still instructs that God deems everyone guilty upon arrival—sinful the moment they're made.

DK: I guess so. Atheist Christopher Hitchens used to say with contempt that, in Christianity, we're all born sick and then instantly ordered to be well.

J: What about those who die as young children? Thrown into hell right along with the unrepentant?

DK: Oh, I'd rather doubt it. Some churches teach that we're protected 'til "age of accountability," which is different for everyone, they say. We're also told that God has compassion and wouldn't punish those without a chance. In fact, a cynical agnostic friend once pressed me on the matter and asked how the Christian God handles the souls of people who died before *you* came along—and what He does with those who died *afterward* but without ever hearing of you. He said if God dooms them despite their known innocence, He's cruel and not very bright. But if non-Christians *are* allowed in heaven because they never had occasion to accept you as their Lord and savior, then the world would've been far better off *without* you. My friend said you condemned nearly all of humanity, just by showing up!

J: Sounds like you're better off living in ignorance. You wonder God hasn't figured this out.

DK: Nonetheless, the church says we're all just pathetically lost sinners, every one, and greatly in need of your grace.

J: Which I firmly *withhold* 'til you hail church doctrine and 'believe.'

DK: According to New Testament writers, yes.

J: And *minus* these remedial measures, billions of God's children will become human glow-plugs in a distant broiler oven called hell.

DK: Yep, that's the story we're given.

J: Going by your very own summary, then, the Inquisition never really stopped . . . and the torture has only been *delayed*. Under Christianity, the world is God's interim observation facility, and most folks are headed for hell as soon as they're born. The Christian faith itself is merely Yahweh's chosen method to give hope of changing his mind about their fate.

DK: I s'pose you could sum it up that way, even if it's cold and unpolished.

J: Thankfully, though, the church says you can *save* yourself from this weenie-roast warrant of death you refer to as life.

DK: Correct. The path of salvation runs directly through your atoning death on the cross. *I* committed the crime, they say—distant kin to Adam and Eve that I am—and *you* paid the consequent price.

J: You mean I paid the price and *then* you committed the crime.

DK: Well, technically speaking, yes.

J: So God had me tortured because *you* would someday be *born*?!?

DK: C'mon, you know the drill: Christ was crucified for *me*.

J: So the church teaches that *you* caused an innocent man's agony, death, and victimhood—and did this roughly two thousand years after he *died*?

DK: I know, it's a cockamamie scheme from the start. But it's still the central teaching of the church: some criminal rapscallion from the boondocks breaks the orders and a guiltless guy from heaven takes the rap.

J: Hmmm . . . let's make sure we've got this dogma by the collar. The church says that humanity's collective soul is automatically inclined to damnation because a couple of kids in antiquity gave in to their instincts and disobeyed meal constraints. And now, everyone on earth must summon Jesus' tender mercies for redemption—and those who won't do it flirt with fire.

DK: That's our predicament, it seems.

J: Basically, then, you're asked to believe that I'll *spare* your miserable souls if you'll invoke me as your 'personal Lord and savior.'

DK: Yes . . . but we can't just *say* it, of course. We must *mean* it.

J: I see. But if you can't—or won't—sign up for this crazy do-or-die theology, you're bound to go suffering forever in a place where the sun don't shine. Is that pretty much how it works?

DK: For the most part . . . though the suffering doesn't start 'til we're dead.

J: Ah. So exposure to God's judgment is put off until the body reaches room temperature—you're safe 'til rigor mortis sets in.

DK: Well, various churches interpret it all quite differently. Some say we first go to Purgatory, where we all sit waiting 'til the final Day of Judgment. The fireworks begin at the Rapture, when *you* return to earth and *really* start kicking some ass.

J: Meantime, though, a hundred billion souls sit around for *centuries* in God's heavenly holding tank, watching the telly and waiting to hear of their fate. He won't judge or harm them before the Book of Life is cracked, and *that* doesn't happen 'til after the Rapture and the time of the Tribulation. That's the official narrative, right?

DK: Possibly . . . though scripture doesn't provide many details. But that's the given story—from the *Christian* standpoint, at least—of humanity's Fall and Redemption.

J: And a bloody great story it is. Plenty of tension and drama spiced with exciting sub-plots and fancies—but I'm shocked there's no mention of Bigfoot.

DK: Hey, it's no laughing matter. The God of Christianity means business.

J: And you're good with this guy actually running the company?

DK: What choice do we have? Scripture says that God is both wise and mysterious and that *his* ways are not often ours.

J: Oh, I'm not sure I'd go *that* far. In the 20th century alone, more than a hundred million people were killed at the hands of fellow human beings—and many died in the name of religion itself. Judging by Old Testament records, God's ways and man's ways are really not all that different. I'll grant I don't see much *wisdom* in those ways . . . but they sure qualify as mysterious.

DK: Lordy, what happened to 'gentle Jesus, meek and mild'?

J: Look where that got me last time.

DK: It's just that we see a man of *your* stature as somewhat pious and proper.

J: Maybe I could throw in a 'verily' or two.

DK: Seriously, what about this scripture thing? I mean a person has to believe in *something.*

J: Why do you need to *believe* anything? Trust in your own natural instincts.

DK: Wouldn't that lead to anarchy, chaos and lawlessness?

J: When did you last watch the news?

DK: Okay, but if everyone embraced Christianity, maybe we'd all get along.

J: You mean like in Northern Ireland or during your own country's great Civil War? Most of the major combatants in the first *world-wide* war were Christian—and it was three largely 'Christian' nations that forced brutal colonialism onto the world, carried out the Holocaust, and first used nuclear weapons on civilians. In the United States, about 75 percent of the citizens call themselves Christian, and 90 percent of Americans believe in a God—yet the country has the highest incarceration rate in the world!!

DK: I'm afraid it's the truth. If you wanna wind up in a prison, there's no place like the land of the free. But I do see your point. Hundreds of millions claim to follow the ways of Jesus and the world is *still* a disgrace.

J: Verily . . .

CHAPTER ELEVEN

DK: So the failure of religion's pretty plain. And it's tough finding the *practical* side of it all. My grandpa would say, in true Yogi Berra tradition, "If it don't really do ya no good, what *good* does it do ya?"

J: Gramps was right. If religion, which claims to be transformative, doesn't really transform, it's worthless—because that should be its number one job. Getting people following a bunch of rules just makes them zombies.

DK: I think the main reason for religion, aside from feeding hope of eternal life, is that living in the world can be scary—some people *need* a God who's in control.

J: Well, I'm not sure how they look at the world and think that God, or anyone else, is controlling it.

DK: Okay, *that* one I'll give sans debate. But even ignoring religion's 'comfort factor,' the Bible teaches that we're all just poor, pathetic sinners and desperately in need of redemption. The Book of Common Prayer has people asking God to save them "From all evil and wickedness; from sin; from the crafts and assaults of the devil; and from everlasting damnation . . ." In the church's stern view, we're somehow *pre-contaminated*—there's something inherently wrong with being human.

J: So this is the Christian perspective on how people should see their reality and no one bothers asking if it's *true*?? The faith has you jabbering on of your sinfulness and then passing it off as humility!!

DK: Yeah, certain religions have *taught* us to see ourselves poorly.

J: That sort of puny self-image is wholly man-made—the child of a guilt-centered faith. Imagine a young girl growing up by herself on an island. The thought of having a blemished soul would never occur to the kid.

DK: But even in a case like that, isn't she still stained by original sin?

J: That's strictly a creation of Christianity . . . God would *laugh* at the idea. Even Pope Innocent III once said, "In our obsession with original sin, we too often forget original innocence." The pope had it right: the purity came first. So it's goodness, not evil, that lies at the heart of your nature, even if it's often obscured.

DK: Well, if that *is* how God sees it, He might've thought to make some mention of it when putting his scriptures in place. Nearly every book in the Bible centers on humanity's shadier side. For Christianity, sin is practically sacred.

J: 'Sin' is just an intellectual label—a reflection of the mind's inclination to judge. Socially, it's purely subjective. What's seen as a sin in one culture is religious obligation in others.

DK: So, we're *not* born straight into wickedness.

J: How could an infant be wicked? In a show of brilliant theological craft, someone in history, probably a priest, decided that people are bad—crosswise with the cosmos from conception. Psalm 51 even has King David endorsing this ridiculous sinful-baby idea: "Indeed, I was *born* guilty, a sinner when my mother *conceived* me." Newborns were seen as spiritually spoiled, even before taking first breath. Though their God had only recently made them, somehow they managed to offend Him while still in the womb.

DK: *Heh heh.* And they got a good *spankin'* for it right out the chute . . .

J: This notion of guilt upon birth long predates even Judaism, but the Jews gave it anchor—it really took hold in their psyche. Centuries later, Christians grabbed the ball and took off. They gave 'original sin' the publicity it needed to become foundational dogma. If ever you dare take the story literally, all of humanity is made guilty because Adam and Eve snub the crystal-clear orders not to eat from the banned Tree of Knowledge.

DK: I always had trouble with that. We're never told much *about* the tree—why its presence was even needed or why its special fruit was unsafe.

J: Nor is it explained why Yahweh is so fearful of his children becoming educated and knowing all the things that *He* knows. Equally baffling is the sudden appearance of evil. A few paragraphs *before* the forbidden fruit fiasco, Genesis states that "God saw everything that he had made, and behold, it was *very good.*"

DK: Was the Lord unaware of the prospect for destruction, do you think?

J: Who knows? It's strange enough He saw the *need* for a plant that could lead to the downfall of Eden. I mean why make all these trees with tempting fruit which no one's allowed to eat?! Then He goes and *plants* the darned things right smack in the middle of the Garden!! Now, in Yahweh's defense, He does warn Adam that the tree's prohibited produce is lethal, and He leaves him with a stern admonition: "for in the day that you eat of it you shall die." As things turned out, though, the prophecy never came to—*heh heh*—fruition.

DK: You're shameless.

J: And not only didn't Adam *die* upon eating the outlawed fruit, he actually went on to live 930 years—a lot of birthdays for a guy not s'posed to make it past his teens.

DK: Maybe Yahweh meant that if Adam ate the forbidden fruit, he was going to die *eventually*. He may have been just warning Adam he'd lose his immortality.

J: Your basket might hold apples if not for Genesis 3. Here the Lord conveys his concern to *some*one—and God only knows who He was talking to—that Adam and Eve will next try to eat from the Tree of Life, in which case they'll both live *forever*. So, human immortality was never part of the plan.

DK: Wow, I never caught that before. Yahweh made Adam and Eve mortal right from the get-go . . . He *knew* their days were numbered.

J: He certainly did. He's *consumed* by the hazard of his unruly kids turning to gods and takes an unusual precaution to prevent it. He guards the path to the Tree of Life with cherubim and—*get this*—a flaming sword that swivels three hundred and sixty degrees.

DK: Hmmm. So He builds a magical sword of fire and stations angelic custodians to keep the kids from nearing the dangerous Tree of Life and eating its Fountain of Youth fruit.

J: Right, and for inquiring minds this should prompt an immediate question.

DK: I think I see where you're going. If this all-knowing God didn't want people eating from the treacherous Tree of Knowledge, why didn't He guard *that* tree in the same way that He later cordoned off the Tree of Life?

J: *Bingo*! I mean He plants the Tree of Knowledge right there in plain sight but tells the naïve young couple not to approach it. Now, anyone with an ounce of parenting skill would *know* that's a recipe for disaster—like a mother putting a box of needles in her toddler's playpen and then warning him not to open it. The moment God created temptation, catastrophe was certain: the full-blown circus of sin and perversion was fully his fault from the start.

62

DK: One could argue that God *trusted* his two young children. He gave them clear instructions and expected their assent. What's worse, I think, is threatening them with death upon *eating* the fruit, when He knew they were going to die anyway. Seems pretty dishonest—and not very godlike, I'd say—scaring his first two children with duplicitous threats.

J: Devious, to say the least. But that's the problem with creators these days—there's no accountability.

DK: So, to recap the story's beginning . . .   Adam gets lonely, so Yahweh yanks a rib from his chest and fashions it into the world's first woman.

J: But why God resorted to invasive surgery I'm not sure—all He needed for *Adam's* creation was a simple fistful of dirt. Anyway, it isn't long after the woman shows up that things *really* start to unravel.

DK: And boy, can I relate to *that*. So now we've got a seductress in the show.

J: Yes, and shortly after she's created, Eve herself is seduced by one of Eden's most unusual residents: a talking serpent. The serpent, generally thought to be a snake, employs his reptilian wiles to convince young Eve that God was just making an idle threat and that eating the restricted fruit won't really cause instant death. Failing to quell her God-given curiosity —and taking what seems like an enormous gamble—Eve munches down the juicy jinx and then bids her bad-boy beau to take a few bites as well. Surprisingly, neither one drops dead.

DK: So the serpent was right!

J: Yep. That poor snake has taken a lousy rap in the history books. Nowadays he'd be suing for millions and a major page one retraction. But pay attention now, because here's where the story gets good . . .
   Soon after ingesting their forbidden fruit cocktail, the two Edenian lovers feel shame for their nakedness and cover themselves with leaves. Later, as Yahweh takes a morning stroll through the Garden, He sees that his first two earthly dependents have begun wearing clothes. Strikingly short of omniscience, the Lord questions Adam on the new fashion trend and discovers that he and his mate have ignored divine orders by eating fruit from the Tree of Knowledge. Abruptly busted, Adam quickly shifts all the guilt onto Eve, while *she* blames it all on the clever, slick-talking snake. Hearing the couple cowardly pass the buck, Yahweh gets really pissed off and quickly begi—

DK: Excuse me, one second here. Did you just say *"pissed off"*?

J: Look, you've gotta get past this 'gentle Jesus' thing or we'll never make any progress. You think I grew up in the grit and grime of my workaday world twenty centuries ago and somehow didn't speak in the vernacular? You act like I never looked on a woman with animal desire, like I never got drunk at a wedding, made politically insensitive jokes or ran a red light.

DK: Uh, ran a red lig—

J: Christians have turned me into some kind of sissified, hyper-religious hall monitor with a 'better-than-you' complex. If I ever write a book, it'll surely be *You Don't Know Jack about Jesus*. I had a different *calling* from others, but mostly I was a pretty regular guy.

DK: I see. Just your average, run-of-the-mill messiah.

J: Well, I didn't walk the neighborhood with hands folded in prayerful supplication and piously quoting the 23rd Psalm. My own daily routine wasn't too unlike anyone else's . . . nor was my use of the language.

DK: Apparently I've seen too many runs of *The Passion*. My apologies—please continue.

J: So the two teen lovers scarf down the banned apple and Yahweh unloads onto Adam: "You sorry son-of-a-deity, look what you've done!! You've gone and ruined *every*thing!! Do you know I had to sweat like a pig for six solid days to pull all of this stuff together!?"

DK: One of the *newer* translations, no doubt . . .

J: Next, as a result of his children's dietary sins, the creator makes one of the meanest, most irrational decisions in the history of religious lore. In a single instant of fury, Yahweh subjects thousands of later generations to strife and sorrow by cursing their lives with toil, suffering, death—and cheap-looking polyester clothing.

DK: He also decides to curse all the women, causing pain when giving birth to their children.

J: Oh, sure . . . as if *raising* them weren't 'labor' enough already.

DK: You've not too much regard, it seems, for the biblical accounting of The Fall.

J: Well, if you stick to its allegorical value, no problem—it's brilliant. In a metaphysical sense, it tells the story of man's unhappy fall into separation and all the needless suffering it's caused. But calling that stuff 'history' would be about the silliest thing ever. I mean I just don't *get* this 21st-century religious gullibility thing. People are typically quite cynical.

DK: It's true that cynicism in modern life is rampant. 'Conspiracy' groups have long insisted the Apollo moon landings were a giant government hoax. I always thought they were crazy . . . but with all the new hidden info coming to light, I'm more and more certain it's true. The irony, though, is that many who had rightfully scoffed at the moon landings are also devoted Christians who accept every mind-bending thing in the Bible.

J: Oh, humans can be skeptical to the point of delusion—they'll deny the existence of a sharp-pointed stick when it's poking 'em right in the eye. But read 'em a story from a 'holy' book and quickly they're pliant as pups. A cosmos created in less than a week? *It's plain as the nose on your face.* A garden with magical trees and talking snakes? *It says so right there in the Bible!* A world gone mad because two young lovers eat a bite of some mystical fruit? *Thus saith the Lord.*

DK: But I think you're ducking some well-deserved blame. It's not like 'original sin' was the brainchild of some parochial school dropout. You've already said it was your very own church that *invented* the concept and made it sellable.

J: Two points . . .
    First, I don't have a 'church.' That's a *religious* thing, and I'm not into spreading theology. The number of Christian sects on the planet now exceeds *thirty thousand.* How would anyone *begin* sorting out that mess? I use the word "church" to refer to it in general, as an institution. It's the same way we use the masculine "He" when speaking of God. We just as readily could say "She"—or even "It"—since "God" refers to something so far beyond intellect that, for all practical value, the word's meaningless. So my terms are just handy conventions of language that people can grasp.

DK: Got it.

J: Second, if you're defending the soundness of an idea by stating that it was conjured up by the church, you're resorting to an especially embarrassing view. History is *bursting* with examples of lunkheaded thinking spewing forth from the sanctums of faith. Religion is usually the last to self-examine, to accept any threatening discoveries or encourage genuine progress. Remember poor Copernicus and Galileo.

DK: You're right, religion's had some pretty sick ideas through the years.

J: And some got a lot of people killed. It's no fluke that the most evangelical religions are also the deadliest. Take the Crusades and the several phases of Inquisition. All by themselves, these two thunderbolts of church-sponsored wisdom inflicted *centuries* of routine persecution, torture and murder onto millions of people. Christianity and other religions have well-established, centuries-long records of violence, bloodshed and death. And the thinking that *inspired* those brutal eras is still going strong—it hasn't substantially changed in thousands of years. We'd likely find reports of 'religious' conflicts in this evening's worldwide news. And all of it goes on as these religions build their power, rake in the money, and cause even *intelligent* people to do whatever faith would demand.

DK: So, clarify something. You acknowledge that humanity can often be more twisted than a stick of black licorice—but you also claim that God knows us only in our state of natural innocence, and not in a state of sin. How does *that* compute?

J: God doesn't see his earthly children as they presently see themselves—little of your current perception is rooted in truth.

DK: If God and his children are one, why has religion been so long focused on sin?

J: Crowd control, pure and plain. And of course a sinful, *fearful* parishioner is a dues-paying, *submissive* parishioner. Promoting a sense of guilt and fostering fear of divine retribution is religion's way of wielding power without using force. Religion wants you always coming back for more. If they scare you into thinking that you're never quite free of your 'sin,' you'll have to keep returning for atonement.

DK: The First Letter of John says, "if we say we have no sin, we deceive ourselves." But later the writer pulls a complete reversal and declares, "No one born of God commits sin." So, I don't follow. Christians say that *you're* the only one technically "born of God." But the author of 1 John clearly isn't referring only to you. He says categorically, *"he who loves* is born of God and knows God."

J: So the New Testament tells you firstly that everyone's a sinner and you're kidding yourself to deny it. Then it says that no one born of God ever *commits* any sin and, further, that anyone who loves is born of God. Using clear New Testament logic, then, everyone who loves is sinless.

DK: Confusing stuff.

J: It's scriptural schizophrenia. The Bible says God is love. If that's true, then love must reflect God's *nature*—pervasive, all-powerful, expansive. No room exists for any judgment, evil or sin because love gives them no energy or reality.

DK: But the Bible is *loaded* with stories of God obsessing over human behavior. And the gospels have *you* making threats of an overcrowded, overheated prison where no calendars are needed, no stays of execution ever granted, and no paroles are approved.

J: Like many other scriptures of the world, those sound like the works of a culture clearly fearful of its God—so it's not surprising that frightened people would adopt such scary theologies. But should sovereign, educated men and women be ceding their power to some musty old papers passed down by a bunch of religious rascals in robes? God's truth is *within* us, and in fact *is* us. Together, *we are* the holy, and *wholly*, living truth of God, and our unity *is* our holiness in a realm where everything is One.

DK: And *there* go the last Southern Baptists . . .

Chapter Twelve

DK: Well, you've definitely caught me off-guard. For centuries, the church has warned of God's wrath and impending doom, constantly threatening non-believers with hell. Sure, it painted lipstick on the skeleton by offering a fate free of fire—but the basic message is still, "You're not good enough, and now you need *us* to *redeem* your ass." But *you* say it was all just a trick to keep the troops in line.

J: Forget my words a minute and reflect on your own experience. Does it seem like God punishes people for sins? When did He ever punish *you*?

DK: Hard to say. There've certainly been times I've felt guilty.

J: Yes, but don't connect guilt with divine judgment. You experience guilt because part of your mind—psychology calls it 'ego'—believes that it separated from Source. This is the mystical meaning of the parable of the prodigal son. And this false belief in separation is what makes you act destructively from the start. Guilt is the belief that you've broken from God and defiled your holy nature. To believe you could do *either* is as arrogant as it is delusional.

DK: Some Christians say that guilt is God's way of 'convicting' us of sin.

J: Only humans convict. Deceptions and denials of love will be exposed and their karmic consequences reaped—this is the law of the universe and the way you expand and find balance. Now, results can certainly *feel* like punishment, but that idea's not relevant in the High Court of Spirit.

DK: A true fundamentalist would say that you're forgetting free will. We always have a *choice* in our behavior, they argue, and God has right to punish if we screw up.

J: Even if He *has* the right, why would He constantly invoke it? He's *God*, for the love of Mike. Can't He just forgive and learn from the experience? That's what He tells *you* to do.

DK: As I understand it, God *does* forgive us—but only if we *ask* Him to. The only real punishment takes place at the Final Judgment, when those who rejected Him here on earth go swift to their deathless deserts.

J: Tell me: what would people think of a mother who wouldn't show her children any forgiveness without them constantly *asking* her for it? Or what of a father who would torture his kids for refusing to adopt his personal philosophy, give him lots of attention, or show sufficient thanks for his grace?

DK: Most would say they're insane and therefore fully unfit for parenting. But somehow that seems different.

J: Oh, you're darned right it's different. The gap in wisdom between adults and their children is *nothing* compared with the gap between God and his sinners. Should regulators not be held at least to slightly higher codes than those they govern?

DK: One would surely hope. But believers the world over have no qualms whatsoever with their faiths' dreadful policies of damnation. The one thing their gods have in common is they don't lightly suffer insurgents.

J: Which is pretty ironic, no? Christians urge all *earthly* parents to endless love and patience with their *own* misguided children—and still they're perfectly fine with Yahweh's hell!!

DK: A valid argument, I think. God should have *at least* as much parental wisdom as *we* do.

J: Even those wallowing in theologies of guilt should expect their 'Lord of love' to be smarter. Somehow they've got no issue with a God who makes it personal and sadistically pains unruly children for infinity in burning pits. Now, if people are honest about it, they already know that Love would never *think* of such things. In a state of harmonious unity, who would be the accuser and who the accused?

DK: You're describing a spirituality of complete benevolence. And of course it's far more *appealing* than a theology of conditional redemption. But my instincts tell me that there *must* be a price for what religion refers to as 'sin.'

J: There's always a price for ignorance. In duality—the realm of good and bad, right and wrong, and so forth—thoughts and deeds have natural results, and especially energetically since everything in Universe is energy. But the word 'sin'—meaning to miss the mark or target—takes on a more *spiritual* tone, suggesting that you and God can be separate . . . sometimes you're *with* him and sometimes you're not. In such a bewildering universe, God would be always joining and then separating from his very own creations—there at your side one minute, He is, and gone like a bandit the next. This kind of thinking is *crazy*, and the world should be asking hard questions.

DK: Like what?

J: Like, how much longer will we pamper this violent God of religion? Is it honest even to call the man 'loving'? According to the scriptures, He judges, condemns and abuses his very own children and then tells the kids to abuse *each other*! But if He's so worried over how folks are living, why not come down and take charge? He micro-managed well enough in the *old* days. What keeps Him waiting around?

DK: You're right, tough questions. I see why the Sanhedrin wanted you gone.

J: Hey, I'm not asking you to go dousing every burning bush or throw out the baby with the baptismal water. To spiritually develop, though, you have to start using your brains—start *questioning*. The Energy driving the cosmos isn't tracking your personal sin-to-sanctity score.

DK: If our basic, unspoiled nature is only good, how do we account for all the bad?

J: Because your basic, unspoiled nature has been distorted. It's not that people don't do evil *things*. Of course they *do*, and religion calls this destructive behavior 'sin.' But if you don't know how Universe works, how can you interpret what you see? Results of evil thinking and behavior are undeniable. But believing in a lasting *source* of evil is to believe that both God and his gifts have limitations—the same as believing that God's *giving* is limited, too. The notion that God withholds his full goodness 'til you've begged his forgiveness and He's handled your mistakes is the phony foundation of some of the world's most powerful religions.

DK: But let's be practical and put God aside.

J: I'll ignore the tremendous irony.

DK: What I mean is that, as far as *I* can tell, God rested on the seventh day and never returned to work. Evil has unfettered run of the store . . . and the owner's nowhere about!

J: Action stems from beliefs: you *behave* as whatever you believe you *are*. Evil is just a behavioral response to a very warped view of reality—a frightened and programmatic reaction to a terribly distorted self-image, and a world that's been misconstrued. Evil is simple unconsciousness or spiritual ignorance. Whenever you set out to hurt someone, it shows that you believe you're something you aren't—in a very real sense, you're walking in a world of dreams.

DK: That could be a loose definition of *insanity*.

J: And often, that's every inch what's happened. Insanity is the state of not being in one's right mind—not knowing one's own reality. And really, an insane man is hardly responsible for his acts. So the answer for this poor guy is not *punishment*, but to get him *sane* again. If everyone were sane in a spiritual sense, your world would be free of evil and everything you look upon as 'sin.' All of it would disappear, since nothing would be left to give it life.

DK: So there's no damnable devil dishing up dupery, destruction and death.

J: Who would've *created* this great Emissary of Evil? I mean where did the fella come *from*?

DK: According to Revelation, Satan was apparently one of Yahweh's top angels who sought to replace the existing adminis—

J: Oh, right . . . *now* I recall the story. But he seemingly tired of euphoric perfection and so rallied together a few other bored-with-bliss angels planning coup against Christ in the heavens.

DK: Yeah, which always makes me wonder about their smarts . . . but after warring against Archangel Michael and troops, Satan and his buddies were defeated and thrown out of heaven. *Now*, say literalists, he's here causing *earthly* havoc and tempting us humans to 'reject' our own creator—whatever the hell *that* means. And I see how this might profit the average short-sighted sinner . . . but how this helps the devil I still can't grasp.

J: So the beginning of Christian theology is that, dead-smack in the middle of heaven, a bloody *shooting* war breaks out—a Pearly Gate showdown with the devil right there at the I'm OK & You're OK Corral.

DK: I know, it's a serious problem. *That* one I never resolved.

J: And instead of being thrown into hell, where they *belong*, the devil and his devious band of demons are summarily ordered to earth —seemingly free to deceive and destroy at will—while Yahweh stands off in the wings making sure that no one flubs their lines and that history goes according to biblical plan. He's *watching* the spectacle but refuses to further engage with Satan and the other angelical ingrates.

DK: Yes, but only 'til their *ultimate* defeat at your Second Coming . . . which, for reasons no one's figured, has been stalled about two thousand years.

J: And all this tomfoolery takes place while God sits around brain-dead like some retiring government bureaucrat and allows it!? Who *invented* this sacred theology? Dr. Seuss?

DK: C'mon, this account of evil's beginning comes straight from the hallowed halls of Christendom.

J: That won't endorse it much. But look . . . darkness is just an absence of light—bring in the light, and dark vanishes back to the void. Same with the shadow of evil: the light of pure love makes it fade. Evil is certainly real enough when it's happening and its scars can't just be ignored. But evil has no lasting existence of its own. The believer looks upon evil and assumes there's a spiritual cause—in this case he's sure it's a devil— and religion's quite happy to exploit its own sinister invention.

DK: Well, bogus Beelzebub. Lucifer's just a convenient, man-made stooge.

J: He's the carefully crafted product of a lie. Christian fundamentalists commandeered the poor clod and made him the great rival of the Lord. But Israelites had no such character in their cosmology, which is why the term "devil" never appears in the Old Testament. The name "Satan" is used about a dozen times—mostly in the book of Job—but he's basically shown to be just a useful servant of God. The one time there's any real friction between the two is in Zechariah 3, where Yahweh only mildly rebukes him.

DK: Apparently old Lucie gets far more attention than he's earned.

J: The truth of it is this: never was there an Old Testament figure named Lucifer, and Jewish scriptures hold no record of Lord Yahweh knowing any cosmic criminal. Few people realize the word "Lucifer" appears in the Bible just once—in the fourteenth chapter of Isaiah. Some versions don't even use it. The tried-and-true Revised Standard Version translates the original text as "Day Star, Son of Dawn" and never even mentions a name. But even though Christians will use that Isaiah verse as 'proof' for the emergence of a devil, it's directed quite specifically to the ruling king of Babylon, and the writer plainly says so in verse four. Five minutes of research would show that "Lucifer" means "bringer of light" or "light-bearer"—a pretty strange name for a "spirit of darkness" from the start. Sometimes the name is translated only as "Day Star" or "Morning Star." Here's a well-kept secret of the Bible: it's just a poetic reference to a specific 263-day window in the 584-day synodic period of planet Venus, which is also the "Evening Star" in a second 263-day cycle.

DK: No kidding!? Seems Lucifer's lucky to have lasted as long as he has.

J: Well, I don't know how you could see that Isaiah passage as the making of a universal villain—you're bullying the Bible to defend a crazy theology. Torture the scriptures *long* enough, they'll scream the confession you want.

DK: Alright, but you're talking *Old* Testament here. The devil has plenty of *New* Testament backing as well—like the gospel account of that high-stakes spiritual tug-of-war 'tween you and Satan in the sand.

J: Ah, right . . . the one you wielded like a crowbar to wallop me in your opening letter.

DK: Yeah yeah, *that* one. And remember, the gospels don't present this story as fiction, so we're seemingly asked to believe it. Hell, they've even made movies about it.

J: My god, doesn't anyone think *metaphorically*!? The desert narrative is a simple allegory on the temptations of the human experience to pull the spiritual seeker off-course. I mean *really*, pilgrim, when's the last time this devil showed up at *your* place? But wait, I can probably imagine . . .

[Ding-dong]

Who's there?

It's Lucifer the devil calling, sir.

What's your business here?

Damnation, if you please. I've come to lure your trusting soul into hell.

Well, I'll have to think about that. What's the latest proposal?

Oh, just the usual stuff . . . a few years of fast-fading wealth, power and fame— maybe some time with swingers if you're lucky.

Gee, Luce, it all sounds very *tempting*. But could you come back a bit later? I'm just hopping into the bath . . .

CHAPTER THIRTEEN

DK: Okay, we'd better get serious or this meeting will have all the standing of a leftist in a Lamborghini.

J: Oh, I'm quite serious, my friend. Christians rattle on of their devil like they've just seen him walking through the woods. So, what experience have you *personally* had with this much-maligned master of malice?

DK: Well . . . none that I'm actually aware of.

J: And yet for *decades* you've carried this childish view of a cosmic bogeyman skulking 'round earth—and not just unsupervised but *unimpeded*, for God knows why—tempting people everywhere to forswear heart and soul and asking everything of genuine value, while nothing of lasting worth is given in kind. *This* is your chosen cosmology? This is your most objective view of reality? Has family been made aware of your condition?

DK: C'mon, ease off a bit. This God-vee-Satan stuff's been shoved down our throats a long time—the devil's a main character in the play. The way *I* see it, the church owes its very *existence* to the guy. Minus him and his burning lake, the need for salvation goes up in smoke and Christianity's more worthless than a sewing article in *Playboy*. I'm telling you, the church critically *needs* the damn devil. Besides, revamping our views of God would mean gutting some of the world's most popular scriptures. Take the Old Testament, for example. It may not contain any running theme of soul damnation, but we both agree that its God is a decadent, cold-hearted guy, who quickly mows down *thousands* when He's pissed. And the *New* Testament isn't much better, because God is pretty somber in *those* writings, too . . . and *you* prob'ly know what I'm sayin'.

J: Wait, I taught my friends and followers to love each other—and *I* think that's straightforward stuff. I urged them always to show patience, mercy and kindness, just as they'd want others showing them.

DK: Well, going by New Testament writings, I'm not sure they all got the message. But really, it's not your disciples I'm *worried* about. In the gospels, *you're* the one who appears so consistently narrow-minded and disparaging. You weren't quite as *violent* as Yahweh—but reading about those scrapes with Scribes and Pharisees, it seems you were equally stern.

J: Threatening sinners with outer darkness and such.

DK: Exactly. Now, after hearing your explanations, I'll ignore those cryptic references to Satan and your infamous threats of "wailing and gnashing of teeth." But *some* of the gospel stories must be based on actual events; and if so, you were something of a moral drill sergeant. You don't appear to have been all that tolerant, either. Sure, you were helpful with folks out boating in hurricanes—or when supplies ran short in the kitchen—but you don't generally seem very *happy*.

J: A real stick-in-the-mud, is that it?

DK: Well, maybe not completely. In the realm of good drama, you were definitely *the man*. And the miracles alone . . . my God, what a glorious show. But seeing how you abused the poor Pharisees who asked you to dinner, I'm shocked you got invited to funerals.

J: C'mon, you're not being rational here. You can't expect to know me from a few dozen third-party stories and a thimbleful of make-believe 'history.' With that sort of limited information, would others get an accurate reading of *you*?

DK: But why all the finger-pointing, tongue-lashing, name-calling stuff?

J: As I said, I didn't write a word of those texts . . . but it's not hard to see how it happened. Humans had a longtime love affair with guilt— my ancestors simply married it and made it respectable.

DK: They certainly did. It shows up in the opening pages of scripture with God's punishment of Adam and Eve. From there it becomes a thematic thread that runs throughout the Bible, right down to John's Revelation. And every step of the way, God wants payback, blood and regret. At first He's happy to settle for altar-smoked animals, but finally He has *you*, his 'only son'—his humanized sacrificial lamb—nailed in agony to a cross.

J: But even allowing for the laughable thought that mere mortals can irritate God, why in the name of anything sober would He lay their guilt onto *me*? To kill a man perfectly innocent as payment for his brother's wrongdoing couldn't possibly change anyone's consciousness . . . it only adds one further crime to another. Give this notion but a tiny bit of thought and you'll see why no deity with brains would ever conceive it.

DK: Actually, the whole atonement scenario is confusing. I never saw how the Jews could bless killing a man seen by some to be Israel's messiah— especially when he hadn't ever harmed anyone and apparently brought healing to many.

J: But I was in fact guilty of *one* thing: threatening their intelligence. At best I was seen as a heretic for brazenly challenging primitive 'holy' law. Near the end, everyone rightly lost faith that I was the liberator many expected. *Their* messiah would've been rankling the *Romans*, not railing at hypocrisy 'mongst his own. Once they saw no savior had come, they rushed me like rabid coyotes. So the Jews hardly considered me the vanquishing knight they were hoping for, and many felt I fully deserved what I got. They were the ones screaming for my death, don't forget.

DK: I still feel that, as "king of the Jews," you really did get the royal shaft. From what I see, crucifixion was absurdly harsh punishment for basically harmless behavior—you seemingly didn't do any worse than question the way things were. Although, come to think of it . . .

J: Every culture has sacred 'codes' of conduct and breaking them is always serious business. By the time *my* day rolled around, Judaism had done a thorough job depicting Yahweh as a visitor of revenge. Theirs was a worldview of judgment, guilt and atonement. Mosaic instruction made perfectly clear that one's moral offenses must be punished—and sometimes paid for with *blood*. Rabbinical leaders felt threatened when I challenged these barbarous beliefs in public . . . and for them this was bloodworthy stuff.

DK: So the Romans *and* the rabbis needed quick solution to squash your support and send warning to every *other* potential pain-in-the-ass prophet.

J: Right, and they got it. For a people long steeped in revenge, my breaking of the sacred law, together with my perceived spiritual arrogance, was plenty of justification for having me killed. This mindset shows why literalist factions of the church had no problem making into 'history' those stories of an innocent savior who dies for a sinful mankind—the age-old tales of guilt and atonement carried on. For the new apocalyptic cult of "Christians," everyone was guilty, God's burning wrath was coming, and choosing me as savior was the fix. I mean, no matter how the church may spin it, this religion's not great for self esteem. And even though Christians said their "new covenant" with God overrode the old intolerant rules of Judaism, their subtler theology still demanded "an eye for an eye." Christians painted my death on the cross as a blood sacrifice to Lord Yahweh . . . and there's no other way to see it.

DK: In a culture stressing vengeance and compensation, then, the loving notion of forgiveness wasn't part of the deal.

J: No, which is why my lessons on compassion weren't as popular as one might presume. And here's good example of what I mean. You know very well of the gospel story of the woman caught in adultery, yes?

DK: Sure. The Pharisees—sort of ancient-day fundamentalists, I guess—bring an adulterous woman to you, wanting to pin you down by reminding you that Hebrew law says adulterers shall be stoned to death. The Jews no longer do it, of course, but in some nations this kind of thing still happens.

J: Well, we all know that if cultures routinely stoned their adulterers, the world would quickly run short of rocks. But the Pharisee is a difficult customer and a hypocrite of highest degree. A Ph.D. in the *letter* of the law, he's a flunkout in grasping the spirit behind it. The Pharisee is an academic tough guy with the sympathy of a junkyard dog and the sense of a drunken frat boy in a new Corvette. And even though he lives in a 'glass house' himself, the Pharisee stands ready to throw rocks.

DK: It's pretty clear the Pharisees were every bit as eager to eliminate *you* as to punish the woman caught cheating.

J: Oh, they would've loved to kill two birds with one stoning. Here was another story of literalists using 'authority' of ancient writings to overrule the *higher* authorities of love, compassion . . . and even everyday good sense. The Pharisees knew that if I openly challenged their scripture, I'd suffer serious blowback from the rabbis. They realized as well—if I *agreed* to the woman's killing—that my choice would make a mockery of my well-known message of forgiveness and would also make me guilty of her death. I would've seemed to my friends and students both hypocritical and weak—a classic no-win situation, and everyone knew it.

DK: So, like a master preparing for checkmate, the Pharisees set the trap.

J: Yeah, they lured me. "And what is *your* opinion?" they asked.

DK: Scripture says you then bent down and started drawing on the ground. What the heck were you doing?

J: I was stalling. I thought I might buy a little time for myself by messing around in the sand. The woman's prospects were bleak and I had to resolve things without getting either of us killed . . . so I doodled awhile.

DK: What was running through your mind?

J: I knew the cowards were too weak to act alone—their force rested strictly on sheer mob strength and therefore thinking like the herd. But blasting their scripture would be risky. I grew up with those writings and knew well how revered they were. So I knelt there thinking a minute, and finally the answer came through. Instead of *dishonoring* the moral code—and they desperately hoped that I would—I stood up to speak and took a chance. I proposed that whoever was free of fault should throw the first stone. I calmly knelt back down and resumed my doodling while the Pharisees stood there confused. I tried not to look at them directly, but I kept a close watch the whole time. As my words went crashing through consciousness and echoed in the edgy lull, the Pharisees finally walked off.

DK: Powerful. A clever strategic victory through peaceful non-resistance—makes Solomon's stuff look lame.

J: I was demonstrating a new way of living—the way of *forgiveness*. You've got to appreciate how radical this was for a people so inclined to revenge. I showed that love neither judges nor condemns, but merely exposes harmful, destructive *thinking* . . . which drags on the collective mind, as well.

DK: Scripture says that when the mob dispersed you told the woman you didn't condemn her. But you also told her, "Go and do not sin again."

J: Not because I'd have *judged* her if she did . . . but because she wouldn't likely be that *lucky* again. And here's something else on the story: although I didn't judge the adulterous woman, *neither did I judge the Pharisees*. It's true that I often raged at hypocrisy and surely didn't hold back my words. But I was only saying what so many wouldn't—what no one else would dare.

DK: You know, for a long time I've thought that you were maybe just another extremist . . . but you're starting to sound almost human.

J: I see I've been getting bad press.

DK: Well, your *biographers* certainly did you no favors—they set the bar too high. They gave us a savior who healed the blind, but *he* couldn't see past tomorrow. He walked on water but couldn't save *others* from *drowning*. He quickened the dead but his threatening doomsday teachings wind up killing practically all of the living. He promised the kingdom of heaven, but mostly we've inherited just a power-hungry, trust-breaking, money-grabbing religious bureaucracy from hell. I hate to break it to ya, chief—but your factory's no longer shipping your first product.

J: That's what often happens when the founder dies: management starts abusing the customers and focusing on the cold bottom line. Then they go and change the bloody formula . . .

CHAPTER FOURTEEN

DK: I have to say, these new perspectives are really shifting my views. But they might not play well down on Main Street—not to those who see you as a prophet of ruin. Most folks are sure they know your story and what you're all about, so I doubt there's much hope of winning them over.

J: Tell 'em about our chat 'down by the riverside.'

DK: Trust me, I *will* . . . but I might as well claim it was Elvis.

J: Ah well, it's never your job to change people. That's one of *religion's* big problems: the faithful often focus on beliefs and intentions of others— and that's *really* missing the point, would you agree? Your task is to seek the truth for *yourself*. Spirit speaks to *you* . . . it doesn't speak to someone else. Correcting errors and revealing truth is *Spirit's* function, not yours.

DK: You talk about human error like it's just a mistake on a quiz. But lots of man's 'errors' have pretty frightful results. Personally, I'm sick of living in a world of warships and missiles, land mines and cluster bombs, napalm, nerve gas and nukes. We can't afford education or healthcare —nor even fill the holes in our streets!—but somehow we've always got *plenty* to fund the latest-model, billion-buck bomber!!

From what I see, most wars are nothing but state- or corporate-sponsored power plays and land grabs aimed at controlling other nations, stealing their wealth and funneling criminal profits into the pockets of the world's banksters, businessmen—and of course the fear-mongering death-squads of the wartime-industrial complex. It's all done for 'spreading democracy," they say, by a nation that calls itself Christian. But me, I've had enough. Like so many others on earth, I'm tired of even *needing* to pay the price of this 'protection.' We've not witnessed even *one single day* of world peace!!

J: I see. Und how did *zat* make you feel?

DK: Very funny, Freud. And by the way . . . this may not sit too well with *you*, but most of us have had it up to *here* with showing 'religious tolerance' to every dangerous devotee with a holy book in one hand and a weapon of war in the other. And we're finished with these elitist, hypocritical, sound-bite-spewing career politicians putting party before country and always turning into little Napoleans. With all the insufferable narcissists who crave it, most of those actively *seeking* high office should surely be disqualified up front. All across the world, these professional leeches will gorge themselves continuously at public troughs, uncreatively keeping the status quo and living like freakin' *royalty* on sweaty tax dollars —and usually voting themselves the cushiest of benefits, of course— while the rest are told to live within budget, suck it up and tighten their belts. We're *done* with these psychopaths' self-serving, war-first, schoolyard bully mentality and *burnt out* on all their secret agenda, secret alliances, secret policies, secret surveillance—and secret damned near everything!!! And always spending *public* funds in ways they'd never *ever* spend theirs.

J: Perhaps you'd like to talk about your mother . . .

DK: And here's somethin' else that baffles. If all of the private funds and government billions spent on space programs—

J: A slight misnomer, incidentally, since the cosmos never held true 'space'—

DK: —but if every last penny were being spent to get the hell off of *this* crazy planet, I might at least get what they're thinkin'. But now we're off exploring, and even talking of *populating*, other planets as well? When still not done spoiling the one we've got? Hell, the daily creation of pollution and rubbish alone is enough to choke our planet half to death— and there are patches of human garbage the size of *countries* floating in our oceans! Maybe these rich, high-tech wiz kids and futurist 'visionaries' could spend more time addressing *that* little problem than they do launching air-poisoning, fire-breathing rockets delivering *still more* future space junk, and spending fortunes to find water on Mars. It's pretty bad when all that'll stop the bleeding and save the earth for certain now is a serious event for *Homo sapiens sapiens*—the proudly self-labeled 'wise' ones— allegedly the smartest and most spiritually advanced species in history!!

And if *all that* weren't headache enough, those of us who still find the will to bother caring are stressed to the max over a world-killing population bomb being blessed by various religions; a soulless capitalism whose only vision for the planet seems to be the building and selling of more and more *stuff* 'til we're *buried* in it; food that's mostly chemicalized garbage; and telephone service reps who don't speak the friggin' *language*!!

So listen, old pal. You wanna do some *good* in the world and make a positive difference? Then set us all free, O heavenly confessor, and liberate us each and every one from the chains of heartless, Big Brother communistic government; paid-for, half-truthing journalism; Earth-ruining corporate exploitation; and the blood-sucking, wealth-sapping vampires comprising the arrogant, philosophically repugnant and largely unaccountable cancers of the Internal Revenue 'Service' and the fully unneeded, transnational, totally reserve-less, non-federal, privately owned Federal Reserve!!!

J: Anything else after you breathe?

DK: Yeah, give us this day our daily bread—but without us having to lay half the loaves into outstretched palms of parasites. Deliver us from evil at the hands of all the self-serving special-interest groups and their sickening, unbroken gush of the latest disingenuous spin. Lead us beside the still, non-municipally-fluoridated waters and make us to lie down in organic green pastures, free from the grip of those sneaky Wall Street gangsters; politically biased legal systems; an ominous New World Order; treasonous self-above-nation 'patriots' . . . and eighty freakin' *thousand* pages of *tax code*!!!

J: Ohhhh, I'm sorry, Mr. Maylor—seems session time is up. I'll just be off to lunch, then, and that'll be three hundred dollars, which you can pay conveniently by credit card on the way out. Please remember to take your medication and I'll see you at the usual time next week . . .

DK: Okay, I got a little carried away. But I can't handle this life-is-beautiful, see-no-evil philosophy of yours. A fat-finger click from disaster we sit— and *you're* all concerned with correcting human 'error'?!?

J: Yes, because that single error, the belief that everyone is separate, is what lies at the heart of all others. Evil is essentially the result of this spiritual disconnect.

DK: So, we harm each other because we don't understand our connection.

J: Well, think how people might behave differently if they knew they're always dealing with the Christ. Who would exploit, abuse or attack when knowing all is one with the Self? Remember: the energy you send out is the energy you get back—multiplied—always and without exception.

DK: I'm not sure I get this 'oneness' thing. Here I am, and there you are sitting next to me. Clearly we're separate.

J: You're referring to our bodies, which do indeed *appear* as separate objects. But surely you've learned that *you* are not the same as your body.

DK: Wait a sec, say *what*?

J: Oh, c'mon . . . don't say you thrived many years in the church and failed to grasp the point of the Resurrection.

DK: Not sure I'm following.

J: Look, if the Resurrection has meaning, it must be that *life is not the body*. What more comfort would it hold?

DK: But the church has made a pretty big deal of the body. They've even made a cannibal-like sacrament of consuming it—"the body of Christ," the most sacred body of all. Christians say our one hope of salvation is the death and resurrection of your body.

J: That's the common view, yes. Let's see if it makes any sense, or whether it even proves helpful . . .

The biblical story of the Passion makes clear that the Jewish and Roman powers believed they were ending my life—and therefore my influence—in bringing an end to my body. What they didn't see, and what many haven't learned even now, is that *we are not our bodies*. The human body is brilliant beyond belief—genius, if you knew the full truth. Still, it's only stardust; frail skin and bones . . . . a brief molecular restructuring of food and water.

DK: Well, there's a cute little blonde at the cleaners whose restructuring is pretty damned impres—

J: I'm only saying that your body is not the same thing as *you*. When energy manifests into the *particular*, the dominion of *particles*, it naturally has to manifest into *something*—into some *thing*. And *in* this manifest world, things do certainly appear to be disconnected, unrelated and separate. But they aren't . . . which plenty of physicists will tell you. This is why you "judge not by *appearances*." All things connect through a common Source, the same way a thousand aspens in a field are a single collective organism through a giant unseen root system joining them together.

DK: So our *bodies* are seemingly separate, but we're not those bodies at all.

J: Right, because we're the ones who are *using* them. Our commonality, our shared and universal 'root,' is Spirit. It was Spirit, not flesh, that outlived the Crucifixion. Why? Because Spirit never died. The life of a body had been taken, but Spirit cannot suffer harm and always 'resurrects' from any 'tomb.'

DK: Then bodies are just temporary tools for our experience and expressing ourselves in form.

J: Yes, and like any tool, they do the job they were made for. But bodies cannot reason, think or decide, and they're powerless to make you do *any*thing.

DK: You ain't seen the chick down at the cleaners.

J: Oh, I admire beauty as well as anyone. But even the world's most beautiful bodies will finally show up at the morgue. Now, form can be *fascinating*, I'll give you that. The human body is dazzling and exquisite and even an atheist should see that it wasn't the chance result of a cosmic *BOOM*. Your body is a direct expression of the vast, ingenious, mind-blowing Consciousness *behind* it. And *that's* the real 'you.' So you aren't the form being energized and animated—you're the energizing, animating force itself.

DK: If bodies aren't ultimately *us*, then why all this raving of resurrection and of corpses flying into the clouds?

J: Because ego links existence to material form. Ego thoroughly identifies with the body—believes that it *is* the body. An ego-based theology would naturally center on the physical and would *need* to have a resurrection to counter the obvious certainty of death. When people speak of eternal life, they're thinking of eternity in some non-destructible *form*. They may talk big on the gravity of tending the spirit, but most of their concern is for the body—*that's* what keeps 'em tossing and turning at night. They praise their religion's glorious heaven . . . but no one's scrambling to guzzle the poisoned tea. Instead they cling to the body for as long as they can, and often at bankrupting cost. Even when the body becomes useless and its quality of life near zip, they'll gladly drive others to poverty so to lay in bed awhile longer to drool on themselves and watch *Jeopardy*. Bodies are thought *vital* to their existence.

DK: But you didn't see it that way.

J: Well, I *couldn't*. I had learned that Spirit's not limited by the life of the form in which it 'lives.' So of course the authorities could kill my body— but I knew they couldn't touch *me*. I knew very well that passing bodies are ultimately no big deal and that fear of death, and all the needless drama that goes with it, is actually quite silly. Someday you'll know this yourself.

DK: Yet you're said to have pleaded from the cross, "Father forgive them, they know not what they do." As if a great crime had occurred.

J: Not that he needs even more of them, but let me play devil's advocate. Why would my killers need forgiving?

DK: They knowingly murdered a perfectly innocent man!

J: But if pre-planned self-crucifixion was God's biblical vision come true, as many Christians seem to believe, all those involved in my arrest, my sentence, and even my death, were guiltless and acting on orders.

They rightly should be seen as faithful servants, dutifully following God's will. From a literalist view you could even say that without Judas, Caiaphas, and Pilate, all humanity would still stand condemned. Instead of being badmouthed and censured, they *should* be made into saints!

DK: Now, *there's* a plan no one's considered, I'll bet.

J: Alright, so I'm kidding. But think about it. You can't say that God, in his limitless wisdom, carefully planned and directed the Crucifixion then hypocritically condemned those who did it. I mean *someone* had to do the dirty work.

DK: If the poor, dead gospel writers heard that, it would *kill* 'em.

J: But shouldn't all Christians be considering this? What sort of deity would function that way? Who'd wanna be at the mercy of this scary eccentric? Certainly not *me*, that's for sure.

DK: So your willing submission to death didn't mean that God was judging us and sees us as stained or corrupt.

J: God was entirely uninvolved. My killing was another try by authorities to conceal the powerful, transcendent nature of man . . . a truth that rarely ever serves the state. These leaders didn't see that *you cannot kill an idea.* They believed all minds are separate, that nothing survives beyond death, that everyone has different interests and some things aren't connected to —or even affected by—everything else. This thought of living apart from the whole has led to the heartbreak of humanity.

DK: But the notion that each of us is some sort of separated body-mind complex seems plain.

J: That the sun revolved daily around Earth once seemed equally apparent. Just as the geocentric model of the cosmos was eventually proven false, your egocentric paradigm as a body-mind will fail when carefully reviewed.

DK: Since you had this 'I am not the body' understanding, did you stay unafraid when you saw that even Yahweh himself wouldn't save you?

J: I didn't fear death in itself because Spirit cannot be killed. I surely was *focused,* of course—nothing puts trust to the test like a few sharp spikes. I knew beyond doubt, however, that bodies aren't needed for existence.

DK: Still, it was a noble sacrifice.

J: Well, it wasn't *intended* as one. Those who insist I was sacrificed at Calvary are clueless. Who would've *asked* this gallant deed? It sure wasn't *my* idea.

DK: The church says it was *God's* idea—but you agreed to do it out of love. You gave your life for ours, it would seem. God killed *you* in lieu of sticking it to *us*.

J: Which means if He hadn't killed *me*, He'd have killed everyone else instead.

DK: So, a strange sacrifice from the start.

J: And especially when you consider who's demanding it. But why should the Lord want sacrifice? If God is everything and all things are One, then who is sacrificing to whom—and for what? Love needs no appeasing, and God only *gives* . . . He doesn't *take*. What would you or I possess that any god would want? And what loving creator would give life in a body then heartlessly rescind it at death? How would He justify this? It's not too much comfort that He might restore life in some faraway heaven, my friend.

DK: I can't see anything was *gained* by your death, I'll admit. But surely something more than a *body* was lost on that dark afternoon at Golgotha.

J: And *that* is the great Christian irony. The point of the Crucifixion is one that very few ever grasp: *nothing was lost*. The one thing possibly 'sacrificed' that day was my body. But why would I offer up my body? How would that *help* the world? Could God find no forgiveness 'til my torture? Why is He always about *pain*? And scripture says I knew I'd be rising up quickly— so what's the big deal going bodyless forty-eight hours? Someday you'll be without one yourself . . . and for a whole lot more than a weekend.

DK: True, but I won't be shedding my blood for a sinful humanity.

J: And neither did I. The Christian church says that I suffered foul murder so that God can forgive his children. Could something be any more insane? This is like a son telling his father, "Listen, dad, I heard that my siblings have been horrid of late and they've really got you upset. Now, I know that you love them quite dearly—so if it helps you forgive them, go ahead and have me destroyed."

DK: Well, I think you're loading the dice. I mean *of course* it sounds crazy when presented like *that*.

J: Yet that's how the church *does* present it—but *they* don't spell it out quite so plain. And what kind of father would *agree* to this psychotic suggestion? A parent who'd condone it would be as crazy as the kid who conceived it, and how this barbarous plan could save someone's spirit or ever help *anyone* is only a clerical guess.

DK: Then what is the body's connection to the spirit?

J: Although spirit doesn't become flesh, it loves to *express* itself through flesh. The body is a brilliant thing for those wanting to know spiritual relationship here in the world of form. By far the most sophisticated technology on earth, the body can be helpful and enjoyable if used well—but often disastrous when it isn't. View it as a kind of learning aid, a useful means of experience and communication. Once it serves its purpose, you lay it aside like an old worn-out suit. *My* body was no more important than yours. I was just functioning at a higher level of being, a higher frequency—the frequency known commonly as love. Love is invulnerable, universal and undivided. It doesn't sacrifice things or ask any sacrifice of *us*.

DK: But the gospels say you *chose* to give in to the Crucifixion scam when a man of your abilities could've escaped. In fact, you mysteriously did this in the gospel of Luke—just before *another* mob you had angered went tossing you over a cliff. So you didn't bother *fighting* the legal charade even knowing you might be killed. And that's fairly sacrificial, no?

J: Millions through history have sacrificed their bodies for others. Even in my era, more than three thousand people died by Roman crucifixion. So my death wasn't nearly unique. Now, I'm the first to say that I didn't *deserve* to be killed since I never harmed anyone and did in fact help a great many. But no one can die for anyone else because, first, there *is* no death . . . and even if there were, it clearly wouldn't transfer like an industrial carbon credit. The Bible states specifically in 2 Kings, and still again in 2 Chronicles, that "every man shall die for his own sin." So God wasn't punishing *me* because everyone else was evil—that is unequivocal insanity. Love doesn't murder to save.

DK: A fundamentalist would argue that, in your case, God gave up his 'only son' to be tortured for *our* personal imperfections—so of course He'd expect *something* for his grief.

J: C'mon, Sparky, try not to reason like a man with a liberal arts degree. What kind of trouble has anyone ever caused *God*!? If the man is rattled by a frail speck of life flittering around on a tiny dot of dust flying unnoticed through a nondescript galaxy in a darkened little corner of a universe spanning billions of light-years throughout . . . well, if you hold such sway over the Lord, my boy, then the *real* God would essentially be *you*.

DK: It's probably left over from childhood, but it's hard to believe that God is so benevolent He accepts us no matter what.

J: And that's one of religion's greatest harms: it keeps you from even *imagining* infinite love. You'll gladly give it to *your* kids, of course— but God won't give it to his. As long as you think this 'God' of religion wants sacrifice, and thoughtless acceptance of astoundingly unholy ideas, even *my* life and message will seem threatening, and God will be feared as a tyrant. Why is this a problem? Because when converts are sure that a deity like this is endorsing—and even *enforcing*—their deadly doctrines, they'll surely keep on judging, persecuting and killing in this god's name.

DK: You realize, no doubt, that you're refuting the entire New Testament. Scripture asserts that you came to stop Yahweh from sending us all to hell.

J: Another good prospect for the test I suggested earlier: "Is it *reasonable?*" Honestly, does the Christian account of God's 'holy' redemption make sense? And how in the heck is it *holy*? His scary plan of salvation's no more ethical or brilliant than his ways in the mid-Eastern desert. How terribly ironic—and *convenient*, for those who use scriptures to justify violence— that the 'Lord of love' so often works his will and gains his goals in the same way long employed by man: through merciless killing of the innocent.

DK: Alright, but your death wasn't only about atonement. It's also said to be proof of God's limitless love for his children.

J: Well, if this 'God' of the Bible really *loves* his children, He's got a helluva strange way of showing it.

DK: So, even though you had a bigger *mission* than others, in heaven's eyes your life was no more important than ours.

J: My life had more of an *impact* than most, since few had attained that level of spiritual vision. But nothing of my *nature* was unique. Whatever I accomplished, so too could others—and I make this perfectly clear in John 14:12. My earthly existence was no more blessed than your own, nor was anything special in my death.

DK: The New Testament says that your death *was* unique since you were the "only begotten Son of the Father."

87

J: Which makes *you* a kind of 'illegitimate' child, does it not? The phrase is much more sensible as "the begotten son of the *only Father*"—an extension of the one and only everlasting Source.

DK: But *that* could apply to *everyone*.

J: Exactly . . .

CHAPTER FIFTEEN

DK: Well, I have to say it again: calling us all divine is fairly progressive.

J: As when Pasteur first told his colleagues to wash their hands.

DK: The thing is, you claim that all human beings are innocent at heart —if not in thinking or deed—yet scripture says the problem of sin was so critical that God required torture to resolve it. And now, the church tells the world, the soul's salvation lies only in "professing the Lord Jesus."

J: There's no salvation in a name.

DK: Then what of that 'turn or burn' stuff? How does this new way of thinking change the old 'Jesus Saves' idea?

J: In the way that salvation is typically preached, it leaves it all for dead. Once more, let's use a little dash of reason . . .

Taking the literalist view, God creates man perfect and then throws him into the Garden along with his much-belabored free will. But this 'free' will turns expensive pretty fast—it basically allows man to destroy himself. Yet if God is omniscient, as claimed, He should've seen the catastrophe coming. Mysteriously as ever, though, He creates humans anyway and then has the gall to grow angry and wounded when they yield to their natural temptations and eat the fruit.

Now, *really*—what kind of God *behaves* this way!? We're talking of the all-powerful creator of the cosmos. We're told that He reigns supreme and that his will simply cannot be hindered. Suddenly, however, his divine plan is shattered and his infinite power usurped by a couple of curious young kids with boundary issues.

DK: Check my thinking here . . . but if Yahweh's intent was to have a perfect creation, and feeble little Adam and Eve somehow ruined it, not only is He proven not omniscient, but He's not *omnipotent* either— a telling divine double-whammy.

J: Yeah, God's two young rebels had *influence*. As you said, they denied Him his utopia—but they also forced Him to do things He hadn't planned. In their effect on the world's destiny, Adam and Eve were every bit as powerful as God. Almost as soon as they're breathing, the pitiful savages make chaos of the Almighty's erstwhile problem-free paradise, which of course took nearly a full week of arduous shift work to produce.

DK: Seems humans made Frankenstein's monster look like a grade school science class gig.

J: Yep. Very early on, God's pilot study of intelligent life spins wildly out of control. By only the sixth chapter of Genesis, He's had more than plenty of the whole sorry arrangement and opts to drown every man, woman, child and beast on the planet—with obvious exception of Noah's small family and their floating homemade zoo.

DK: But even *that* didn't settle the mess.

J: Unfortunately not. Like most of Yahweh's crackpot schemes, drowning his earthly children and all *other* land life on the planet was a bloody boondoggle from the start—and nothing productive ever issued from the watery mess. Noah's offspring were just as idiotic and violent as their hooligan antediluvian precessors.

DK: So now man ruins God's earthly heaven *again.*

J: Correct. He clearly needs a more effective plan. On giving it some thought for, oh, a couple thousand years, God finally has a brainstorm He's certain will work. He brings in a divine Superdude—that's *me*—who's fully incapable of sinning, it seems, and perfect in every respect. Now, why He couldn't make *everyone* this way is a riddle. But I digress . . .

So, for several centuries God ponders the problem of sin, and suddenly the hot idea strikes. "I've got it!" He shouts. "Jumpin' Jehoshaphat, what a stroke of brilliance!! Why didn't I think of this before!? I'll fix it so they'll torture and kill my son, and then I can finally know peace!!"

DK: And next, through some trumped-up charges in a Roman kangaroo court, your Father in heaven watches over your crucifixion, allowing your torturous demise because He loves us.

J: But if I'm one with God, as claimed, then by Christian theology you'd have to say that God actually killed part of *himself.* No escaping *that* conclusion, right? I mean *He* had to have some skin in the game, did He not?

DK: I may have to think this one through . . .

J: Well, anyhow . . . as churches tell it, God in his mysterious wisdom deems that I should die a terrible, sacrificial death to atone for the dark, blackened soul of mankind. Steeped in my heavenly virtue, I come down and suffer for *your* sorry butts, doing *for* you what you simply can't do for yourselves.

DK: Despite the sneering, perhaps Yahweh saw the real *need* for symbolic atonement—it seems to rule a pretty big part of his life.

J: But let's be honest: it's not a big God who goes nursing his grudges and tracking his children's mistakes. Salvation wouldn't be needed at all if not for the dull-minded deity who thought of the silly idea— an honest, half-brained high-schooler could've told Him the plan wouldn't work. And what kind of father makes a world for his children where the poor kids' foremost concern is to dodge their dad's pre-planned abuse? Think about it and you'll see that Christian 'salvation' is just a divinely devised loophole to escape its Mastermind's own wickedly sadistic nature.

DK: Certainly a creative new slant.

J: But it's true: the need of absolution is debatable from the start. And even if the Lord *did* desire an officially sanctioned act of forgiveness, He simply could've descended in a whirlwind of glory and declared the job done: "No problem, folks, you're all forgiven! Let's eat!!"

DK: Though that wouldn't have asked any sacrifice or effort from *us*.

J: Neither did my crucifixion.

DK: So you're suggesting that Yahweh might've worked out a *non-violent* solution—a one-time, no-exclusions, non-expiring nullification of sin.

J: Well, why not? He's *God*. He can do as He pleases, right? Who's gonna stop Him? But no . . . the God of Christianity just cannot bring himself to forgive and move on with his life. He's sorely offended by his naughty delinquents and makes it a major affair. But why does He internalize it all? And how does any *God* derive so darned much satisfaction judging mortals of his very own design? The man complains *constantly* of his *kids*!!

DK: Yeah, so what's all *that* about? Why's He so self-centered about his children's rambunctious behavior? They certainly have little mindfulness of *Him* when they're out breaking rules and transgressing.

J: But there's the very problem, you see? Yahweh doesn't suffer defiance. And He doesn't handle offenders with mere lectures or a slap on the wrist. He often seeks *blood,* so they'll know He's not at all pleased. He wants *them* feeling the burden of his *personal* load. So He plans my crucifixion many centuries in advance—you can't rush into these things—to ensure his wayward subjects fully realize the dire implications of sin. If they wanna know salvation, the little devils, they'll have to pay a dear price in *guilt*.

DK: I can't explain the logic, but heaven surely knows that some are far too young or guileless to have a *conception* of sin . . . and some will never *hear* the Christian 'Word.' Others are raised in conditions that would make it nearly impossible to *embrace* such a theology if they heard it.

J: Doesn't matter, say the literalists, and each one's as accountable as the next. God is a God of *justice*, they'll say—as if spending forever in hell for having a different perspective could ever be seen as 'just.'

DK: Okay, but even the God of literalism will sometimes show grace. Some say that even if a person wasn't Christian at death, a few special, cooperative cases might still qualify for heaven. God also judges the *heart* is how they explain it.

J: If God were the judge you've been told He is, then judging people's hearts might show at least a bit of good sense. In sketchy schemes like *that*, however, good works and professions of faith could well be moot.

DK: According to one Christian camp, even if a lifelong killer repents on his deathbed and takes you as his Lord and savior, he's quickly absolved and happily taken into the fold.

J: Here again you're describing a 'deity' who's not very sharp. First He commands his children to follow strict moral standards based on fairness, respect, and the highest of ethical order. Those who flout these laws will pay profoundly, and possibly 'til hell freezes up. But then He has the entire system—no matter how badly abused—fully annulled in a moment through an easy, back-door escape of his own devise. If Christian New Testament theology can be trusted, salvation is a mere technicality.

DK: Growing up in the church, I was so thoroughly programmed by the teachings that I never mulled the *idea* that God might forgive us without your death. Or that He might not judge us at all. Or that He didn't even *exist*.

J: And how telling of the power of ideologies that these thoughts never crossed your mind.

DK: No, they really didn't. I was raised under the ominous warning of Hebrews: " . . . without the shedding of blood, there *is* no forgiveness of sins."

J: And there's your Christian theology all nicely wrapped up in hot dogma. Somebody spoon-feeds you this biodegradable waste and you swallow it like a baby slurping down strained peas. And it reeks with the stench of hypocrisy. The Bible says that God wants his children showing love and forgiveness—but no one is disturbed that the Lord himself will rarely "turn the other cheek" when *his* fragile feelings are bruised. When *heaven's* disappointed, all *hell* breaks loose!!

DK: It seems the Lord's not happy 'til He's dished out some meaningless violence. You'd think He'd take the *quiet* path now and again.

J: No, sir—not Yahweh. He's a card-carrying God of retribution: someone's gotta *hurt*. Throughout the Old Testament He's beating his chest and handling human frailty with mean intimidation, nasty threats, and the use of lethal force. "I'll send down *plagues*!" He thunders. "I'll strike you *dead* if I have to—you impudent bunch of free-willed reprobates! Don't you know who I am!!?"

DK: But *you* showed up, centuries later, and Yahweh had mellowed a bit.

J: Well, his redemptive 'justice' still centers on guilt and revenge—but He does start taking a less violent, more manipulative approach. *"Now* look what you've made me do," He tells humanity scoldingly. He acts as though his only road to compassion and justice is having me brutally killed . . . as if there was no alternative. He 'lovingly' puts *me* through a torturous hell so that *you* then gain entrance to heaven. All of it perfectly sensible, don't you agree?

DK: You know, I felt a little guilty when flaming this stuff in my letter. But now, after talking it out, I think I was far too kind—the whole salvation arrangement is *wacked*! The God of Christian literalism has the temper of a crabby librarian, the patience of a hound-cornered fox, a brain about like a walnut—and an *ego* the size of New York!!

J: *Heh heh.* An oversized public official. . .

DK: I'm beginning to like your suggestion that God might've skipped all these pointless earthly theatrics by making *everyone* perfect—like you. It would've nixed the *need* for salvation.

J: "No, no, no—that'll never do," says God. "This calls for serious drama. Before they'll gain entrance to *my* place, the pitiful little hellions will have to earn it. Besides, if they aren't free to *spurn* my kindly grace, how will I know if they love me?" So here's the omnipotent king of creation with neurotic insecurity that makes Deputy Barney Fife look like Bond.

DK: Well, He likely didn't want mere androids walking the planet—but God really dropped a fork in the blender with humanity's dangerous free will.

J: And *here*, in the Christian scenario, is where *I* step in. By harshest reading, those who 'believe' in me are saved . . . and those who *don't* will toast to a golden crisp. For the vast number of earthlings, God's celebrated plan of 'salvation' leads directly to eternal affliction. Thus has God's wisdom grown oh-so-mysterious that it's now nothing less than insane.

DK: So it's clear why religion has flourished: the fear factor is strong. And certainly it worked in my case. I realize now that I clung to my uncomfortable religion to avoid the still crueler sufferings of Hades. Given all the insanity in the church, however, there were times I didn't see too much difference.

J: Ha! 'Tis truly a narrow border 'tween heaven and hell. In the story of Lazarus and the rich man, the two spots are within shouting distance.

DK: Hey, now *there's* a paradisaical paradox: angelic choirs on the one side, with wailing and gnashing of teeth across the way.

J: Yes, and this makes for *another* vexing theological puzzle. How will heaven's holy ever get a wink of sleep with that infernal *noise* next door?

CHAPTER SIXTEEN

DK: So you've made a good case for re-thinking the Crucifixion and the meaning of salvation . . . but I still have a hitch with resurrection. Rising from death isn't your average parlor trick—yet the whole of Christian religion hangs on its truth. And even many *Christians* don't believe it, even as the church stays with the story that it's fact. And that's a ballsy claim these days.

J: Not necessarily. Other traditions have saints resurrecting from death and appearing to followers here and there. Even thousands of the non-religious report visions—and sometimes full-on manifestations—of deceased friends, relatives and others. And medical archives hold hundreds of cases of people clinically dead returning to life.

DK: Not after two solid days, I'd guess.

J: No, but by gospel standards for 'Most Days Dead Before Resurrecting,' I don't even hold the record. Scripture claims my good friend Lazarus was resting in Abraham's bosom a full four days before *his* big bounce back to life.

DK: You're right, I forgot about him . . . he outlasted you by a mile. Did things get a bit tiresome on your weekend excursion to hell?

J: I bored of all that wailing and gnashing of teeth.

DK: *Heh heh*. Are you sure I've got the right Christian messiah?

J: You're shocked that I laugh and have fun.

DK: Well, the gospels pretty much paint you as a sourpuss. Offhand I can't think of a single church teaching even *suggesting* you had a normal sense of humor. For a good part of my life I would almost hesitate to have any fun because religion makes one's faith seem so serious.

J: Forgive me, Father, for I have grinned.

DK: Exactly . . . and *your* Bible persona's not much different. I don't recall a reference to you ever having a chuckle or cracking a smile.

J: It's true. Never am I shown to be a light-hearted, good-natured guy just reveling in the moment with no sense of wrongness or concern. Instead, everything's lecture, lesson, and warning . . . and the reader doesn't sense that this 'Son of man' fella would be too uplifting or very much fun to hang out with. Not once do I tell a group of my followers what a great job they're doing and they're perfectly loved and accepted just as they are.

DK: Actually, nowhere in the New Testament is there any real emphasis on the present moment or the simple, sweet savoring of life.

J: No, the spotlight's on a *future* existence where the fortunate redeemed will somehow derive unending pleasure giving endless attention to God. You're taught to make sure He knows how truly grateful you are that —unlike *other* people you know—He won't be sentencing *you* to spend the rest of eternity in whining to Satan of serious buyer's remorse.

DK: It's that kind of programming, I think, that gives so many Christians and other believers a sense of unworthiness or shame.

J: Sure, their religion makes 'em guilty just *being* here . . . I mean whose bloody fault was that!?? But I enjoyed my life thoroughly—and some found that downright disturbing. They saw me as almost a hedonist and resented that I mingled with prostitutes, drunks, and other groups frequently shunned.

DK: But we've got no stories of you really cutting loose with those folks. The gospels show you mostly as a lecturing parent, not a patient, compassionate teacher—they give you just a *whisper* of humanity. If not caught up in some death-defying drama, you're moralizing on mountains or fighting with local religious groups.

J: Remember, the gospels are just stories of my life *as passed on by others—* entirely third-hand stuff. And the writers naturally fixed on what they felt was most important. Which is only sensible, really. No one wants to read of Jesus mowing the backyard or telling jokes about Roman elite. But you won't ever know me through scripture. Reading the gospels, you soon get the feeling that whenever this Jesus shows up, a scuffle or sermon breaks out.

DK: What *bugs* me is the vote was unanimous. Gospel writers all describe the same surly savior, in desperate need of an oil massage and a few good puffs of God's weed.

J: Depicting a serious Christ was no accident. Scripture had to prod folks to join—and a jovial, laid-back messiah would never do it. Throw in some threats of a hell and a looming apocalypse, and there you've got a brand new religion.

DK: Well, like I said: to know a bit of your life, the Bible's about all we've got.

J: But try to be practical, too. I lived more than *thirty years*. Yet, take each quote ascribed to me in scripture and you'd read the whole collection in a night. Add the fact that much of it's concocted and you'll soon find you've too little turkey and way, way, *way* too much stuffing.

DK: I do know the four gospels weren't written until long after you died, which is cause for suspicion from start . . . and, interestingly, *not one* is written in the first person. Aside from a couple of vague lines in John, the gospel writers never speak of you with familiarity and relate no stories of camaraderie or personal friendship. In the introduction to Luke, the author *implies* that some of his material was obtained from people who knew you—but strangely, he doesn't *say* that. Instead he says he got it from "eyewitnesses and ministers of the word," which could mean something different, I admit.

J: Well, as you say, New Testament authors penned their writings long after I passed. None of them was an original disciple and all their *initial* works are gone. The ones used now are generations removed from the first.

DK: Nevertheless, the Apostles seemed ready to meet their maker on your account—they must've been confident they were right.

J: Though wouldn't you say the same of a suicide bomber? Militance tends to reveal an idea's *weakness*, not its strength: only the *theoretical* needs *enforcing*. For thousands of years, millions of devoted souls —acting for religion, please remember—have laid waste countless cultures and killed untold millions of resistant non-believers. So far off in their thinking were the infidels, believers insisted they die. These murderous 'defenders of the faith' were deeply 'devout' and zealously gripped by their cause. But were their convictions either proved or made valid in their keenness to kill or be killed?

DK: Clearly not . . . but excepting Paul's merciless oppression of Christians before his conversion, the Apostles weren't hurting anyone. They were just preaching what they understood as the message of God's salvation. No harm in *that* effort, right? And all seemingly done in good conscience.

J: Virtue can rarely be known by one's conscience, which is usually no better than the ideas that shaped it. Even extreme violence is often done quite freely within bounds of the perpetrators' own 'good conscience.' You shouldn't assume, when someone is 'serving' religion or country, that all their ways are noble or blessed by God—you've ample proof of it *now*.

DK: So you *reject* the message your followers were spreading.

J: Depends on which message . . . and which followers. You'll recall that I warned my friends before my arrest that they would soon misinterpret my teachings. Sure enough, they drastically twisted my words and intentions through fears, hopes and personal inclinations. A few centuries later, my simple ideas about life had morphed into a monolithic religion. Christianity became another mainstream institution, flexing its political muscle while pulling in charlatans and authority hounds in droves. As usual, ignorance and power proved a dangerous blend.

DK: It does seem that whenever religion shows up, it leaves a mountain of bodies behind. Within a century of Europeans landing in the Americas, natives by the millions had become what is now euphemistically called 'collateral damage.' When not having their culture choked out of them by God-loving Christian missionaries, native peoples in the United States were murdered systematically at the hands of U.S. soldiers, settlers and others, many of whom considered themselves faithful stewards of the church. The battle cry, apparently, was "Kill a heathen for Christ!"

J: But again, we can't single out Christianity. It certainly isn't the only faith with disgraceful records of violence and coercion—many other religions have left trails of blood in their paths. And talking about it as history tends to make it sound merely academic. But the same insanity is still playing out today. By their nature, ideologies cause separation and disagreement, or feelings of specialness and advantage . . . that's hardly what I had in mind.

DK: Okay, but apart from conflicts brought about by religion, maybe *some* of our violence is justified. When some chump slaps you upside the head, don't you have to wallop him right back?

J: *I* didn't.

DK: Well, I'm not sure we can really compare your situ—

J: Listen, my friend, we may as well face the facts. The ethics of the average Christian these days have shamefully little connection to the so-called 'teachings of Christ.' Almost from the beginning, Christians have conveniently looked past the unmistakable instructions in Luke 6: "But I say to you . . . *love* your enemies, *do good* to those who hate you, *bless* those who curse you, *pray* for those who abuse you . . . And as you wish that people would do unto you, do so also unto them."

DK: Morally challenging stuff, no doubt.

J: Yeah, try floating *that* in the next State of the Union address.

DK: I'll relay it to the relevant party . . .

J: And speaking of the book of Luke reminds me of something else I'd like to clear up. In Luke 22 the writer has me quoting a line from Isaiah 53—an Old Testament passage frequently said by the church to hold prophecies of *my* life and mission. But the prophet's words have nothing to do with me and no Hebrew scholar worth his weight in matzo would say different.

DK: Hang on while I read it through . . .

Well, the passages *are* pretty confusing. And *vague*. The writer is mostly referencing things that had already happened. A few verses seem to match *aspects* of your life—but others aren't relevant at all. And I see how the authors of the gospels might well have *written* their stories to match with Old Testament texts. So I get your point: even if the words *are* connected to you, how would that ever be proved?

J: With so many scriptures around, you can make any argument you want. The 'God-said-it-I-believe-it' bumper sticker folks have intellects on cruise control. They take an easy path by skipping the first requirement of those who seek the truth: *thinking for yourself.* Always challenge ideas that ask you to check your discernment at the door. God is neither cruel nor stupid—but to mesh with religion's insane belief systems He'd surely have to be *both*.

DK: It's true, and I always resented that God would command *me* to be infinitely loving to the relatively few people in *my* life, while *He* condemns *billions* to eternal complaint!!! God's hell isn't just heartlessly vicious—it's grossly hypocritical, too.

J: With what you've made of *this* world, hell would be overkill.

DK: I think some folks feel gratified believing in hell. They kinda *like* the thought of people they despise getting poked with a fiery rod. Others may not fully *believe* in a hell—but it *is* a New Testament theme. Christians think, in *accepting* the teaching, they're just being holy and humble.

J: Well, be it ever so humble, there's no place like hell. Nor is there a separate site called heaven. These things aren't locations, but *states of mind*. If it exists at all, it can only exist in the now. And those who live a genuine hell here on earth know how real it can be and that nothing much worse could wait in a burning hereafter.

DK: But at least God offers *escape* from those pyrotechnics. All He really wants, it seems, is the simple confession of *Him* as undisputed creator —as if there's competition for the post—and of *you* as the 'one begotten son' of the Father, nailed to a cross for the sacrificial saving of souls.

J: Sacrifice is a telling perspective of relations between God and man . . . it's 'the art of the deal' in extreme. Christians will call human sacrifice 'primitive' but don't seem to realize their religion is *founded* upon it— they don't bother asking why their God must be mollified with blood.

DK: Literalists argue that a gift like salvation bears a cost and that God can't offer something so valuable for free.

J: So their God is like a schoolyard drug pimp. He may dole out a sample or two—but He surely wants return on his investment. The God of the Bible offers violent forgiveness and then demands nonstop praise because He gave it. But try to see that God has no ego, no emotional requirements— no need to hear He's terrific. You can't *earn* your way to heaven and don't need to. Think of it like this: do parents show blessings to their children even if the kids don't always deserve it?

DK: Well, sure . . . I think *all* good parents do that. It's just the way love works, am I right?

J: As a matter of fact, it is *exactly* the way love works. How sad, then, that the world's mortal parents show more graciousness and compassion toward *their* children than this 'God' of Christianity gives his.

DK: Some Christians say it's a very 'cheap' grace that has no sacrifice or pain.

J: Huh?? Think about that madness from an *earthly* view. Would a mother reject her guilty son until she first punished her innocent daughter who agreed to suffer for the brother's poor behavior? The guiltless are penalized in place of the guilty, and the overseer says this makes *sense*? This is the core of serious Christian theology? This is the story of God's 'grace' as recounted by one of the world's most successful religions? Brother, if that's not outright *crazy*, what other label would you give it? But, look . . . if it's really 'cheap grace' you're worried of, rest calm— the Christian version of grace is definitely *not* a grace without cost. Quite the opposite, in fact—your payments for it never come to an end. Christianity calls for each and every receiver of its grace to worship, throughout eternity, a totalitarian ruler in the sky from whose vigilant, reproachful gaze one can never escape. Biblically it's sealed, across even the furthest of time, that God's 'saved' will never be free of his binding 'grace.'

DK: Pretty discouraging stuff when you spell it out.

J: Oh, but it's far *worse* than that . . . because even the most personal *thoughts* of these blessèd few will be forever surveilled by this wary watchman called 'God.' So the price of your divine Father's grace is actually costly beyond calculation. It's living in fear this celestial warden will one day stem his mercy and turn his back. Not only is this grace not 'cheap,' but it's giving up your freedom as a sovereign child of Universe and yielding all allegiance to the führer. And even putting this cartoon theology aside, it denies the very *nature* of grace to have to earn your way in.

DK: Well, it's not like we have to *earn* it, exactly. The church says that all God is asking, at heart, is for each of us to accept your sovereignty and give you honor. It's only this that makes Christian grace conditional.

J: Any way you slice it, there's something fairly ungracious in conditional grace. The Christian version of grace now has a *God-father* doing the bargaining: "Live and believe as I say," He warns the world, "and I'll think of not *torturing* you later."

DK: So it's an offer we can't refuse.

J: Right, and how 'gracious' could He truly be if you've got to obtain his approval through submission, adulation or barter? Do you honestly *like* this small-minded, big-headed, fast-dealing God of the Bible?

DK: After I left the church, I never really gave it much thought. I squashed all the doubts because I probably feared God would punish me for losing my faith. I dunno, maybe we *have* been duped . . . it's hard to believe we can just stop sweating this hell-and-no-water idea. Judging by many religions, this good news of yours seems slightly too good to be true.

J: For people whose God is supposed to be loving, their hell is too *dreadful* to be true. An eternity of torment for a few years of ignorance? How much respect can you *rouse* for a deity so cruel and unfair!? I mean *someone's* fixin' to *burn* because they weren't quite as wise as the all-knowing God of creation!!!

DK: So, naturally they've got to be *punished* for their mortal mistakes.

J: Yes, and the punishment will be *forever*. A curious thing, really . . . that the God of Christianity, the alleged designer of the universe, just can't figure, when dealing with earthly sons and daughters, how the heck to develop a win-win solution . . . a scheme in which nobody loses.

DK: No, and He's made it quite clear that, throughout all time, He never intends to forgive his ungrateful children.

J: But c'mon . . . even if this juvenile image were true, could you ever walk in peace through streets of heaven—smiling and joyfully strumming your golden harp—with billions screaming "Heaven, please help us!" in hell???

DK: Well, of course not—no one with compassion possibly *could*.

J: But the God of religion's okay with it all.

DK: Literalists say that God doesn't *like* condemning to hell but He's a God of absolute justice—so He *must*.

J: Ah, more of that Christian 'justice' thing. God is *morally obliged* to torture his wayward children—*philosophically bound* to be a jerk.

DK: As I've said, I was taught that God's ways are forever loving and that everyone has opportunity to accept Him. But of course we're also free to reject Him by rejecting *you* as the Lord and redeemer.

J: Whereupon you're quickly sent to this always-loving God's flaming hell. He feels really awful sending folks to burn in anguish, but somehow thinks He *owes* it to 'em, eh?

DK: Apparently it's the Christian thing to do.

J: But if this loving God of the Bible is so concerned of his errant children's spiritual salvation, why doesn't He personally intervene?

DK: We're told that's what He did when He sent *you*.

J: Even if you're right, that was two thousand years ago. Meantime, his kids are dropping like flies. As you pointed out in your letter, *billions* are incurring damnation by his neglect. I mean the *devil* must be *delirious* with this deal!!!

DK: Well, I guess God figures your appearance in Palestine was enough. *Now* all He can do is spread the good word and trust that we'll make the right choice.

J: You mean hoping for the best is God's only remaining option? If so, then Christianity's theology is this . . .

First, God creates man happy, frail and ignorant. At the unexpected Fall in the Garden during the very first week of its opening, Yahweh predestines every one of his children to hell on their day of arrival. Many centuries later He offers a remedy which—and let's be honest about this—most of the world's population is apt to reject. As all of this drama's unfolding, He lets Satan steal as many souls as possible while *He* stands back watching the show, waiting to see which of his precious creations will self-destruct.

DK: Maybe God doesn't see it that way. Christians say He provided a clear solution and salvation is a free will decision.

J: So God, in his deeply mysterious way, gives his children the choice to accept Him or reject Him—which, technically, means accepting or rejecting a particular church's doctrinal theology. Those who do 'accept' the God endorsed by their church are given white robes and wings, while those who *don't* will forever long for a little cold beer and a breeze.

DK: A wee bit waggish, I'd say . . . but yes, that's the hardline Christian view. There's heaven or hell and that's it.

J: Therefore, by threat of eternal discomfort, God's teeny-weensy prison of 'free will' allows you just a single view of reality. Love it or loathe it, you've one choice and one choice only.

DK: Right, we're essentially forced to *submit*.

J: Effectively, then, God's message to man has been this: "Take me or leave me, your call—but don't forget those blazing pits of fire!"

DK: That's how the church lays it out.

J: Well, what kind of useless free will is *that*? Sounds more like spiritual extortion. It's little different from an earthly parent telling his children, "You're each free to live as you please. But if you don't do as I ask and give thanks for all that I've done, I'll disown you, hunt you down, then lock you away and torture you for the rest of your life."

Now, please be fair: would you look past this obvious derangement by concluding that the father is abusing his children because he *loves* them?!?

DK: Of course not, I wouldn't even have the guts to *say* it.

J: Then why go so easy on God? You see, this is the literalist's dilemma. A loving God can never be reconciled with hell. If either one exists, then the other, by definition, cannot.

DK: So if religion's God is loving, He wouldn't create a hell—and if He *did*, He's definitely not loving.

J: No two ways about it. A God of goodness can't also be the author of the definitive evil and the ultimate child abuse.

DK: Perhaps this God of religion isn't 'good' in the usual way. His goodness may transcend our typical view—*his* thoughts are not *ours*, they say.

J: Well, maybe you've got a point there. Let's look at scripture and see . . .

Psalm 145 says, "The Lord is gracious and merciful, slow to anger and abounding in *steadfast love*." And who's to gain from this flood of divine beneficence? The Psalmist tells in no uncertain terms: "The Lord is good to *all*," he declares, "and his compassion is over all that he has made." He goes even further and says the Lord is "gracious in all his deeds," "just in all his ways" and "kind in all his doings."

Now, ignoring that none of these attributes is the least bit accurate in describing the God of the Bible, the *claims* of his nature seem pretty darned clear, would you say?

DK: Hell, there's no further need of review . . . He's Santa Claus on steroids.

J: So the Bible firmly states that God is 'good' within typical meanings of goodness and, moreover, says that God is good "to *all*." But wait— what's *this*!? Just before closing up shop, the Psalmist slips in a single but critical disclaimer to keep us on edge: "The Lord preserves all who *love* him," the writer assures us, "but all of the *wicked* he will *destroy*."

DK: Okay, now *that* part's a little disturbing, especially when you're iffy about everything God finds "wicked" . . . and given his *own* sketchy background, it's not always easy to tell. It also implies that anyone who doesn't 'love' God, whatever exactly that *means*, is wicked from the start and hangin' by a thread already.

J: A similar thing lies in Exodus 34, where the Lord claims for himself the same qualities ascribed by the Psalmist: merciful, gracious, fully in touch with his feminine side and so on. But lest we breathe a sigh of relief, God also declares He will never absolve the guilty and, even more, that He'll punish the sins of the parents *by way of their children*.

In Deuteronomy 5 He's even more unforgiving and warns that he'll lay the personal sins of the fathers not only upon the fathers themselves— but also on their children, their grandkids . . . and even their *great*-grandkids!

DK: Boy, talk about holding a grudge.

J: And here again we've got the innocent footing the bill for the guilty— and not just for a while, understand me, but for three generations to come!!

DK: So, going by the Bible, God is loving but hateful, kind but vindictive, and slow to anger but quick to destroy.

J: Or so says the 'internally consistent and inspired Word of God.' But never mind scriptural double-talk. If the Lord is so lovable and compelling, why must He threaten cutting his kids from the will to get the rascals home for Thanksgiving? And how is He driven to dispatch all the radicals to the choking-hot, lung-searing, sulphuric combustions of hell? I mean why always *drama* with this guy? Wouldn't He get the exact-same result just condemning them to a summer in Houston???

CHAPTER SEVENTEEN

DK: Let's talk a bit more of the classic Christian hereafter. To me, hell is critically important because it sits at the heart of Bible literalism. The church can talk all day long about God's *love*—but that don't mean *diddly* if salvation is only escape from his loving *torture*. So hell deserves a little deeper look, I believe.

J: Alright, back to the flames we go. But first, a quick test. Where in the Old Testament is the record of hell's creation?

DK: You're baiting me . . . I don't think scripture describes it.

J: Clever lad! And do you know why it *doesn't*? Because Israelites considered themselves Yahweh's elect. They never would've dreamed that their God might condemn his own people, and the *Christian* vision of hell would've been absurd. For Israelites, divine vengeance was tied primarily to the *immediate* world—you'd better start worrying *now*.

DK: Yet the Old Testament does make mention of hell.

J: Yeah, many times . . . but later Bible versions changed most of the original King James "hell" passages to better reflect early Hebrew ideas such as "Sheol," the oldest reference to an afterlife in Jewish scripture. Sheol can be translated as "the pit," "the grave," or "the abyss," and various Old Testament verses state that both the wicked *and* the righteous are there. Passages containing the word "hell" are relatively few and vague, and writers who used these terms were clearly unfamiliar with the fiery, devil-ruled enterprise of Christian literalism.

DK: What about the *New* Testament? On top of the word "hell," you've also got terms like "Hades" and "Gehenna." Most Christians think that they're all the same thing: God's place of eternal distress.

J: Just like the Old Testament terms, each of those words has its own subtle meaning and you don't always know the intent. So, biblically, hell is a truly mixed bag—a real mystery. A few passages certainly do imply a place of punishment, while others suggest only a purgatory where souls are cleansed and purified . . . as gold might be refined by fire. Some texts insinuate a mere resting place of inaction with not too much going on— like your apartment. So you'll need to request clarification when someone tells you to go to hell.

DK: I'm guessing it won't be long . . .

J: Historically, Judaism didn't have any fixed dogma regarding the concept of hell. Many Jews did *believe* in an afterlife, but the laws of Moses don't threaten the guilty with unending next-world punishment. Instead they promise *earthly* woes—both for the criminals and their unfortunate descendants.

DK: So the Israelites had no clear postmortem theology.

J: No, and *I* certainly didn't go preaching one. I knew that no religion or belief system influences the destiny of man's spirit. I was an early advocate for separation of church and fate.

DK: Then the notion of hell was never part of Jewish cosmology.

J: It wasn't part of their thinking. My family and I grew up with the Torah, which never reports creation of any hell. Now, if you're Christian, this should really grab your attention. If God created a place of eternal torment for his billions of insurgent children, shouldn't they be told a little bit more *about* it? And why is it the only option other than heaven? Can't there be some kind of rehab to work out the kinks?

DK: I think you're right. We need a more thorough *description* of the place.

J: Exactly. I mean, okay, so there's a lake of fire . . . which always makes for tricky boating, of course. But couldn't God provide a few more details on the sufferings in store for those who don't make the team? He might also tell why He's committed to harming his children in the first place, doing it *forever,* and why He would use such cruel, sadistic means to get it done. And shouldn't He explain above all how behaving so diabolically could bring Him any justice, satisfaction or peace?

DK: But we agree that we wouldn't expect Yahweh to go defending himself or asking for anyone's permission. His rulings are pretty much unilateral— a done deal. The man doesn't do any focus groups.

J: But still . . . a place like hell you don't reveal at the very last second like a pop quiz. Milking hell for its true deterrent role means it has to be publicized—you've gotta get the *details* out and scare up a little obedience. Printing a few vague and discordant scriptures isn't enough. And it clearly doesn't accomplish the task: all you've gotta do is read the headlines in this afternoon's news. To *really* get peoples' attention, hell would need widespread pre-release marketing to drive home the point.

DK: Ah, *now* you're thinkin' like a capitalist.

J: And the issue of hell burns very much deeper than its mere lack of scriptural specifics . . . because *someone* had to *build* it. I mean it didn't just pop up from nowhere—and religion's made plain there's but *one* universal creator. So now we've got *another* serious snag. If Yahweh did in fact create a hell, then when, precisely, did He do it? If He made it right away, during Creation Week, you'd have to wonder, "Hey man, why the hell is God creating hell!?" Know what I mean?

DK: Not exactly.

J: C'mon, Maylor, don't embarrass your family. If God constructed hell at the very outset, He must've seen a *need* for the place. See where I'm goin'? If Yahweh knew that hell was required, He must've known his forbidden fruit tree would quickly trigger man's ruin. So if He didn't want his naturally curious children fully using their perilous 'free will,' why give it to 'em at all? Surely He'd know they would soon give in to allure.

DK: True, but Yahweh didn't give the two lovers any inch-thick, leather-bound Garden Conduct Manual—even the lewdest public displays of affection were no problem. There's one lousy rule . . . and they break it.

J: Okay, but let's say this Bible God *is* omniscient, as many people believe, and can in fact look into the future. As you said, He must've foreseen The Great Fruit Disaster before it happened. And if He *knew* that Adam and Eve would stumble and 'fall,' why didn't He draft a different *plan*? Why not axe the tree of temptation altogether? What sort of father plants a garden for children that's rife with potential for harm?

DK: Maybe God *didn't* create hell right away and established it when He saw the rebellion. It may have been management by crisis.

J: C'mon, we're talking of *God*, not the government. Religion's God is said to be all-knowing. He knew his children would rebel and misbehave and He knew his plan to save them would implode—but He chose to follow through nonetheless.

DK: Divine privilege, I suppose. Not everyone can be among the chosen.

J: Oh yeah? Why not? Who told God to send his stubborn children to hell? That's not the only alternative, you know. If they're so bloody distressing, He could zap 'em from existence and save 'em all forever from their free-willed, free-thinking pain.

DK: I guess that makes sense. What God has created, He can quickly rub out.

J: And mind your previous thought: the New Testament says that *your* mercy must always be without bounds. How baffling, then, that God puts such a pitifully low threshold on his.

DK: Yes, and that *really* rattles my cage. We mortals should have *at least* as much right to hypocrisy as God does.

J: And consider this: If God created hell, how did He do it?

DK: You're losin' me again.

J: Okay . . . according to scripture, hell is some fairly serious agony, right? You gotta think it's a pretty grim arrangement—dark and sweltering, gloomy and depressing, nonstop stream of complaints to upper execs. Probably no tablecloths, either. But how, exactly, did God *forge* the place? Is it fully stocked with old-time quartering racks, fiery beds of coal and dungeons of pain? Or do they just play hip hop 'round the clock?

DK: I see the problem, alright. No loving being would ever *conceive* the idea.

J: That's my point. Picture God sitting there *pondering* this plan. Here He is, like the wicked witch hovering over a crystal ball, plotting and scheming against his earthly foes, rubbing his hands with evil cackles of laughter in delightful anticipation of the horrible sufferings to come. *"Now* then . . . how best to bring affliction and regret to my mutineers?"

DK: Maybe we're going too hard on the guy. I can't believe God carefully *configured* his place of punishment or eagerly planned its grand opening. We're told He condemns people sadly, with great disappointment and pain.

J: Sorry, but that won't cut the cake, my friend. Doesn't God have any free will of his own? It makes no sense to say that sending his children to hell really bums Him out—like He's got to do it 'cause He has no *choice.* But again, He's *God.* He's not union, so no one's *forcing* Him, right? Why not, as the old song says, just call the whole thing off? So, once again we've got a slew of theological dilemmas . . .

First, either God knew that people would sin and created them anyway, knowing they would burn if they didn't turn Christian before death. *Or,* He suspected they *might* sin but still rolled the dice with their souls. *Or,* He thought they *wouldn't* sin, in which case He was woefully mistaken and therefore isn't omniscient, and doesn't know his mortal children at all. Take your pick.

DK: Not a very pretty set of choices.

J: There's an even more pressing concern. If God sees the future, He already knows the Judgment Day rankings and who's gonna draw the short straws. The moment someone is born, He *knows* if they're destined for hell—and Revelation 13 *says* it. So He'd spare the poor blokes an eternity of horrors in just skipping their lives from the start.

DK: Hey, *there's* an inventive solution: the no-risk, non-existence option. No *benefits*, perhaps . . . but no *pain* of any kind as well.

J: And here's *more* Christian theology based on a true story. The church tells the world that its God feels the pain and suffering of his children. But will He be feeling the pain and suffering of those He hurls into hell? If so, He's condemning *himself* to an infinity of torture and anguish. But of course He's not going to *do* that, right? We've got to assume God *ignores* the cries of his children from the bright-blazing depths of remorse. And in that case, he's no better than a dictator who sleeps perfectly well at night, knowing that his death camps are stuffed with people groaning in grief. So, how is this God less monstrous than his demonized devil? The Christian 'God of love' is rather hateful, I'm sorry to say.

DK: I've always heard that God *hates the sin* but *loves the sinner.*

J: Well, whether this God of the Bible actually *loves* his sinners is still a wide-open debate. But here once again is an obvious double standard—for when dealing with God and his flaming hell, *you're* instructed to *hate the torture* . . . but *love* the bloody *torturer!!!*

DK: Maybe God *isn't* all-knowing and didn't think we'd be such a curse. Prob'ly thought his test would turn out peachy.

J: Then why did He bother with hell? In case things got too rowdy at the fair?

DK: He may not always know what's in the cards. He may see only *parts* of what's coming—*bits and fragments* of tomorrow.

J: Pretty tough to make that argument if, as many Christians believe, God's prophets predicted my life—and even the course it would take—hundreds of years before. With pinpoint precision like *that*, you'd have to know almost every step someone could make.

DK: You're right. After all, we're talking of *God* and not a traveling carnival gypsy. But, still . . .

J: Actually, it's quite within bounds of scripture that the Bible God *isn't* all-knowing. You mentioned the book of Job in your opening letter and had fun with the fact that Yahweh asks Satan more than once where he's been and what he's been up to of late.

DK: Another allegory, perhaps?

J: Not if we're talking about the 'literal word of God.' Symbolism really blurs the line between fact and fiction. You can't say the Job story might be fable but the Resurrection is fact—though *both* of them require clearing pretty serious hurdles of faith.

DK: So if all Bible stories are *literal*, God's knowledge is limited at best. He's not as informed as we think.

J: And these tales of Yahweh's blind spots arise periodically throughout the Christian Old Testament. In Genesis 18 Yahweh freely tells Abraham He doesn't know a *thing* about the shameful realities taking place out in Sodom and Gomorrah. Start reciting at verse twenty.

DK: Un momento there, padre, some of us look to the text . . .

"Then the Lord said, 'Because the outcry against Sodom and Gomorrah is great and their sin is very grave, I will go down to see whether they have done altogether according to the outcry which has come to me; and if not, I will know.'"

J: Well, there you have it. In the Bible's very first book, God grants He's not always clued in. This point is important—and big in particular if He's preaching on the future of the planet or what lies inside peoples' 'hearts.' Not sure what's happening at present, He sees things still centuries away.

DK: I personally don't even *care* if He's omniscient. Either way, I have a hard time finding space for any 'God' who isn't gratified until his enemies *hurt*— especially when He's always telling *me* to *love mine*!! I may come to grudgingly respect this guy but I sure as hell don't like Him.

J: You respect Him like an animal respects a cruel owner—you *fear* Him. At its core, religious fundamentalism demonstrates a terrible, ungodly fear of a terribly fearful God. And let us be honest: you cannot love something you fear. You may *resign* yourself to this tyrant . . . but never will you really *trust* Him. Secretly you'll wonder if, someday, like a disloyal Doberman, He'll turn and rip you to shreds.

DK: I always had trouble with those stories of God's cruelty to humans— but for years I couldn't make myself say it.

J: So you gave this fearsome God your forced compliance. Frightened and deeply unsure, you gathered whatever backup troops you could find and called it evangelism.

DK: I did what I thought was right, I suppose.

J: "Nothing in the world is more dangerous than sincere ignorance and conscientious stupidity." That's Reverend Dr. M.L.K., the junior.

DK: Still, as vexing as I was with my witnessing, I always felt I was truly serving the Lord.

J: Pascal said that men never do evil so thoroughly and cheerfully as when done from religious conviction.

DK: You're a living quotation book, dude. But you're grinding sacred cows into sausage, you know. This won't go well with born-agains.

J: But like they say: you've gotta make sure that the 'second birth' doesn't squeeze all the air from your brain . . .

Chapter Eighteen

DK: So you've smothered the fires of hell and we can all breathe calm. But your view on the 'born again' thing is a bit queer. In John's gospel, you tell Nicodemus: "Except a man be born again, he cannot see the kingdom of God."

J: Right . . . you won't *see* it. But religions view the kingdom, or heaven, as some other-worldly locale in a distant corner of the cosmos— a place where right-of-entry is determined by God once the physical body gives out. *Absurd.* You're always 'in' the kingdom but you don't always 'see' it.

DK: Then *your* version of salvation is conditional, too.

J: It's conditional the way a man wearing blinders must remove them before he can see. But this isn't saying that *love* is conditional, which it most surely is within Christianity and all faiths based on scary gods.

DK: *Religion's* salvation, though, is all about safety of the soul. They're selling something they tell us we can't live without: eternal life insurance.

J: Yes, and it usually centers on acceptance of certain creeds or beliefs, said to have issued from God and his earthly ambassadors. The promised redemption doesn't actually kick in until sometime after one's death, keeping the faithful naïvely dependent on data that cannot be proved. This 'pay-now, collect-later' proposal is the favorite sheep-herding tactic underlying so many religions. You may or may not get virgins and harps— but that's what you're promised up front. And the message is always to do as you're told while you're living, and you'll wake in a heavenly dreamland after you're dead.

DK: And you see it all as a sham.

J: It's a bloody fool's game—there are no hidden altars in God's temple. He doesn't keep joy from his kids in the present to see if they'll deserve it later on. Believing true fulfillment waits exclusively in heavenly utopias, you're flatly declaring that life's most rewarding achievement . . . is *death.*

DK: So then, what becomes of religion's private yacht club for the few?

J: It fades back to irrelevance as it should. Religion's notion of heaven has another incriminating flaw: the idea that timeless reality will somehow be kinder to the future than it has been to the past. But where's the comfort in this? Religion's God sits unconcerned in heaven for several millenniums while his only acknowledged children in the cosmos suffer obvious hell here on earth. Why should He pay more attention anytime soon?

DK: Some Christians claim that God was waiting for Israel to officially become a nation again. But now it's many decades since that took place, and nothing has really changed—some would argue things are even worse.

J: So Yahweh lets his non-chosen stepchildren 'round the world suffer practically forever, while waiting on a small number of Jews to settle a reserved patch of Middle Eastern land barely bigger than the state of Massachusetts?!? And in one of the very few spots in the region where you can't just drill holes and strike oil?!?

DK: Zionists say that it's all part of God's special plan.

J: God doesn't *make* any plans. His 'timeline' is *now*, and He doesn't wait for certain things to pass before sharing his full goodness with creation. Now, it's true that the *world* will change for better and for worse— but reality is always perfect and always exists only in the here and now. Once you've had this 'rebirth' of sight, you'll see as you've not seen before. In 2 Corinthians 5, Paul states that "anyone who is in Christ becomes a new creation." Even Saint Thomas Aquinas, one of Catholicism's finest minds, found that his transforming mystical episodes had turned his most brilliant thinking into dross. Now born again in the truest sense, Thomas confessed: "All that I have written seems to me like so much straw compared to what I have seen and what has been revealed to me."

DK: I know that Buddha, Krishna, and other spiritual standouts have openly stressed enlightenment . . . but *you* never even mentioned it.

J: I had to use other terms: kingdom of heaven, salvation, kingdom of God. Most people of the period were still dealing with a terribly ill-tempered, humanized God who was always busy doling out punishment and reward, according to one's obedience to the law.

DK: So you met them on their own cultural terms.

J: Of course. But not much remains of my original teachings in the hacked-up maulings of the Bible. Gospel writers have me droning of a sinister devil and his blistering hell—what a joke. Pushing theology like that to everyday Jews would've quickly gotten me laughed from the Temple. All of that soul condemnation hype was added long after I was gone. Though it's not like I gave no clues on the meaning of salvation. I likened it to a hidden treasure or a lost precious gem . . . things that were out of sight and had to be sought. If grace rested solely in professing the name of Jesus, what would there be to *seek*?

DK: In Matthew 15, you do allude to a lower-state consciousness when you tell your disciples that *worldly* affairs are not the true source of our ills.

J: No, because the *outer* troubles rise from what's happening within the mind. I warned of "the leaven of the Pharisees," an obvious swipe at their hypocrisy and their savage, judgmental thinking. I spoke of the five wise maidens with oil for their lamps—another hint at the state of heightened awareness.

DK: But why conceal your 'good news' with cryptic stories and masks?

J: There was no safer way to do it. *Attaining* this mystical knowledge would take one far beyond the 'law'—a very dangerous thing in the eyes of power. So the message had to be encrypted. It was there for those with "ears to hear," but not very many had ears . . . they balked at their own liberation.

DK: Can't a person be good with finding happiness in simple *earthly* indulgence and leave all this spiritual flap?

J: It's a fine question: *Can* you? I mean, worldly pleasure is all well and good— but its shelf life is pretty darned short. Take sex, as a case. One minute you're screaming for God or whatever and then craving root beer and chips.

DK: But why seek knowledge if ignorance is bliss?

J: Ignorance isn't often bliss at all—except as it may blissfully profit those who exploit it. At heart, people long to know their own reality. And unlike the pleasures of the world, the bliss that comes from *knowing* can't be lost and doesn't fade with circumstance or time. It frees you from exploitation and suffering, from disillusionment, from guilt, manipulation and fear. It's the pearl of great value in Matthew 13. As soon as he finds it, the merchant sells *everything* to secure it.

DK: You paint a compelling picture.

J: That's how it is with the truth. You embrace it and release all attachments—everything of worth is now yours. You're free to enjoy the blessings of life as those who clutch and control can never do—the passing from bondage to freedom. So spend a little time each day getting quiet and then turning quietly *within*. Self-awareness is the first requisite sign of wisdom.

DK: The Bible says *"fear of the Lord* is the beginning of wisdom."

J: Fear is the beginning of *neurosis*. Humans need fearful religions and deities like chickens need ravenous wolves.

DK: Then what's the need of religion from the start?

J: Religion at least recognizes that there's something beyond the limited human persona. It's an early step on the never-ending path of knowledge.

DK: So religion *can* be useful in returning us to the real.

J: It certainly can point the way—but all too often it loses *the point*. Religion is often used for political reasons, taming the masses, or even to generate cash. For the individual, it can be a mere social event. Some use religion to relieve their guilt, manipulate others, or even to bargain with God in hope of striking a binding deal.

DK: To be fair, lots of religious people are solemnly sincere.

J: Sure, but sincerity alone isn't helpful—your good intentions aren't enough. You also must learn to recognize progress as ever-increasing wisdom, peace, and unflappable inner strength.

DK: I think, for many people, religion's just a way to form social bonds, help them feel connected, and navigate the challenges of life.

J: But why would I choose to start another religion when I spent so much time blasting those already in place? In this regard, here's a few relevant questions for the modern believer . . .

Would you practice your religion if no one else were doing it and everyone thought it was crazy? Would your theology have occurred to you naturally if you had never heard it before? Is it something you'd find rational on your own and without someone else's support? Does it harmonize fully with mind and heart—and does it really make *sense*?

DK: So religion should be a private, personal thing and examined *objectively*.

J: Well, coming together in gratitude and reverence isn't worthless. But fellowship is one thing and joining in mass delusion is something else.

DK: That raises the issue of religion in the media. A lot of religious endeavors these days are crimes against human intelligence.

J: District attorneys can sometimes see 'em as crimes of a *different* sort.

DK: Yeah, we've certainly witnessed some shocking hypocrisy through the years. Jim and Tammy Faye Bakker's 'ministry' had its own 2,000-acre theme park. Turns out the two flashy evangelists were living sordid lives of wild excess on donated funds from the chumps. Even the Bakker family hound had an air-conditioned, high-dollar doghouse. All of it was finally shown as a fraud—and overnight the couple went from grandstanding to grand jury indictments. I believe ol' Jimbo did five years of state-enforced penance on that account. I guess you could call it 'doing some time for Jesus.'

J: *Heh heh.* It's a short trip from the penthouse to the pen . . .

DK: I also recall—it was back in '87, I think—when TV evangelist Oral Roberts told *his* followers he had to raise eight million dollars or the Lord would call him "home." He finally brought in about nine million bucks—but *not* before missing the deadline. Somehow, though, he managed to avoid being taken.

J: If only the poor *donors* were so blessed . . .

Chapter Nineteen

DK: So you're sure we don't need religion to find God.

J: Do dolphins need a compass to find water? The irony of 'seeking for God' is that you're swimming in Him every passing moment. "In Him I live and move and have my being," your scripture declares.

DK: You're citing the book of Acts. I thought you were an anti-Biblicist.

J: I only reject lack of *discernment*. The Bible contains hundreds of beautiful gems of wisdom and inspiration and it's *full* of instructive buried treasure. Very few Christians or Jews know how much insight lies hidden in their scriptures. But some of these biblical texts are not just unhelpful, they're actually counter-productive. So we have to distinguish, I think you'll agree, the sublime from the clearly inane.

DK: But, with the Bible, mustn't you take the bad with the good?

J: No, and neither must you. Those who insist on the all-or-none approach to the Bible could hardly know a thing of its history. Even a *trace* of honest learning proves the literalist position absurd, and anyone endorsing that view is disgracing himself. If properly schooled on the subject, he wouldn't dare *call* it 'the word of God' since he prob'ly couldn't say it straight-faced.

DK: That's certainly not the view from church experts.

J: An expert's just a fella from out of town.

DK: Well, the 'experts' within Christianity say that *some* of it just requires blinded faith.

J: Not good enough! Blind faith may be *faith*—but it's still *blind*. When the unquestioning explain the unknown through the unprovable, it can only result in the terribly unbelievable.

DK: You're bucking every realm of religious authority, you know.

J: Religious authority!? A blatant oxymoron, for sure! Those who lust for power are the very last ones to be given it—and anyone seeking it through religion has sailed seriously past the port. True holiness lies *within* and seeks influence over none. It lives in the heart, radiating only peace, asking for nothing and enveloping all. The Christ spirit is compassionate, loving, humble . . . and usually pretty quiet.

DK: Wait, I asked you in my letter of a story in the gospel of John about you going berserk one day at the Temple. You call that little riot *compassion*!? Scripture says you overthrew some furniture, upended the cash registers—and ousted the offenders by assault with a deadly weapon!

J: C'mon, it says I used a bloody *whip*, not an AK-47.

DK: Well, either way, it doesn't sound too gentle and loving to *me*. And I doubt that it happened very *quietly*. If the Christ is so hang-dog humble, how do you explain your little temple-tantrum at church?

J: Look, I can't defend every water cooler rumor you hear. As I've said, I had nothing to do with the documenting of my life. And anyway, what of it? You can't know another man's consciousness from a state of ignorance.

DK: They say that a man's actions speak volumes.

J: Depends on who's doing the interpreting. What does a toad in the canyon understand about the ways of a soaring hawk? No one living in spiritual darkness knows the mind or motivations of the awakened. In fact, Buddhists have a tradition known as 'crazy wisdom' in which the master will do things that seem entirely bananas. He knows that shocking his students with unusual behavior can free them from the strait-jackets of their culturally entrained—some would call it 'civilized'—programming.

DK: You're dodging the issue here. Did you really go Indiana Jones on the vendors in the mid-Eastern Temple of Doom?

J: Why would I do *that* when I had spent my whole ministry trying always to teach people peace? My one function on earth was to serve as the way-shower for my brothers and sisters. Anger, violence and retaliation wouldn't show them any ways very different from the ones they knew.

DK: I press the point only because the church instructs us to imitate Christ. Do you agree? *Should* we strive to pattern our lives after yours?

J: Given the serious clashings of the Bible, that's a confusing task. I mean which Christ does the church advise imitating? The one who nobly *forgives* the sins of others? Or the one who takes their sins personally, threatens their pitiful souls with hell's fire, and whacks 'em around with a whip!?

119

The main thing is *intention*. All effort given to knowing more of your godly nature is fruitful—and isn't that what most religious believers claim to want? So, even if mimicking someone is fairly useless, absorbing a teacher's *wisdom* can pay big. The timely words or actions of a saint are powerful and may be precisely what's needed to spring you free of any ideological prisons. You learn to stop *reacting* to things and to calmly respond from peace and genuine detachment. It really is possible to do this. Just start noticing when you're habitually reacting to emotions, thought, or circumstance. If you catch yourself unwittingly reacting—to upsetting feelings of fear, doubt or anger, for examples, or maybe negative thoughts about some possible threatening future—bring your attention back to peace and calm. With a little bit of practice and awareness, you'll quickly realize you could spend your whole life reacting to things instead of enjoying the moment or simply *being*. Don't let your thoughts and emotions get bigger than *you*.

DK: From where *I'm* sitting, that kind of mastery seems a long way off.

J: How far could you be from reality? Trust me, it's closer than your very next breath and nothing can keep you from it—not even the finest religion.

DK: You make a lot of distinctions between religion and spirituality, but isn't there some connection?

J: The mind may associate 'spirituality' with religion, but there's no direct causal relationship . . . and each can make the other seem pointless.

DK: Some insist we honor *all* spiritual paths and religions.

J: Even if they're clearly insane?

DK: But you'll admit that religion *can* lead to a greater spiritual awareness, yes?

J: Sure, but so can a heart attack. And given a choice *between* the two, I'd have to think awhile . . .

CHAPTER TWENTY

DK: You don't show much regard for religion.

J: Religion's not shown much regard for *people*—think of all the millions it *killed*. So, I see it like this: the *knowledge* might be sacred, and the *seeker* is most *surely* the sacred . . . but not the religion, which is only a tool at its best.

DK: Once again your view doesn't jibe with the scriptures. You're quoted telling Peter, "On this rock I will build my church." So it seems you were planning something big. The boys in the Church of Rome surely thought so.

J: Well, you'd almost need a theologian's help to miss the statement's obvious metaphor—and only one gospel even quotes it. You'd think something so important would've garnered more attention from the press. Using that one cryptic sentence to build a mammoth institution seems a bit over-zealous, don't you think?

DK: But did you, in fact, choose Peter as the very first pope?

J: Peter was no more important than anyone else. In the ninth chapter of Mark—showing total lack of spiritual understanding—the disciples argue about who among them is "greatest." Clearly *they* didn't see any pecking order in place.

DK: Still, the Catholic Church points mostly to that single story of Peter's scriptural promotion to justify its powerful papacy.

J: My *own* goal was to bring in a 'higher' law to replace the intolerant laws of form. I definitely sought change—but within the *individual*. No one sat above anyone else and I sure wasn't starting a formal movement.

DK: So how do you *view* the pope now that his post is firmly established? Is he truly incapable of error?

J: Does a bear genuflect in the woods?

DK: Well, is the pope at least acting as spokesman until you return? And isn't his selection the will of God?

J: Let's take a look at some interesting Catholic history and see how much entails 'God's will' or if popes speak for anyone but themselves . . .

Firstly you've got to know this: even though the Catholic Church insists that Peter went to Rome to lead its Christians, the church can show no proof this claim is true. Clement of Rome, writing only thirty years after Peter was allegedly there, gives no indication he knew anything of it— even though Peter's 'Roman ministry' is said to have been quite effective. Nevertheless, the church has pushed the papacy forward, and over the centuries more than two hundred sixty men have headed up the Holy See.

DK: Are you serious!? Two hundred and sixt— Hey, wait a minute. Headed up the holy *what*?

J: The Holy See.

DK: I'm prob'ly a big time pope dope, but what exactly is the Holy See?

J: It's the formal term for the principal episcopal jurisdiction of the Roman Catholic Church . . . it's what you might call 'Popeville.' The Holy See— a sovereign entity of international law, by the way—is presided over by the Bishop of Rome, commonly just called the Pope. It's the central body governing the Vatican and representing Catholicism in its worldly affairs. So whether it's to be, or not to be, if over land or over sea, the Holy See will oversee most all things Catholic, from A to Z. From sea to shining sea, *ami*, the Holy See is sovereign. *Oui*?

DK: I think I've got it now. *Merci* . . .

J: So, more than two hundred sixty men have now filled the papal throne, also called the Chair of Saint Peter, and their histories contain all the blood and murky intrigue of a mystery thriller. The Catholic Church was so embarrassed by some of these papal putzes that it actually began calling them "antipopes." A number of them muscled or even *murdered* their way into the job. Some lasted only a few months—or, in one case, not even a couple of weeks—before being ousted, killed or inexplicably going missing . . . and not by getting lost in the woods, if you know what I mean. Some of these guys were up one day and down the next.

DK: Holy See-saw!

J: The first part of the 10th century was an especially enthralling time for the papacy—and probably its darkest hour as well. Referred to even by Catholic historians as the "Pornocracy" or the "Rule of the Harlots," it was a period dominated mostly by two Roman noblewomen: Theodora, wife of the powerful Count Theophylact, and her daughter Marozia. They weren't really prostitutes, but in some ways they came pretty close. And even the bishop historian Liutprand of Cremona—admirably following my instructions not to judge—did actually refer to one of them as "a shameless whore." But you don't need *me* for this stuff. You can read it in the writings of the former priest and Catholic scholar Malachi Martin.

DK: Ah, c'mon, don't tease me with that lead and let me hang. Let's hear some of the backstory.

J: Well, Marozia's life was especially charming, in a seriously *dysfunctional* sort of way. As a teenager, she gave birth to a son fathered illegitimately by Pope Sergius III, and later—with the kid barely a step out of boyhood—Marozia had him installed as Pope John XI. But Marozia's papal pipeline went further. In addition to her son by Sergius, Marozia had two grandsons, two great grandsons, and one great-great-grandson who all became popes.

DK: Hmmm. I can maybe see obsession with rock stars, heroes or actors—but freaking out about *popes*?

J: Oh, you wouldn't believe the ghoulish drama surrounding the papacy during the days of these two schemers and their hand-picked pontiffs. It was one long succession of papal thrills and spills—a regular pope opera. Between Marozia and her mother, this powerful family controlled papal politics for more than fifty years. In one span, the two vexing but prominent women helped install nine popes in only eight years. They also had a hand in *removing* their revolving-door papal puppets. Two of the nine wound up strangled to death; four were deposed and died under mysterious circumstances; and one was outright suffocated, the same violent destiny awaiting one of the two shrews herself years later.

DK: Vixens of Vatican! A pontifical parade of death!

J: Actually, Vatican City—the world's tiniest sovereign state, by the way—wasn't really established until 1929, the year leading to the Great Depression.

DK: Well, *whatever* they called it, the place had better drama than most *networks*.

J: And there's plenty more to come. Years before Marozia came to power, Pope Stephen VII, nowadays called Stephen VI, was installed on the throne by another power-crazed noblewoman: Ageltrude, Queen of Italy. Soon after Pope Stephen's consecration, Ageltrude and her son Lambert II urged the new pontiff to exhume the body of their longtime enemy and one of Stephen's predecessors, Pope Formosus, who by then had rested peacefully underground in his casket for almost a year.

DK: They dug the poor guy from his *grave*!? What was *that* all about?

J: Well, it seems that Lambert and Ageltrude, belatedly taking revenge on Pope Formosus, wanted his corpse carried to the Basilica of St. John Lateran and placed on trial—*posthumously*, please understand—for crimes during his relatively short tenure as pope. As Ageltrude's pawn, Pope Stephen, diseased and mentally unstable, fast and loyally responded. Along with several of his criminals— er, that is, his cardinals and bishops, Stephen had the unearthed Formosus fetched over to the Basilica, where they dressed the old boy in his full pontifical garb and then sat him down on a chair, preparing for 'trial.'

DK: I've heard of reviving dead cases . . . but *that* is some loon-crazy shite!

J: Yeah, this bizarre event is famously known as The Cadaver Synod. It involved Pope Stephen and a papal accuser actually shouting allegations at Formosus—even cross-examining him—while a group of cardinals looked on and a trembling teen-aged deacon stood aside the dead pope and responded with a pre-written script.

DK: Oh my god, that's hilarious! A ventriloquist and a dozen live dummies!! If all of this was really God's will, however, He's sure got a great sense of humor . . . even if it is a tad dark.

J: And the freak show wasn't yet finished. Once they were done with the grisly proceedings and the papal pronouncements of guilt, several of Stephen's cardinals charged immediately at Formosus' decaying corpse, ripping the formal vestments from his body and savagely tearing off the first three fingers of his withered right hand—the ones typically used for papal blessings.

DK: *Sheesh*. Gives whole new meaning to the 'non-digital' age. And this was the friggin' *pope*, for godsakes. I'd hate to meet the *felons* back then! So, what happened next? Formosus does county fair dunking booth?

J: Well, they dressed him back in layman's clothes then hauled him outside and dragged him down the road whilst cheering Roman crowds pummeled him freely with stones and mud. Lastly, Pope Formosus—or what remained of his remains—was ingloriously dumped into the River Tiber where his story literally ended with a splash.

By the way, Marozia was also in attendance that day. Only a child at the time, she was brought to witness the event by Ageltrude, who seemingly meant to provide some early training to the lass in the proper ways of life amongst nobility. Marozia would put her learning to good use in later years. No one recorded if the young girl was near when Cardinal Sergius presented Queen Ageltrude with the truly gruesome 'gift' she had requested of Pope Stephen just *before* the zany affair: the violently severed fingers of her former rival. What a conversation piece *that* must've been.

DK: Good lord, I never realized that the papacy could be so colorful—or so *dangerous.*

J: A pretty rough period, for sure. One papal candidate felt he just couldn't stomach the brutality and bloodshed that might develop should he himself ever become pope . . . so he quit the priesthood and joined up with the mob.

DK: *Heh heh.* Of all the outrageous messiahs, *you* take the prize—no contest. So, any other lurid pope tales? This stuff brings out my shadow.

J: Well, there's some interesting history concerning three other popes of the era. First was Leo V, who lasted all of one month in July 903 before he was thrown into prison by Cardinal Christopher, who had Leo strangled in the pokey and then replaced him as pope. Unfortunately, Christopher himself was later imprisoned by Cardinal Sergius, who soon gave Chris a taste of his own remedy, having *him* strangled in stir as well.

DK: You're pullin' my leg here, right? Makin' it up as you go.

J: Perhaps you'll believe the Italian historian Vulgarius. That's *his* account.

DK: So Leo the Five gets strangled by Cardinal Chris, who naturally succeeds him as pope. Then *he's* overthrown by Cardinal Sergius, who quickly has Christopher strangled too.

J: You got it. As last man standing, Sergius then murders all the cardinals who opposed him and has his enemies on the papal court strangled as well.

DK: Seems the local rope makers stayed pretty busy those days. So Sergius, having basically run 'unopposed,' wound up in the chair of Saint Pete.

J: And took the name Pope Sergius III. He also took on the sexually maturing Marozia as his favorite mistress. Only a mere teenager then, she later bore him a child who, as I said earlier, would one day himself become pope. Her mom Theodora, no doubt, was proud as a parent could be.

DK: Whatever became of this mother-daughter team of papal power brokers? I think you said one didn't fare very well.

J: Theodora went on to a quiet death, but Marozia's pathetic ending was far more dramatic. After years of cruel imprisonment by her own son —it's a long story—the elderly Marozia, wasting and barely alive in her bleak prison cell, was finally suffocated and her sorrowful soul released "for the well-being of Holy Mother Church."

DK: Clearly an act of Christian charity. They say that parents shouldn't smother their children—but Marozia probably wished that she *had*. I guess in a family like *that*, nothing's so warm as sending dear old mom to the brig . . .

J: On the night of her church-sponsored murder, Marozia was nothing but a pile of skin and bones on her prison cell floor. The poor shriveled woman was forced to listen to a scathing list of her sins along with those of her grandson Octavian—son of Alberic II—who 'served' as Pope John XII. Now, I should stress that neither Octavian *nor* Marozia would ever win the Good Samaritan award. But weighed with the crimes of her grandson, Marozia's corruptions were trivial breaches of etiquette. With his evil and lecherous lifestyle, this Octavian kid probably set the low mark for the entire history of the papacy—or at least the world should hope so.

DK: Let's have the gory details . . . this wacky will of God's got me hooked.

J: Well, after being deposed by a Holy Synod and replaced by Pope Leo VIII, Octavian was quickly driven to flee Rome. He never meant to live in exile, though, and later returns to Rome to bump Leo from the papal throne. He then sets out on a terrorist mission of revenge—one that would keep the coroner busy for weeks. Octavian, once again operating as Pope John XII, might have impressed even a modern-day crime family. His sins against the emperor and 'Holy Mother Church' were legion: treason; perjury; looting the papal treasury; cutting off the nose, tongue, and two fingers of a Cardinal-Deacon; skinning a bishop; severing the hands of a notary; and beheading no fewer than *sixty-three* Roman clergy and noblemen, the holy will of God be praised.

DK: Wow. Pope Terminator the First.

J: But as the young bishop in the prison had painfully reminded Marozia, her grandson's negative karma did finally come calling one night when His Holiness—a man with a penchant for adultery and kinky sex— was caught giving his fully unclothed papal blessing to a married woman whose spouse had appeared unannounced. Dispensing with the usual pontifical formalities, the irate fellow then promptly began bashing the promiscuous pope's skull with a hammer.

DK: So the pope came and went, all in one night. Funny how so many betrayed husbands will often go after the *man* . . .

J: Meanwhile—back in the dark, musty dungeon—the 20-something bishop concludes his list of accusations against Marozia and her evil grandson, Pope John XII. On conducting the rite of exorcism to cast any lingering demons from Marozia's soul, the bishop then accepts her confession, cancels her longtime excommunication and, lastly, grants her the total absolving of her many sins. But Marozia was unaware that she had just been primed for a visit from two mysterious strangers who would make their way into the darkened, candlelit prison later that night, bringing with them the notorious, telltale red cushion that would be used to snuff out what little life was left in Marozia's pitiful *corpus miserabilis*.

DK: *Incredible.* Apparently there was lots of high drama surrounding these old-time leaders of the church.

J: And some were practically poster boys of spiritual and moral decay, constantly abusing their office and expanding their wealth. Exactly the kind of thing you might expect from a position that was—at times, anyway— just a powerful political post.

DK: Well, thankfully those days are over.

J: One can only pray. And certainly it's not true that all popes have been up to their skullcaps in graft and corruption. Some were brilliant thinkers who performed noble works and inspired worthy deeds. But the pope still packs as much punch in the world of politics as he does in the realm of religion. An office of nearly unlimited power, a pope issues edicts almost at will. He lives like a king in a palace that some kings would envy, he's seldom harshly challenged by subordinates, and even world leaders will defer to him.

DK: There's only been a handful of popes during *my* life—most are pretty old by the time they're chosen. Why do they wait to select these guys 'til they're clearly too pooped to pope? And I never cared for their strange, misogynistic banning of women from the priesthood or their baffling, arbitrary morality—like prohibiting or discouraging birth control in a world now *smothering* with people. They seemingly care more about *growing* the flock than nurturing the one that they've got. But the popes are generally presented in ways that make them *seem* decent enough . . . though doubtful much fun at the beach.

J: They surely must tire of wearing the same clothes every day.

DK: Hey, as a longtime bachelor myself, I can relate. But you're right. *Just once* I'd like to see the pope down at Saint Peter's Square in a ragged old T-shirt with flip-flops and faded Bermuda shorts. It'd make him a little more *accessible*, you know? There's something not right about a powerful spiritual leader wearing all those flashy, ornate threads —and living a life of privilege and opulent luxury, I should add— while preaching to the *rest* of the world on simplicity, grace and equality.

Television made the pope a rock star and he and his entourage are celebrities wherever they go—the ultimate satire. The 'humble' pope is zipped around the world in private jets and limos and even has a bullet-proof Popemobile. The Vatican itself is basically a militarized compound protected by a special battalion of Swiss guards—some of the best-trained warriors on earth. I mean where is the advertised *faith*?

As head of the Vatican, the pope presides over a multi-billion-dollar empire of high-rent real estate, thousands of elaborate churches and cathedrals, magnificent artwork, priceless jewelry . . . and hoards of other immensely valuable stuff. From what I gather, the Vatican and its advisors control huge wads of cash and even business and investment portfolios. They've got a Secret Service and their own bank as well. The Vatican Bank has been accused of money-laundering scandals for years. Amid claims of connections to organized crime, the bank has engaged in suspicious and secretive transactions involving huge sums of money and has played legal cat-and-mouse games over the years to elude the crippled arms of the law.

J: And all of this madness goes on as Catholicism's faithful Third-World followers are striving for survival in poverty and filth? When half the world can't run themselves a warm bath?

DK: So, none of it was ever the plan?

J: Even with my slanted portrayal in scripture, do these sound like things I'd encourage? Nowhere in the Bible is the pope or the papacy mentioned. That single, hazy story of Peter's career advance is the most-leveraged scripture in history—and building a religious superpower upon it is unreal.

DK: To be fair, though, Catholicism certainly isn't unique. A pretty large part of Christendom runs much like a multi-national conglomerate. In many ways, that's essentially what it is . . . but with way better tax breaks, of course.

J: Where did people get the idea that I was starting a retail religion? I urged my friends and followers to share news of their spiritual renewal. Somehow I got incorporated.

DK: What set the tax exemptions rolling?

J: The starting point was Christianity becoming the official religion of Rome and its far-reaching empire. Next, of course, came the money—bishops took charge of the cash box. Then the religion *really* gathered steam. I'm not sure how it was justified, though, since I taught a faith to be practiced quietly and out of the public view. I instructed people to pray *in private*—which clearly *wouldn't* include saying prayers at public sporting events, in classrooms at public schools and so on. I often lambasted religion back then, and it should've been clear that I wasn't creating another.

DK: Even though I played the game myself for many years, I now wonder why any of this stuff is believed.

J: Well, because religion implies that *it* knows—far better than *you* do—the truth of your reality and what's best for you and *Oh, by the way, could you possibly write us a small check?*

CHAPTER TWENTY-ONE

DK: Okay, I've been wondering about something: how did you come to all this knowledge and wisdom? What was the professional secret?

J: Well, I simply recognized early in life there's nothing to cling to in the world—nothing that *saves* anyone. So I began thinking about what *does* last and started questioning *everything*. I spent time with sages and drank from the wells of their wisdom . . . and yes, from a few of their wine bottles, too. I learned to shift my focus from the outer world and to meditate and bring my gaze inward. I then saw that, whatever appeared, *I* had to be there as witness. Before a single question could be asked—even about God himself—*I* had to be there to ask it. And wouldn't this be true of you as well?

DK: And his disciple was greatly confused, saying, "What the hell are you *talking* about!??"

J: The mystical meaning of John 8: "Before Abraham was, *I am*." Abraham represents the physical world. Therefore long before the world, a powerful manifestation of Consciousness, was the One—the changeless, formless, nameless primordial Source. You are the belovéd child of this Energy and a creative expression of it. And here's a way to prove that you and the body-mind are not the same thing. Ask yourself open-mindedly, "*Who* is experiencing this body? *Who* is having these thoughts?"

DK: The answer seems obvious: *I'm* the one in this body. *I'm* the one with these thoughts.

J: Yes, but who is speaking?

DK: What the heck do you mean? *I* am speaking!

J: But again, who is this mysterious 'I' you'd have me acknowledge?

DK: Oh c'mon, it's *me*, you messianic mule—the guy sitting right here beside you.

J: You're pointing your finger at your chest and referring me to your body. My question is, who is the one pointing and referring?

DK: You should've been a lawyer.

J: No, *really*—addressing the question "Who am I?" can actually be pretty revealing, and will leastways show you what you're *not*. In fact, try this fun little experiment: tonight when you climb into bed, close your eyes, be still, and quietly consider one question. "Who—or what—is lying here?"

DK: And why should I do *that*?

J: Because you'll find there's no inarguable answer. What you are can't be located or labeled—you're not a particular *thing*. But still, what do you notice? Who is the one that's *aware* of a body on a bed? Can this invisible energy be called this or that and be proven so in a balanced court of law? It sounds a little strange, perhaps, but it's the wisdom of Galatians 3: "There is neither Jew nor Greek, there is neither slave nor free man, there is neither male nor female; for you are all one in Christ."

DK: The thought of being nothing in particular is strange . . . and even a little scary, truth be told. I fear I can't so easily snuggle up to the mystery.

J: Say what!?? You do it when snuggling up to your bloody *pillow*!! Every time you doze off to sleep, you dive head-first into deepest dark water and not even certain you'll ever resurface again.

DK: I never thought of it that way.

J: Well, *think* about it. In the state of dreamless sleep, your whole self-ish world disappears and every part of your 'reality' goes with it. Normality is rolled up like a strip of old carpet and you lose all attachment to your life, your existence and your 'self,' with no sense of fear, loss or destruction. Good or bad, your world is gone with the wind, your ego is dead . . . and suddenly you're perfectly content in this problem-free state of nothingness—the restful condition of no-*thing*-ness.

DK: Still, I have my history to trust. Believe me, I always snap out of that 'state of *nothing*' when the alarm reminds me of *something*.

J: Sure, but the point is that when hitting the sack each night, you fall quite happy and helpless into the Void, not sure it won't swallow you up forever. And really, you're only betting with the odds by assuming you'll awaken with the clock. You know the day is coming when you *won't*.

DK: You're referring to death, I assume?

J: Of course. What happens *then* to the 'you' who's been living your life?

131

DK: Well, I've always figured that *God* would handle it all and there wasn't much I really needed to know.

J: O ye of groundless faith! Your thinking entails a pretty long string of disturbing, unproven—and *unprovable*—assumptions. The biggest one, of course, is that a God exists outside of you and separate . . . a cosmic Wizard of Oz behind the curtain, throwing all the switches and running the show. This means that your God created you *as a body*, with careful planning and thought, and hence brought you onto the planet at his whim— which then clutters the gutters once again.

DK: That's true . . . as I said in my letter, He couldn't have asked my permission if I didn't yet even exist.

J: By Christian theology, then, you're victim to God's own, self-centered agendum. If God created you as a body—and did so, remember, at his sole, uncounseled discretion—He allowed you no input at all in choosing your birthplace, your parents . . . or even the main religion of your culture. And may God himself help you if it wasn't primarily *Christian*. Now, any Bible literalist should see that, by forcing your engagement in his little earth-drama, God has knowingly placed you—and all those you've loved— in danger of eternal damnation. And if God has made *you* in this fashion, others arrived to the same soul-endangering environs. And what of those born into squalor, oppression, neglect or abuse? Cursed from the gun by your all-wise, all-loving deity. "But that's life," says the God of the Bible. "*My* ways are not *your* ways, you know."

DK: You must've been a blast at family dinners.

J: Just call 'em the way I see 'em . . .

DK: But I have to agree with your point: it's totally unfair that a relative few *are* given lives of luxury and ease, while billions have been born into hell. Or that God would give some folks eighty or ninety years of life to 'repent,' while others get maybe fifteen or twenty . . . and many get even less. Now that we view it more closely, I see that God's curious soul redemption gamble is limited by the same time and space restrictions as anything else in life.

J: Then salvation's just a matter of luck.

DK: Apparently so. And many situations aren't *conducive* to the Christian message. I mean how could a struggling child of the ghetto understand the idea that you long ago died for his sins? It's just not realistic.

J: The God of the Bible is pretty much removed from all that. He still holds everyone *accountable*, of course—but He's not too concerned about his children having food, some decent shelter, or a safe, fruitful land in which to live. He's no longer messing with things like wars, famines, and plagues. He's no more time to fret of volcanic eruptions, those killer tsunamis and hurricanes or the latest science-borne 'virus.' He mostly stays busy building his brand and basking in his own vainglory, watching his troops like a hawk and hitting his quotas. And that's the *one* way He's always been consistent: ever gauging the attention you're giving to *Him*.

DK: Okay, so the *problem* is pretty darned clear: our understanding of God is a mile off mark. But what, O font of wisdom, is the *solution*?

J: Well, as I see it, you basically have two choices. Resign yourself to this self-absorbed, learning-disabled God of religion, or throw Him out on his deafened, insensitive ear. If I were the average human, I'd fire Him on grounds of incompetence alone—send Him back for remedial logic or a course in personnel management.

DK: I trust I'll have your protection when the angry mob arrives . . .

CHAPTER TWENTY-TWO

J: I hear those sprockets grindin', pilgrim . . . say what's on your mind.

DK: Well, I'm thinking what if they're right? The literalists, I mean. What if they're right about reality? Don't we have to give some weight to *their* view? This 'God' concept is ancient—so maybe there's something to it. My aunt would say that even the *thinnest* pancake will always have two sides. So, what if this quick-tempered cuss of the Bible really exists? Shouldn't we mortals tread lightly? 'Cause He's pretty darned testy when He's not had his sleep.

J: C'mon, we're talking about the great Mind of the Cosmos . . . the force that creates quasars, black holes and supernovas, whirling galaxies and star systems light-years across. Even your body is utterly imbued with intelligence, flawlessly processing trillions of functions per second, all without your slightest effort or thought.

DK: No argument here: the universe is truly a living miracle that appears to have no connection with religion. And the whole spectacular show seems somehow harmonized—from the macro level of a solar system down to the subatomic world of the quark.

J: Then we agree that a mysterious, vast and brilliant Hyper-Intelligence seems pulsing through all existence.

DK: All but Capitol Hill, I'd say.

J: So are you telling me this Cosmic Magnificence called 'God' is a guy who takes personal interest in your sex life?

DK: Hell, I wish *somebody* would.

J: But, *really* . . . is it right to think this Universal SuperMind would have you out bemoaning your sins and clinging to the ol' rugged cross while sending off chunks of cash to some slicked-up preacher at your favorite media megachurch?

DK: Man, if you were this cocky twenty centuries back, it's no wonder you teed off some folks.

J: It ain't Aunt Thelma's bridge club . . .

DK: But I'm starting to glimpse some truth in what you're saying. I see how third dimension may be nothing but a passing play of consciousness—even a few branches of science seem to confirm it.

J: Yes, but the beauty, love and intelligence that *infuse* the material world are all deathless aspects of the high, eternal realm that gives it life. In this sense, the world could well be called divine. Seen from the wider view of love, there's nothing evil or clumsy about it. The same could be said of *you*. If you grant there's one foundational energy or 'stuff' in the universe —and that everything in life arises *from* it—then *you* must have arisen from it too. Call this creative force 'God' and you just proved your own divinity. A good tree doesn't yield rotten fruit, a point most all religions would deny.

DK: How do you think these views will be received? I mean even most *liberal* Christians will find them challenging. As for conservatives . . . well, I prob'ly won't be welcome at church conventions.

J: To worship at The Church of the Open Bible and the Closed Mind is always your personal right. But if you're unwilling to *examine* your thoughts, you're condemned to continue *thinking* them. Ego's very nature is to resist anything threatening—especially information contradicting its opinions on 'reality.' Almost by necessity, then, ego's worldview is largely black and white—some ideas simply cannot, and *will not*, be considered.

DK: Then it's *ego* that creates all our dogmas, not Spirit.

J: Yes, and it blasts them into the ears of each believer, warning him that —should he ever *question* these ideas or reject them—there will certainly be hell to pay. Within Christianity, the penalty for leaving the faith is the risk of damnation. In Islam they don't wait around or leave things to chance: your fate for apostasy is *death*. These scare tactics spring from religion's rightful fear that intelligent, educated people, if left to their own reflection, would surely come to see things another way. And *that's* not good for business.

DK: So, even from the start, there's a lot working against the enlightenment of those who operate from doctrine.

J: Right, and they've been well-assured by their clergy that these teachings are 'the truth,' with little incentive to think it through for themselves. In short, folks are pretty objective about topics they regard as what you might call 'psychologically neutral,' bu—

DK: —but once we have a personal stake in the race, or fiery feelings arise, *that* shifts the rules of engagement.

J: Yeah, the more emotional you get, the less objective you become—and nothing's more emotional than religion. For instance, if you see the Christian Bible as a collection of God's personal diaries and I say there's no proof that Moses ever parted the sea, you're suddenly insulted and upset. At this point you might offer 'evidence' for the story—but if I still reject it, you break from rational discussion altogether and begin demanding obedient acceptance. If I *still* resist, you're soon accusing me of doubting 'God's word' and giving me the grim climate facts on underworlds.

DK: What you're saying is that we're always perfectly happy using reason—but only if it works to our advantage.

J: Well, most people do like to think of themselves as reasonable. But the moment reason fails them and dogmas collapse from its weight, they run to their trusty fallback position: *This* kind of thing calls for *faith*!

DK: And maybe it does.

J: But if religion—or science, medicine, education or politics—claims any 'truth' that can't be proved through simple reason, research, intelligence, or even just plain common sense, why on earth would anyone *believe* it? If people can't agree with your position on metaphysics, don't go losing your temper and waving some holy book as though you've just provided court's evidence. You're not doing yourself any favors.

DK: I've heard it said that if you're angry at one who doesn't accept your religion, your religion has serious problems—and *you're* the living proof. Who could really argue the point?

J: And why *wouldn't* a rational thinker have concerns about world religions? Consider the Bible . . . a book of claims and stories that can't be verified and often don't even make sense—yet it's the heart of two major religions! The fact that these crazy stories are 'scripture' doesn't prove anything of the stories, but it *does* provide good reason to question the scripture.

DK: A scary thing to do when you're told it's from the High Command.

J: Sure, it's human nature to protect embedded ideas. This is notably true of *spiritual* ideas, which many feel obliged to defend. British Nobel laureate Bertrand Russell said that one of the biggest barriers to progress is the religious or political idea that various doctrines are one's 'duty' to believe.

DK: I see how that would discourage honest discussion.

J: Yes, and it's not a point of sincerity, because people desperately *want* to believe and many tell themselves that they *do*—but few are really convinced it's all true. This is why religious and political militants will spend so much time making converts. They boost their own fragile beliefs by gathering other soldiers of the faith who, like themselves, will never ask questions and won't take "No" for a stance. If something is plainly outrageous and can't be verified, its backers grow all the more zealous. Like a schnauzer pup yapping at a grizzly, sometimes the side with the weakest position is the one that makes the most noise.

DK: Reminds me of an old story about a preacher's wife. She's sitting there Saturday evening scanning her husband's planned Sunday morning sermon when she circles one of the paragraphs in heavy red ink and makes a note: "Weak point. Yell louder."

J: *Heh heh.* Once you're dug in to dogma, you fight like a devil to hold ground. But even if you're a genuine, certified genius, please understand that *true* intelligence constantly self-corrects and objectively adjusts to new data. Two of its most critical traits are an open mind and intellectual honesty— the willingness to hear other views without feeling angry or threatened, then *acknowledging* what's true and what isn't; what can, and clearly cannot, be proven. Those with dark motives or weak ideologies are seldom able to do this . . . like politicians who never allow that the *other* side might have a point worth making. But is it not outright *hubris* never thinking that you might, just possibly, be mistaken? Strong response to dissent can often expose inner doubt. So, be very cautious with someone who constantly has all the answers. It's like that old saying about the masters: Those who know rarely tell, and those who always tell rarely know . . .

CHAPTER TWENTY-THREE

DK: Say, I don't mean to be quarrelsome but there's something I'd like to nail you down on.

J: Not a wooden beam, I hope.

DK: Sorry, poor choice of words.

J: No problem, hammer away.

DK: Well, you continue insisting that the material world is nothing but a mind-made illusion—and I admit that even science is starting to lean in that direction. If correct, this would force us to rethink our entire existence. But we don't yet know for sure that it's true, so why should someone believe it?

J: The *better* question, I think, is why should they *doubt* it? Even poets have been expressing this thought for centuries. Edgar Allan Poe wrote, "All that we see or seem is but a dream within a dream."

DK: Words you might *expect* from a poet, no? Especially one who was high.

J: C'mon, aren't you curious why so many masters across history would teach that the world is a projection of consciousness? They have no reason to deceive you—there's nothing in it for *them*. Why not take their advice and do some exploring?

DK: Listen, you might sell that 'projection' stuff to the guru worshipers—but not to us working stiffs. For us the world is all too real.

J: To which world do you refer?

DK: To this world *here*, of course . . . the one *you're* experiencing, too.

J: Hey, don't cast projections onto *me*. The world *you* perceive is your own *private* world, closed and inaccessible to others. Universe, remember, is an 'equal opportunity' creator—creation takes place in the state of unity where everything is shared. Anything seemingly 'yours' is only part of the passing fancy of form, and this should be obvious even to casual observers.

DK: But there must be *some* link between dreams and reality.

J: Of course, and it's the only one there *could* be: You.

DK: This 'dream world' thing is a mind-bender, for sure.

J: Even Einstein said, "Reality is merely an illusion." And physicists have already proven that anything solid viewed from the deepest level is about 99.9999% empty—there's practically nothing there! It's a world of weightless, subatomic wonders, whizzing around at warp speed, flashing on and off billions of times *per second* and with no apparent stability whatsoever. Scientists say just *observing* these things seems to alter their curious behavior. At the quantum level, the physical plane disappears— a 'reality' short-lived and razor-thin. It's all just perception and projection.

DK: If the world really is an illusion, why didn't you just *say* it centuries ago?

J: Wait 'til this interview hits the street and see for yourself . . .

Chapter Twenty-four

DK: Okay now, wait up. Even if I did—perhaps in a long distant past— make soul-level choices to experience the world of form, the physical world of 'illusion,' why do I not remember it?

J: A funny question from a guy who can't find his keys half the time.

DK: But why would I or anyone else choose a life so potentially painful?

J: For the same reason you'd risk going rock climbing, diving off cliffs, or majoring in the liberal arts. You know the decision can lead to disaster— but you're willing to chance it for the *experience*. It's true that life entails challenge and danger, but the prospect of short-term 'victory' drives you on.

DK: If it weren't a bit treacherous, it mightn't be nearly as fun.

J: Well, consider how often you've taken risks that could've brought you great pain—each time, with one motive or the other, you elected to do it. The choice to experience duality wasn't much different. And this choice was perfectly within your nature to explore—there's nothing wrong with that. The problem was the sense of separation that arose. But you're never apart from the One, and nothing you do, or *don't* do, can threaten the immortal *Self*.

DK: I'm still having trouble with 'oneness.' I don't recall you teaching it to your students.

J: Perhaps you have a short memory. You asked me at the start about my statement that the Father and I are one.

DK: I thought you were speaking of you and *God*, not you and everyone else.

J: But God *is* everyone else . . . we're all *connected*, don't you see? You and I are not two separate beings who are magically joined in unity. We're the *same being* individuating in different *forms*. Every being is part of the One Being, and all living things are one. A quote from John 17 will make the point: "The glory which thou hast given to me I have given to them, that they may be *one* even as *we are one*, I in them and thou in me, that they may be *perfectly one*."

DK: When I was a believer, I never gave that verse much attention.

J: Very few Christians do. Instead they talk of sin and bein' "washed in the blood o' the Lamb." But the unity argument is both simple and compelling. If the Father and I are one, and if *you* and I are one, it's logically irrefutable that you and the Father are one. If A equals B, and B equals C, A *must*, in every case, equal C.

DK: Divinity by rational deduction, eh?

J: But it's all theoretical mush until you know it.

DK: I still say the average person is fairly happy and has no *need* to question the earthly reality. He's got his religion or his personal philosophy and seems mostly fine with it all.

J: Even bailing wire and duct tape won't keep *that* view intact. Nearly every place on the planet contributes to its enormous illegal drug trade. In your theoretical world of contentment, chemical liberation's in big-time demand.

DK: A valid point, I suppose. And let's not forget the *legalized* cartels— the mighty pharmaceutical firms. These folks make street pushers look downright inept; they're selling addictive anti-depressants, anti-psychotics, sleeping aids, painkillers, sedatives and 'mood enhancers' by the *ton*.

J: No doubt about it: misery loves a drug company.

DK: Booze does a pretty brisk business, too. The earth has more than two hundred million alcoholics. Recently I read that alcohol is now considered the world's most dangerous widely available hard drug. It's so physically damaging and addictive and has such far-reaching negative effects on society, it's right up there with heroin, nicotine, meth and cocaine.

J: Well, I think you just proved my point. Unless folks are feeding a diet of liquor and joy pills to their pets, it sure sounds to me as if *someone's* unhappy.

DK: Okay, you've got me pinned to the mat—many folks are obviously trying to *escape* their sufferings. But life can be difficult. Who could blame us for wanting some help to cope?

J: The one lasting answer to the world's insanity is going beyond it entirely by connecting with reality directly—and for that, you've gotta get quiet. So don't be one who constantly runs from stillness. Slow down, quiet your thinking, and listen for what *Life* has to say. The voice of wisdom inside you is subtle and cannot be heard o'er the deafening din of the world. There's a reason that so many avatars, sages and mystics spend time sitting in deserts and caves—prolonged silence can be powerfully enlightening.

DK: In younger years I'd constantly have a TV or radio going, even if I wasn't paying attention. I've noticed *lots* of people do that these days.

J: It's been said that people's problems rise mostly from the fact that they can't sit happily alone doing nothing in a quiet room. You've got to make time for stillness just the same as for anything else. Life, after all, is a matter of one's priorities. So, taking a peaceful walk in nature is at least as important as surfing the internet, right? As so many humans have discovered in life, God frequently speaks through the natural world.

DK: This thought of a cosmic intelligence communing with us and working for our expansion and fulfillment makes the 'God' force a lot more relevant. More *practical*.

J: And it *needs* to be practical, too. For many people, an historically isolated Christ is too vague to be truly helpful—and the traditional teaching of my story is surely no blessing. Nor is it even intellectually sound. How could death, which doesn't exist, possibly establish life, which exists forever? Even in Christian theology, the Crucifixion didn't establish the Atonement: the *Resurrection* did. The Crucifixion in its traditional sense is a meaningless solution to a problem that never was real.

DK: I've heard it put this way: as the symbolic equivalent of an ancient-day animal sacrifice ritual for the purification of sin, your death cleared the path for our redemption.

J: Well, it's strange and convenient 'redemption' when *someone else* must pay your tab at the bar . . . and two thousand years in advance, no less!!

DK: Generous beyond your time, for sure.

J: But, c'mon . . . do you honestly find it rational that I was murdered because of *your* personal imperfection!?? A wonderfully healthy life was destroyed because someday *you* would be *sick*?!?

DK: I can't defend the *intelligence* of it—but like you said, those were the rules. Atonement was big in those cultures, right?

J: Yet, what kind of God would need bloodshed and suffering to *forgive*? And why is He judging his children in the first place? It's bush league theology for the weak. A spiritual bypass. An insane escape from owning your power and a life-limiting denial of who you are. Refuse to be anything less than holy. In other words, *"be* perfect—as your heavenly Father is perfect." Because *you*, just as you are in this moment, do not need 'fixing' and are ever God's perfectly Accomplished. Therefore you need only release anything *hiding* it . . .

CHAPTER TWENTY-FIVE

DK: So you've pretty much destroyed all those crazy ideas about your life and its related events—especially the Crucifixion. But that leads to yet *another* concern . . . because with all you've said about the 'Christ within,' I'm now questioning the need for your Second Coming. Lots of Christians are talking about these likely being 'the last days'—the time before your predicted return to earth. With all of the high-drama news in the world, some folks claim that we are indeed witnessing the prophesied 'end times.'

J: A literal reading of the Second Coming is lame right out of the gate. Would I show up to get myself killed so to then revel in glory more than two thousand years up ahead?

DK: A bit overdramatic, perhaps.

J: The New Testament refers many times to my grand return—and everyone expected it *quickly*. Matthew's gospel has me telling a group of disciples that some of them would still be alive when I came back. The Apostle Paul, too, warns his extended church families to stay alert and live exemplary lives. He cautions of my nearing arrival, and his first letter to the Thessalonians provides some intriguing details. Open to chapter four, verse sixteen.

DK: Okay . . . "For the Lord himself will descend from heaven with a cry of command, with the archangel's call, and with the sound of the trumpet of God. And the dead in Christ will rise first; then we who are alive, who are left, shall be caught up together with them in the clouds to meet the Lord in the air . . ."

J: So here's the Almighty playing horn on my descent, and Christians —in sudden defiance of gravity physics—floating off to heaven on an angel's wing and a prayer. Now, this was all hoped to happen while Paul was alive. But if Paul claims to have gotten this privileged intel through divine inspiration, what shall we make of his source? And even though his letters were written long before the New Testament gospels, it's clear that Saint Paul—and others before and after—were expecting my fast and glorious, triumphant return, with rapturous resurrections and ascensions, and accompanied by a traveling chorus of angels. In 1 Thessalonians 3, Paul tells his fellow believers, "May he strengthen your hearts so that you will be blameless and holy in the presence of our God and Father when our Lord Jesus comes with all his holy ones." Notice he's not telling them all to chill out because they've still got loads of time to clean up their act.

DK: So, Christians have called for your return engagement from the start. You'd think that simple honesty would at least make 'em wonder if they've possibly missed something here. Instead they're handing out a bunch of moronic pamphlets with those ludicrous scenes of the Rapture and the great Second Coming.

J: Their goal, I guess, is to scare the bloody hell out of earth's unsaved heretics and heathens by showing them what a loving and generous God they've been ignoring. Never mind that He's planning to boil their butts in a burning lake if they won't profess what a great humanitarian He is. It might be amusing if it weren't so disturbing to think that billions of humans have *believed* it. This thinking reflects the idea that God created you as a body and He'll raise—then condemn or redeem you—*as a body*.

DK: That's how the Apostles seemed to see it, and they got the idea *somewhere*.

J: Well, they sure didn't get it from me. I never *belittled* the body—but neither did I exalt it, as made clear in the Sermon on the Mount. I taught that your life is far greater than the body, and 'the kingdom' isn't found in the world.

DK: Yeah, you once said that *your* kingdom is not *of* this world.

J: That's true—but neither is yours. God's children are not travelers through 'outer' realities, and nothing outside *themselves* can hold their inheritance.

DK: Are you saying that earth offers no hope of redemption?

J: I'm sayin' it's a bloody worthless 'redemption' that hangs on the *weather* next year! God's grace is never withheld, and freedom lies only in the now. *A Course in Miracles* says, "God has no secrets," and "He does not lead you through a world of misery, waiting to tell you, at the journey's end, why He did this to you."

DK: So we're already saved, it would seem.

J: You're never in danger and were created free—*in* Love, *by* Love, *as* Love— and this truth never wavers. Why would you believe that *someone else* must arrive before joy can reign over the earth? It's a dangerous idea because it shifts the burden from *you* and lays it on a forthcoming god from the sky. This hasn't been a very effective strategy in bringing you peace on earth.

DK: Then why all the noise from the church over your long-prophesied reign down here on the earthly plane?

J: As you observed earlier, many religious believers want security in a world they often find threatening. They long for their God to make sense of the insanity and finally put things right.

DK: Heck, what's wrong with *that*? I think we'd *all* like to believe there's a force backing some kind of order in the world and keeping everything tidy.

J: Perhaps you've confused God with Martha Stewart . . .

CHAPTER TWENTY-SIX

J: You look baffled. What's up?

DK: Well, I still say that some Christians won't take kindly to the view that they're not being judged and they're one with God, that you weren't killed because *they* were bad, and the rest of that "fear o' the Lord" madness.

J: How strange that people turn angry on hearing they're free. And yet this freedom is precisely the 'good news' of my teachings. No matter how it's been interpreted, my message wasn't about giving your attention to *me*. We're not *different* from each other, you and I—we're *individuating* in the unity of the One. It's startling enough you *resist* this idea, but the interesting part is *why* . . . and it's quite astonishing when you see it. You believe a reality of love is simply too good to be true.

DK: The point certainly can't be denied. A lot of believers seem comfortable enough with God torturing his children in hell. They figure that if God deems it needed, then it must be okay—this is how they sell it to themselves. In many religious circles, damnation is highly respected theology.

J: *Theology? Bah!!* There's the logical and the *theo*logical—and the two are barely acquainted. Theology seeks to know the nature of the sun through assiduous study of shadows. But God will never be captured in the net of the intellect, and spiritual intuition is worth far more than mental gymnastics.

DK: What about the view that Christian salvation, including the penalty of nonstop suffering in hell, is a strange kind of celestial 'tough love.'

J: It's tough to call that any kind of 'love.' Love doesn't punish and it never opposes. But some people just can't handle a reality of goodness. Parting the ocean? No problem. Raising the dead? Of course. But speak of their oneness with a God who's pure love and they'll yank you from your warm bed at midnight to hang you in the nearest tall tree. Give 'em religion crammed with guilt, judgment and fire, however, and they flock like geese to a pond.

DK: I'm definitely in no position to judge. At one church I attended, we all sat glued to our seats for half an hour, never raising a question while the preacher roared hellfire and dread. Looking back on the spectacle, I'm actually pretty embarrassed. We lapped it up like hot, thirsty horses, drinking from a cool-running stream. And to think I was giving this guy and his church a full tenth of my annual wage!

J: So you *paid* him to suffer the assault.

DK: I'm afraid so. A fool and my money are soon partners.

J: It all goes back to the separated mind we call 'ego' and its feelings of guilt. Ego believes it offended God in its quest to be 'independent' and figures that God has an ego of his own—that God thinks exactly the way that *it* thinks. So God is seen as defensive, judgmental, vindictive and quickly upset. This same kind of projection is reflected allegorically in the tale of the prodigal son. The son thinks he angered his father in leaving and returns fearing vengeance and grief. But dad never held the slightest grudge.

DK: So, ego believes it's battling God and that God feels ego betrayed Him.

J: Absolutely. Ego views God as the ultimate foe and 'knows' that He wants retribution, just as an earthly parent might. Ego believes that the guiltless are guilty and that even the mere *suggestion* of human purity is profane. Ego springs from belief in separation and thus harbors judgment, fear, and guilt. This pained sense of guilt is unbearable, though, so ego projects the guilt outward. Its primary premise is that guilt is for real, and *some*body *some*where has bloody well got to pay up. Project this kind of thinking onto a deity and you'll see how some theologies arose—they're all about guilt and atonement.

DK: And here, by the *Christian* theology of guilt, is where *you* take charge.

J: But not right away, don't forget, since lots of time would pass without a remedy before *I* stepped in. So, prior generations had to *improvise*, and it might've gone something like this . . .

Somewhere in early human history—in a land far away, of course—a holy man sits staring into the fire one summer night, wondering why the rains won't come, and suddenly he has an idea. If the tribe has somehow offended the gods, their wrath might be quelled and their help reacquired with a little guiltless blood offered up. He tells his fellow clansmen about it, they talk it over awhile, and everyone agrees that it's genius. I guess it must've rained soon thereafter and the idea stuck. First to be sacrificed were the animals, of course. Next it was people. Eventually, tribal priests invented the ultimate in sacrificial lambs: God himself.

DK: Then belief in the need for sacrifice has persisted for thousands of years.

J: Right. And even as man begins exploring the cosmos, he's still claiming deities of blood ransom. Billions across the world will reject any notion that the Energy they call 'God' doesn't judge them. A deity who won't keep notes on their behavior? Forget it, they can't sign on to benevolence. They believe a God too good to his children is indeed too good to be true. And to *really* boil their blood, try telling 'em they're *one* with this 'God.' With dangerous messages like *that*, you're lucky to live past lunch.

DK: So we cast off a God of love for one whose love is largely provisional.

J: Well, many God-fearing believers assume that any God worth fearing is probably as judgmental as *they* are. It's why religions have so many stories of a petty, hypocritical God of anger who constantly sows vengeance and pain. The writings simply reflect the traits of the writers.

DK: I know *one* thing for sure—if the scary God of the Bible were human, we'd lock Him up and melt down the key. He'd be seen as a threat to society.

J: That or a promising contender for high office . . .

CHAPTER TWENTY-SEVEN

DK: Ever go hiking in the mountains?

J: Hiking in the mount— Wait a minute, did I miss something?

DK: Sorry, just a little joke. The topics were getting a bit heavy and I thought I might lighten things up.

J: Okay, I'll go along. Here's a quick one . . .

A middle-age Jewish woman is sitting on the beach, quietly watching her five-year-old son splash happily in the shallows near the shore. Swiftly and without enough warning, a giant wave roars in and sweeps the poor kid out to sea. The mother is frantic, of course, so she turns toward heaven and wails: "Oh God, how could you take my only child, my precious baby boy—the one true light of my life!?? Please, God . . . bring him back and I'll do what you want! I'll visit the temple three times a week and start giving twel— no, make that a full *fifteen percent*! I'll even stop nagging my husband!!" You know, the whole nine yards of desperate contrition.

DK: [I'm already chuckling] Uh-huh . . .

J: Seconds later, yet another huge wave washes in and dumps the boy right at her feet. He's rattled and coughing up water but basically okay. *Now* the woman's crazy with ecstasy, right? She's hugging and kissing her shivering son and shedding tears of joy at her fortune. Suddenly she sees the kid's wrist and turns serious. She looks back to heaven and shouts: "He had a watch!"

DK: *Heh heh*, cute. The Anti-Defamation League will *love* it . . . By the way, today is Easter. I'm wondering how *you* might see it.

J: A big deal for some. For the awakened, a total non-event. *Now is now*, you know?

DK: But all around the world, Christians are lauding your Resurrection.

J: And most aren't giving a single *thought* to their own. If I were preaching a sermon today, I'd say that focusing on *me* has really thrown Christians off-course. I'd say that I'm here to shake people up, to give them higher visions of themselves and their reality.

DK: What, no 'love thy neighbor' pronouncements?

J: The problem there is no one wants to be the first to *risk* it. Anyway, love for others is the *result* of understanding, not its cause—and it isn't something conjured on demand. You can't fully love someone before first loving *yourself*. Also, I'd remind everyone that attacking others is, in essence, a kind of spiritual suicide, and doing it in the name of religion is the ultimate self-destructive insanity.

DK: Keep purging, releasing works wonders for the soul . . .

J: Well, next I would tell believers everywhere that to be of any 'service' to their God, they'll have to—as Saint Paul himself once advised— quit any sniping or bickering and start being a little more *god*like. I'd warn that following divisive ancient writings will continue bringing disaster upon everyone. And lastly, I'd challenge religion to make itself *relevant*. If it can't do any better fostering peace and enlightenment than it has for thousands of years, they should blow out the candles, board up the stained-glass windows and go home. Forever and ever, Amen.

DK: Wow. A rant like that could go viral. But don't expect it to play during family hour—you just took religion and gutted it. Your message of man's union with God is certainly *reasonable*, though . . . and a very much more *uplifting* one for sure. I mean who'd reject a sensible gospel like that?

J: You'd be surprised. Millions will kick and scream about theology that tells them they're holy—*they* won't see it as 'good news' in the least. They'll fight to the death defending their story that everyone's deplorably sinful and fully deserving of God's everlasting reproof. And seemingly He's waiting to *give* it to 'em—good and hard—on his dreaded day of doom. That's when He'll open their mouths, examine their teeth, and see which horses are worth keeping and which become glue.

DK: Let's look under the hood of this Last Judgment thing. It sounds like pretty scary stuff.

J: Well, it *would* be—if it were *true*. For thousands of years, religion has used fear of God's judgment to keep the sheep moving quietly on the trail. But the 'last judgment' is made not by God, but by *you*. This is when your vision moves beyond all time-bound, fear-based thoughts of your reality— you'll no more be *tempted* to judge because then you'll finally *know*. So God isn't waiting around for his famous Last Judgment since He never even made the first one. Why would He always be judging his own creations?

DK: Christians say the Last Judgment is God's valuing of spiritual *worth*— it's based on our beliefs and our behavior. As you implied, the climactic finale is that end-of-the-world arrangement when the Book of Life is opened and God parts the faithless from the true.

J: The Bible's Last Judgment scene is a perfect example of an ego's desire to be special and its constant need to be 'right.' Projecting its guilt onto others, it delights in the sufferings of its foes. But very few souls would be gloating after the Final Judgment since only a *smidgen* ever sneak past the Pearly Gates.

DK: So the odds of strolling the golden streets don't appear very promising for *any.*

J: And that's why every Christian on the planet should be praying his religion is *mistaken.* The visions of Revelation make it practically a given that he and his closest friends and loved ones will be screaming in the scourging fires of hell, while the minuscule 'redeemed' are singing praises to their savior in the clouds. If Revelation is *right*, the billions of believers who thought themselves saved . . . were *wrong.* In fact the church should change the words to its famous old hymn: "When the roll is called up yonder, I'll be damned."

DK: You make a mockery of fundamentalist 'salvation.'

J: Their salvation makes a mockery of *intelligence.* But please forget *my* view and ask any literalist if he *likes* the idea that his heaven, if he gets there, will have a populace roughly twice the size of Bermuda's, while a hundred billion others—likely including all those *he* ever cared about— scream ad infinitum in God's hell. Ask him to explain why this is sensible or loving, and see if any part of you as a rational being accepts it. And even if the literalist is deluded enough to think that he'll *win* the spiritual lottery and be chosen one of the very few 'saved,' ask him how he could ever come to see this cruel arrangement as any kind of 'heaven' or why he'd worship a god who would ordain it. I mean, *really* . . . who would even *want* this 'salvation'? Religion's heaven is a twisted and sadistic version of hell. Instead of doing the suffering *yourself,* you're forced to *observe* it for a few trillion eons or so. What a kick *that'll* be, eh?

DK: But sin, guilt and liability are the crux of the Christian scriptures— they're unavoidable. Therefore the need of atonement.

J: That kind of atonement says that God must be pacified by blood before He forgives—which holds that He was somehow personally offended and couldn't get past it 'til some blameless bloke was rubbed out. This thinking rose first among frightened people whose God was somewhere outside of them, judging them from afar. Next we're told that He's perched on a throne up in heaven with me by his side, reading last rites over most of humanity and sending them off to his hell. Now, this is nothing less than eye-gouging, mind-killing literalism, and it hurts you every moment you believe it.

DK: But afterlives of punishment or heavenly reward are ideas that've been here forever . . . and well before *you* came along. The gods of religion seem to want both winners and losers.

J: The notion of God as a separate being is the basis of most big religions. Even *using* the word 'God' implies that this force has a separate existence along with personal egoic attributes, just like you. But a simple whiff of logic should put a stop to this divided thinking of God as a discreet personality: a limitless universe cannot have been created by a limited point *within* it. This is like saying that a single drop of water is also the entire ocean and, even more ridiculous, that the droplet *created* the ocean. How sensible is *that*?

DK: Well, if God is no individual being and there's no day of judgment marked in on his cosmic calendar, what's with all that end-of-time stuff in religion? The theme is so common, there must be some *message* behind it.

J: Symbolically, the end of time is the end of any past or future—or the end of the belief they have meaning. Time is dualistic and exists from a *relative* view: it's relevant to the world of *things and places*. Just as with the notion of distance, you've gotta have something to *compare* it to. The mind, through memory or anticipation, lays an imposed sense of linearity onto timeless eternity. Whatever happens, though, and whatever *will* happen, must always take place in the timefree *now*. Each new instant stands free of limitations to time.

DK: Now that you bring it up, it's obvious that this moment is all there is— or ever *could* be.

J: Of course. What you think of as 'time' is really just a perpetual flow of *is-ness*. So learn to make is-ness your business. Your point of power is always in the present.

DK: Surely it's wise not to fret of imaginary futures . . . but if we abandon the past, our history, how would we know ourselves?

J: The mind and its shifting thoughts don't form your identity. You are what you are and the mind is uninvolved. Without understanding the world you perceive—and you won't 'til you understand *you*—using past learning to *interpret* the world will prevent you from seeing what's there.

DK: A bit hypothetical, perhaps. Got any tips to suggest?

J: View your surroundings, from most familiar to least, and look upon all with 'new eyes,' free of old opinions and ideas. In Matthew 18 I instruct to *see afresh*. This means observing with detachment, wonder and without any judgment . . . just as a child would do. Even with people you know well, act as though it's the first time you've met. Just like you, everyone continuously evolves, so pay them careful attention and ask yourself this: who are they *really*, and what is our true connection? Your discoveries may surprise you. And whenever any upset arises, try not to come from reaction, but calmly step back and observe with greater detachment so you won't become a prisoner of the mind and its endless chatter. And always remember this critical truth: "Whatever crosses my awareness, *I am only the witness.*" Be faithful in it and new realities will dawn.

DK: I hear all the words but I've still got my doubts.

J: That's *good*. Doubt what you cannot be sure of, until you know its truth for yourself. The beauty of reality is you needn't take anyone's word for it. Questioning what you're told—whether by government, society, science, religion, school, or the news on TV—is the crucial first step to real freedom. Ask if what you're hearing can be proven . . . or is it merely someone's own perspective? I taught that knowing the truth sets you free. That is, you don't 'do' anything with the truth. The freedom comes merely from knowing it.

DK: So, put every claim to the test.

J: Well, you're workin' in the blind if you don't. Refuse to settle for anyone's slanted opinions and ask the essential life questions: Who am I and where did I come from? What was I before I was born? What will I be when I die? How did I come to be a frail little body in a haywire world of woe? Ponder these things. For years you've invested energy on the 'outside.' Now spend some time turning inward; you may find some of your treasured assumptions off-beam. And remember, when lost or confused, that love and the brilliance of all creation go with you each step of the way and are always working in your favor, when you *let* them . . .

CHAPTER TWENTY-EIGHT

DK: Well, it's good to hear your loyalty never expires. For most of my life I was taught that your patience runs out with the Rapture.

J: Some people think they couldn't possibly deserve my untiring effort and resolve. They think I have a line in the sand or a breaking point, projecting onto *me* their distorted images of 'self.' But I don't see them the way they see themselves. I understand their reality, and I'm never limited by opinions of what's possible nor deceived by ideas of what's happened. My patience is measureless—I don't just give up. It's not the *well* who need the doctoring, but the *sick*. I mean even *non*-Christians would have a hard time envisioning Jesus thinking, "Forget it, these clowns are hopeless."

DK: Still you have to admit that, in so many people, the Christ spirit's less than a fog.

J: But that's when it's most sorely *needed*, n'est-ce pas? The story of my birth suggests that the Christ is often 'born' where least expected—in danger and darkness, unworthiness, fear or self-doubt. It doesn't need perfection before birthing, but just needs a little 'virgin' ground—a pure hearted, open-minded willingness to explore. And the world scarcely *knows* the holy 'child' when it first appears, for the child spends its early days in shadows and in lower states of awareness. This is symbolized in the Christmas story as a manger, often mistaken as another word for stable. But mangers are just animal feeding boxes and were sometimes used back then as cradles. And since we're on the subject, I wasn't born in a barn or a cave nor does "stable" ever appear in the gospels. Matthew 2:11 says, "and going into the house, they saw the child with Mary his mother . . ." So, be realistic, dude. No one calls a smelly cattle barn a *house*.

DK: Great, *now* you've done it . . . you've gone and de-stable-ized the Nativity.

J: But the stable symbol's useful, even so. When Christ energy 'births' into people's lives, they're often surrounded by the stench of suffering— stinking of metaphorical manure.

DK: So much for the beauty of the lilies and your birth across the sea.

J: It's true that the Christ's beginnings are frequently quite humble. As the years pass, however, it grows "in wisdom and in stature." Eventually it turns 'savior' to the world by showing that life's real meaning lies *beyond* the material world. And please don't fret if your inner spark seems dim. For someone in darkness, even the least ray of sunshine is backed by the full magnificence of the sun—and catching even a *glimmer* of light is enough to prove light exists. Helping you *see* it better is pretty much why they pay *me*.

DK: Well, surely there's more to it than *that*. Aren't we asked to help relieve pain and suffering—service to fellows 'n such?

J: Clearly so; bring an end to suffering where you can. But also put *yourself* beyond need. When a student tells the master that he wants to help the world, the master will often say, "First help *yourself* and *then* tell what problems you see." The master knows that the student is sometimes deceived and is badly distorting reality. He knows that a student gives more help awakened than ever he could while asleep. In *that* state he's mostly a pest.

DK: So now the Good Samaritan's obsolete?

J: Of course not—but you're missing vital parts of the story. The kind-hearted Samaritan wasn't *looking* for someone to help; it strictly was a matter of fate. And he addressed only the man's *worldly* needs. There's no effort to save his lost soul, instill new beliefs, or change the guy's mind about *anything*.

DK: Evangelicals won't like hearing *that*.

J: No, probably not. The evangelist focuses on the presumed insufficiencies of *others*. Instead of dispelling his *own* ignorance, he's slashing through some hidden jungle to bring 'salvation' to a tribe that's done just fine without him for seven full centuries, thank you so very much. The missionary walks from the forest and informs the tribal leader that he's come to share his religion. But the poor chief doesn't know the facts and cannot *possibly* imagine the calamity that now lies ahead. For if he knew the truth of it all, he'd quickly send the guy on his way: "Why would we want your religion? Look what it's done to *your* world."

DK: But as the title implies, a missionary *is* on a mission.

J: Yes, but in so many cases he isn't content with just feeding the hungry, nursing the sick and helpless or sheltering the poor—not when there are souls to be salvaged and longstanding cultures to trash. The religious World-Saver is cocksure *positive* he's armed with the truth and now seen the heavenly light. Of course when *he* was a non-believer he would've been *outraged* to have some cocky religious fanatic come knocking at his door—uninvited—

trying to get him cozy with 'God's truth.'

DK: But somehow that was different.

J: Yeah, because *he's* got it all figured out now, you see, and he's hell-bent on *sharing* his 'knowledge' with any hapless victim he can corner and every sap who can't see him coming. Not happy tending to folks' *earthly* concerns, World-Saver wants to play God. He's confident he can shape a man's spirit, remold his sad character—fully take charge of his life. The World-Saver is *sure* he knows more of God's plan for this fella than the poor man himself can know.

DK: Well, I can say from experience that the thought of shifting the fate of a spirit is a much bigger ego boost than giving out sacks of grain or helping some volunteer dentist pull teeth. When *I* was out evangelizing, I too felt superior when knocking on doors or 'sharing Christ' with some guy at a bar. I know now, of course, I was mostly a thorn in the side. Still, you can't be too critical of someone who's just trying to help.

J: Perhaps. But when religion provides 'help,' it usually comes with a price: perplexing moral obligations and constant threats of punishment and hell. So what kind of help is *that*? Many people don't yet know what real help *is*, and are far more likely to cause pain—every murdering tyrant in history, after all, did fully believe he was 'helping.' Progress lies not always in doing what's 'good' but in caring to "first do no harm."

DK: Then what's to be learned from the parable of the Good Samaritan?

J: That you walk your path and deal with what appears. If someone needs help and you're prone to assist, trust your inner guide to show you how. But you've got neither wisdom, right nor power to go fashioning anyone's spirit, the one part that needs no adjustment. You're not here to be out finding people to save—and least of all if *you're* the one drowning!

DK: So, no sense *searching* for problems, eh?

J: Well, why do *that* when so many show on their own? "Therefore do not be anxious about tomorrow. . . Let the day's own trouble be enough for the day."

DK: But large parts of humanity are hurting and so much needs doing. Suffering goes on day and night—and we know it.

J: Did it keep you from savoring your last meal? Anyway, there's a big difference in treating a kid for parasites and 'saving' his sad, lost soul.

DK: But Christians were specially instructed to travel and spread their faith.

J: Not by me they weren't. Leading people to freedom is not at all the same as teaching them what to *believe*. Telling them what to think is like saying, "*This* is the way to see the world and no other views are allowed." Think of the sheer *arrogance* of that. The same sort of conceit prompts radical regimes to persecute millions of their very own citizens as 'subversives,' political 'agitators,' or 'dissidents.' Ideologies, dogmas and creeds are the cause of every conflict and lead even intelligent people to unthinkable atrocities for their countries, parties or religions. They figure that those who don't see things from *their* angle do fully deserve to have their villages bombed, their heads cut off, their families murdered and their lives destroyed . . . since something's plainly wrong with their *thinking*!!!

DK: I'm loath to keep pressing the point, but with a single swipe of the sword you've destroyed two thousand years of tradition. New Testament writers are clear in urging Christians to share their beliefs.

J: Well, what would you expect? The New Testament came from crusading evangelists who warned of a coming apocalypse—they thought the bloody *world* was ending! This is why most of their writing is in fact apocalyptic in tone. But scaring people with fire was never the plan. Let's examine my gospel parable where the king tells his faithful stewards, "For I was hungry and you gave me food; I was thirsty and you gave me drink; I was a stranger and you welcomed me; I was naked and you clothed me; I was sick and you visited me; I was in prison and you came to me."

DK: From Matthew, I think. For some reason the king's whole life was a disaster—the man's always in need of *something*.

J: But do you notice anything unusual? Because you certainly should, especially if you're an evangelist. All the actions praised by the king —who, in this story, represents God—were related to folks' *physical* needs. Just like the parable of the Good Samaritan, no word is said of particular ideas or beliefs . . . or even of religion in general. From the Christian view, the king is conspicuous in omitting any reference to doctrine.

DK: So the king gave no praises for professions, converts or creeds.

J: None of it was even important. The primary factor in their fate was, "How well did you *love*?" The faithful stewards' deliverance lay in unity— they saw their connection to *everyone* and not just to those of their kind.

And the help was always given with no word of politics, God or religion.

DK: Then the key was showing compassion and easing suffering.

J: Yes, and no one *suffers* from lack of beliefs . . . they suffer *because* of them.

DK: A truly encouraging message, I'm sure. But perhaps you've forgotten the main point: the story has all the deadbeats going to *hell*!

J: Just another ploy to get converts to 'sign on the line'—and a poor choice of endings, for sure. The king becomes a true sadist hypocrite. He's far more callous than his subjects ever were and infinitely more barbaric than those He'd punish. Eternal pain is a frightfully harsh penalty for ignorance— the careless ones never saw what union was about. They ask the king, "When did we see *you* hungry, naked or lonely?" They honestly didn't know—they didn't understand *oneness*. Their blindness was unfortunate, perhaps, but no loving king would *scourge* them for it, and least of all forever.

DK: The stunningly harsh sentence doesn't *near* fit the crime, and there's surely no doubt about that. But scripture is clear. Come judgment day, you're slated to be God's number-one cowboy, feverishly separating the men from the sheep . . . or *something* along those lines.

J: All we need now is a campfire and hot bowls of beans.

DK: You don't savor being a wrangler of souls?

J: I'd sooner take a thirty-year mortgage and lay bricks.

DK: So you won't ramrod the Big Roundup, driving the faithless mavericks into the Condemnation Corral.

J: I'm no judge and jury, hoss, but a heavenly hand riding lead over the Great Awakening. I come not to *brand* humanity but to *free* it on the open plains of truth . . .

CHAPTER TWENTY-NINE

DK: Okay, let me be totally frank. This notion of unlimited forgiveness, even coming from *you*, is far from our usual thinking because it's not how you're frequently pictured in the gospels. The biblical Christ isn't always that kind and forgiving—so we don't always see you as perfectly non-judgmental.

J: Why is the notion of grace so hard to accept? I forgave those who *killed* me. Would it make sense to judge far lesser acts of ignorance later on? Am I not quoted in Matthew declaring that *all* of man's sins will be forgiven?

DK: Well, it totally muddies the issue of salvation and it used to drive me *nuts* when I read it . . . but yeah, that's what the short passage says.

J: Nor does it limit the promise only to Christians.

DK: That's true, but you did make one notable exception to your generous offer. Three of the four gospel writers have you warning that blasphemy against the Holy Spirit will *never* be forgiven—not in this life or in the life to come. I'm not sure what blasphemy against Spirit might be, and you didn't specify the penalty, but the clear implication is a fully non-negotiable, one-way bus trip to hell.

J: You have to grasp that all of God's creations are *joined* with Him. *Forever.* To think that any short-term ignorance could lead to separation is silly. *Your* being and *God's* being are *one*—and God doesn't punish himself.

DK: Another sharp negation of the Bible.

J: Doesn't it depend on the scripture? First Timothy 4 says that God will be the savior of *all*, even if other Bible teachings would dispute it.

DK: You're right, another scriptural muddle. That one made me crazy, too.

J: Remember that words are not the reality. Even my own gospel character is a baffling mix of confusing and bizarre contradictions. On one side I'm depicted as a loving and compassionate friend and redeemer. On the other, I'm more like the Old Testament war god Yahweh—an angry, obsessive moralizer. Sometimes I show as much mercy as a hungry lion for pigs.

DK: So, to a degree, gospel writers created you as a humanized version of the old Hebrew god.

J: True, but those later authors toned it down a bit. Instead of promising imminent *earthly* suffering, as per Yahweh's bent, the writers have me using the subtle but far more *alarming* threat of soul conviction. If keeping people psychologically leashed is the goal, scaring them with fire is pretty effective. However warped it became at the hands of others, though, the gist of my original teaching was finding the light within.

DK: Yeah . . . makes sense, I guess . . .

J: A faraway look's in your eye. What's up?

DK: Oh, I've just a got a million thoughts bouncing 'round—like a bunch of screaming kids on a trampoline.

J: So, *vent.* Suffer the children to come unto *me.*

DK: Well, I was just thinking that most of what you taught had been presented by other great teachers many centuries before you were born. Telling us that love is the answer was hardly a lightning flash of fresh wisdom—and even preaching virtues like charity, tolerance, and forgiveness was nothing unique. But if you didn't come to save us from burning in hell, what did you offer that was so inspirational or new?

J: Urging mercy for one's enemies was fairly novel at the time . . . though I see it's no more popular now than then. Focusing on forgiveness over judgment was radical as well. But basically I taught the world of *unity.* Aside from that, I came and left mostly bare-handed.

DK: You'll surely not be blamed of padding your stats.

J: It's not that my life made no difference. Clearly it did. I was the first human to fully embody *and demonstrate* Christ consciousness. And even if not always for good, my life changed the world, did it not? It opened that doorway for all. Why? Because consciousness is *one.* Whatever could be said of reality upon my arrival, though, was true before I showed up. And you're right: who didn't already know that one should treat others as one would be treated? Confucius had a version of the Golden Rule *five hundred years* before mine. A few decades before me, the great leader Rabbi Hillel declared: "Whatever is hateful to you, do not do to others. That is the whole Torah. The rest is merely explanation." So, yes, it's mostly intuitive stuff—but the world needs reminding it's the only way that *works.*

DK: Well, *something* must lie in your message that carries such ongoing, widespread appeal. The annual expenditure on Christmas gifts alone dwarfs budgets of most small countries.

J: Now you see why the church clings so tightly to its claim that I'm 'God's only son'—it has nothing else to offer. And they sell this arrogant notion not through any kind of love, but through fear. It's firstly about saving yourself from fire and *only then* can we can talk of fringe benefits. Ironically, the success of the Christian religion has no connection to the primary focus of my life—self-empowerment through connecting with the divine. My story is a dramatic demonstration of the eternal nature of *Being*. I saw through the falsity of fear, separation and death. Other great messengers have seen and taught exactly the same things. I was the first way-shower to *Christ* consciousness . . . but each age has its spiritual pioneers.

DK: Do they still experience life's pleasures?

J: Sure, and also its pains. But they aren't seeking the one or fearing the other. So the difference is they no longer suffer.

DK: Most of us are a long voyage from *there*.

J: Don't draw conclusions about things not yet concluded. Insights can shift you in the span of a minute, and forever—and that's how it happened for me.

DK: But of course *you* had a little extra help.

J: Not so! I was no closer to Source than you are . . . I was just more *aware* of it. Otherwise I was mostly an average Joe.

DK: Well, Joe, that's a major downgrade from your Christian designation as "God Junior."

J: Ah well, the church has *its* objectives and I've got mine. As I've said, I'm no different from you except that I'm in full awareness of the 'God' connection, and you, for a while, are not.

DK: Let's follow this path a minute. Even though lots of Christians show you special esteem, as far as I can tell you never requested it.

J: If scripture has me asking anyone's homage, you'll know from the start that it's bogus.

DK: Then no legitimate teacher would ever think of demanding or seeking it.

J: No legitimate teacher would even *want* it. He wants his students paying attention to *themselves.*

DK: All the same, lots of people do basically worship you. How do you respond?

J: To worship is to show reverence, honor and devotion—and I receive it in the same spirit of love in which it's offered. But any honor given me is always returned in full. In the way I just defined it, you'd have to say that I worship you, as well.

DK: Now, hold up just a minute. In the first of the Ten Commandments, Yahweh instructs the Israelites to worship only Him.

J: Why should worship be for Yahweh alone? And how can you even think He deserved it? The ones who *did* worship Him exclusively didn't often lead lives of happiness, luxury and success. And is Yahweh so plagued by disinterest and rebellion that He *threatens* his children to secure their undistracted allegiance? Are they not allowed their spontaneous expressions of love? Isn't there enough to go around?

DK: I can't really say. He calls himself a *jealous* God.

J: Well, who the heck is He jealous of? And why is He always warning not to follow other gods if there are no other gods to follow? Besides, if Yahweh is so likable and so quickly inspires devotion, why the need for an order from Him *requiring* it?

DK: Considering his poor disposition, He may not be so naturally endearing. Even the *chosen* weren't always inclined to his worship.

J: In which case commandments would do no good.

DK: You're right—coerced devotion would effectively be hollow.

J: And that's exactly my point. Millions of Christians believe that God expects their constant devotion and wants them always talking about Him and even getting others to start talking about Him too. But, oy . . . what if you had a *friend* who needed that kind of outrageous attention? How long would you want him around? I mean genuine, spontaneous reverence is a beautiful thing—but compulsive glorification is worthless. God doesn't need people's praises before He'll be happy and *like* them.

DK: You no doubt realize these ideas will be fervently attacked. I could name a half dozen big-name preachers who'll rant with fury at these things.

J: Then let them prove the voice of reason *wrong*.

DK: But these are some powerful, well known Christians.

J: So was Adolf Hitler. He was Catholic. And though he would go on to quickly try destroying Christianity in Germany—and was later only *informally* excommunicated, strangely enough—as a young man he rose to the top of his class at monastery school. And Joseph Stalin, really just a hardened atheist whose only real religion was communism, actually earned a scholarship to seminary and spent some time studying there. He too was well familiar with Christian teachings. Between them, these two deranged monsters caused the murders of many *millions*.

DK: You're comparing hard-core evangelists to history's greatest madmen?

J: Well, they certainly have similar behavior. When someone is thrashing his arms and thundering his 'inspired' message, you'd best hide your wallet, grab your family, and run for the nearest safe cover. That kind of preaching plays directly on emotions and discourages all critical thinking—it's pure manipulation and leaves no room for reason.

DK: Some would say that zeal in pursuit of the truth is no vice.

J: And defending stark ignorance with proverbs is no virtue! When a man becomes so sure of his 'truth' that he's pressed to start gathering converts, you can bet the *farm* there's gonna be trouble.

DK: Is fervor in one's faith never befitting?

J: Perhaps, but 'tis a short, slippery slope between the fervor and the fanatic. Fanatical *thinking* breeds fanatical *behavior*—and that's not good for *anyone*. The world's been awash with the blood of the blameless, killed without mercy by religious 'faithful' who saw themselves as God's chosen army. In true Christian spirit, Pope Innocent III once commanded subordinates to "use against heretics the spiritual sword of ex-communication; and if this does not prove effective, use the *material* sword."

DK: *Heh heh.* Christendom's version of gunboat diplomacy.

J: Religion's arrogance seemingly knows no bounds, and history spills over with examples of religious terror by those who were absolute-God-ordained *certain* they had it correct. The attitude was, "See things *my* way . . . or die."

DK: A lot of Christians feel *obliged* to make converts—just as *I* did many years ago. True evangelicals point to the Great Commission, where you tell all your followers to wander the world and preach.

J: Like many scriptural 'quotes' of mine, the words never crossed my lips. The Great Commission appears only twice in the entire New Testament—first in Matthew and again as an add-on section at the end of Mark, where it's usually listed as a footnote. This is where I reportedly tell my disciples, "Go into all the world and preach the gospel." Scholars *know* it's not part of the original text and never should have been included. Christians haven't really thought it through, but any instruction to 'preach the gospel' couldn't possibly have referred to the New Testament. At *that* time it didn't even *exist*!

DK: What about the last part of Luke? You're quoted saying, "Thus it is written, that the Christ should suffer and on the third day rise from the dead, and that repentance and forgiveness should be preached unto all the nations."

J: That one's worthless, too—but it's even *more* problematic, so let's come back to it later. This leaves just Matthew 28:19 as the one valid gospel verse containing the Great Commission. Given the importance of this mandate, it's terribly strange that most Christian writers left it out.

DK: Well, *someone* sure took it to heart. Over the centuries, the church wound up with several *billion* 'defenders of the faith.'

J: The truth doesn't need defending, and whatever *does* need defending will weaken you. I never taught people to label themselves, and calling yourself Christian doesn't make you like Christ, just as dressing up like a doctor doesn't make you a surgeon.

DK: I'm not sure about religion, of course, but I would think we should stand firm in *something*—if only to help us know who we are.

J: But this is where folks miss the turn: beliefs do not *aid* self-discovery, they *obstruct* it. The one statement made with absolute surety is, "I am." Anything after that is up for debate . . .

Chapter Thirty

DK: These things you say are not the usual message in the average megachurch blasting *Jesus!* into the skies. The pastor typically teaches that God protects us from harm and grants material blessings if we think and behave certain ways—which of course implies giving some hard-earned cashola to his church. Creating 'abundance' is one of Christianity's few attractions. "Ask anything in the name of Jesus," they shout, "and he'll bring it to your door as you trust!"

J: So in *this* little scheme, a Mercedes beats a meditation and a parcel's as good as a prayer. Sounds like private enterprise religion—salvation gone Form 990.

DK: But you did make that affirmation, did you not? It's right here in John 14, in black and white. Or—*heh heh*—in red, as the case may be.

J: Yeah, I'm said to have declared "And whatsoever ye shall ask in my name, that will I do . . . If ye shall ask *anything* in my name, I will do it."

DK: Right, pretty much like a blank check. The 'ask what you will' guarantee.

J: The key is that, in biblical times, a thing's name typically symbolized its *nature*. Asking 'in my name' is to ask *in alignment with my nature*. The foundational energy of Life is perfect love—the highest frequency and 'vibration' of all—and this was the 'nature' I embodied. Things envisioned by those living from this state of love do indeed tend to manifest in form. But even from the viewpoint of duality, where you and God are separate, what could need doing that a loving, all-knowing, all-powerful creator wouldn't already be addressing? What would He need *you* to be telling Him?

DK: Well . . . nothing, I guess. But if that's true, then why ask for anything at all? It appears that most prayers are just silly requests asking God to be something He's not.

J: It isn't that the force you call 'God' doesn't respond to prayer. It does. But It isn't deceived by your delusions or bound by contract if you spout a prayer for a hundred billion dollars and conclude 'in the name of Jesus.' Take care you don't impose your Western values onto God.

DK: Maybe you're riding us too hard. After all, life can be a real bitch—especially when you're broke. It may have been the great philosopher Marx who said, "I've been poor and I've been rich. Rich is better."

J: You sure that was Karl Marx?

DK: I was referring to Groucho.

J: *Ah.* Well, as I've said, God is pure benevolence and abundance, and these are a part of your nature. You run into trouble, though, in believing that abundance is all about money and that money will be your salvation. Save all the money you want, old pal . . . but the *money* will never save *you.* Although you may think of yourself as 'spiritual,' most of your everyday life revolves around *material* gain and comfort. Even your own *language* has been stained with corruptions of capitalism.

DK: I'll buy that.

J: Here's *my* counsel: do what you feel you must to make your way in the world—but at least develop awareness of what *drives* you. What is the *purpose* of your life and mission in the world? I mean, it can't be all about money, right? So at least give some thought to what faith you've placed in your savings.

DK: You can bank on it . . .

CHAPTER THIRTY-ONE

J: Talking of misdirected faith . . . you're familiar, no doubt, with my caution not to build your proverbial house on the sand.

DK: Of course—you said it leads to the proverbial *crash*.

J: Right, and that brings us back to a topic that'll easily make you the life of the party on New Year's Eve.

DK: Ah, so we've come back to *death* once again. You know, a lot of people are really turned off by that. They say that your focus on the afterworld takes most of the fun out of *this* one.

J: Despite what you've read, I wasn't focused on death and I didn't preach of an *after*world. The doomsday Christian religion may teach it—but I taught of the *only* world, where you and Creation are one.

DK: In the gospels, you're selling futuristic Nirvana for the faithful and hellish fires of vengeance for the damned.

J: I wouldn't have suffered that sorry, two-bit theology. I say, postmortem *schmortem*. Reality is always *now*, and betting on some rapturous tomorrow is a mug's game.

DK: You did warn us, though, not to get too settled here on earth—it's one of the central messages of the Sermon on the Mount. Or were we bamboozled on that one as well?

J: Most of it is fairly sound—but not so well understood. I wasn't pointing to some heaven in the sky, but merely reminding you that, right from the moment of birth, the body is marked indelibly 'Return to Sender.' It's truly a wonderful thing, the body, but it's no reliable refuge and was certainly never your 'home.'

DK: Then I'd have to agree with the critics: you do come across a bit morbid. Why so much attention to the grave?

J: A fair question . . . but it would take some explaining.

DK: I've way more time than mammon.

J: Okay, but don't blame *me* when your speaking fees dry up. Like a cockroach on the wall at dinnertime, no one wants to deal with this stuff. Everyone knows they'll leave the Body Motel eventually bu—

DK: —but they don't want the owner always coming around to *remind* 'em.

J: No, it's not something people wanna hear.

DK: So we hang "Do Not Disturb" signs on the doorknobs of our minds.

J: Yeah, you focus on certain *parts* of the illusion, not fully thinking it through—like customers buying sirloin steak at the store. They're perfectly fine with the packaged product, but not so much interested in a tour of the slaughterhouse, thanks.

DK: This is starting to sound serious.

J: Well, yes and no. To the ephemeral self, the person you *believe* you are, it'll be like opening the morning paper and finding your own obituary. To the true Self that's *really* you, it's only pure entertainment—a little light diversion for a good cosmic laugh. And it can't be a *bad* thing, I don't believe, to frankly discuss the most impactful event of your existence subsequent to birth, and to fully grasp its implications as you travel through life.

DK: Alright, I'm braced for anything. Fire away . . .

J: I'll start with something that may sound unnecessary since it seems so very self-evident. I assure you, however, that, despite your *intellectual* understanding of it, you've yet to grasp the import of the following words:

You . . . will . . . die.

DK: You're right, it's an obvious fact. I don't see where you're going.

J: Well, for decades you've witnessed the 'obvious fact' that everyone dies. Some live longer than others, of course, but all of them die in the end. No exclusions, right?

DK: Not as far as I know. Although, one of my few Old Testament memories from Sunday school is that Enoch was "taken" by God. It's strange because everyone else in those stories is clearly said to have died. Also, the New Testament book of Hebrews claims the high priest Melchizedek was "without father or mother or genealogy, and has neither beginning of days nor end of life . . ." And *that* is one helluva résumè.

J: Okay, but we have no clue what the biblical writers were describing. I mean the words are fairly mysterious, no? The scripture says, "Enoch walked with God; and he was not, for God took him." But let's be blunt: that's about as clear as the fine print on aluminum siding contracts. And the writer of Hebrews is equally vague. He doesn't explain why Melchizedek alone should be immortal or how the man managed incarnating with no father and mother.

DK: An extraordinary claim, for sure—even more impressive than being born to a virgin, I'd say. It seems you were bettered in your ability to bypass parents.

J: Well, my people *are famous* for removing the middleman . . .

DK: I'm not sure about Melchizedek, but the New Testament says that Enoch was a man of great faith.

J: All I can say is that plenty of people have faith. But the faithful suffer the same inevitable destiny as anyone else. Even *I* was no exception, true?

DK: Sorry, didn't mean to split any hairs. I get your point: I'm not likely to be the next Enoch.

J: Then you know with full certainty that your body-mind persona —the thing you affectionately call 'I'—will eventually perish.

DK: Of course. But again, why labor the obvious?

J: Because you don't really *believe* it. Consciously, death is quite undeniable. *Sub*consciously, though, it's a very different game. You know beyond doubt that what you *imagine* as 'you' will one day disappear in a blink. But ego can't bear the thought of extinction—the notion that it won't endure. So, it rationalizes. "Death happens to *others*," it says, "but not to *me* . . . or at least not for a very long time."

DK: So we shove the file in the shed and shut the door.

J: Yeah, you stay *busy*. And you live as though you'll be here forever. You're quite aware, of course, that all things material will end. Still, you pour a lifetime of spirit and vigor into building an acceptable image, an *imagining*, of your one authentic Self . . . then you watch it all disappear. This is the story of the body-mind.

DK: I always think it adds *permanence* to life when I triumph at something, reach a lofty goal, or buy some big-ticket thing . . . it's like I'm establishing who I am. It seems the more I gain or accomplish, the more *stability* I feel.

J: Sure, that's why you spend your whole life 'making a name' for yourself. Psychologists call it the 'id.' They say you make up your own id-entity.

DK: And that's where the trouble starts, eh? We trust in things that don't last.

J: But let's be clear: enjoying the world and all the surprising events and journeys within it was the goal of the incarnational plan. Not a problem. The deception—and the irony—is that you seemingly believe you're creating real security for yourself in a world where nothing is secure. But somewhere in the darkest corners of the mind, lost among its tedious ruminations and incessant reverie, a subtle voice calls out like an echo from a faraway canyon, and you hear it every time you watch the news: *You. Will. Die.*

DK: No arguing the point, of course. I mean how can anyone ignore it? The older we get, the louder the damned echo becomes.

J: Yet you suppress it and do all that you can to avoid it. But still this voice follows you like a shadow—and you know that what it's telling you is true. You know that your world will someday implode and that none of your idols will save you. All in the world is a momentary picture on the movie screen of life. In the end it's more flitting than a campaign pledge before the vote.

DK: Man, is our situation as bad as all that?

J: Let me lay it out for you in terms only a lawyer could skew . . .
   You are going to die. It may be tonight, it may be next month, or it could be decades from now—but you *are* going to die. So, see your pale corpse stretched out in a ripoff-priced crate and with ill-fitting clothes with a smudge of cheap mortuary makeup on the collar. *Because it's going to happen.* Right? And whether it's sooner or later won't matter by then. When the last day arrives, it'll seem you lived no time at all.

DK: Yeah, I've read that the dying often feel that their lives, in retrospect, were nothing but transient dreams.

J: It's true. One of the common deathbed perceptions is that life lasted only a blink. As death creeps up and the facing of finality sets in, the dying take one long look back. Suddenly they realize that life was a mere flash of consciousness—a disappearing burst of breath on a cold winter's night.

DK: Okay, now *that's* gettin' pretty depressing.

J: That was the *cheery* part.

DK: You mean it gets worse?

J: *Oh* yeah. It's like the guy who gets a call from his doctor. "I've got some bad news and some worse news," says the sawbones. "The bad news is, we received your test results and they indicate the condition of a man who's got about twenty-four hours to live." Naturally the guy is aghast. "My god, doc, what could possibly be worse than *that*!?" The doctor stalls a moment, then responds: "I forgot to call you yesterday."

DK: Ha!! Thanks a hundred for the comic relief.

J: Who wants a savior that can't get a laugh?

DK: Alright, so give it to me straight. How does the story get worse?

J: Well, because not only will *you* die, but *everyone you know* will die, too. All of your heroes, your friends and your enemies . . . those you admire and those you despise. All of them will die. The supermodel, the actor, the big ball player, the rich business boss. The lovable saint and the most loathsome sinner will each die the same endless death—no exemptions. They'll all fade faster than a crippled mare at the Derby.

DK: It's really strange to think that everyone I know and care about, and everyone I've ever seen or met, will one day disappear forever—and all of 'em at once if I'm buried first!!

J: And few will die quietly in their sleep and in fairly good health at the ripe old age of ninety-five. Some will die young. Some will die of dreadful diseases, while others will be killed in accidents, wars, murders, and bizarre mishaps or disasters. Some will even take their own lives. But whether it happens peacefully after a long and productive life or in the midst of painful suffering and despair, one thing remains fully sure: you *will* die. And when you go, you'll leave everything—and I do mean *everything*—behind. Nothing in the world of form in which you now take pride or pleasure will go with you. Think of that. *Absolutely nothing.*

DK: Well, you were right . . . it's pretty dismal stuff. Compared with you, a mortician is a nightclub comic.

J: But isn't it true? No one gets to stick around for long. Take your favorite sports heroes, entertainment stars, corporate wizards—or anyone you envy or admire. In fifty or sixty years, barely a *blip* on the screen of eternity, they'll either be well on their way to dying or already stiffer than a Lutheran's martini.

DK: By then, I'd imagine that few people will ever think of them.

J: Yes, and fifty years after that they'll be long dead for sure, and even their descendants will not have known them. A century later, if they were truly exceptional, a small percentage of people might know their names. It won't do *them* any good, of course, since they'll be dead and only of historical interest at best. Most of the world will have never heard of them . . . and never will. A mere thousand years later, it'll be as if they— along with you and your entire civilization—had never even *existed*. I mean let's be realistic: there won't be any football hall of fame in the year 3000.

DK: Wow. I should've stayed home and watched *Grapes of Wrath* or a fun documentary on the plague. After listening to *that* little speech I'll need a fire-and-brimstone sermon just to perk up. I'll bet you were big loads of fun at bar mitzvahs . . .

CHAPTER THIRTY-TWO

DK: Let's make sure I'm up to speed before ending this spiritual buzzkill: we're all gonna die. Have I missed anything so far?

J: To this point comprehension is brilliant.

DK: But why harp on something so obvious?

J: Because you don't believe it applies to *you*—or leastways not anytime soon. Gripped by your desire for immortality, you don't like hearing that your physical 'reality' won't last. Now, I've said that God's creations cannot die, so maybe you should do some reflecting. What is it that *does* die?

DK: Well, the answer's pretty plain by now. What dies is our passing *illusion* of ourselves—we give up the *roles* we've been playing.

J: Give the man a cigar . . .

DK: But is our existence just a vanishing puff of steam? Are we nothing but a false impression?

J: It's not that *you* are an illusion. But you aren't anything *in particular*—and you can easily verify this. Imagine developing a sudden case of amnesia and not recalling a single thing before that moment. Who would you be *then*?

DK: A politician being grilled under oath?

J: *Heh heh.* That's one possibility these days . . .

DK: Well, I'm not sure who I would *think* I am. But obviously I'd still be me.

J: Yes, but can we agree that you'd no longer be the 'person' you presently assume? Of course you would still be *you*, as you say, since nothing of your *essence* would've changed, but you'd lose any sense of yourself based on history. I'm advising to leave the past in the past and pay attention to what you are in this moment. Stop defining yourself with this I-am-the-body nonsense and consider that when you say 'I,' you aren't *really* sure what you're referencing.

DK: You're right. I actually have no idea who or what 'I' am . . . or, *is*.

J: So, notice the hilarious irony. All your life you've referred to yourself as 'I.' Yet now you say—when you reason it out—that you haven't a clue as to who, what or even *where* this 'I' character is! And if *you* aren't sure of your identity, think how wrong *others* must be in *their* assessments of you. Let's say you ask twenty friends and family to describe you by writing out a couple of pages each. You'd surely get twenty very different responses—and all of them based on the past. Some might even conflict.

DK: Sure, I can see that. Everyone's perception is different.

J: Now let's go a step further. Suppose *you* were to write a description of yourself and then do the same in twenty years. How close would the two accounts be, do you think? Suppose you had written one thirty years ago. How near would it be to the one you write today? What if you had written a summary of yourself at age five? Can you reasonably say that you're still the same 'person' you were then?

DK: So all this philosophizing means what?

J: It means that there's no such thing as a 'person'—not really. A person is much better seen as a *being*—individualizing as transient form, ever in flux, always morphing and expanding. The word "person" comes from the Latin *persona,* meaning a mask or a character in a play. This is no accident. The wise have long acknowledged that "all the world's a stage."

DK: It first seems crazy when you say it . . . but I'm starting to see its truth.

J: You're learning that you're neither defined by nor comprised of your accomplishments, your viewpoints, circumstances, experiences, memories or beliefs. We've already shown that you can't be your mind or your body, because *you're* the one who's *using* them. There must be something more primal from which it all arose—something there from the start. Get in touch with that *something* and your questions will soon fall away.

DK: *Alllllll-righty, then.* What say we go bowling?

J: I know it all sounds a bit strange—but really it's nothing so new. Lots of spiritual teachers over the centuries have helped their students see these truths for themselves. Thinking yourself to be a person is to mistake your identity with the ephemeral body-mind. And because you see yourself in this manner, you see others this way as well. Sure, you may know someone's history and personality and all . . . but you can't know his fundamental nature if you know very little of your own. Nothing you perceive about yourself or any 'others' will survive the cruel ravages of time.

DK: Does dis-identifying from the body help improve our self-image?

J: Any self-image is only choosing a different *confusion*. One self-image is as delusional as another, and each of them rice-paper thin. A small, perceived slight; a cutting comment; the loss of a job; a serious injury . . . or even just a menacing glance from a stranger, and instantly your self-image can shatter. As long as you relate to an *image* of yourself, you'll strive to maintain and protect it. Feeding this imaginary self kills authenticity and keeps you from knowing life in its deeper dimensions—you're locked into a prison of deceit. This misinterpreting of Self is the primary cause of most people's suffering.

DK: The Buddha said that life *is* suffering.

J: Yes, but only from the standpoint of the limited, mind-made self. Pay attention and you'll see that you suffer most when viewing things as a 'person.' You defend your self-image, fretting over what might happen, what people will think and so on . . . and *because* of all this madness will a molehill turn into a mountain. Everything shifts, however, when you scrap all judgment of yourself and others and bring *presence* back to your life.

DK: How is that different from our usual mode?

J: When fully absorbed in the instant at hand—with things that demand concentration, for instance, or merely doing something you love—you're simply *being* and not judging or thinking as a limited, time-bound persona. In moments like this, neither past nor future exists, and even the notion of death disappears. Death is a *future*-linked concept that's irrelevant to spirit but makes ego fret like a spinster. Death becomes meaningless, though, in the lovely aliveness of *now*.

DK: In Texas we say to clear out the brush and get to the sod.

J: I'm urging you to seek your real nature. You can see, as I did, that reality *transcends* ideas of life and death and it has no connection to suffering. Though it's true the real 'you' cannot die, you *can* confuse yourself with things that do. If you think you're a body, you live with a fear of death. The fear may be faint if you're beautiful, healthy and strong—but it grows fast with age, and soon you come to see clearly that "time's running out." As death's forbidding footsteps draw near, anxiety can turn to despair, depression or even panic—the dying often fear they're being extinguished. They sometimes turn angry and cause a lot of needless drama because of it.

DK: You're right, and I've noticed that those around them can do the same.

J: Sure, because they're watching a painful reminder of their mortality—flustered as they helplessly stand by and watch. The process can be scary for the dying and cause lots of painful suffering for those who share it. But none of it is needed. Death is only rarely the unpleasant thing it's perceived to be, and thousands of joyous and enlightening near-death and post-death stories from across the world have proven it.

DK: Still, the fact remains that we all have to die—a real existential bummer.

J: Once you've seen the falsity of the body-mind 'person,' you'll have 'died' long before physical death: "He who *loses* his life . . . will *find* it." Die to the false self *now* and you'll finally know true life and see why the body's conclusion isn't nearly so 'grave' after all.

DK: That's a long day's walk from religion, which has caused quite a scare about the gravity of bodily death. In Christianity we're taught that our souls go flying off to Limbo, patiently awaiting some word of salvation or sanction at the opening of the Lord's Book of Life. It's the grand finale—the dreaded Day of Judgment when a hundred billion souls will be condemned or redeemed as they stand afore the fearsome throne of God.

J: You forgot the part about the magic dust, an evil witch, and the dance of the sugarplum fairies.

DK: Don't be so glib, this is straight from the boys of the Bible.

J: They showed twenty centuries too soon, I would say, 'cause they'd fit perfectly fine out at Disney. I'm telling you, your spirit isn't another thing among things. It's the *essence* of you—the essence of *God*. Spirit isn't limited by form, and it certainly isn't trapped in the body. You might say that it's temporo-spatially inapposite.

DK: I'm not sure I *could* say that. In English, please.

J: Time and space don't control it. If the soul were a *thing* with its own existence, and if it were being 'housed' in the body, I guess it'd have to go *somewhere* after you die. But where would it go? Off to some galaxy called heaven? If so, then why wait around? Why not build a ship to fly you there now?

DK: First of all, wise guy, we don't know where it is . . . the cosmos covers a pretty broad swath, know what I mean? Secondly, maybe *multiple* realities exist, all at once. Even some scientists think so.

J: So God whipped up this crazy earthly dimension as a kind of real-time proving ground to see if you pass inspection, while dangling a far *better* one before you like a spiritual carrot on a stick. Definitely bizarre . . . perhaps even sick and sadistic. And folks say this religion brings them *comfort*?

DK: C'mon, just spit it out. Do humans have souls or not?

J: So what if you do? It still begs the question. If you're making the claim, "I have a soul," then my challenge again would be this: who, what, or where is this 'I' you're telling me of? Who is the soulless one claiming to have a soul—get what I'm sayin'? There must be something *apart from* or *prior to* the soul for it to declare, "I have a soul."

DK: I see what you mean. But still . . . call it a gut feeling or whatever, I have to conclude that some kind of 'soul' does exist.

J: Alright, but even if it does, why stuff it into a body? If the soul is a separate *thing*—with shape, character and identity—it's really just another kind of body. So, why the need for two bodies at once? As I said before, wouldn't it be more sensible for God to create you as a perfect soul and place you into heaven directly?

DK: What about our free wi—

J: Hold it, hold it. You can stop *right there*.

DK: What's the problem now?

J: Look here, amigo: give me your tired, your poor, your huddled masses. Give me liberty or give me death. Give me a home where the buffalo roam. If you just can't control yourself, you can even gimme that old-time religion. But *please*, for the love of sane thinking, don't give me more of that ridiculous *free will* junk.

DK: I seem to have struck a raw nerve.

J: Here's the thing: It's true that all power in heaven and earth is yours through the energy you call 'God'—but neither you *nor* God possess powers that don't exist. Free will doesn't mean that you're free to destroy yourself or free to change what God created perfect. As people think of it, free will applies only to the dream state: you're free to choose between illusions and the truth. But don't waste time believing you've made chaos of unity or separated yourself from the all-encompassing Source. You're always free to *use* the laws of Nature—but never to break them.

DK: Surely God doesn't want robots. Wouldn't He have to allow for rebellion?

J: If Bible creation mythology were true and God was set on allowing his precious dependents to 'reject' Him, He might as easily have placed everyone in heaven with the option t—

DK: —to freely get the hell *out* at any time!! Now, *that's* a damned good perspective.

J: Well, I mean what was the bloody *point*? Instead of creating his kids and then releasing them straight into heaven, He sends the poor saps on a perilous involuntary mission wherein all of 'em risk limb, life and soul whilst running about like maniacs 'round some second-rate testing site in an off-the-path little solar system spinning in the deep, dark belly of a cosmos so big that it's *scary*. Where's the need for this dangerous detour into other dimensions of reality? There's just no discernible *sense* in it.

DK: Maybe you're right. I'm not all smiles in jumping through hoops to prove worthy to my own creator. Forcing us all to suffer life here on earth before inheriting some heavenly afterworld would make God an intellectual slug. But what can we do about it?

J: Go beyond your ideas of death by finding the thing that's deathless. Then you'll know with certainty that you and God are not what you've assumed and that *his* immortal life assures your own. *A Course in Miracles* explains, "When your body and your ego and your dreams are gone, you will know that you will last forever . . . The Holy Spirit guides you into life eternal, but you must relinquish your investment in death, or you will not see life though it is all around you."

DK: And how do we relinquish our "investment in death"?

J: You simply disinvest in the evanescent.

DK: No one likes an omniscient show-off.

J: You relinquish your investment in death by refusing to invest in things that die. Each day, as often as you can, hold your attention on that which time can't destroy. This place of peace and safety is the Self— and to know it, move gently towards I AM . . .

CHAPTER THIRTY-THREE

DK: You look sleepy. Shall we take a break?

J: Well, it does take time to adjust to the physical plane. But the ground is muddy and I didn't bring a cot—so, alas, the Son of man has nowhere to lay his head.

DK: Hey, I don't wanna be that guy who blew the interview with God. Let's shift gears and get back to Christianity.

J: Thy will be done . . .

DK: Okay, earlier we talked about the Crucifixion. But now let's focus on the *other* side: the Resurrection. My own feeling is that the Resurrection is Christianity's keystone. I mean if the story ends with you buried and forgotten, you're lucky to make page twelve of the *Judean Times-Herald*—and prob'ly just a blurb with a catchy header.

J: "Crucified Messiah Still Dead"

DK: Precisely. The reason you were headline material was due to the exceptional claim by your disciples that you sprang back to life after you died. Scripture says you then appeared in the flesh to several hundred of your supporters in the emotional days that followed. Now, I don't need to tell you that *some* folks have real problems with that story—they've no frame of reference for rising after death and entombment. Some even say your crucifixion didn't actually kill you.

J: Oh? On what theory?

DK: That you were taken from the cross—now *seemingly* dead but in fact just barely alive—and nursed back to health over the following several days. There's guesswork that the nurse was your friend Joseph of Arimathea. Others say it was Mary the Magdalene, who some insist was also your girlfriend or wife. Adding to the mystery of it all, turns out there's quite a volume of old literature detailing claims that you later traveled to India, where you lived out the rest of your life teaching love and continuing your ministry under the sacred name of Saint Issa, with 'Isa' being your Arabic name in Islam, and īśa meaning 'the Lord' in Sanskrit. And despite the great controversy around it, you've even got an official burial place in the Roza Bal section of Srinigar in Kashmir.

J: I believe there's one in Shingo, Japan, as well.

DK: Yeah, but nobody takes that one seriously since their claims are made without a speck of proof.

J: Well, as far as that goes, the two most revered burial sites claimed for me in the Holy Land are nothing but pure speculation. The Garden Tomb *and* The Church of the Holy Sepulchre have both been rejected by scholars because there's no good evidence for either.

DK: Alright, but my point is that a lot of people—Christians included— have wondered why you didn't make the rounds after 'resurrecting' and show yourself to *everyone* . . . certainly would've been more convincing. I mean why not, in true messianic fashion, hop right back on that doggoned donkey and ride victoriously through Jerusalem, as you did just prior to your arrest. In fact, why not go knocking on the door of Pilate himself? Wouldn't you have loved to see the look on the poor fella's face?

J: You should be writing spy novels.

DK: No, no . . . I can already see it up on the silver screen. There you are, standing before the guy ultimately responsible for your death. Calmly and without flinching, you look Pilate straight in the eye, slowly extending your upturned palms with their freshly healed wounds. Finally, with a condescending smirk, you speak: "Hi, remember *me*? We recently met here at the Praetorium." Now, *that*, my friend, is the fabric of box office legends!!

J: Next I'll be kung-fu kicking the high priest . . .

DK: But really, what about this Resurrection thing? Because without *that*, you're just another martyr with an attitude.

J: Let's clarify something . . .
    When discussing the 'Great Commission,' I suggested we come back later to the verse you alluded to from Luke 24. And here's why: The Resurrection has no foundation in Jewish scripture.

DK: *What*?!?

J: It's true. The Jews never expected their messiah to be killed and then raised from the dead—nor would he be so easily stamped out. So the Christian Resurrection was no fulfillment of some revered Old Testament prophecy, because there *is* no such prophecy in those texts.

181

DK: Wait up a sec. The Luke passage says, "Then he opened their minds to understand the scriptures, and said to them, 'Thus it is written, that the Christ should suffer and on the third day rise from the dead . . . '" Apparently the Resurrection *did* fulfill some ancient divination of the future.

J: Nope, there's not a single Old Testament passage predicting any messianic resurrection, and even back then it was a joke. No serious Jew would've expected the messiah to be rising from the bloody *dead—* not after two days, not after two weeks . . . not even after two jugs of hooch. The Old Testament never calls for the raising of a coming savior-god, and the gospel writer quotes scripture that doesn't exist.

DK: I was taught that you were referencing Hosea 6:2, which says, "After two days he will revive us; on the third day he will raise us up."

J: Well, if that's what the writer of Luke was dealing, he really was stacking the deck. Read from Hosea chapter four and you'll see that God was just scolding his sheep once again. The passage is Yahweh's prediction of what his rueful nation will be declaring when they realize the errors of their ways. They'll proclaim, "He'll revive us . . . He'll raise us up."

DK: Yeah, they're speaking in the plural.

J: Of course—because they're talking about *themselves.* No smallish hint of any future messiah nor magical rising from death.

DK: I'm sorry to say it, but in all my years as a Christian, I never bothered checking it out for myself.

J: Don't feel bad, your ignorance gains you membership in a pretty large club.

DK: Well, this is yet *another* blockbuster reveal, then, because Christians believe that the focus of the Resurrection was your body. But *you* say your body was no big deal.

J: We've got the same challenge with the Resurrection that we had with the Crucifixion: the idea that my body was special. But even a resurrected body would still be only a body . . . and no *body* was ever savior to the world. Bodies are the perfect vehicles for the reason you choose them— but you don't need them in order to *be.* So the Apostles' Creed is 'dead' wrong: resurrection of the body has *no relevance* to life everlasting. And rising from the grave is improbable from the start, is it not?

DK: And yet, there you sit!

182

J: When I appear to people, which I do now and then, they have no idea what they're seeing. They don't know who or what I am, where I came from or how I got here—they can't even answer those things about *themselves*. And my appearances don't prove or confirm *any*thing of the Bible, or even of what someone believes. But like I said, in Palestine the notion of a literal resurrection would've never been taken to heart. Just because we're talking of an *ancient* society doesn't mean that people were stupid. No one expected my rising when I was crucified—and even my disciples didn't huddle with bated breath aside my tomb. In fact, they all took off running when things turned south: they feared the cops might soon be coming for *them*. Their fervently held faith faded fast.

DK: True . . . but scripture does indicate that those who saw you after your tomb was found empty were ultimately convinced of your godhood. And for many it's an inspirational story—but some of us find it pretty hard to accept. I guess it just requires a leap of faith.

J: Well, that's one *giant leap* for mankind. Luckily it's not a leap you're required to make. One of the earliest Christian writings, used as seed material by the authors of Matthew and Luke, is a popular text called The Synoptic Sayings Source—also referred to by scholars simply as "Q." This record, like The Gospel of Thomas which contains confirming parallel information, was written within twenty years after my death, while the four New Testament gospels were composed much later. This is big since neither "Q" *nor* The Gospel of Thomas consider my death at all important to the faith, and they make no claims of resurrection— instead they emphasize my *teachings*, which is where the focus should be. Christian reports of resurrection didn't rise until decades after my passing, and that should tell you some things.

DK: Our doctrines may need some fine-tuning . . .

J: From my view, a bulldog grip on doctrine is nothing but close-minded conviction that won't be shaken by facts. Religion insists that unqualified faith is the key to its marketed 'salvation,' so this discourages scrutiny and keeps folks from digging too deep. But even if I say the Resurrection happened exactly as claimed, what difference would it make to *you*? I mean how would that *help* you in life? How does it bring you closer to Self-knowledge? In that sense it can't help at all. So whether you take your scriptures for history doesn't really matter in the least— life is not impressed by your conviction nor offended by your doubt.

DK: The gospel of John says that even your friend Thomas was skeptical when first seeing you post-Resurrection—rising from the dead simply wasn't part of his paradigm. He didn't believe it was you until he touched the wounds on your palms.

J: But again, for you that's only a story. So, clearly you've got two options: stay doubtful or accept it all on faith. Either way, it's got no connection to my message of spiritual liberation. For *that*, you'll need a very *different* sort of personal, 'hands-on' experience . . .

CHAPTER THIRTY-FOUR

DK: I s'pose it's no shock that your story would cause so much flak. First off, there's no biblical record of anyone confirming you dead—nor was there a single eyewitness to your resurrection. We're told only that an obscure centurion informed Pontius Pilate you had died, and that your friends Nicodemus and Joseph of Arimathea then removed your body from the cross and took you to Joe's family tomb. So maybe the conspiracy folks are right. In theory, at least, it's possible you hadn't fully expired.

J: Ah, the old trick of fooling the medical examiner by stopping the heart and going the day without breathing.

DK: It's not all about vital signs, though. The writer of Matthew reports that a strange, untimely darkness descended upon the earth for three hours before your death. He also says there was an earthquake the minute you died. Unfortunately, neither of these astro-geological events has ever been substantiated by any *non Christian* writings.

J: Picky, picky, picky . . .

DK: And here's the *real* zinger. The gospel writer makes the remarkable claim—which, again, remains unproven—that when you breathed your last breath, lots of old corpses rose up from their graves to go visit their pals in Jerusalem! And so, it would seem, the rising dead in Palestine that week were effectively common as camels. And finally we're told that, several days after your death, you popped in sporadically on friends. The book of 1 Corinthians says you first went to Cephas, or Simon Peter, and then to all twelve apostles . . . which I assume included Matthias, who took the place of Judas after his death. Scripture alleges that you then appeared to five hundred people at once. One can only *guess* how much wine was conjured for *that* gig.

J: If derision were a gift of the spirit, yours would need shipping by freight.

DK: But there is good reason for wonder at that claim. Suspiciously, we've not found one first-person account from that crowd. Five hundred folks had seen a miracle like never before—and no one among them thought to write it down or *tell* a few people about it!? Even the gospels themselves are mysteriously silent. Not one of their writers says, "Oh, and get this: I ran into Jesus 'bout a week after entombment and he was livelier than a scalded cat!"

J: No diaries stashed away in secret caves, eh?

DK: Not so far, it appears. What's worse, not a single known historian of the day confirms *any* of these extravagant claims. Surely the era's most respected record-keepers would carefully note the earthquake, three hours of midday darkness, and the stunning resurrections of the long-deceased. And did no one write of dead relatives coming 'round for meals? I mean we have enough data from that era to fill a freakin' *library*—but none of the writers ever talk about *you*. Instead all we've got are the Christian accounts, written no sooner than decades after your death . . . and we don't even know who *wrote* 'em!! Now, truly I say unto thee: that's pretty fishy journalism, dude.

J: Hey, gimme a break . . . not a stroke of those ancient writings was mine. I knew that future cultures couldn't verify events of my life. Would it make sense to have your spiritual advancement hanging on your will to believe, with no fleck of credible evidence, these wackadoo claims from the Ages of Bronze and Iron?!?

DK: All I know for sure is that the Resurrection is Christianity's bedrock—without it, the faith has no point. But the church says the soul's in some serious hot water and your famous return from the dead is all that'll save it.

J: Nonsense. Again I ask, even if you accept the Resurrection story exactly as recorded, what obvious good does it do *you*? Does it merely give hope that, despite your own death, you might one day make it to heaven? How in the world could that ever bring benefit *now*?

DK: Well, like you said, at least it provides some hope.

J: Hope is an item that's way overbought. If hope is the best that religion can offer, it's time you went shopping somewhere else. Hope only blinds you with the mud of anticipation. It's waiting for God to do something *tomorrow* He *should* be doing *today*.

DK: If hope isn't all that helpful, what good is hoping for resurrection of the body?

J: It's a thoroughly useless idea. Resurrection's true relevance transcends the belief that life is of the body. And it isn't important if I *was* resurrected—the past is dead. I *am* the resurrection and I *am* the life. *And so are you.* If this weren't true, then what would be the point of Christianity? A Christ who keeps others submissive, dependent, and not as fully empowered as himself would never be a Christ worth having, nor one that you would ever even want.

DK: But now we're back to the basic Christian dilemma. The church says that your physical resurrection is *fact* and the soul's single hope of repose. The only other option is hell.

J: How could my desecrated body ever help your *spirit*? And wasn't saving your spirit always the goal? In traditional Christianity, the Resurrection proves that I was special . . . *better* than you. Somehow more divine. And now your own acceptance as a child of God hangs strictly on your willingness to *accept* that idea. For the church to claim that I was something you can never be is a shameful perversion of my teachings. Never let religion demean your worth or cause you fear, for religion has much to gain in the deal and *you've* got a lot to lose if you believe it. Love has no limits, preconditions or judgments, nor must it be called in through any broker.

DK: And I think the church *does* see itself as the broker. It warns that our acceptance of you as 'God's Son' is fundamental to our spiritual salvation, and only Christianity can give it.

J: So the church says you're saved or condemned by your beliefs. But *how*? Beliefs are just thoughts . . . they never change your essence. You surely can't be Christian—or Muslim, or Hindu or whatever—*by nature*. There's nothing of the Self that could be found, identified or labeled. And *believing* it to be something it isn't surely doesn't make it so in *fact*. Lay a corpse on a slab and prove to me scientifically that it's Catholic, Buddhist or Rastafarian. It can't be done. And if it can't be done with a body, how would it be possible with Spirit? You're certain that you're this thing or the other only when you're actually *thinking* about it. When you *don't* think about it, it's irrelevant. Now do you catch my drift?

DK: Oh, I'm *drifting* alright.

J: Maybe another example will clear it up. Let us say you touch a hot oven by mistake and you're suddenly in excruciating pain. For all practical means, in that moment you're no longer Christian, Jewish, Scientologist, or even a human being—you're not *aware* of yourself in those terms. When attention's fully focused on the now, you basically become the experience . . . in this case, extreme physical pain. In every living instant, you're essentially the experience of your awareness.

DK: So, upon burning my finger at the oven, I wouldn't be thinking of myself as a Christian—not until initial discomfort had passed and I finally regained all my senses. Only then could I resume the conceptual idea that I'm Christian.

J: Or, for that matter, any concept at all. Every concept is still just a thought, and it's got to be *recalled* to have relevance. Take your most cherished opinions, ideas or self-images, and see how meaningful they are the next time you're having an orgasm.

DK: I'll make a note . . .

J: This stuff may sound peculiar, but you enter this selfless state each day on awakening. For a brief period during initial grogginess, there's only pure awareness. *Time* is required before thought or the notion of 'I' and your 'story of me' comes to life. So your religion, like any idea, is relevant only when you think about it—when you're *aware* of it. On busy days, you're often blind to yourself as any kind of devoted 'believer.' Where does the believer *go?*

DK: On the other hand, I 'gave my life to God' when I was a kid. I'm sure the church would argue that my choice brought a change in the spirit, if not in the body-mind complex. . . though how they could actually *know* this I really can't say.

J: But thoughts don't alter your eternal reality, and this is where religions crash and burn. The essence of religious salvation is that God will either love his children or abuse them—and all of it depends on their *thoughts!!*

DK: Right, the Christian church teaches that we're judged by what we think and believe—by what goes passing through our minds.

J: But if God has left salvation up to you, He's just another figure in the story and can't save with any assurance—Satan's as likely as Spirit to win the match. Biblically, therefore, something doesn't click. One minute God is thinking that the whole of creation's "very good." Then, without vote or even prior notification, He's brewing up flammable water for his fiery lake.

DK: Yeah, He's inconsolably troubled by our inherited evil nature—which *He* actually made possible, of course, in giving us free will and then double-dog daring us to use it.

J: Yet the moment you take *me* as your 'Lord and savior,' God is rendered happy once again as He lovingly unlatches the gate.

DK: Well, that's what they *tell* us, at least . . . and for me it holds little of cheer.

J: Breathe a giant sigh of relief, my friend, 'cause it's all ecclesiastical swill. God never sees you as less than your holy Self, and He hasn't since your *creation* in Holiness.

DK: Shouldn't we allow that God—when given sufficient reason, of course—*could* change his mind on our worth?

J: Only if we allow that his creations can be defective, his assessments mistaken and his highest of visions derailed. In the case of humanity, God either has lousy foresight or He made you imperfect from the start. If the first is true, He has no business issuing prophecy or scolding folks for *their* lack of vision. If the second is true, He has no right to judge. And if *either* is true, He's not the God that religion would have you believe.

DK: So religion's 'salvation' is baloney if we're always looking for paradise past the grave.

J: It's a game of spiritual Three-card Monte . . . and *you're* the gullible dupe!

DK: Religion's more bizarre than I've imagined. And I'm starting to see that our spirits never needed redeeming. But what sort of saving did you bring?

J: If you grant that human ignorance has resulted in what is often a hell on earth, it's obvious that the 'good news' of redemption must mean this: freedom from the hellish state of ignorance.

DK: Spiritual things aside, we often need saving from *material* states.

J: But what if saving grace is withheld? The God of religion may work the occasional miracle, yes—but He also stands idle while pandemics, wars, and catastrophes kill millions at once. If religion's God takes credit for saving you from periodic need or disaster, He also gets the blame for all the tragedies and failings as well. Given the oft-cruel nature of earthly life, how much concern could God really have for a body? And certainly a *body* has no need of spiritual redemption.

DK: So, in reality there's nothing to save.

J: Nothing at all. You could view salvation as liberation from the belief that you ever for a moment *needed* saving. The entire separation-from-God idea was only a passing error in judgment—in fact a genuine dream, as hard as it is to believe. And you should darn well *pray* that the world, *as it is,* would never be the highest vision of a loving, all-powerful God . . .

CHAPTER THIRTY-FIVE

DK: This idea that the world is a product of the mind has been taught through many sages, intuitives and mystics for thousands of years. But the challenge of *accepting* it stretches most of us too thin.

J: Well, all of it exists in the sense that you're experiencing it and that it presently affects and influences you—that's why you chose to show up. But none of it is ultimately binding because consciousness can't be bound. An experience of a different reality makes *this* one disappear in a flash.

DK: Early in life I might've said that kind of talk was crazy. But it sounds like something from several years back during one of my life's more depressing periods. I was sitting on the sofa one night feeling rotten when, somehow from nowhere, waves of bliss welled up within me like a fount— I went from hell to heaven in a flash, just like you said. Inside those timeless minutes of revelation, if that's indeed what it was, the world became quickly irrelevant . . . it barely had a tinge of reality and mostly I gave it no thought. Whatever caused the world to fade that evening was the thing that was far more real—and infinitely more fulfilling and meaningful, too. The main impression was the marvelous joy of existence, and the one thing I wanted was to share it with all of creation. It surely must've been the most 'self-less' moment of my life . . . no ego-mind even existed. All things felt 'connected' as I gushed out thanks to that unseen force we call 'God.' To me it was grace pouring in, and life seemed to know what I needed. The experience was healing beyond words—and on so many levels, as well.

J: And that's how it is in the original state of union. Most people can't understand it because once they move beyond childhood they don't experience it—society can send the soul into hiding. But you *are* as you were created. So either your eternal state has changed—a clear contradiction— or something made you *believe* it has.

DK: A challenging point—suffering and divine perfection are poles apart. But if the world *is* just a movement in mind, then what of the hoping millions who are counting on you to save them after they die? Scripture says that you'll raise their lifeless bodies during 'the last days,' at which time they'll be taken up to heaven 'midst angelic choirs and those blaring introductory horns.

J: Was the writer describing a theology or maybe just a plot for cable TV?

DK: Hey, it's salvation, Christian style—and all of it straight from the Holy New Testament.

J: Which also states that *"Now* is the day of salvation." Again, the notion of any future redemption is meaningless and beliefs are just a lazy replacement for brains.

DK: Look, I apologize for over-pulling the taffy, but I've gotta press you on the Christian party line and the claims about you and your life. For example, the New Testament says that, sometime post-Resurrection, you mystically ascended to heaven. What can you tell us of that?

J: The Ascension carries the same issue we had with the Resurrection. Making it literal and thinking it's only for me, your wagon's wandered way off the trail. Ascension is the transformation of *consciousness.*

DK: So you're not asking us to believe in a *physical* rising from the dead.

J: I'm not asking you to believe *squat.* Every belief is based on uncertainty, and uncertainty is mere ignorance of the Self. I'm suggesting that you make the trip 'inward' to the place of true knowing where you won't limp around on the crutches of belief or assumption.

DK: I'm starting to see that your agony on the cross was never required.

J: Well, sadly I wasn't offered early retirement—those who wanted me dead were in no mood for barter. Besides, it would really ruin the rhythm of the Apostles' Creed: "He suffered under Pontius Pilate, was defrocked, and went on to *fortunes* in the wine trade."

DK: But really, after all that you've said so far, wouldn't you expect us to conclude that you died in vain?

J: I expect you to realize that *I did not die.* Not because I was *the* Christ, but an expression *of* the Christ—the full embodiment of its holy, celestial nature. The word "Christ" derives from the Greek CHRISTOS, "the anointed." I became what you and your brothers and sisters can each become: fully empowered, awakened children of Universe—'anointed ones' for whom even the thought of death is no concern.

DK: Once more you're reversing some long-held doctrine on your nature. I'll refer again to the famous passage from Philippians which declares,

191

"at the name of Jesus every knee should bow" and "every tongue should confess that Jesus Christ is Lord." Literalists say that those not submitting to you thusly are damned to maltreatments of hell.

J: *Holy mother-of-pearl!* Ask any literalist if *he* would employ that system and abuse *his* children like that if *he* were God. If he's dumb or dishonest enough to say yes, ask him to explain and then see if you can make yourself *believe* it or keep from laughing. If he's honest and says no, ask why it's fine for his *God* to be any less wise. If he waffles by saying that he can't be certain since he isn't God—showing he knows that answering yes would make both him *and* his argument sound crazy and answering no means he's fully *aware* that it's crazy—then just be bloody grateful that he *isn't* God since he can't even spot stark *madness* when he sees it. In any case, you're sure to have some real fun with this one . . .

CHAPTER THIRTY-SIX

DK: Hey, before I forget: you never went on about your possible connection to India. Apart from the camp that claims you fled there after surviving the Crucifixion, other writers say that you were traveling the Far East even during those early 'lost' years—long *before* you began your ministry in Palestine. Many people say that some of your teachings are Buddhist. And the Bible gives reason to think this theory of your overland ventures might be true. The gospel of Matthew says, "and *coming to his own country, he taught them in their synagogue, so that they were astonished, and said, 'Where did this man get this wisdom and these mighty works?'*" So it's clear that you were gone a long time and that folks back home were impressed with the knowledge and power you'd gained.

J: Why should anyone doubt that I would seek far and wide to learn more about the mysteries of life? I wasn't born a preloaded data bank, you know. As you said in your letter, the gospels fail to account for a pretty big chunk of my history. Growing up in the Middle Eastern desert, I was naturally attracted to the mysteries and traditions of the Far East. Through travel, study, meditation, and tapping into the ancient wisdom of others, I grew . . . I *expanded*. I finally saw that everything I was seeking was tracking me like a shadow—the treasure I sought had lain hidden beneath my nose.

DK: So your studies weren't confined to the sacred writings of Judaism.

J: I always honored truth *wherever* I found it. On top of the many Far Eastern teachings, I also gained knowledge from the Essenes.

DK: I've read a bit about the Essenes. Weren't they considered a cult?

J: Hey, now *there's* a winning strategy: discredit something by labeling it. When another group's philosophy threatens your own, just call it a cult and you instantly kill its good name—one of the oldest plays in the book. In fact, pull out your dictionary and read the definition of 'cult.'

DK: Let's see here. . . . "cult: A group of followers. A sect which adheres to a particular set of practices or rituals."

J: By *that* description, then, even a society is a cult—a *cult*-ure, if you will— and major religions are the biggest cults on earth. My own disciples would easily have qualified as a cult in the eyes of both the Romans *and* the high rabbinical authorities. For many years following my death, if any group could rightly be called a cult, it was Christians. After all, they were the new kids on the block. So it's quite hypocritical for Christians to exalt themselves by calling the Essenes, or anyone else, a cult. Study the true origins of the twelve tribes of Israel and you'll know a lot more of Essenes.

DK: Anyone familiar with the gospels will recognize groups like the well-known Sadducees and Pharisees; but not many know of the Essenes because the New Testament never refers to them. Researchers say that's a very strange thing, since the Dead Sea Scrolls—some of which pre-date your birth by more than two hundred years—show that an ancient group of devotees was practicing a kind of prototype Christianity many generations before your disciples. A number of Scroll scholars think it was the Essenes, and academics have suggested that even your cousin John the Baptist, evidently a very learnéd man and spiritually advanced himself, was an Essene who grew up in Qumran.

J: And the Essenes, along with other non-traditional, pre-Christian groups, had quite a few rituals that the church may find uncomfortably familiar. They practiced baptism for the remission of sins and performed healing by the laying on of hands. They had a communion consisting of bread and wine, and their internal structure was practically identical to church government as described in the book of Acts. They even called themselves "the meek," "the poor," "the New Covenanters," "the chosen ones" and even "the elect."

DK: So these groups were using Christian-like rituals, ideologies and even the faith's vocabulary long before you or the Christian religion ever existed.

J: Yes, and the timing wasn't even close. Essene-type teachings had been revered for at least five centuries before my birth, with some evidence dating back even as far as the Sumerian glyphs—around 4000 BCE. The fingerprints of these early traditions appear not only in Christianity but in *several* of the world's big religions. So the New Testament's failure to mention the Essenes and their teachings must certainly have been by design since they were widely known in the day.

DK: Some scholars believe the Essenes, or perhaps their offshoots, actually *were* the original 'Christians' and that *theirs* were the first Christian texts. And some of those early papers did in fact reference the Essenes—but nervous church clerics quickly laundered them out.

J: Bear in mind that most of the New Testament was written *outside Judea*—and some of it a century or more past my death. So it's clear the New Testament couldn't possibly hold the earliest Christian writings, unless no word was written of me for thirty years after I died. You've got serious issues between the first Christian writings and the first books of the official New Testament—they're not at all the same. And assuming the most popular of those early works had some sort of meaningful impact on the later ones that wound up in the Bible, you have to account for other distortions as well. Not only did the subtleties of language evolve during the decades following my death—causing problems for translators when deciphering what those early writers intended—but plenty of opportunity remained for critical redactions, embellishment, or outright hanky-panky.

DK: *Unless*, of course, each word came from Yahweh himself.

J: In which case He's got some explaining to do . . .

CHAPTER THIRTY-SEVEN

DK: Okay, I've got a problem. Your view of Christianity clearly challenges the general favor it enjoys across so much of the globe. Now, no one can deny that the world is a mess and the church hasn't successfully 'saved' it. And we're in full agreement that religions have caused as much conflict and bloodshed over the centuries as anything else one could name . . . most *all* of 'em need a serious kick in the frock. But maybe we're not giving credit where due. Perhaps there's merit to the church's claim that, despite its many failings, its influence on the world has still been mostly positive—if not so firmly on the *physical* plane, then possibly on the spiritual.

J: Hey, let's not beat around the burning bush. Going strictly on history, there's no cause to think that Christianity or any other religion provides large-scale solutions to *anything*—their polarizing views very often just add to the grief. Bertrand Russell compared literalist Christianity to Communism and said their most dangerous features are frighteningly similar: "fanatical acceptance of doctrines embodied in a sacred book, unwillingness to examine [them] critically, and savage persecution of those who reject them." Russell said "the whole contention that Christianity has had an elevating moral influence can only be maintained by wholesale ignorance or falsification of the historical evidence."

DK: I guess you'd *expect* that from a guy who wrote *Why I am Not a Christian*.

J: But was he wrong? I mean, *really* . . . what has Christianity given the world that the church finds so terribly essential? Which of its noble works would be wasted without the religious trappings?

DK: Well, I won't try to argue that Christianity—or any other religion—brought some sort of goodness to the world that wasn't already available. I also won't argue that Christians help ease the world's suffering by feeding the poor, caring for the sick and all that, because then you'll say that kindness surely didn't start with the church and that we shouldn't need religion before showing compassion. But what about the great Christian architecture, literature, music and art?

J: A pretty lame offering for the faith's many centuries of oppression. If it meant avoiding their cruel demise, I'd guess that all those tortured and killed as heretics or heathens would've happily deprived the world of the Sistine Chapel and the singing of *O Holy Night*.

DK: Well, heck . . . at least Christianity helped establish the Western calendar.

J: I was looking for a bit more substance—and they broke the *calendar,* too.

DK: What about monotheism? Weren't Judaism and Christianity the first religions with only one God?

J: Even though he couldn't make it stick, the father of the Egyptian boy-king Tutankhamun, Pharaoh Akhenaten, is generally credited as the first in recorded history to attempt establishing full-scale monotheism. The great Persian empire also had a one-god religion that can be argued to have preceded the Hebrews. These facts are largely moot, though, since it's well known among scholars that the Old Testament refers not just to *one* so-called 'god,' but to *many.* When original text contains the Hebrew word *elohim*—which, if researched, reveals some deadly serious extraterrestrial earth visitor implications—it's usually translated as "God," in the singular. But it doesn't mean "God" at all, and some have claimed it can even indicate angels. Anyhow, there's a huge theological difference in worldviews from a passage that reads, "And God said . . ." if the writer *really* meant, "And the *gods* said . . ." Most people think that Jewish Old Testament heroes take a monotheistic view of reality in every case. But that's not true, and the famously fickle Solomon himself is a perfect example.

DK: Apparently the Israelites changed perspectives on the divine quite often over the centuries before adopting Yahweh as their god.

J: As you'd expect with such a long and complex history, their beliefs were all over the map. Old Testament scriptures may appear to focus on only one 'deity,' but Israelites weren't always thinking in terms of monotheism, which is clear from their behavior. And even Yahweh himself never tells them that no other gods exist—He merely orders not to give them *attention.* But never mind Judaism. I'm curious to know how you figure that Christianity is monotheistic.

DK: I already know where you're going. You're gonna say that Christianity technically has *three* deities: the Father, the Son, and the Holy Spirit. The church says that's not polytheism, though, since all three are joined up as one.

J: Alright, but how is that different from, say, Hinduism? As a single ray of light produces infinite colors in passing through a prism, the various Hindu gods and goddesses are seen as just different expressions of the one supreme source, called Brahman. Christianity, with three distinct members in *its* Godhead, is essentially claiming the same.

DK: I think that's only fair. Taking that view with *any* religion means having to allow it with others.

J: And let's not forget that the God of the Old Testament and the God of the New Testament have virtually nothing in common—they seem different characters entirely. So Hinduism and Christianity are both either monotheistic *or* polytheistic, depending on how you see it. But either way, so what? Surely the church offers something more helpful than having just one man in charge. I mean how is that really of use? As long as he's getting what he wants—or especially when he *isn't*— a fella doesn't *really* care if there's one god or six hundred thousand.

DK: The church would say its chief contribution—the carrying forth of the Christ story—brings hope of salvation to the world.

J: Well, nothing's too innovative in *that*—religion has promised soul-saving from the beginning. It's very peculiar 'salvation,' incidentally, that leaves so much death in its wake. Going by headlines, religions are as likely to *destroy* the world as they ever will be to redeem it . . .

CHAPTER THIRTY-EIGHT

DK: So the lesson is we don't need any religion since we're always united with God, even if we haven't yet seen it. And certainly it's a wonderful *idea*, don't get me wrong . . . but the faith of the average believer will never allow it.

J: The teaching of cosmic unity has been around for thousands of years and was essential even in early Greco-Christian theology. Two of the church's most respected Greek theologians—Clement of Alexandria and his student Origen Adamantius—were both well-versed in the principle of oneness within variety. They saw the inseparable linking of all things to what the Greeks called "First Cause," their somewhat scientific term for God.

Clement wrote of being "brought together into one love, according to the union of the essential unity . . ." He urged Christians to "follow after union, seeking after the good Monad." He spoke of "the union of many in one" and "the production of divine harmony out of a medley of sounds and division."

Origen had similar views, and he asked of a particular passage, "what can the meaning of Scripture be except the harmony and unity of the many?" It was Origen, by the way, who referred to me specifically as "the Sun of Righteousness" and taught that those who followed my example would unite with me and would themselves become full Christs. An early writing called Gospel of Philip states the same regarding those who achieve a state of "gnosis," which we'll cover in further detail in a bit.

DK: I still feel that something sets you apart. The gospels are jammed with so many tales of your godlike powers and crowd-stirring charisma that *some* of 'em must surely be true.

J: Even so, I wasn't the trailblazer most Christians seem to envision. The average Christian has no idea that the biggest parts of his faith were 'borrowed,' shall we say, from other, far older traditions. Some had existed for centuries, or even millennia, when Christianity was still wearing diapers.

DK: What's the poop?

J: It all starts with the old-school Mystery religions and the surprisingly common story of a slain-and-risen godman who saves the world from sin. The Mysteries spread like fire 'round the ancient Mediterranean, and this supernatural being was widely revered for wielding miraculous powers, unjustly bearing death at the hands of evil, and ultimately resurrecting back to life. Having now paid for his followers' transgressions, He returns in ascension to heaven and redeems them.

DK: Seems like you copied the dude's résumè. Who *was* this godman guy?

J: Well, he had lots of names through the centuries but was always the same basic mythical being in different cultural garb. He arose first in Egypt as the solar god Osiris, and his story appears in pyramid texts written twenty-five centuries before me. The Egyptian *Book of the Dead* says that Osiris—also the god of resurrection and of the underworld—came to save the fallen, who now resided outside the Garden of Eden. In true godman fashion, Osiris is unjustly murdered and his body then cut into pieces and scattered across the land. Later, he's reassembled by the goddess Isis, who then wraps his corpse in white linen. He's quickly resurrected, thereupon granting rebirth and eternal life to the faithful. Osiris had lots of names, but some will be quite relevant for Christians: "King of Kings," "Lord of Lords," "the Resurrection and the Life," and even "the Good Shepherd." Osiris was said also to cause people to be "born again."

DK: Sounds like you saviors follow some kind of script . . .

J: And later, in Greece, Osiris was fused with the popular wine god Dionysus and his stardom became widespread. In Persia he was called Mithra. In Italy he was Bacchus. In Asia Minor he was Attis . . . and so it went. As legends of these gods entwined, their traits grew too consistent to ignore. That's why, nearly three hundred years before my birth, this popular godman was referred to by the dual name Osiris-Dionysus.

DK: So when *you* were born, other saviors were already in business.

J: The deities of the Mysteries had been revered for centuries, and Palestine was swarming with followers of these various religions. Christianity came relatively late to the party and was started by people already comfortable with the notion of a world-saving godman. So even though Christianity was partly based on Judaism, much of its character—and several of its *characters*—came straight from the legends of the great Osiris-Dionysus.

DK: I don't get it. What does the biblical Christ have in common with those mythical muckety-mucks of the Mysteries?

J: Some examples . . .
   The various pre-Christian myths of Osiris-Dionysus depict him as part god and part man. Born of a virgin, his birth is often heralded by a star, and his birth date is given as—are you ready for this?—December 25th.

DK: Wait a minute. The guy is born of a virgin on the same day we celebrate Christmas!?? I'm growing suspicious.

J: Oh, it's no mere accident, my friend: it's *why* you celebrate Christmas on that day. And here's *more* exciting stuff for next week's sermon . . . Surrounded by twelve disciples, Osiris-Dionysus turns water to wine, helps fishermen fill their nets, casts out demons, heals the sick, calms raging waters and conjures miraculous meals for his friends. He rides triumphantly through town on a donkey and is later betrayed for thirty silver coins — historically the going rate for the deed — a theme also linked with the cruel death of Socrates some four hundred years before me. Finally, the godman is crucified for the moral shortcomings of the world, his bloodied body then wrapped up in linen and duly anointed with myrrh.

DK: I'd say we're far past statistical coincidence.

J: True, and we're not even finished. Osiris-Dionysus resurrects on day 3, appears in the flesh to his followers and finally ascends back to heaven, waiting to judge the unbelieving masses at the end. In some versions of his mythology, Osiris-Dionysus dies and resurrects on the same two days that early Christians sometimes chose to mark my *own* death and resurrection: March 23rd and March 25th.

DK: Well, it's no great puzzle why the church sweeps its history under the rug. Its storyline painfully matches the old pagan motifs.

J: And we've only just abraded the surface. In many ways, Christianity and paganism are practically identical twins. Three thousand years before me, the sun god Horus was a powerful figure in Egypt, and parts of the Horus mythology will sound quite familiar to Christians:
Horus was called "The Good Shepherd," "The Lamb," "The Son of Man," and "The Word made Flesh." Sometimes he was even "The Anointed One," which, again, is the literal meaning of "Christ." The Horus myth also has him struggling with his arch-rival Set, the Egyptian god of the desert and of chaos. This theme is reworked in the gospels as "Temptation of Christ" accounts in which I struggle in the desert with Satan—Christianity's ruler of *spiritual* chaos—where we too engage in a scuffle of Good-versus-Evil. Horus was said to have resurrected and to bring eternal life to the loyal.

DK: So it's plain that Christianity was basically a cut-and-paste version of the religions of ancient Egypt and later ones known as the Mysteries.

J: Yes, and the *biggest* mystery is why gospel writers weren't sued for plagiarism. You can bet your bottom shekel that these copy-cat themes are no fluke. Christian literature contains *loads* of thematic elements lifted straight from the pages of paganism. Believe me, Christianity isn't just *any* old religion. It's a genuine Mystery . . .

201

CHAPTER THIRTY-NINE

DK: I just got a call from your agent . . . says crucifix sales are *plummeting.*

J: I realize I'm rockin' the boat here—but facts are facts. Christianity was strictly an offshoot of paganism, and the gospel version of my life is just a clever clerical clone job. Taking the Christian saga literally is ridiculous and you might as well do the same with Aesop's fables.

DK: How did the story of your life get so screwed up?

J: Well, after hundreds of Christian sects were forcibly consolidated under the fantical Emperor Constantine into the rigid, powerful Church of Rome, all the preceding *mystical* forms of Christianity were mostly destroyed. From there on, literalists manned the presses, so to speak, and henceforth styled their religion as they damn well pleased.

DK: So Christianity basically put a Greco-Jewish twist on a very old tale.

J: It was paganism with a new pair of shoes . . . fresher variations of those Mystery themes. One of the better-known groups with this view came to be called the Gnostics, a name derived from the Greek GNOSTIKOS, indicating the "known." Not all Gnostics were Christian, of course, and groups that *could* be called Gnostic were as divided in opinion as the countless sects of present-day Christians—and modern Gnostics as well.

DK: What was their common thread?

J: In general they were striving to renounce the flesh and gain insight into the great celestial mysteries, both spiritual and scientific. This was the desired state of *knowing*, or gnosis. Gnostics knew that the godman stories of old were meant to lead initiates beyond the shallow waters of formal religion to an inner revelation of the divine. And because of these venerated savior-god legends and their underlying mystical importance, even factions of the early Christian church understood enlightenment. Just before Easter—during the vernal equinox and the festival of the 'resurrected' sun—many Christians would conduct a baptism ritual called PHOTISMOS, meaning "illumination." Now, this was not the behavior of any fire-preaching, heaven-and-hell literalists.

DK: Yet *you* never said a thing about gnosis. As far as I know, the gospels don't even mention it.

202

J: Oh, I discussed it *plenty*. But remember, the New Testament is only a small sliver of the early-Christian literary universe and was heavily edited to purge any remnants of Gnosticism. Many of its censors didn't *get* this "gnosis" thing, though, so they failed to see what the renegade writers were teaching—genuine Gnostic thinking had slipped through the cracks. If you know what to look for, Gnosticism is staring you in the face right there in the gospels.

DK: An example, perhaps.

J: I once said that unless you become as little children, you cannot enter the kingdom. And why is this so? Because "the kingdom" comes to those who are open-hearted, unpretentious and totally void of guile. This was not a literalist view of salvation but rather a Gnostic one. Childlike innocence, wonder and trust are among the traits needed for awakening.

DK: Ah, okay. Therefore blesséd are the meek and the poor in spirit.

J: Yeah, the pure, the humble . . . the *authentic*. Not all of the 'kingdom' parables are that simple, of course. Others are quite involved and require some wisdom to grasp—but all of them point to a radical rebirth of spiritual perspective and the qualities most conducive to its coming. Even Saint Paul, himself a quasi-Gnostic and the earliest of the New Testament authors, makes occasional reference to this new perception. In 2 Corinthians 12 he speaks of the time, years earlier, he met a man who was "in Christ." But Paul knew *hundreds* of Christians—why would he mention this guy? Only one answer makes sense: because of the powerful revelation on his famous trip to Damascus, Paul had experienced enough of the Christ presence that he certainly would've recognized it in others. Whoever the man was, Paul knew he was living in that higher state of awareness. It's true that he was transformed on the road to Damascus—but Paul's writings show he hadn't yet transcended the beliefs of duality. The man he refers to probably had.

DK: And all of that relates to this thing called gnosis?

J: What else *could* it mean if "God's kingdom" lies "within"? In the original Greek text, 1 Corinthians 12 has Paul referring to gnosis as a spiritual gift.

DK: So the New Testament is indeed partly Gnostic.

J: Yes, and in ways that most Christians would find shocking. In fact, much of the gospel of John is essentially a Gnostic composition, starting with its very introduction positioning me as the new LOGOS—a concept handed down from ancient Greece. And these hints of Gnosticism are scattered throughout the New Testament. Another example appears in Mark, the oldest of the four gospels, and likewise in Luke, where I tell my friends, "To you it has been given to know the secrets of the kingdom of God; but to others only in parables . . ." And this passage prompts a relevant question. If salvation through 'acceptance of Jesus Christ' was all anyone needed to know, why would I teach my disciples things *in secret*?

DK: I can't imagine. Why?

J: Well, lots of people saw my teachings as a threat. Their gods and authorities would suddenly be made obsolete along with most of their doctrines and beliefs. The prospect of radical change can be scary because it means that one's view of reality is horribly warped. Ego finds this quite frightening and doesn't wait long to attack. So it wasn't the sort of thing you'd discuss in public—not with those gripped by theologies of fear. But I had a job to do. I held great respect for my people but ultimately told them, as a clever wag once quipped, "You go Yahweh and I'll go mine."

DK: And yet your more 'spiritual' approach was apparently well-grasped among Gnostics and other groups mystically inclined.

J: Right, and they fully respected obvious symbolism and rejected Christian literalism as kid's stuff. But even the Gnostics weren't sailing uncharted waters. Five hundred years before me, philosophers were already scoffing at people still taking the old godman stories as fact.

DK: Did any prominent Christians hold that view?

J: Clement of Alexandria comes to mind. Venerated as a saint in some factions of the church and traditionally viewed as a literalist, his thinking was far closer to that of the Gnostics. He said outright that my words were often meant to be symbolic and he called Gnostics the "true" Christians, fully endorsing the process of gnosis. Other important church leaders held similar views and didn't appreciate the growing Christian practice of turning popular ancient legends into 'history.' Another Catholic saint, Dionysius of Areopagite, said that, apart from the wisdom of their *encoded* meanings, the gospels were childish myths.

DK: And they actually *sainted* this guy? I'm surprised they didn't hang him as a heretic—a word which, I recently learned, derives from Greek and just means "able to choose." Pretty funny when you think about it. Anyway, who else didn't march lockstep with the regime?

J: Clement's student, Origen, certainly didn't. Here's another respected early-Christian writer whose work is far more liberal than traditionalists care to believe. Church apologists will sometimes quote Origen to strengthen their case—but Origen's philosophical stance was miles from Christian conservatism. He wasn't Gnostic, though, and in fact wrote treatises refuting a few Gnostic creeds. But he did believe that *all* people would eventually attain salvation which, to him, was a purely intellectual realm where the soul would forever probe the secrets of the Cosmic Divine.

DK: Plainly no fundamentalist.

J: Not in the least. Origin cleanly admitted that many gospel stories were obviously allegorical and that some were not only untrue but were "utterly impossible." He said that even the writings of the Apostles were not "purely historical" and held "incidents that never occurred." Origen felt that literalist Christianity was strictly a product for the simple-minded rank and file. He viewed the subtlety and sophistication of respected pagan philosophy as an exquisite, spiritual high cuisine, whereas the literal form of Christianity was what you might call a kind of fast-food religion for those not wanting to *think*. So Origen viewed literalism as nothing but a pacifier for the masses. He fully realized —and therefore taught his students—that a thorough understanding of Christianity required some solid historical knowledge of the old *pagan* world.

DK: I'm still grappling with the idea that Christianity's roots took hold in the soils of what Christians call 'paganism.'

J: Paganism suffers a lousy reputation that's mostly undeserved. Originally, 'pagan' just indicated someone from the country. Christians began using it derisively for anyone or anything pre-Christian or, *after* my era, *non*-Christian. It basically came to mean "heathen" or "non-believer."

DK: When *I* was fundamentalist, we used the word pagan all the time. The implication was that something or someone outside the *Christian* orbit is lesser in the eyes of God—somehow less valuable or loved. We got these ideas from the Bible, of course, so that's *literally* how we saw it, you could say. Anything 'pagan' was beneath us.

J: It's pretty strange for Christians to belittle such a wide swath of wisdom by maliciously calling it pagan. They sneer at the notion of prayers to the sun, which at least can be witnessed and felt, but won't think twice sending their *own* prayers and reverence off soaring through the darkness of space— to 'the Son.' Still, they spew the word pagan like a curse. This is pure ignorance, though, since Christianity itself is fundamentally a pagan religion.

DK: But surely you'd agree that a lot of pre-Christian religions do certainly hold elements that now seem quite primitive and vile.

J: Sure, but so does Christianity. A good man bears a bestial death before God grants forgiveness or boon? Is this not the very *idea* behind human sacrifice? And what about the Eucharist? Eat my body and drink my blood!?? Sounds kinda primitive to *me* . . .

DK: Many Christians see those words as *symbolic.*

J: And they're sure all the pagan stuff wasn't?

DK: I yield the point.

J: Don't be so tough on paganism. It's not a synonym for witchcraft, you know.

DK: But aren't a lot of pagans avowed atheists?

J: Some are, many aren't. Anyway, what if they are? Atheism carries no inherent iniquity—it's an honest current perspective and nothing more.

DK: Okay, but what do you say to someone who doesn't believe in God?

J: I'd say, which God is it that you don't believe in? Because *I* probably don't believe in that God, either.

DK: Then you're not necessarily down on atheists?

J: I'm not down on *anyone.* I do have trouble grasping, though, why atheists are so bloody sure of their position—they won't allow for even the *prospect* of a 'higher power' nor any *other* truth beyond the known. But is it objective or intelligent to view Life's harmonious brilliance as just another happy turning of fate? At heart, the atheist is one who believes that a living, interactive cosmos—and the idea that he's a direct embodiment of it and critical to the overall scheme—is just comforting, egotistical thinking for spiritual dreamers who can't come to grips with their death. The atheist admits he's not sure how the universe works . . . but he's certain that he knows how it *doesn't.* "It's all evolutionary kismet," he says, "and none of it is miraculous to *me.*" For a being of such high state and consciousness to shun the mere suggestion of a universal life-force is almost comical—like a child in the womb disparaging the ridiculous notion of a mother.

DK: So far, we're on the same page . . . but lots of scientists aren't nearly so inclined, I'm afraid. They say they're atheists *because* of their science.

J: Since the dawn of the modern age, atheists have frequently used 'science' as their nightstick to pummel all supporters of the God theory. And hey, no one could *fault* the atheist for rejecting, even *without* science, the preposterous, violent and senseless gods presented by world religions. But let us agree, as evolutionary science affirms, that species are constantly evolving . . . and not just in form but in *powers of mind* as well. Human beings are a perfect example. Let us further agree—given millenniums of compelling evidence which can no longer be ignored—that there are indeed other civilizations in the cosmos, that a handful have in fact interrelated with humans over the centuries, and that at least one of these 'alien' groups is a mere one million years ahead of you in both scientific technology *and* in the 'technology' of consciousness.

DK: Well, science currently puts the universe at 14 billion years old, and some say it's much older than that. So your premise is not far-fetched. On scales of billions, a million is a pinprick in time—pocket change. I've no trouble thinking that if there *are* more civilized worlds out there, some would very likely be much, much older than ours.

J: Alright, now consider how far humanity's technical knowledge has advanced in just a few hundred years. Can we agree that, to someone in the 1700s, your science would be nothing short of magic?

DK: No doubt it would.

J: So we already know that technology and understanding will continue to expand exponentially . . . that is, at a faster and faster rate. And given how fast things have progressed scientifically on earth in just a few centuries, imagine my proposed ET society with another million years of evolution under its belt and the drastically different reality theirs would be.

DK: Well, we're talking of a species *ten thousand centuries* more advanced. Their knowledge and life would likely be more than we could dream— they might not even be human or even need bodies.

J: Then why would any fair-minded thinker dismiss off-hand the possibility of a godlike being? Humans aren't far from this already. Isn't it *likely* that a creature from a world so radically progressed past your own would seem to present-day earthlings to be, for all practical purposes, a god? With so many ancient, cross-cultural tales of visiting "star people," does it really seem reasonable, given the exceedingly high odds *against* it, to think that such a super race—or even *Homo sapiens*—arose haphazardly, through trillions of cosmic conjunctions, from sea gunk and goo from the swamp?

DK: For me the answer is no. But plenty of scientists, skeptics and other empirical types seem comfortable enough in believing it.

J: It's interesting that science, like religion, holds plenty of strong but unproven beliefs. The only real difference is that the scientist refers to *his* beliefs with a much more dignified term: *theories*. One of them says that a cosmos exploding into existence—and void of all consciousness or life—did somehow create a paradisaical planet whose various systems seem ingeniously connected and birth one startling species after another, many of which have astonishing beauty and intelligence and communicate in ways that make *human* language seem downright primitive. And all of it unfolded through a magical process called "natural selection" during astonishing multi-billion-year streaks of beginner's luck.

DK: Yeah, science says that's how it happened. A while back, a Swedish astrophysicist calculated there are 700 *quintillion* planets in the universe. That's a 7 followed by 20 zeros! Yet, some scientists say that the earth is likely the only planet of its kind. Why anyone would even *believe* this is a topic for another day . . . but if they're right in their current 'theories,' then the chance of life here on earth was roughly 1 in 700 quintillion—which makes winning the lottery seem like a surefire, dead-certain lock. Even so, many people insist there's no miracle or aim in the evolution of life and that Mozart was no more meant than a mosquito.

J: But if this kind of complexly developed world arose against the impossible odds science has claimed, it basically would *be* a miracle, no? I mean you certainly wouldn't be crazy or even 'unscientific' to wonder if it's all just a child of *bonne chance*. Let me share an idea that might help even the skeptics give thought to at least *some* type of cosmic intelligence or 'God' force . . .

Consider the miraculous nature of your own consciousness. Here's an invisible, cohesive energy that is inherently meaningful and self-aware, simultaneously analytical and intuitive, and seemingly limitless in its power to expand, explore, experience and ingeniously create. And if all that stuff weren't wild enough already, this unseen energetic field of awareness you refer to as 'I' can, itself, have powerful 'spiritual' experiences, moving it instantly into other realities while often appearing to skirt the 'laws' of physics.

Impressively, human consciousness can direct its attention, on demand, to anything in its known existence. It can speculate on things it hasn't experienced and can see into past or future with astonishing precision. It relates telepathically to other people—or even to other *species*—sometimes with perfect clarity and regardless of barriers or distance.

It deduces, infers, and, astoundingly, can even tap into knowledge without having learned it, and parts of it are even measurably electro-magnetic. And *this*, the great gift you call *conscious*-ness, is something scientists say takes place within a three-pound chunk of cellular mass called "brain," and evolved—by mere fortune and with no thought or intent— in a universe with no intelligence or life, and solely through this magical science-made mystery called natural selection.

DK: Or at least that's what *some* of 'em claim.

J: But if someone—or some *thing*—did *intend* this amazing wonderstuff called consciousness, which seems the only *sensible* conclusion, think how powerfully brilliant this Force must be.

DK: Well, you make a pretty good point. In my view there's a big difference between healthy skepticism and cocksure insistence there could be no 'intelligent design.' This seems especially unfitting when considering that earthly science is still in its relative infancy. It seems only logical that if a design is truly intelligent, it would *have* to imply a pre-existing *intelligence*. Things that are ingenious, purposeful, coherent, significant—and often even beautiful and compelling—cannot, by definition, happen by chance. Now, the fascinating structure of a beautiful piece of quartz could very well have been a random occurrence. But a human being and the complex genetic code that creates him? I doubt it. I mean, c'mon . . . are the 'realists' arguing that sexual orgasm was really just a biological fluke? Just a happy—let's call it 'shot-in-the-dark'—result of natural selection? With no intelligence directing or even *influencing* the whole shebang? You gotta be *joking*.

So while I do have plenty of questions on how it all came about, here's where I part ways with the average atheist. Because a Marilyn Monroe doesn't come into existence on a lark. For that kind of beauty and elegance to arise, there *must* be a mind that first pictured it. I can't *prove* that, of course. But likewise, if *science* can't be sure that there *isn't* some cosmic intelligence at play—even as more and more physicists are thinking there might be— it should at least stop *saying* there isn't. And even scientists will confess that the world contains things which at least *seem* mind-bogglingly brilliant . . . yet they swear it isn't backed by intelligence!! This conclusion is so far from honesty and reason, so weird in its refusal to concede the obvious, I marvel at those who still babble it like it ever made some kind of sense.

J: When you gaze into microscopes too long, you sometimes overlook the bigger picture and forget the one doing the gazing. To assume something doesn't exist because it can't be gauged or computed is plainly absurd.

Love itself has never been proven in a lab—but even a scientist knows it's real, and I doubt there's an atheist anywhere who hasn't felt it. So science and spirit are not incompatible just because spirit isn't yet measured by machine.

DK: Still, for many in the scientific community these days, the topic's not even respectable—there's no debate to be had.

J: It's scientific pride at its worst. "Yes, yes, we've heard all this before," they'll tell you, as if dismissing an idea without firmly establishing anything has settled the matter and rendered it no longer relevant. "Trust us," they say . . . "we're *scientists.*" The original flat-earthers themselves, it's the same group that smugly gave you a static, earth-centered universe and later figured out the entire paradigm was *wrong.* So it's rational to respect what science can prove—but not to take its word for things it can't. And remember that a *description* is not the same as an *explanation.* Science may tell you something *happens* but it may not know how or why and it surely doesn't see the full truth. The scientist knows next to nothing of his own consciousness—but he's *sure* it's all in his head.

DK: I think it's just the emotional charge of the word "god," and the nutty ideas that surround it, that understandably put off most atheists.

J: Sure, the atheist hears the word "god" and thinks of some mythical, magical character from ancient religion. Naturally he's repelled, which is indeed a sensible response. But why would he assume, in his worship of the 'true god' of science, that a seemingly supernatural being could never be accounted for in terms that are strictly scientific? And never mind that there may be civilizations in the cosmos *many* millions of years advanced beyond earth. Would they not be gods by comparison?

DK: Oh, I doubt there would be any dispute. It'd be no different from our modern capabilities compared with Neanderthal cavemen—and *that's* a difference of just thirty or forty *thousand* years. What happens over a million is only a guess.

J: Of course. So the atheist can be as righteously narrow-minded as any believer he's scorned. He'll gladly wave the proud banner of 'science' . . . but only until it's used *against* him. He asks where a godlike creature would've come from, never thinking it might have evolved by the same 'scientific' means that led to the atheist himself. Now, the atheist may argue—incorrectly, as he'll one day discover—that there's no reason to think that *individual* consciousness implies one that's universal. But when the atheist demands to know how this vast cosmic consciousness arose, one might fairly respond by asking, "Well, how did *yours?*"

The atheist finds the universe inherently chaotic and aimless . . . mindless, blind, deaf and mute. But if so, how did a tiny, single-celled amoeba crawl out from the river and grow into a graceful gazelle? I mean talk about great ambition! And science says the cosmos tends always toward "entropy"—disorder, upheaval and breakdown—not toward intelligent systemization and evolution. How and why did it organize and advance unaided for billions of years? Somehow it churned out a species so brilliantly put together, so self-aware and autonomous, so ingeniously inventive that it now builds intricate, high-tech spacecrafts and sends them rocketing off to other parts of the galaxy with arithmetic precision. How did this all take place without direction? Could it be that natural selection is actually *part* of some intelligent design?

DK: Great questions.

J: But, to answer them, the atheist is forced to spout the most inane, theoretical, jargonistic gibberish you've ever heard. He foolishly insists on either evolution *or* intelligent design, not allowing that the great Life Force is quite skillful using both things at once. In fact, are the two not *bound* together? Even humans must wait for technology's 'evolution' before conceived designs are perfected. You don't go from wagon to Ferrari in one leap . . . but would anyone say there was no *intelligence* in the wagon? Yet, when discussing the evolution of man from beginning to present, that's basically what science has concluded—and not just about the wagon, amazingly, but also about the Ferrari!!

DK: So the atheist is a walking paradox.

J: He's a living marvel, amusingly insisting that he's nothing but billions of stupendously fortunate steps removed from slime.

DK: Agreed. And who's to say the slime wasn't part of the early plan? I mean every creation, whether human *or* cosmic, has to start *somewhere*. That kind of 'scientific' dogmatism seems to go beyond mere theories and sometimes seems to trigger something deeply and personally *threatening*. I always wonder at someone blind to the obvious brilliance of the natural world. . . even while he himself stands as a rather remarkable example.

J: How ironic, though, that a godlike being of such potential power and genius prefers to see himself instead as just a fortunate fickleness of fate: the universe belched, and out popped a self-confirmed atheist!

DK: Personal perspectives will differ, of course, but I know lots of atheists with really sharp minds.

J: Oh, absolutely. Nor can the atheist be *blamed* for his disbelief. If he's not had a cosmic experience, how can he hope to accept or take seriously all that such experiences imply? And really, the atheist is often the most honest soul in the room. Religion offers him an assortment of deities, all with strange penchants and quirks. Finding no proof for the truth of these beings, nor very much sense in their reported words and behavior, he simply chooses to ignore them—and surely nothing's unreasonable about *that*. Actually, there's not much difference between the atheist and the Christian. The Christian has chosen to reject all gods but one, while the atheist won't make that final exception.

DK: I would guess nearly all of us have questions on the God concept— I've certainly had *my* share over the years. I think we skeptics would do well to release old religious ideas of those ill-tempered, dictatorial gods and to think more in terms of a responsive, intelligent, universal *something* that somehow connects everything. How else could we explain our mental telepathy and other psychic affairs?

J: Modern physics may be taking you in that direction . . .

DK: But paganism, atheistic or not, has a pretty dark history at times.

J: A good part of pagan history is no darker than Christianity's— and some of it far *less* so. Lots of pagan societies were quite spiritually advanced, and the pagan world boasts some of the greatest cultural, intellectual, scientific and artistic accomplishments ever. Consider some of humanity's most brilliant minds: Socrates, Pythagoras, Hypatia of Alexandria—she who was lovingly murdered by a mob of Christians— Marcus Aurelius, Hippocrates, Plotinus, Aristotle, Diogenes. All of these great thinkers were essentially what Christians call 'pagan.'

DK: Okay, you win . . . paganism doesn't suck. But tell me further how it ties to your life in the gospels.

J: C'mon, I already gave you a dozen examples of specific parallels between the stories of my life and those of Osiris-Dionysus. What more proof do you need, Señor Cynic?

DK: As much as you can muster, Master.

J: Alright, let's go back to the Eucharist. The concept of divine communion through consuming the god is older than heartburn. It's found even in the *Book of the Dead*, which predates my birth by centuries. Common in the Mysteries, too, it gave initiates a chance to 'unite' with Osiris-Dionysus.

DK: I thought the bread and wine thing started with the famous Last Supper.

J: Don't confuse the Last Supper with the first communion. Long before Christianity were the Mysteries of the Greek god Mithras, who's vaguely linked to the earlier Persian deity Mithra. The religion celebrated a "holy communion," and its bread wafers often bore the sign of a cross. And the brotherhood to Christianity goes further. The Mithras sect had at least half a dozen sacraments that were later adopted unchanged by the Catholic Church, and overt pagan symbology runs throughout the Vatican. But don't think for a second that insiders aren't aware of what it means. Even the pope's miter headgear symbolizes the ancient Babylonian fish god Dagon, said to have been worshiped by the Philistines in Judges 16. The pope's pinecone-tipped staff directly represents the pineal gland, which philosopher René Descartes referred to as "the seat of the soul" and esoteric groups have long considered the location of the "third eye" of spiritual gifts and wisdom.

DK: Sounds basically like a cult of the occult. And let's discuss the virgin birth a bit more. Until you told me about Osiris-Dionysus, I thought *that* was strictly a Christian thing as well.

J: You should spend more time in libraries. Ancient religions are so pregnant with stories of virgin mothers that you'd think the Holy Spirit was hopped-up on horny goat weed. In the pre-Christian Mysteries alone you've got Dionysus born of the virgin Semele; Aion of the virgin Kore; Attis of the virgin Cybele; and Adonis of the virgin Myrrha. And that's to name just a few.

DK: *Godfrey Daniel!* A lot of miraculous pregnancies for one planet.

J: And we've not even really warmed the engine. Virgin birth stories are connected with names from Alexander to Zoroaster. Divine or supernatural conceptions are also attributed to the mothers of Buddha, Krishna, Plato, Pythagoras, Augustus Caesar and the boy-king Tut. In one account, even the mother of Mongol mass murderer Genghis Khan claims that her child is the son of the *sun*, while another story says he was the product of an interspecies mating between a gray wolf and a white doe. Centuries of virgin mother mythology has women knocked up by everything from gods, spirits and animals, to planets, lotus flowers and mystical wisps of wind.

DK: Well, I have to admit that some of the pagan virgin birth stories are no more unlikely than Christianity's.

J: The simple truth is that claims of my mother's sexual virtue were nothing special. The sexless mother idea's been around since Egyptians worshiped the virgin goddess Isis, whose depictions sometimes show her suckling the infant Horus. Centuries later, this well-traveled image was directly stolen by Christians in their nearly-identical portrayal of 'Madonna and Child.'

DK: The Immaculate Conception is starting to sound like an immaculately conceived hoax.

J: Hang on there, my Protestant friend . . . you're confusing the doctrine of Immaculate Conception with the doctrine of the virgin birth, and they aren't the same thing at all. The Immaculate Conception idea says that my mother—despite her own normal beginnings—was nonetheless free of original sin. And in one respect the claim is at least logical: if you swear to the world that your guy is the Divine Dude incarnate, you'd better ensure he's from really respectable roots.

DK: So you paint his mother white as the 'virgin' snow and portray her to the masses as a model of moral perfection.

J: Can't be avoided. Most mother of God legends depict her as perpetual maiden since God's mother must be entirely without the 'urge to merge' in the bedroom. But religion's done women no service by making the ideal woman into a 'virgin mother.' The very phrase itself is conflicting.

DK: So this virgin mother theme has been around awhile.

J: As old as political corruption, I'd say. For a true godman, a requirement on the application.

DK: Okay, what other Christian/pagan ties have ya got?

J: Oh, I could talk for hours about pagan elements that were melted in the fires of the church and recast in the Christian mold. And not just the 'son of God' idea. Christians were picking pagan pockets from the start. They stole every fable, symbol, legend, myth and sacrament they could —pardon the pun—lay their hands on. From cradle to cross, gospel stories of my life are based largely on models from paganism, including the Nativity and its attendant wise men; water baptism; the Holy Spirit; the Alpha/ Omega; and of course your basic heaven and your hell. Even the founding image of me as the LOGOS incarnate was a centuries-old pagan model, and the Greeks referred to the herald god Hermes using this very title.

Also inherited from pre-Christian traditions were the cross, the sign of the fish, salvation from soul corruption, springtime crucifixion and resurrection, three hours of daytime darkness, a short descent to the underworld, ascension to heaven . . . and Apocalypse with a Final Judgment.

DK: Then none of these themes originated with Christianity?

J: Nope, nor even with Judaism. The Jews never thought of mystically uniting with any slain-and-resurrected messiah. That part of the Christian motif came straight from the Mystery traditions and, before that, the ancient religions of Egypt. So this stuff was purely 'pagan' —if you choose to label it that way—and most of it existed *centuries* before Christianity.

DK: Well, shoot . . . at least Christians have their Easter eggs.

J: Actually, that little ritual has its roots with an old Germanic fertility goddess called *Ēostre*, or *Ostara*. So Christians own neither Easter nor its beautifully decorated eggs.

DK: Damn, *another* sacred holiday scrambled. You're raining all over the Christian parade. I put this stuff in print and we'll need riot gear . . .

CHAPTER FORTY

DK: I clearly should've been more careful checking my religion. For me, this heavy Christian-pagan correlation is a shock.

J: Well, it's no shock to scholars and theologians. Some of this stuff's been known for many centuries.

DK: Evidently, Christian writers weren't aware of it.

J: Are you kidding? Lots of 'em knew all about it. But as religious faithful tend to do, they didn't let facts disrupt their agendum and frequently obscured the truth. Take the Christian historian Eusebius of Caesarea, for instance. He's one of the faith's most glowing champions—some will call him the father of church history. But *as* a church father he was a pretty dysfunctional parent and was hardly the pillar of goodness you'd expect. At one point, Eusebius was even condemned as a heretic. A good bit of boot licking later, however, he was chosen to be the official biographer and historian for the infamous emperor Constantine the Great. Eusebius' *main* Christian 'achievement' was that he deviously concocted a fake chronology of the church, which others, including Saint Augustine, later based their *own* writings upon.

DK: So anything centered on the work of Eusebius was built on a platform of twigs.

J: Unfortunately so. The man was such a world-class liar he could've easily made high public office. One scholar calls him "the first thoroughly dishonest historian of antiquity." In fact, it was Eusebius who magically produced a work attributed to Josephus that no one had seen before. Josephus, of course, is one of the more prominent early Jewish historians.

DK: I've read a bit about General Josephus, a common source of first-century background on the Jews—even if some have questioned his reliability. Some people reference his work to help prove up *your* existence.

J: But until Eusebius came along, Christians didn't resort to the records of Josephus. Why would they? Josephus never talked about me. But then Eusebius shows up with a 'new and improved' version of the man's writings. Suddenly the long-dead historian is declaring that I was the messiah while giving previously unreported 'facts' of my life—even about my appearance before the Roman Prefect Pontius Pilate.

DK: Apparently it fooled the young church.

J: But it didn't fool modern-day researchers. Whoever doctored the writings of Josephus was a little too ambitious. In a real explosion of creativity, the mysterious editor has Josephus claiming I miraculously cured Pilate's wife of an illness, so Pilate decided to release me. Adding even more *blood* money to my story, he says the Jewish priests then secretly bribed Pilate to proceed with my execution nevertheless.

DK: A total contradiction of the gospels.

J: Yes, and that's not all. To refute the anti-Christian argument that my friends took my body from the tomb, the Eusebian version of Josephus makes another astonishing claim. It says thirty Roman centurions stood guard at my tomb along with *one thousand* Jews. Now, if all this were true, you'd have to wonder why no biblical writers bothered recording it.

DK: Okay, it's pretty obvious that Eusebius was a true Christian patriot. But should his 'finagling' of the facts discredit the man completely?

J: Well, it should at least discredit him as an unbiased source of reporting. And it should certainly cause the world to wonder why so much Christian dishonesty through the centuries has even been *needed*. But no, Eusebius' heart wasn't made of granite. In some ways he proved to be quite brave, finally confronting the powerful Constantine on the openly fraudulent nature of the Nicene Creed. Despite his involvement in structuring the Creed at the First Council of Nicaea, Eusebius later wrote to Constantine and confessed that he and his bishop buddies had committed a serious hypocrisy in signing it. The Nicene Creed was a coerced work of fiction, and Eusebius later admitted to Constantine that he endorsed it only because he feared what might befall him if he *didn't*. As it happened, his suspicions were well-founded, and every bishop who rejected the Creed was soon after exiled as criminal—by direct orders of the emperor.

DK: Then perhaps Eusebius wasn't a fraudster after all. He may have been just showing some political savvy.

J: No, I think Christendom should wake up and smell the snake oil here. Eusebius once wrote that it was an act of virtue to mislead people if it would further the cause of the church and, of course, the victims' own spiritual well-being. In one of his works he's got a section called "How it may be Lawful and Fitting to use Falsehood as Medicine, and for the Benefit of those who Want to be Deceived." In other words, it's alright to lie when our 'truth' won't suffice.

DK: I see what you mean. He doesn't exactly inspire unwavering trust.

J: And Eusebius was no isolated case of some overzealous convert forming his own 'truth.' Other notable Christian apologists were every bit as deceitful and one-sided. Justin Martyr, another guy whose work the religion looks to for validation, once declared that anything noble or worthy that may have emerged from paganism was in fact the rightful property of the church!

DK: *Heh heh.* A little over-the-top, for sure.

J: And not to be outdone in Christian conceit, Saint Augustine declared boldly about two hundred years later that if Plato and other pagan philosophers had said anything "in harmony with the faith," Christians were to resist the earlier teachings and reclaim these truths from those who had taken "unlawful possession" of them.

DK: Hmmm. I'm beginning to wonder what these nutty church fathers were smokin' . . .

CHAPTER FORTY-ONE

DK: If it makes you feel any better, I'm beginning to see your point—that is, the need to distance yourself from this ongoing Christian insanity. I've witnessed some half-baked stuff from the church in my day and I did learn a bit of its history . . . but I never knew this humbuggery happened right off the blocks. I'm starting to see I've led a sheltered life.

J: And I haven't told ya the *worst* of it.

DK: Hey, if you've got the dirt, my friend, I've got the shovel and cart.

J: Okay, then, back to Justin Martyr. He may be a respected church father but he was straight from the cuckoo's nest. Martyr, among other Christian defenders over the years, embraced an idea called "Diabolical Mimicry"— a beautifully imaginative theory devised to explain why many Christian doctrines and practices so closely resembled those of old *pagan* traditions. The premise was that Satan, in a brilliant preemptive strike, plagiarized Christianity *before* its arrival to disgrace it when it finally showed up.

DK: Oh, now *that's* priceless. The Greatest Story Ever Foretold.

J: And Martyr wasn't alone in his delusions. Many thousands of Christians were no more reasonable than he—thoughtless faith had killed intellect, honesty and sense. Even now, in the modern age of deep-space voyaging, things haven't changed very much. Billions of religious believers are just as naïve.

DK: I'm stunned there was so much historical and philosophical fraud among church 'intellectuals.'

J: But don't throw 'em all in one heap. Ancient Christians were never just one big, happy clan of saints and martyrs agreed on each written 'truth.' You basically had two camps. On one side were the literalists, who swore that every piece of *their* godman story—with me in the starring role— was absolute historical *fact* and the world was soon coming to an end. Churchmen like Eusebius, Augustine and Martyr held this view. Across the street were the symbolists, like Gnostics, who understood that most of the elements in Christian scriptures were figurative and based on the old pagan myths.

DK: How'd the church come to take the literal view?

J: In a nutshell, Christian and pagan Gnostics were practically pummeled from existence. This was accomplished systematically by the upper Roman establishment with the help of rulers like Constantine and, decades later, emperor Theodosius—the guy responsible for making Christianity the official religion of the empire. The Gnostics were generally peaceful folk and mostly content with striving to attain enlightenment. Somewhat elitist in their thinking, they didn't do very much preaching, so they weren't out converting people or fighting to lay the groundwork for institutions— exactly the kind of thing they *didn't* want. But literalists, especially those with influence or power, were very much interested in establishing an *imperial* religion that would strengthen their political control.

DK: So they built a scary, soul-threatening faith that kept everyone servile and meek.

J: Yes, and they brutally wiped out the 'competition.' You hear lots of talk about Christians being persecuted—but they've done their share of it, too. By the time Arcadius took the throne in 395, his Christian predecessors had run roughshod for decades over prominent groups of pagans by saddling them with burdensome laws, inhibiting their social advancement and, to *really* wipe out the vermin, disallowing their heirs any estate inheritance.

DK: How very *Christian* of 'em . . .

J: At the extreme, Roman Christians would even confiscate pagan holy sites, looting and sacking their religious treasuries and sanctuaries while public officials often did nothing to stop it. Many are the fearful who've uttered the prayer, "Oh Father, please save us from Christians!!"

DK: Man, what ever happened to that oft-touted Christian tolerance?

J: Oh, don't be fooled. Some of these Roman administrators were Christian in name only. Constantine, a man more accurately called a Christo-pagan ruler, was a virtual dictator. And though he was Rome's first 'Christian' emperor, he *might* possibly qualify as a member of history's Top 100 tyrants. Like emperor Theodosius after him, Constantine wanted a 'catholic,' or universal, religion for his empire, with him unchallenged lord of state. But, ruthless as he was—the guy would've been a *terrific* 10th-century pope— the merciless emperor naturally preferred a more *peaceful* way to manage and manipulate the masses. And though it wasn't peaceful very long, literalist Christianity seemed to be just what the doctor had ordered.

DK: I've read that even under some of Rome's so-called 'Christian' regimes, Christians weren't necessarily spared from persecution.

J: No, not even by other Christians. And Christian-against-Christian violence is a familiar theme. Have a look at history and you'll find that, through wars and various other settings of sheer bigotry, Christians have died at the hands of their fellow believers about as often as they've been targeted by governments. Until about 250 CE, even *Roman* abuse of Christians was relatively light. When Emperor Decius came along, however, oppression of Christians went mainstream and lasted decades.

DK: But Constantine's rule apparently changed *everything*.

J: Definitely. After three centuries of staunch rejection by most Romans, Christianity at last began spreading when Constantine himself formally professed it—the religion got the big boost it needed to start permeating the Holy Roman Empire decades later. And for some it was an easy transition since Christianity was so like the familiar old Mystery paths. But there *was* a critical difference: this newer, literal version was authoritarian and left no room for dissent. All other views were blasphemy, said the church, and God would punish the faithless soon enough. That is, I suppose, if the church didn't handle it first.

DK: I do know the New Testament is big on obedience. The faithful should submit to the government, wives to their husbands, children to their parents and such.

J: Right, and it's quite informative that the New Testament even instructs slaves to obey their masters. In Christianity the believer is indeed a slave to the faith—good stewardship is believing and doing as you're told. For a huge control freak like Constantine, endorsing a new religion of subservience encouraged unquestioning support for authority— by direct instructions from *God*, no less! In contrast to the Mysteries, which were practiced by many of the day's most respected philosophers, literalist Christianity quickly dispensed with those pesky non-conformist intellectuals who advocated freedom . . . and free *thinking*. They were dangers not only to the faith itself, but to the empire. They tended to decry Rome's oppression tactics of guilt-based religious 'obligation,' political and physical bullying, and—if all else failed—unrestrained out-and-out terror.

DK: Like the powerful leaders who advanced it, then, the Christian religion required absolute obedience and loyalty—and not just to the church itself, but to the *state*. First Peter 2 urges submission to *every institution and king*.

J: Yes, and because of rulers like Constantine, Christianity's historical shift from inner authority—the Holy Spirit—to outer authority had begun, tragically destroying in its path any accent on purification and self-liberation.

DK: But you've gotta give the guy credit. Constantine had far more impact on the world than he ever *dreamed* of having. Who would've thought this villain would play such a big role in one of history's most popular religions?

J: The man was a colorful character, for sure . . .

DK: Another story about him has always had me stumped. Long after his so-called 'conversion' to Christianity, Constantine claimed that several years earlier, just before a significant battle, he and his troops had seen some kind of cross or Christogram showing in the noonday sky. Next to it, he claimed, were the words, "In this sign conquer." He went to bed baffled by it all and says that you then approached him in his dreams and told him to wipe out his enemies by having his warriors paint the cross symbol onto their shields. He later won the battle decisively.

J: So, if we can believe Constantine, he dutifully murdered his fellow human beings under instruction, guidance and protection of the 'Prince of Peace.'

DK: I guess you could see it that way . . . onward, Christian soldier 'n all.

J: It makes for a good story, perhaps, but it's more of that God-is-on-*our*-side kind of thinking—like Constantine declaring that Lord Jesus helped him slaughter his brothers. You couldn't mangle my message any more than that.

DK: Even so, Constantine's war victory apparently gave him motive to spread his newly founded religion through the realm.

J: Well, his motivations were *suspect*, to say the *least*. But all things considered—during his lifetime, anyway—Constantine's plan to convert the empire was pretty much a bust. Even Eusebius, who died shortly after Constantine, could name only a few Christian townships in the entire Holy Land. The main thing is that Constantine did whatever it took to enforce allegiance, brutally eliminating any and all opposition— political *and* philosophical. He wanted a compliant citizenry and hoped Christianity would help provide it.

DK: Hard to believe this very same savage had such a huge impact on the shaping of the scriptures and the Nicene Creed.

J: The Creed, like the young church itself, was every bit as political as religious. Literalist by design, it was directly meant to help Constantine and his bishops consolidate power. The Nicene Creed was a blatant work of heresy—and the bishops knew it. At the time it was ratified, very few Roman citizens gave the Creed any concern. Having been raised on the symbolism of the Mysteries, most Romans wouldn't have believed a literal godman story—though few would risk publicly denouncing it, of course. Even after its substantial modifications during the First Council of Constantinople in 381, it would still be many generations before the Nicene Creed became widely accepted church doctrine. Now it's recited by millions of Christians each week. Ironically, they can credit a wickedly brutal Roman dictator for much of its tone and content.

DK: Evidently, Constantine was his era's version of the Christian right wing.

J: But with him there *was* no other wing—it was his way or the graveyard. Lemme tell ya what a sweetheart the guy was, this man referred to by Catholics as *Saint* Constantine and so revered by the Eastern Church as to be christened "the Thirteenth Apostle." Once he was happy with proceedings in Nicaea, Constantine went home to embark on a monstrous killing spree, wiping out a lengthy list of longtime friends, associates, and theological foes in Nicaea. He even had his wife Fausta murdered along with his own son Cripus and his sister's son Licinius, who was just a young boy.

DK: Ah, the familiar conservative emphasis on family. It seems the poor Gnostics and pagans never stood a chance against a killing machine like the Thirteenth Apostle.

J: Nope. And even though Gnostics were among the earliest Christians, they were bedeviled to near-extinction by Christian literalists before ever getting their historical day in court. Even most of their *writings* were destroyed.

DK: And since history is written by victors, it's no big mystery why we don't read much about Gnostics.

J: No, in fact if Constantine and some of his successors had gotten their way, the world might never have known much about them. Luckily for Gnostics, though, a funny thing happened on the way to oblivion . . .

In December 1945, an Egyptian farmer stumbled upon a stupendous archaeological bonanza: thirteen ancient leather-bound papyrus codices buried across the river from Nag Hammadi, a town near the east bluff of the upper Nile River valley. Known now as the Nag Hammadi Library, or the 'Gnostic Gospels,' these old Coptic writings comprise about a thousand pages and represent more than fifty separate manuscripts, some of which are actual Gnostic scriptures. The newly discovered works provided important information about Gnosticism and its wide-ranging views on philosophy, religion and life. Some were even brought into use by early Christian communities, which took the various texts and then plugged in changes where needed.

DK: So Gnostics finally had a confirmed place in the evolution of Christian history.

J: True, but their bearings were oceans apart from the literalists. Gnostics viewed literalists as the ones who were misguided, and they considered Christian literalism mindlessly superficial and half-witted. They felt it fostered an "imitation" church that mistook symbolism for history and encouraged blind faith without imparting much spiritual wisdom.

DK: So each group saw the other as heretics.

J: Right. And I should mention that 'Gnostic' is just a convenient umbrella term for a spiritually diverse bunch of sects that sometimes clashed. But Gnostics were on the right track. They sought an *inner* knowledge— a supernatural joining with the divine that couldn't be shaken or lost. So Gnostics were considered a threat since they saw no need for religious organizations and hierarchies. Indeed, many Gnostics viewed matter as evil and the greatest barrier to their ascension. They were seeking a spiritual kingdom *within*, while literalists were busy building an *earthly* one.

DK: Hey, the literalists did a damn good job of it, I can tell you that. Several years back, TIME magazine said the Catholic Church alone was generating billions of bucks in revenue every year. Running the Vatican is serious business.

J: Well, imagine the fortune *any* institution could amass given centuries of diplomatic immunity, a private bank with questionable oversight, and total exemption from any and all world taxes. Did the article give a figure on court settlements?

DK: I know this much: Christian organizations have owned or held interest in everything from theme parks and golf courses to beach front retreats and hotels. They're also into radio, TV, merchandising, manufacturing— even international banking. There's really no doubt about it: Christianity is a thriving endeavor.

J: Surely Saint Constantine would smile . . .

CHAPTER FORTY-TWO

DK: So it's pretty clear that Gnostics and other ancient spiritual groups had huge effects on the development of the Christian religion. The new faith wasn't just a branch from the tree of Judaism.

J: No, and even the *Jewish* impact was a complex mix. Religions can shape cultures, it's true—but cultures shape religions as well. Many thousands of exiled Jews were profoundly affected by the great pagan societies of what was then called Babylonia, or present-day Iraq. Egyptians across the Sinai left their mark in the region as well. And don't forget the Greeks: they too had influence on the Holy Land. By the time I was born, Galilee was so rife with foreign bias that Jews sometimes called it "the land of the Gentiles."

DK: That's interesting, because Biblical Palestine is usually thought of as an obscure, mostly barren country with practically no ties to the outside world.

J: Many people have that impression—but we weren't the isolated backwater hicks that most of them envision. Palestine was really a cultural melting pot. In Gadara, there was a school of pagan philosophy. On Galilee's southern border in the town of Scythopolis sat a center for the Mysteries of Dionysus. Not far from Jerusalem, the cities of Ascalon and Larissa produced 'pagan' philosophers who were known even as far away as Rome. But of course, having been Christian so long, you already knew this, right?

DK: My ignorance is dwarfed only by my embarrassment.

J: Well, you're not alone in that ignorance. Most Christians don't venture far beyond traditional Bible groups. They memorize verses and learn some historical background but seldom ask how their religion *evolved*. They don't examine its foundation.

DK: But even if Christianity was a blend of what appears to be a kind of Greco/Judeo paganism, wasn't your personal message of salvation something new?

J: Not in every sense. Long before me, the ancient Persian prophet Zoroaster proclaimed: "I am the Way, the Truth, and the Light." Lao Tzu and the Buddha said nearly the same thing. And these, along with other great teachers, came well before the Christian era. Earlier we discussed Mithras, the god of fire and light and the central figure of Mithraism.

Mithras was widely reverenced by Romans, and his worship was spread by Roman soldiers to the farthest reaches of the empire. He was known as "the Way," "the Truth," "the Light," "the Life," "the Word," "the Son of God," and even "the Good Shepherd."

DK: Exactly the names later assigned to *you*.

J: Yes, and Mithras was frequently pictured with a lamb, just as I am, and his followers—like mine and those of Osiris-Dionysus—celebrated their god's birthday on December 25th. And there's a *reason* all these deities of light show up in late December. It's the time of the Northern Hemisphere's winter solstice, when days are shortest and the 'high noon' sun makes its lowest zenith of the year. This period signaled the end of the bleak 'days of darkness,' as the daylight hours would soon increase after solstice. Grateful to their saviors for 'bringing light to the world,' ancient worshipers, like Mithras devotees, honored the special occasion with gifts, candles, bells and hymns.

DK: Lucky for the church there's no trademark on pagan rituals . . .

J: The Mithras legend also states he was born from a rock and laid to rest in a rock tomb called PETRA, the proper form of the altered PETROS, or Peter, the name I assign in the gospel to the "rock" of the church. And the Mithraic atonement legend is suspiciously 'Christian' as well. In the cave temples where Mithras was often worshiped, the most prominent image is a *tauroctony*—a scene in which the godman slays a sacrificial bull, thereby giving eternal life to the faithful through the age-old theme of spilling perfectly innocent blood to bail the guilty. Importantly, the atonement stories of both Mithras and Jesus carry heavy astronomical *and* astrological allusion. And surely not by coincidence, both 'events' take place near the vernal equinox, historically a time of adoring the 'resurrected' sun.

DK: So, again, Christianity and the Mysteries share a bunk.

J: Yes, and much like Christians, Mithras' followers also believed in a final 'day of judgment' when their savior would descend from heaven and condemn all non-believers to their fate. Not surprisingly, the deceased *faithful* were to be resurrected and delivered into 'paradise,' a word that derived from the Persians. Had enough, or would you like another serving?

DK: Heck, no point in holding back now. You've gone and stirred the embers so you may as well fan the flames. And why not? Now I've lost the Catholic *and* the Protestant endorsements, both. No one's left to offend . . .

CHAPTER FORTY-THREE

DK: Well, congratulations, my long-revered friend. In one afternoon you've knocked ninety percent off your stock.

J: But isn't it time to get this stuff on the table? The church keeps selling me as God's Superman, so my message gets lost in translation. I'm seen as an idol with unlimited powers but use them only to save a few thousand humans from hell. What a colossal con game! And not even very creative— that soul-saving scam had been around practically forever.

DK: So, ancient cultures had *often* laid claim to various saviors, messiahs, prophets, or so-called 'messengers of God.'

J: Right, and many were said to have had miraculous births, performed great wonders, risen from the dead and all that. Most of these characters were strictly mythological—but some were quite historically human and preceded me by hundreds of years. Christianity was built upon myths that were very much older and firmly established at the time of my birth. To complicate things still further, not one claim about me in the Bible is a proven historical fact . . . *not one*.

DK: There's certainly no arguing *that*. After centuries of archaeological and other scientific study, support for your very *existence* remains slim and theoretical at best—some say we have far better evidence for *ghosts*. And even though the Romans typically kept meticulous records, we've not found any Roman writing showing you ever encountered Pontius Pilate. Skeptics say there's no real proof you ever lived and, even if there *were*, it wouldn't confirm a single claim in the Bible except that you did exist. And that brings up still another deal breaker. Nowhere outside of the Christian religion is there any validation of your life. Nearly thirty well-known, non-Christian authors wrote either during your lifetime or within a hundred years after, and none of them references *you*— not even the great Jewish philosopher Philo Judaeus. About fifty of his works still survive, but the guy never mentions your name—which he surely would've done if he believed the Jews' messiah had arrived.

J: Maybe I wasn't the celebrity you've been sold.

DK: But that worries me. You'd think that the very first earthly appearance of 'God's only son' would command a bit more coverage by the networks. Except for conflicting New Testament accounts, we really know nothing about you.

For instance, what about the historical record penned by Justus of Tiberias? He was one of Philo's contemporaries and lived near Capernaum, a place you were said to have visited quite often. Justus composed a history dating back to the days of Moses and extending through his own lifetime. If anyone were likely to write of you in that region it would've been him— 'specially with you out raising the dead 'n such. In all of Justus' works, however, *your* name never pops up. And you already explained that the passages about you in the writings of Josephus were phony and inserted by someone else.

J: It's true that Josephus didn't write about me. And even Origen admitted that Josephus would never have accepted the Christian claims of my godhood since he sided with the Romans in rejecting any Jewish messiah. Josephus thought the Emperor Vespasian was the true, divinely blessed political world ruler. And the Church wasn't pleased with his candor. A couple centuries past his death, they censured poor Origen as a heretic— which is too bad, really, because Origen was as loyal as they come. Figuring that I'd like him better without testicles, the poor guy actually neutered himself in a show of religious submission: his emasculation proclamation.

DK: *Ouch.* Self-inflicted castration—the unkindest cut of all! Now, *that's* what you call giving it up for Jesus!!

J: *Heh heh.* Nothing more devoted than a eunuch in a tunic . . .

DK: We don't all have the *faith* of an Origen, though—and from my view there's every cause to *doubt.* By comparison, we've got trainloads more info on the life of Islam's Muhammad than we do about you. As you say, not a single bit of your life has ever been proven, and most Bible scholars say that none of the New Testament writers even *met* you . . . which is obvious from the tone and structure of their work. New Testament expert Rudolf Bultmann once said that it's hopeless to know anything factual about you since the gospels are too patchy, inconsistent and legendary to believe. So, historically speaking, you've hardly got a wave to walk on. Even the brilliant doctor Albert Schweitzer—himself a serious Christian and a decent theologian, in fact—referred to you as an "ineffable mystery." Schweitzer said the Christ of the Christian gospels can't be proved.

J: Well, he was right. The biblical Christ is a *composite* figure—a mythological fusion of pagan-based godmen from antiquity. I wasn't that man at all. I was sharing a message of love and forgiveness, teaching even higher things to those who were ready to hear. Once I pulled chocks and left town, all kinds of claims began spreading in Christianity's quest for new converts. A few decades on, I'm made into a kind of Jewified, apocalyptic version of Osiris-Dionysus, the godman of the Mystery religions.

DK: Then you weren't the guy we read about in the gospels.

J: How *could* I be? The combination of a dozen fictional characters rolled into one is . . . well, nothing but a cartoon star.

DK: This won't be big at church camp, I can tell ya.

J: But these are the cold, hard facts. Myths that for centuries had been seen as allegorical were suddenly made into 'history' by Christian literalists.

DK: I think the world just lost a hero. A lot of folks take comfort in a fella who can alter the weather, summon the sleeping dead and turn water into Shiraz.

J: Making me special is the trap. It keeps you from questioning the church's 'truth' and hinders your spiritual growth. The goal is to give up dependence on 'authorities' and follow your heart instead. So much that's written after a teacher departs is just gossip that can't be confirmed. As stories make the rounds over the years, saints can wind up sounding like heroes from a comic strip.

DK: I guess every field has its spin doctors. Yet I don't see how Christianity is so wildly successful with its obvious pagan descent.

J: It's verifiable fact, nevertheless. The church's uncomfortable truth is that every important claim about me was made of other 'deities' long before. Scientifically, the Christian story is no more defensible than the others, and most major gospel themes are found in pre-Christian traditions— even heralding stars, angelic annunciations . . . and of course those ever-convenient, specially informed shepherds.

DK: Okay, why don't we finish this multiple messiahs bit with a few of the more *famous* ancient figures who've been honored as blessed or divine.

J: Well, two of the best-known names, of course, would be India's Krishna and the very first Buddha of Nepal. Then there's Osiris, Horus and Thulis of Egypt; Zoroaster and Mithra of Persia; Baal and Taut of Phoenecia; Indra of Tibet; Bali of Orissa; Thammuz of Mesopotamia and Attis of Phrygia.

DK: Ye gods!

J: We've also got Quetzalcoatl of Mexico; Quirinus of Rome; the sun goddess Amaterasu-Omikami of Japan; Hesus of the Celtic Druids; Crite of Chaldaea; Muhammad of Arabia; and Prometheus of Greece.

DK: Saints deceased! With so many prophets and saviors coming and going, you'd hope for not a sinner in sight.

J: And that's a really short list of nearly *four thousand* documented figures that various groups or cultures over the years have exalted as special or divine. So you can't really blame any skeptics for mocking the claim that I'm "God's one and only true child." There's several thousand years of *history* on their side . . .

CHAPTER FORTY-FOUR

DK: You know, if we're honest about it, maybe people *need* a good savior. Most of us aren't very godly.

J: Not too surprising. Even from childhood, billions are taught that they're sinful, unworthy and lacking. From the sacred halls of Christendom they're told of their Maker's longstanding annoyance with them for a mild act of rebellion in Mesopotamia—several thousand years past—by a couple of kids with not a *trace* of meaningful, on-the-job experience.

DK: The doctrine of original sin.

J: Yeah, the church teaches that all kids bring guilt upon arrival—sullied from the start for the damnably presumptuous act of being born. In the church's mind, this random event, though fully out of their control, makes them all deserving of God's infamous wrath and its never-pleasant results. Even spending forever in fires of penance isn't reckoned too severe for underperforming after this dangerous gamble called birth.

DK: We usually live what we learn, I suppose, so it only makes sense if we take on the junk we get from the world and its religions of judgment—garbage in, garbage out, as they say. And scripture does state consistently that we're flawed. I'm a sinner, this I know . . . for the Bible *tells* me so.

J: And again religion teaches that God couldn't get things quite right. It seems He's not omnipotent after all and can't *really* have anything He wants. In Eden, we're told, all in God's creation was "very good" . . . *except*, apparently, for the most *important* part: his kids. They're constantly in need of policing and never quite acceptable as they are. This old archetypal story has been hammered into the collective awareness for many thousands of years. Religion has made guilt into a *virtue* and teaches that you're only showing humility in feeling corrupt. But *genuine* humility acknowledges your holiness by affirming the following: "I am whole and perfect, just as God created me, and nothing in the world can change it."

DK: I'm prob'ly squeezing the life from the lemon, but I still feel you're somehow unique. Even your closest friends seemed to agree.

J: The enlightened always appear special—or even crazy—to the ignorant. The caterpillar looks upon the butterfly and never even *imagines* having the same kind of stellar potential.

DK: Still, it's not every Tom, Dick or Hyram who's hailed as the 'son of God.'

J: Actually, the term was pretty common. They used it for kings and great philosophers, national heroes, miracle workers, holy men and others. The long-known "son of God" idea pops up even in the Old Testament. In 2 Samuel the Lord says of David, "I will be his father, and he shall be my son."

DK: Nevertheless, no one but you has pulled it off. In all of Christendom, not one single person, no matter how saintly, has commanded the church's reverence in quite the same way as you. Well, except for maybe your mom.

J: The idea that I was 'God's only child' was never suggested until many years after my death. It's referenced only a few times in the New Testament, and most of those books were written decades after I'd gone.

DK: Let's dig a little bit deeper here. The New Testament's first "only Son" reference appears in John 1:14. The writer says, "we have beheld his glory, glory as of the only Son from the Father."

J: In other words, it was the kind of glory that an only son might receive from his doting father. The *first* work might even have said, "glory as of a father's only son," or possibly "glory as of the only son from a father." See there? Change the determiner and change the whole meaning. Discerning the original writer's intention after all of the many translations is a roll of the dice at best.

DK: Okay, there's another "only Son" reference further down, in verse 18. It reads, "No one has ever seen God; the only Son, who is in the bosom of the Father, he has made him known."

J: But what if the *original* text was misinterpreted or even changed? Because a Gnostic may well have said it like this: "No one has ever seen God; only the Son, who is in the Father's bosom, has made him known." By switching "the only Son" to "only the Son," the words become meaningful and smart: the invisible Absolute, or the 'Father,' is made known, or manifest, only through the expression of Its creation— figuratively called "the Son." This notion of the shifting, relative world as a reflection of the unchanging eternal is what wise ones have been teaching for centuries.

DK: I'll confess that I consider this 'God's only son' thing the screwiest concept ever. Quite frankly, a lot of people find it insulting to human intelligence . . . and even many *Christians* don't believe it.

J: I said early on that God's offspring, or his 'son,' is a metaphor to describe his creation. God creates only by extending himself. So the 'son,' by necessity, is always in the Father's 'bosom'—that is, *united* with Him. Why ignore meanings that are perfectly sensible for ones that makes no sense at all?

DK: Well, the church doesn't give us the option—its doctrines aren't up for discussion. But, who knows? Maybe this interview will finally move clerics to change stance.

J: If *money's* involved, I wouldn't wait around by the pulpit . . .

Chapter Forty-five

DK: By the way, we haven't covered the New Testament's most *famous* verse calling you the "only son" of God—John 3:16.

J: Ah, right . . . the preferred passage of sign-bearing Christian sports fans everywhere.

DK: Yep, when the camera scans the stadium, you'll often see a few scattered Christians waving poster boards with John 3:16. "For God so loved the world that he gave his only son, that whoever believes in him should have eternal life." Now, *some* Bible scholars believe those words are yours, but others insist they're the words of the gospel writer. At this point I'll side with the second group since you've made it clear that you weren't preaching salvation that hangs on beliefs.

J: If I had embraced the thinking *behind* those words, why wouldn't I come right out and say, "For God so loved the world that he sent *me*"? I mean, what idiot goes around speaking of himself in third person?

DK: A few puffed-up celebrities come to mind.

J: C'mon, the Force behind creation is not an egoic personality, and the thought of it having a single legitimate child is absurd.

DK: But, biblically, your status as God's sole next-of-kin seems conclusive.

J: What are you trying to do, get arrested for impersonating a journalist? The Bible's very first book, Genesis, *twice* refers to *all* men as "sons of God."

DK: Well, alright . . . but that's *Old* Testament.

J: Are we not talking about the collection of works the Christian church refers to as unchanging, infallible and internally consistent words of God?

DK: I should've expected that one . . .

J: And the Book of Job, too, makes several references to the many "sons of God," while Romans 8 even defines who qualifies: "For all who are led by the Spirit of God are sons of God." So it's time again for some logic.

If only one 'Father' exists, and if all of his children are created in his image and likeness—that is, created with the same *nature* as the Father—all would be divine and equally loved, would they not?

DK: A touchy topic, to be sure. Saint Paul suggested that everyone but you is "adopted."

J: God created you and later decided to *adopt* you? How smart is *that*? And how is it different from a mother giving birth to her child then declaring that the kid was adopted? Everyone has potential for divinity, and this hidden fact of human magnificence was *announced* to the world thousands of years ago. Psalms 82 says it clear: "You are *gods*, sons of the Most High, *all* of you." Christians forget I remind them of this in John 10.

DK: So, it can't be *said* any plainer.

J: Right. And yet the single Bible passage telling them exactly what they are is one that literalist Christians just *can't* bring themselves to take literally.

DK: If it's true, Psalm 82 contradicts just about everything the church has preached for two thousand years and makes Christianity pointless.

J: And if it's *not* true, then every passage in the Bible is up for debate and, once again, the entire Christian religion's at risk.

DK: I can see why that verse from the Psalms would be shoved aside. Most churches focus on *our* humanity and *your* divinity.

J: Well, you can't give the impression that everyone can be just like Jesus. I mean, who'd pad the plate for a message like that? With spooky religions like Christianity, you've *gotta* scare 'em half to death or why in God's name would they *stay*?

DK: There's one other scripture calling you 'God's only son.' It's 1 John 4:9. Some Bible scholars attribute that letter to the same person who's often credited with authoring the fourth gospel—although it's now been proven that the writer of those two books was definitely not John the Apostle.

J: But still, a huge problem remains. You haven't got an original document for any of the books in the Bible. And even if you did, how would that prove they were inspired? Resolving their 'holiness' is no more possible now than it's been for the thousands of years since they were scribed. Every book of the Bible has loads of scholastic or theological challenges, and *each* of these works had many nameless 'editors' through the years.

DK: All a big crapshoot, eh?

J: Pretty much. And since you reference the book of John, I should mention that some New Testament scholars have serious concerns about the authenticity and reliability of that gospel because it differs so radically from the other three. John takes on a more mystical tone than Matthew, Mark and Luke. As with several other books of the New Testament, some church officials didn't want John's gnosticized gospel included.

DK: Hey, some didn't even want the Old Testament. Interesting to speculate how Christianity would look if John's gospel *had* been omitted—makes me wonder which verse they'd be using on those ballgame signs. But I'll give 'em credit for one thing: the image of John 3:16 is forever burned in our brains.

J: Despite its popularity, though, that verse is just a lead-in to one of the single most depressing ideas in the Bible. The sentiment of John 3:16 may sound promising at first—that is, if you fully ignore what it implies— but Christians overlook the critical but less-promoted corollary thought, coldly summed up just two verses later: "he who does *not* believe is condemned *already* . . . "

So you may as well stop all the fretting about Judgment Day drama, 'cause there shouldn't be any surprises. According to New Testament writers, for those who don't blindly accept official church doctrine *the judgment is already done.* And you can see why the church might omit this small point from its marketing plan. Going by scripture, God so *hated* the world that He set up a system wherein the vast majority of his children would damn themselves to their own eternal torment through legitimate ignorance, bona fide doubting, or outright disbelief. Try *that* as your poster board slogan, see how many converts you get.

DK: Are you sure you're ready for a tent revival ministry down south?

J: Look, it's clear that your world is in need of a radical shift. Your worn-out ideologies are clearly the *problem,* not the solution.

DK: Maybe we find it easy to accept a God of judgment because we see the world's insanity and think, "Well, if *I* were God, *I'd* be pissed off, too." We figure any forthcoming punishment has been well-earned.

J: Yes, but like I said, a creator who grows piously angry and pretends to be surprised when his children go rogue is a creator undeserving of defense. Strict scriptural literalists say that the God of the Bible knows *everything*— future included. He must know beforehand what's coming, am I right?

236

DK: Well, if He is truly omniscient, then I don't see any way around it. And He certainly claims to be so in the Bible. And how could He hope to make accurate prophecies if He's *not*?

J: But Yahweh's reaction to rebellion denies omniscience. When man soon gives in to curiosity and temptation—something that would've been foreseen by just about anyone, and surely by an all-knowing god—the Lord grows indignant at the insult, spewing threats of terror at his children and later on dishing up *smorgasbords* of cruel and unusual abuse. At first the penalties are confined to *this* world. But later, by way of the New Testament, they're taken into eternity . . . the vengeance never stops. Now, seriously, where's a thread of sense among the bloody *psychosis*!!? We have the God of creation cranking out defective merchandise and then having the unbridled chutzpah to badmouth the goods!! I mean, who's in charge of quality control around here!!?

DK: *Heh heh.* Talk about refusing to assume product liability.

J: You ain't kiddin'. This has gotta be the most blatant case in history of the need for a factory recall. If God were a corporation, He'd face a line of lawyers even longer than Methuselah's memoirs. But things get crazier still—in several Bible passages, Yahweh is actually the *cause* of man's disgrace. In Exodus chapter fourteen He resolves to "harden Pharaoh's heart," a theological nightmare implying that God can fully control someone's thinking. Verse eight surely seems to confirm it: "And the Lord hardened the heart of Pharaoh king of Egypt . . ." Later in the chapter, Yahweh says that He'll punish the stubborn Egyptians by wiping out Pharaoh's army. On conceiving his genocidal plan, He does a bit of bragging to Moses: "I will harden the hearts of the Egyptians so that they shall go in after [the Israelites], and I will get glory over Pharaoh and all his host, his chariots, and his horsemen." He's really looking forward to the gig.

DK: So Moses invokes the Lord to part the sea and the Lord complies, thereby helping his people to cross the soggy seabed unharmed.

J: And with Egyptian forces in hot pursuit, Yahweh steps in and clogs all their chariot wheels with mud. As the Israelites arrive safely on the other shore, Moses stretches his arm once again, staff in hand, signaling his god that it's now safe to finish the job. This brings the great walls of seawater crashing down like monstrous tidal waves upon the suckered Egyptians as the Lord, in a fit of heavenly vengeance, immediately *drowns* the whole hapless, hard-hearted bunch.

DK: And the rest, as they say, is history.

J: Actually, there's no proof *any* of it is history, so maybe I'm a revisionist. Here again we have scripture describing a deity who takes his dear creatures' lives about as seriously as a bloody spelling bee—not even the poor *horses* were spared. And the Lord God makes certain that He receives full credit for this shocking feat of programmatic victimhood and hatred.

DK: So even though it was Yahweh himself who caused the Egyptians' heartlessness, He chooses to drown them all anyway?

J: That's what the holy scripture says. Yahweh has little tolerance for disobedience, rebellion or ignorance. His answer for those with poor vision, quite often, is striking them blind in full.

DK: Is it possible biblical writers were speaking *symbolically* in declaring that Yahweh had 'hardened' someone's heart? Perhaps they meant only that He *allowed* for their obstinance, knowing He'd be victorious in revenge.

J: Even at that, it's not a very *godly* choice . . . or even a godly *God*. Does it ever dawn on this celestial grump that instead of going around hardening people's hearts, He simply could choose *softening* them all instead? Surely if He does the one, He can easily do the other.

DK: Perhaps it was only a one-off event, brought on by grave circumstance.

J: 'Fraid not. Once again let's look to the scriptures. This time we'll consult the book of Joshua, a work recounting a far-reaching campaign of war and terror—an odd inclusion for a 'holy' book, no?—with Joshua's army razing kingdom after kingdom and killing most everything that moves. Very few cultures got along with the Israelites and in Joshua chapter 11 we learn why: "For it was *the LORD himself* who hardened their hearts to wage war against Israel, so that [Joshua] might destroy them totally, exterminating them without mercy, as the LORD had commanded Moses." "I mean, after all," say the chosen, "they started it!"

DK: Yep, you're right—there's no wiggle room. The great Heart Hardener is workin' overtime.

J: So, again, Yahweh is clearly the instigator of wars against Israel's foes. In fact, it sounds like He wants to set 'em up so that later He can brutally knock 'em down. And notice the Lord expects Joshua, as He did with Joshua's cruel mentor Moses, to be merciless when slaughtering the enemy.

DK: And what, I hesitate to ask, was Joshua's response?

J: I'll quote: "Joshua took all these royal cities and their kings and put them to the sword. He totally destroyed them, as Moses the servant of the Lord had commanded . . . The Israelites carried off for themselves all the plunder and livestock of these cities, but all the *people* they put to the sword until they completely destroyed them, not sparing anyone that breathed. As the Lord had commanded his servant Moses, so Moses commanded Joshua, and Joshua did it."

DK: Seems Joshua wasn't too soft-hearted himself.

J: No, and it was Joshua who went on to lead Israel after Moses died.

DK: Well, he certainly sounds like the perfect guy for the job.

J: But consider the utter hypocrisy of these tales. In the Exodus account, Yahweh secretly programs the Egyptians to be aggressive and unyielding in pursuing his favored people during their famous flight from longtime foreign internment. So he's fully prepared and waiting when the Egyptians perform as precisely instructed through his mysterious psychic encoding. Seemingly delighted at the result of his own crafted scheme, Yahweh kills every man in Pharaoh's army by drowning the full brigade in the sea. Now, what kind of half-cocked, gladiator deity are we *dealing* with?!?

DK: I'll tell ya what: if He's anything like that in heaven, I'd just as happily take my chances down south.

J: It may not be a bad choice. Believe me, hell hath no fury like the heartless, heart-hardening God of the Christian Bible. Anyone who follows *this* cantankerous character had better go see a cardiologist . . .

CHAPTER FORTY-SIX

DK: I'm starting to see how little I know of the Old Testament. Apart from some of the more famous stuff, I never really gave it much time because it frequently seemed so dreadfully dry and dull.

J: Oh, not at all . . . the thing is bloody *full* of great crime stories.

DK: Well, I was so confused over the *New* Testament, I chose to ignore most of the Old. To me it never made any sense—and that Exodus story's a good example. It's all I've grown to resent about religion's usual picturing of God. I just can't fathom the Lord inducing his children's ignorance or causing their sinful demise.

J: It's fairly common in scripture, though, and even Moses indulges the idea. He angrily tells his tribesmen, "to this day the Lord has not given you a mind to understand, or eyes to see, or ears to hear." Moses is maddened by his people's dark vision but says *God* is withholding their light.

DK: Hardly seems fair.

J: Fair? You expect this lunatic god of the desert to be *fair*? Oh, that's *rich*! In 1 Kings 22, He's busy streaming faulty forecasts to false prophets: "Now therefore behold, the Lord has put a lying spirit in the mouth of all these your prophets . . ."

DK: Yahweh caused other prophets to *lie*? How could they ever stay in business with a shoddy data feed like *that*?

J: Well, they weren't misleading anyone *intentionally*. If you constantly made bad predictions back then and nothing you said panned out, you quickly lost all standing and were forced to become an economist.

DK: So the prophets had nothing to gain by lying.

J: But with *God* against 'em, however, the poor schmucks never had a prayer.

DK: At least now we know that the Bible's false prophets were genuine.

J: But you've gotta wonder why the Lord saw a need of *distributing* those deceptive divine downloads. Because you can't just say the false prophets were unscrupulous, since it wasn't as though all the *chosen* doomsters were ever the salt of the earth. In the second chapter of 2 Kings, Yahweh's prophet Elisha grows downright furious when a large group of boys pokes fun at his baldness. Scripture says he then "cursed them in the name of the Lord." I'll bet we can guess what *that* sounded like.

DK: A bit short in self-composure, perhaps . . . but it sounds harmless enough.

J: Unfortunately that's not where it ends. If a 'holy' prophet cursing kids 'in the name of the Lord' isn't weird enough already, the story turns downright grisly, you might say, when God quickly *vindicates* Elisha's great trauma by sending two adult bears from the nearby woods to maul and mutilate *forty-two* of the insolent little imps to bloody shreds.

DK: You're not serious.

J: It's all in the word of the Lord, my son.

DK: I should've joined those Old Testament groups after all—I missed out on all the *good* stuff. But at least I've gotten a taste of prophetic psychosis.

J: Oh, but there's plenty more to sample, lad. In Jeremiah 18, for instance, the 'godly' prophet is madder than a riled hornet.

DK: Aren't they always?

J: Well, in this case Jeremiah's miffed because the people are ignoring him and aren't showing gratitude for all his intercessions on their behalf. So he calls up the Lord for revenge. He wants Yahweh to kill all the fathers and to starve and murder their children. "*That* should teach 'em to appreciate me," Jerry says to himself.

DK: I'm surprised that was seen as fit behavior for a man of the cloth. I guess ol' Jerry wasn't big on being led beside the still waters.

J: Still waters? Ha! Some of these prophets were likely to live near raging rivers of *blood*. And since you allude to the Psalms, let's examine a snippet from Psalm 137—another Bible work sometimes attributed to Jeremiah. In this piece he lashes out against the Babylonians: "Happy shall he be who takes your little ones and dashes them against the rock!"

DK: Huh? Smashing enemy children against the rocks will bring *happiness*? What's this hothead got against innocent kids?

J: Actually, biblical stories of savagely murdered children aren't that rare. Many other Old Testament stories use the same kinds of lethal language. And the prophets—who, like their deity, nearly always felt neglected—really seemed to thrive on churning out forecasts of hateful violence. Interestingly, two of these kill-the-kids prophesies bear the same chapter number and verse. Isaiah 13:16 threatens the usual mutilation and killing of children—but with the additional promise that the women will be raped as well. *Hosea* 13:16 predicts the same brand of madness but goes a step further and warns that pregnant women will have their unborn babies slashed from their bellies.

DK: *Heavens to Hannibal*!! Such dashing, smashing and slashing! You're right, these touchy prophets sound dangerously like to their God: they aren't just incredibly violent, these guys, but they seem to need one helluva lot of attention.

J: Yeah, very much like the deity they rep, the prophets will not be ignored. In Jeremiah chapter 16, Yahweh again rails in anger at his dull-minded people and leaves no threat unexpressed. They'll die and be left as dung on the earth. They'll perish by famine and sword—two of Yahweh's more favored methods of killing his belovéd children. He spitefully declares that his victims' corpses will lie rotting as food for worms.

DK: Boy, how did anyone tolerate this bruiser? I mean a fella can take only so much steadfast love.

J: The shocking thing is the *reason* for the Lord's deadly distress. Start reading the passage at verse ten.

DK: Lemme see here . . . "And when you tell this people all these words, and they say to you, 'Why has the Lord pronounced all this great evil against us? What is our iniquity? What is the sin that we have committed against the Lord our God?' then you shall say to them: 'Because your fathers have forsaken me, says the Lord, and have gone after other gods and have served and worshiped them, and have forsaken me and not kept my law, and because you have done worse than your fathers, for behold, every one of you follows his stubborn evil will, refusing to listen to me . . ."

J: So Yahweh is consumed with a venomous wrath against his very own nation because their parents didn't like Him and ran off, and those who stayed behind won't *listen*. And once again his chosen children are shopping around for new gods—said by Jews and Christians not to *exist*. Now, this evokes critical questions that can no longer go unasked . . .

First, why is Yahweh incessantly worried of other gods? Who *are* they? And why do they make Him so consistently uneasy that his number one published announcement from Sinai is a rule prohibiting their worship? Are these the same gods He first viewed as peers in Genesis 3?

Next, if these other gods do exist, shouldn't we at least hear them out? *You* know, see what they've got to say—maybe they've got some value. If they *don't* exist, why is the Lord always denouncing them and warning you to keep them at bay?

And lastly, but most importantly, if Yahweh's nurturing leadership is ever prone to make his followers thrive, why are they always out searching for superior gods???

DK: With all of the violence and drama that followed Him, I can see his poor reception in the market. But maybe those ancient prophets channeled 'gods' of their own creation to vent *personal* partialities and complaints. It certainly seems true with Jeremiah. Nothing in his story is even slightly encouraging or godly—and his 'righteous' anger is more apt to bring *death* than deliverance. He also takes a strange delight calling mean, violent curses onto kids . . . and *that's* gotta be some seriously bad karma.

J: Ironically, biblical calls for vengeance against enemies' offspring directly oppose many *other* passages instructing that children shall not pay for the sins of their parents—Ezekiel 18 covers this in quite some detail. It's hard giving that any credence, though, when Yahweh himself warns in Exodus: "for I the Lord thy God am a *jealous* God, visiting the iniquity of the fathers upon the children . . ." The man simply won't bury the hatchet.

DK: So Jeremiah's veins are pulsing with murderous rage against his clan and he's fixed on making blameless children bear burdens of mom and dad's debt.

J: Right, he's keenly set on manifesting carnage and death. These days he'd be called a terrorist and labeled certifiably insane. And even though Yahweh frequently complains of those irritating, lying 'false' prophets, He constantly picks guys like Jeremiah for his reps.

DK: Pretty crazy, for sure. But why was the Lord so hard on those reviled prophets? Instead of *confusing* the competition, it might've made more business sense to *recruit* 'em. If Yahweh had specific instructions, why not visit the oracles in person, so to speak, and tell 'em all exactly what to say. Assuming He had proper I.D., of course, He surely could've spun the phony forecasters a hundred and eighty degrees.

J: He clearly had no intention of turning a prophet . . .

DK: But Yahweh had mellowed a bit when *you* came along. In the gospels, He seems to have more self-control and compassion. I mean at least He's not always out whacking people.

J: But the Bible God's spiteful behavior isn't limited to the Old Testament. Second Thessalonians 2 shows that even in the *New* Testament, He's still using the same old tricks: "Therefore God sends upon them a strong delusion, to make them believe what is false, so that all may be condemned who did not believe the truth . . ."

DK: I'm well familiar with that one since it always made me squirm— but of course back then I couldn't bring myself to admit it. Just as He did in the Old Testament, God is causing his people's deception when they're plenty confused as it is.

J: Yes, and He takes a kind of smug satisfaction in condemning all the saps who believed him. Hoodwinked into hell by their own creator!

DK: Hard to find much value in a crazy teaching like *that*.

J: Heck, we've only touched the tip of the terror. Sort through the records and you'll find a lot more of the Bible God's screwy behavior. He seems to be just a bigoted, juvenile hypocrite who's fruitier than a fresh peach daiquiri, meaner than a bullied badger, and even more bewildering than a full joint session of Congress . . .

CHAPTER FORTY-SEVEN

DK: Okay, it's pretty clear that the Bible simply cannot pass for truth in every case. I don't believe for a moment that God—whatever we conceive Him to be—actually hates anyone or ever even *said* that He does. But if *some* Bible passages need deciphering and don't always mean what they say . . . well, then we've *really* got grief.

J: Right, so the church can never allow for this kind of mushy approach to its scriptures. To say that scripture often leans on inference, opinion, or deduction—and that some is just preposterous or wrong—would also mean proving that *its* inferences, opinions and deductions are the *right* ones and they alone have power to make the calls. They'd be blasted so fast it would make their heads spin. So the church sticks to its story that scripture means what it says, even when absurdly ridiculous, and any discrepancies are handled by the boys at the top.

DK: Well, it's bad enough this Bible God's so petty that He hates his own children and treats 'em like fleas on a dog. I mean we're talking about a serial mass murderer here. But I don't see the need to immortalize it all in scripture. And how does He *arrive* at these judgments?

J: A good question with no good answer. It's like the Genesis story of Sodom and Gomorrah. Yahweh decides to burn and destroy the two ill-famed cities because the people are of low moral character—and yes, just think about the irony of *that*. But the Lord spares the life of a man named Lot, even though Lot, in a desperate move to save two 'angelic' house guests from imminent sexual attack by all the adult males of Sodom, had cowardly pacified the brutes by offering to have his two young girls gang-raped instead. So *there's* a guy who merits divine favors, eh?

And then there's the famous tale of Jacob and Esau where the younger son Jacob steals his older brother's birthright from their father. Jacob was one of the true scoundrels of the Old Testament. Esau, by contrast, was a pretty upstanding citizen and was always taking care of his family while Jacob lounged around in the tents. But still it's the trickster Jacob who inherits the father's fortunes and basks in the biblical fame.

DK: I can't explain the Lord's fondness for Lot—but with Jacob and Esau, I can only figure that Esau did something that really got Yahweh cranked up.

J: But what was it? What did Esau do that was any worse than *Jacob's* chronic dysfunctions? The Bible never says. What we *are* told, however, is that Jacob

—at the urging of his sneaky mother Rebecca to dress like a wolf in sheep's clothing and thus carry out the scam—not only stole his brother's birthright by dishonoring and deceiving their father Isaac, but also showed serious sexual indiscretions and made some horribly poor lifestyle choices. Scripture recounts Jacob cheating his uncle, practicing bigamy with two of his cousins and fornicating with two of his housemaids. The guy was lucky the Ten Commandments hadn't yet come around because he practically made a *living* from breaking them. So in my opinion, that whole Jacob/Esau disaster is one big, baffling contradiction. Yahweh's animosity toward Esau —He says in Malachi 1 that He *hates* him—is every bit as confusing as his strange and passionate affection for King David.

DK: Whaddaya mean? David is considered a genuine biblical hero.

J: Well, I don't know why, because the Bible paints him as just another despicable dictator. Like the god he claims to be serving, David is a monster. Prior to becoming ruler, David is a traitor who lives among his enemies the Philistines under protection of their king—plundering and pillaging local inhabitants with his army and even *killing* them to cover his tracks. He lies to the king continuously to stay in the crown's good graces and gladly offers to fight alongside the Philistines against his very own countrymen!!

DK: Now, *this* part they never taught us in church.

J: Well, it's all right there in 'God's word,' old boy. In one revealing scene from 1 Samuel, David is extorting a wealthy livestock owner named Nabal. David, who isn't yet king and is still relatively unknown, wants Nabal to give him certain gifts and provisions as repayment for not harming or thieving from Nabal and his workers while they lived near David's army. David basically tells Nabal, "I didn't steal your stuff or murder your men. You *owe* me."

DK: So it was something of an ancient-day offering of Mafia-like 'protection.'

J: Right. But Nabal refuses to be strong-armed like this and boldly tells David to shove it where the sun don't shine. David turns furious and vows to take his army and kill Nabal and all the other males on the property. Nabal's wife, Abigail, hears of the plan, goes groveling to David with a mule train of gifts, and shamelessly begs his forgiveness for her husband's boorish behavior. David then backs off and assures Abigail that he won't follow through with the slaughter of Old MacDonald and the others. A few days later, though, Nabal is mysteriously found dead. David quickly announces that, because of his high-nosed arrogance, Nabal has been "smote" by the Lord.

DK: Smote?

J: Summarily whacked.

DK: I see . . . I'll assume the story's ending contains some kind of moral instruction.

J: Not so much. The minute David hears that Nabal is dead—if indeed it was truly a surprise—he sends for the rancher's wife and sleeps with her, later on making her wife number 2 and a part of his growing collection.

DK: *Crikey.* Going from Sunday school memories, David was almost a god.

J: By scriptural accounts, though, he's a cold-blooded killer who sadistically slaughters thousands of men, women and children in the beastliest ways you could think. David is also a sex-crazed polygamist with at least eight wives and a harem of concubines to boot.

DK: And I can't keep a freakin' *girlfriend* . . .

J: Hey, compared to his son, Solomon 'the wise and moral,' David was a relative monk. First Kings 11 says that Solomon had 700 wives— which, to any man who's been married, probably doesn't seem all that wise. He also had 300 concubines . . . which doesn't seem all that moral. Solomon is also said to have kept a few princesses wandering through the palace in case things slowed on the weekend or he wasn't too busy building shrines to a bloody *boatload* of those other, more desirable gods.

Still, it was Solomon's father, King David, who really took the prize for debauchery, depravity and death. Vulgar in his treatment of ladies, David is a raving drunkard who exposes himself to helpless housemaids and then explains later to Michal—his first wife and the daughter of his rival, King Saul—that he was merely giving thanks for his kingship by "dancing before the Lord" in celebration. It's interesting to note that David had secured the princess in marriage by killing two hundred of his former Philistinian comrades then hauling their mutilated foreskins back to her father Saul, who no doubt was doubly delighted since he'd previously asked for only a hundred.

DK: What!?! Why in creation's name would they do *that*?

J: Well, to kill off some of Saul's enemies, of course, and because . . . well, *you* know, nothing proves a guy's love for a woman and wins the favor of her family quite like buttering up the old man with a bagful of severed private parts from two hundred massacred tribesmen.

DK: Of course—I should've guessed. And so *practical* a gift as well . . .

J: But if all the wives and concubines weren't plenty to quell his craving for fresh sexual conquests, David is also an adulterer who steals Bathsheba —the wife of one of his most faithful and honorable soldiers—gets her pregnant and then has her husband Uriah the Hittite killed in battle, along with many *other* of David's troops so as not to be too obvious, to *conceal* the illicit affair and protect his *own* hide. The king soon marries her, positioning himself as the hero who takes in the poor, dead soldier's grieving wife. Bathsheba then later gives birth to Solomon. And this, as recounted faithfully in holy scripture, is the miserable truth of King David.

DK: Well, I see why they gave him the palace and crown. I mean who'd want him living next door?

J: Even Lord Yahweh is wary of David's violent nature—and *that*, my friend, is really *saying* something. In 1 Chronicles 22, David tells his son Solomon that the Lord has now forbidden David to build a tabernacle for Him because David has shed too much blood.

DK: And this is the man the church proudly proclaims to be the start of your family lineage?!?

J: Yeah, the very same hero on whom the book of 2 Samuel confers the title of "the sweet psalmist of Israel." To get a feel for the psalmist's sweetness, read a few verses of Psalm 109 sometime. It's a work that some scholars have attributed to King David. Whether David wrote it is doubtful, but it sounds like something that one of Yahweh's 'favored' would pen. The writer invokes the Lord, prophet-like, to inflict one calamity after another onto his enemies. He wants their children made fatherless and begging for food in the streets.

DK: Boy, what is it with these Old Testament characters calling curses onto innocent kids? It seems these biblical leaders weren't always the towers of spiritual strength and moral integrity we've come to believe they were.

J: Well, in David's case, the man wouldn't have known an ethic if it kicked him in the shin. And in fact *many* of Israel's leaders practiced the famous "works of the flesh" so strongly reviled by Paul in Galatians 5: immorality, enmity, strife, jealousy, anger, selfishness, dissension, envy, drunkenness, and carousing. And with *David*, that was only the *small* stuff. Read the last part of verse 21 on Paul's grim caution of the afterlife fates awaiting violators.

DK: Okay. . . He says, "I warn you, as I warned you before, that those who do such things shall not inherit the kingdom of God."

J: But, astonishingly, in the Book of 1 Samuel the Lord proclaims proudly that David is his kinda guy—a man after his heart, He declares!!

DK: Well, considering God's *own* alleged behavior, I can see where He'd feel that way—the two had a lot in common. To balance the ledger, though, I could argue that you've cited just a handful of examples from a book of a thousand pages.

J: Yes, but these are not isolated accounts. The Old Testament is *stuffed* with stories of the Lord and his prophets showing fear mongering, intolerance, double standards, and trifling mean-spiritedness . . . and here again, that was only jacks-for-openers. Many passages contain flare-ups far more serious, including massacres and holocausts of entire tribes and kingdoms.

DK: My Sunday school teacher would sometimes say Lord Yahweh's power knows no bounds.

J: Yeah? Well, neither does his destructive rage. He's constantly starting wars or cursing large populations with various hardships and plagues, and his victims include even the Israelites themselves. He seems to find special delight in causing hunger and starvation, frequently sending down plights of famine, years of drought, waves of crop-killing insects— and hosts of other societal disasters and griefs. As we've discussed, Yahweh is often credited with annihilation of entire cultures. And the Bible descriptions of these holy terrors are psychotically similar to the horrific 'ethnic cleansing' events with which your world is now sadly familiar.

DK: The God of the Bible seems to *focus* on judgment and revenge— like that's what gets Him up in the morning.

J: The irony is that He's constantly telling humanity to show compassion and forgiveness, while *He* maintains a zero-tolerance rule.

DK: Well, He did warn us when He said "Vengeance is mine."

J: But who thought He'd make it a full-time job!!? And all of it to prove that He's the one and only, irreplaceable, undefiable and indisputable *Boss*. It's crazy, but this Bible God would just as gladly fry their fat in the fire as to really try *saving* someone. He's perfectly happy being pictured as a cosmic hit man—so long as they get his name correct in the papers.

DK: But again, that's all *Old* Testament, right? God's *New* Testament nature, allegedly demonstrated through *you*, seems far more centered on love.

J: How can you make that argument when Christianity's central theology has most of God's children suffering timelessly in a soul-scorching hell!? You call that insanity *love!!*? If the gospels can be taken for truth, my friend, the creator's most chilling behavior still lies ahead. If you don't make his final-day roster, you're sorrowfully sentenced to his eons-long payback in hell. Behold, dear mortals, how thy biblical God doth *love* thee!!!

DK: Now, wait a minute. Paul says in the ninth chapter of Romans that we shouldn't even *question* God's motives. In fact, he specifically mentions the story of Jacob and Esau because *he* had trouble with it too. But Paul says God has every *right* to be fickle because . . . well, just because He's God.

J: Ahhh, got it. So if Paul says that God has the right to abuse his children because it suits Him, who are *you* to go questioning. *That's* what he's tryin' to say?

DK: Fundamentally, I think.

J: Well, what a terrific strategy *that* is. Throw in a verse that God's ways are above reproach—no matter how cruel, idiotic or hypocritical—and that settles it, eh? "We'll clarify as we go," the church tells you, "but please don't impugn the Holy Bible's divine emanations."

DK: So this 'don't even ask' policy, one that's pretty common in religion, discourages all intelligent appraisal by implying that anyone who *does* question their scripture will be subject to the wrath of the Lord.

J: Right, so most believers choose not to let these sleeping lies dog them.

DK: But Paul doesn't quit in his Christian justification of God's ways. He writes, "What shall we say then? Is there injustice on God's part? By no means!" He quotes the Lord as proclaiming, "I will have mercy on whom I have mercy, and have compassion on whom I will have compassion."

J: Then Paul is basically arguing that God's bizarre position is a really sick twist on the Golden Rule. In effect the Lord is telling you this: "Whatsoever I would that you should do unto *me*, you had better bloody well *do* it. And anything I wish to do unto *you* . . . *that* will I damned well do!"

DK: It's possible I'm not doing Paul full justice. He further explains, "So it depends not upon man's will or exertion, but upon God's mercy . . .

He has mercy upon whomever He wills, and He hardens the heart of whomever He wills. You will say to me then, 'Why does He still find fault? For who can resist his will?' But who are you, a man, to answer back to God?"

J: So, asking obvious questions is forbidden and it's straight predestination, plain and clear. Your devotion means *nada* since it's all up to heaven now, and nothin's left that anyone can do.

DK: But not many Christians would dare challenge scripture that way—their *Bible* gives 'em a fairly healthy fear of their *God*.

J: There's nothing healthy in fearing God . . . and living in fear of *anything* would still mean living in fear. Using the world's religious books as the ultimate moral authorities is a pretty dangerous game. Some of the writings do certainly show the wisdom, warmth and beauty you'd *expect* from sacred works, while others teach hypocrisy, hatred and violence—they end up causing fear and separation. At the extreme, they're even used to justify first-degree murder.

DK: It's confusing, because parts of the Bible, and other holy books too, seem actually to *encourage* judgmental thinking.

J: I advised my disciples to "judge not"—and nothing's confusing about *that*.

DK: Well, I fear your noble instruction not to judge has been buried by hundreds of *other* scriptures about a God who judges almost everything. And it's not just within Christianity—other religions have the same kinds of scary-ass gods. It's why so many believers live from fear, I think, and do things in the name of their faith that no *sane* man or woman would consider.

J: And no wonder so many *Christians* are confused. They've got demons with godlike powers and a God who's very often demonic. He favors a few but forces others into lives of evil and even condemns them for it. Old Testament stories in particular show this character as a mean and whimsical flake. Under *his* rule, it's quite possible—as with Esau—to play your position near perfectly and still get kicked off the team.

DK: Didn't Christianity change that?

J: It doesn't really offer much relief. Christian theology of 'guilty by birth' just *compounds* the guilt by putting *you* at fault for my death. The holy scriptures say that refuting these things is presumptuous and should be avoided . . . they imply that anyone who does so will surely regret it on crossing the River Styx. Now, does any of this sound reasonable? Or intelligent? Or *loving*?

DK: First Thessalonians 5 advises Christians to "test all things."

J: Wouldn't that have to include their Holy Bible? How many Christians, or those of *any* religion or ideology, apply that rule to their *personal* views? The Bible urges people to be wise, yes, but never encourages neutrality or critical thinking regarding its *own* ideas and doctrines. This kind of 'faith' is downright deadly and history proves it out. Blind compliance with 'inspired words' has brought centuries of pain into the world, and man has suffered forever at the hands of religious believers —Christians, Hindus, Muslims, Jews, and others—firmly persuaded by ancient writings they were faithfully serving their God.

DK: I certainly won't argue the point. Along with many other religious or political institutions, Christianity—which is *both*—has a sorry record of rights abuse against those who reject it. They say that if you've gotta make your argument at gunpoint, you've likely got a pretty weak case.

J: Christendom's whole belief paradigm comes directly from the Bible, a book that practically sanctifies intolerance and confirms man's worst ideas about reality. Millions of religious faithful across the world have assumed that if God can treat *his* enemies like maggots—as taught in their revered holy books—there's no reason they can't do the same. They figure that God shares their righteous indignation toward those who rub them the wrong way or question their dogmas and creeds. For many of the faithful on earth, scripture has become their war guide.

DK: I don't know about devotees of other religions, but I know from experience that the average Christian has very little in-depth knowledge of how his holy scripture evolved. Even those quoting it inside and out often act like it came straight from God.

J: Yeah, the Ten Commandments phenomenon. Christians seem to believe that the Bible was divinely compiled, fully laid out in their language and ready to go. I recall one dear gal in particular—a sweet old widow with poor sight. She'd faithfully read the four New Testament gospels each month. Once, during nightly prayers, she offered up thanks to God for making things easier for her by printing all of *my* words in red . . .

CHAPTER FORTY-EIGHT

DK: I probably shouldn't point fingers at the fundies. For nearly twenty years I thought the Bible practically fell from the sky—so I mostly focused on memorizing various verses. On doing some research, I learned that compiling it actually dragged on for centuries.

J: Not one of my favorite topics. And you could fill a few *boxcars* with books on the history and development of Jewish and Christian scripture.

DK: I'll grant the subject *is* a little bland. With the Bible's importance to both Judaism and Christianity, though, it's certainly worth some time. Maybe we could skip through the tedious details and focus mainly on highlights.

J: Ah, the *Reader's Digest* edition. Okay, you start and we'll go from there . . .

DK: Well, my first surprise was learning that the Old Testament in present form didn't even exist until at least five or six decades after your death.

J. True . . . but the Hebrew scriptures, from which the Old Testament is taken, were around long before my birth. And it would still be another century or more past my death before the Jews finally settled on their official holy books. But even though Christians started calling the Hebrew canon the 'Old' Testament, for Jews it remained the *only* testament. They saw Christianity as pointless and didn't agree that I was the prophesied messiah.

DK: No, and they still don't.

J: A real irony, right? Christians have built their religion on the historical and scriptural foundations of the very ones who disavow their claims.

DK: It is a little odd, now that you mention it.

J: Odd? It's like an attorney in a murder trial arguing his client's innocence by producing six witnesses who saw the guy pull the bloody trigger!!

DK: Okay, I stand corrected: it's *very* odd. I suppose the coupling of Jewish and Christian scripture actually is a pretty strange pairing.

J: In the view of most Jews, it's senseless—there's no legitimate tie between the two. This is why terms like 'Judeo-Christian' and 'Old Testament' are

253

often met with jeers by many Jews. These labels are useful for Christians, perhaps, but I wouldn't go tossing them around in the local temple.

DK: Thanks . . . always good to know what's politically correct.

J: Now, the Christian 'Old' Testament was, again, derived from the ancient Hebrew writings, so establishing its contents was fairly simple. But even though the standard Old Testament holds 39 books, that arrangement's not agreed upon at all. The Catholic canon, for instance, uses an Old Testament of 46 books. And differences like this apply to the New Testament, too. The Syrian Church, as an example, uses a New Testament of only 22 books instead of the usual 27. And though Christians respect and employ the Old Testament as sacred scripture, the Jews don't reciprocate with any Christian texts. Within mainstream Judaism, the New Testament isn't used nor is it seen as divinely inspired. For Jews it's irrelevant, and most consider it heresy. Only *Messianic* Jews—those who think I'm the messiah—give any credence or import to the Christian New Testament.

DK: I would imagine that during the earliest years of Christianity, everyday Jews must have been appalled at what was developing.

J: Many were. And it didn't help that Christians were using their 'customized' versions of various Old Testament passages as 'proof' for the prediction of my Palestinian coming. As their new sect expanded, Christians hijacked ambiguous old Hebrew texts and used them as the basis for their new religion, claiming that even the Jews' own scriptures saw their Jesus as the great messiah. One critical case of some scriptural sleight-of-hand involves the popular Christmas verse from Isaiah 7. Christians knowingly mistranslated the Semitic word *almah*—indisputably meaning only "young woman"—to the Greek PARTHENA, meaning "virgin." This clever switcheroo allowed Christians to claim that Hebrew prophecy called for their messiah to be born of a virgin, a concept quite common in the Mysteries but totally foreign to Judaism. In writing me up as a virgin-born man, Christians could therefore argue that their central character was God.

DK: Well, that's a fairly serious problem. The virgin birth is the church's first claim in defense of your special nature—the very starting point of the Christ story. If it's bogus, there is no more Christianity. And I have to be blunt: even a lot of Christians are uneasy with the virgin birth. There is a phenomenon in nature called *parthenogenesis* in which certain creatures can reproduce through development of an unfertilized ovum. For skeptics, though, that just won't do in explaining the virgin birth. There's not a single scientifically verified case of human partheno—

J: Excuse me for cutting in on your gripping biology lecture, which has me just *riveted* to my seat with its rockets' red glare and bombs bursting in air—

DK: Go easy, now . . .

J: —but I would point out that I never even talked about my birth. As I've explained, the virgin mother idea was standard fare in the Mystery religions and that's how it landed in the gospels. But honest Bible scholars will tell you that Jewish scripture never refers to any savior-god messiah nor to anyone born of a virgin—the Jews would've found it all absurd. Not once did I make the outrageous claim that my mother was still a virgin at my birth. Only two gospels, Matthew and Luke, even *tell* the virgin birth story, while no other New Testament writers ever suggest it.

DK: Interesting. Especially given the shocking nature of the claim.

J: The gospel of Mark was the original document from which the other two "synoptic" gospels of Matthew and Luke were derived, but Mark doesn't include the virgin birth. The edit was added later by Christians working hard to find converts. They sought to build their new religion's power by putting as much salt in the sack as they could. But there's no *non-Christian* report of a miracle birth in Bethlehem from that period —and none but my mother could've possibly known for sure if it was— and even Christian accounts of it weren't written until decades later. None of this much matters, really, since I wasn't *born* in Bethlehem, and anyone who's researched the historical defects of the first verses of Luke chapter 2 would know this—the writer simply conjured a more convenient version of 'history.' The very same shenanigans gave rise to the virgin birth.

DK: I do know that the Apostle Paul, bent as he was on spreading his special version of the faith, never refers to the story of the virgin birth— which he surely would've done if he believed it.

J: Paul's letters were written a long time before the gospels, and his writings show he was unaware of the stories that wound up in Matthew, Mark, Luke, and John—his letters contain no parallels to those accounts. Paul had strong Gnostic leanings and saw me as more of a *mystical* figure. He never refers to my parables, my run-in with the Romans, my sermons—or anything else that would show he knew the 'historical' details of my life. He never uses my sayings in his letters, even when doing so would clearly bolster his point. The only time he bothers quoting me is in the eleventh chapter of 1 Corinthians. Few Christians know it, but what he's citing is the ancient Mystery formula for Eucharist.

DK: Paul was familiar with the Mystery rites?

J: *Intimately* familiar. In 1 Corinthians 2 he writes of imparting a "secret and hidden wisdom" to "initiates"—and this isn't something you'd hear from a strict Christian literalist.

DK: So even if he'd known of the virgin birth story, it's not very likely that Paul would've bought it as fact.

J: Not a chance. Paul could be fanatical in many ways and sometimes was pretty pigheaded . . . but even Saint Paul had his bounds.

DK: You surely know that debunking the virgin birth is no small thing. It's not like declaring you were actually blond or something—we're talking major revisionism here. Nearly every Christian church on earth teaches that God magically impregnated your mother and that you had no true earthly father . . . it's one of the main pillars supporting the claims to your godhood. People find it *crucial* to believe that you were cosmically created, or you would be essentially like us.

J: Oh, now wouldn't *that* be awful.

DK: You don't care if folks see you as an equal?

J: *Au contraire, mon ami.* I'll sleep much better when they *do* . . .

CHAPTER FORTY-NINE

DK: So you've smashed yet another sacred shrine: the virgin birth. Christendom puts you squarely on the pedestal of divinity and *you* keep jumping off! I see you won't be happy 'til you get yourself dethroned.

J: I'll tell ya what: since we're examining the Bible's evolution and the Christians' forced coupling of Old Testament and New, let's take a look at the famous Christmas passage in the first chapter of Matthew. We'll see if there's any scriptural agreement or prediction of some virgin-born god . . .

Matthew says, "All this took place to fulfill what the Lord had spoken by the prophet: 'Behold, a virgin shall conceive and bear a son, and his name shall be called Immanuel.'" But as I said, the original Semitic word was actually *almah*, indicating only a young woman, not a virgin. Any Hebrew writer wanting to convey virginity would use the term *bethulah*. The gospel's claim about the Jews' predicted virgin birth of a god —the very *heart* of the Christian religion—is based on a prophecy having nothing to do with virginity and no obvious ties to any god. And by the way, no one ever called *me* Immanuel.

DK: It is curious that in the Revised Standard Version of the Bible, Matthew's quote from Isaiah does cite the word "virgin." But when you look up the actual verse in Isaiah, the passage reads only "young woman," as you say it should. Apparently, even using the very earliest text, translators wouldn't give in and use the word virgin.

J: Of course not—they knew darned well what the writer meant.

DK: Even so, in some Bible versions New Testament translators did add a footnote saying, "or 'virgin'."

J: Only because they were dealing with a political hot potato and were appeasing the few promoters of the virgin birth. And incidentally, that prophetic Old Testament passage I just quoted from Matthew is taken from the seventh chapter of Isaiah. The words were written around 735 BCE and were intended to comfort King Ahaz, who was distraught over Syria threatening to attack Jerusalem. If worse came to worst, Isaiah's prophecy would strengthen his people's wavering courage by promising victorious revenge in the years ahead.

DK: Nonetheless, the church still says Isaiah was paving the path for *you.*

J: But the prophecy referred only to the *near-term* future . . . and even Isaiah's own countrymen never took his words as the predicted birth of a god. So it's clear that nothing in the passage even *hints* at my own arrival centuries later. And what would've been the point? How would Ahaz find reassurance in his hour of crisis by learning that a great redeemer might vindicate him many generations after he's *dead*!?!

DK: No consolation in *that*, I suppose.

J: No, it would be like Isaiah telling Ahaz, "Things may look bleak at the moment, Your Highness, but don't fret: a kid from Nazareth will even the score *lickety-split* in approximately seven hundred years!"

DK: *Heh heh.* Hardly cause for Ahaz to stare at the sundial.

J: The thing is, the people of Isaiah's time, like those of my day, were hoping for an *earthly* savior, not a heavenly one. They wanted a vanquisher—someone to settle accounts with the enemy *du jour*. But they weren't thinking of some future *divine* leader who would set about the preaching of love and lecturing on the lofty merits of peace. The Jews wanted *vengeance* and they clearly wanted it *now*. One of the famous Dead Sea documents, the War Scroll, even lays out a specific battle plan for the expected clash, predicted to occur at *har Megiddo*—now popularly known as Armageddon. Ironically, it was the site of one of the first recorded battles in history, and more than thirty conflicts have been fought there. Some Christians claim Armageddon will also be the spot for history's *last* battle as well—the end-of-the-world storyline in Revelation. But the War Scroll is clear that the prophesied confrontation was to be solely between humans, with no celestial ties in the least . . . apart from the fact that of course Yahweh would be on *their* side in the fray.

DK: Then the War Scroll doesn't reference any devil or heaven-and-earth struggle for control.

J: Not a word of a cosmic clash between goodness and evil. The expected fight was to be strictly between the "Children of Light"—the Jews—and the "Sons of Darkness," their derogatory name for the Romans and other inimical groups. The Jewish hope was that a powerful, God-ordained emancipator would rise from their ranks and lead them on to military victory. The War Scroll says the envisioned messiah will serve in the mighty battle as Israel's supreme martial commander—the kind of thing Isaiah had in mind when he made his famous prophecy to King Ahaz. But though they've labeled several 'messiahs' in their history, the Jews were still waiting for their hero more than seven centuries later when *I* was born.

DK: And some are waiting *still*.

J: Well, I can tell you this: even if their newest messiah does emerge, he won't have any connection to Isaiah's prophecy, since that was expected to play out relatively quick.

DK: If Isaiah wasn't referring to *you* and never even mentioned a virgin, then what's the bottom line on your mother's pregnancy?

J: The bottom line is my beginnings were never any different from yours. There's no serious scholarly support—and *zero* evidence, of course—for the gospel's virgin birth account. *I* never talked about it, the Old Testament doesn't predict it, and the *New* Testament all but ignores it.

But as we've seen, the virgin birthing of gods was pretty common in the Mysteries, so it's not unusual that Christians adopted it too . . . especially given the allegiance to it later on by various leaders in Rome.

And you have to realize that the gospels were written by men and women who were Christian evangelists. The writings were meant to encourage new converts by creating an atmosphere of urgency, mystery, and divine authority. They show the kind of passion you'd *expect* from avid disciples.

DK: But if the virgin birthing of a Christ was indeed widely known and believed, it's very strange that most New Testament writers failed to use it—it would've been their most compelling material.

J: Don't lose perspective. The books of the New Testament were written independently over the decades following my death. Never intended as affiliated pieces of a collective work, they differ radically and often conflict.

DK: Yet here's the church, now twenty centuries later, still talking about it like . . . well, like it's *gospel*.

J: In the years after my death, things which at the start were only myth, symbol, or opinion did ultimately become Christian dogma— all hustled as 'fact' by an infant religious sect eager to expand its impact and save the world from the heavenly destruction at hand.

DK: So the church has used the Bible to slip us a wooden nickel.

J: Well, there's no doubt that the Christian story of my life is a superficial hodgepodge—and plenty of scholars know it. The gospels were written and pieced together long after I was gone and were revised not just for decades, but for *centuries*. Like the famous Christmas narrative, the result is hardly more than a folk tale. Fragments of my life were strung together, exaggerated, commingled with ancient pagan themes and artificially linked with various unrelated verses from Jewish scripture. The whole concoction was then glossed over and dispensed as a unified whole. For credibility, right up there with the Tooth Fairy, a campaign promise, or a major White House press conference.

DK: You're blasting pretty big holes in mainstream beliefs.

J: Beliefs don't *establish* the facts: they *distort* them and keep them veiled. As with the virgin birth, religion floats ideas that should trigger the doubts of thinking people everywhere. Threatening pain and eternal torture for the faithless, religion still fearfully guards the gates to the Tree of Knowledge.

DK: I hope you know you're really *killing* my chances for a future guest appearance on the news . . .

CHAPTER FIFTY

DK: Wow, what a trip. Religion has thrived for centuries selling sinners on a God who's never quite happy. Now *you* come along and raze one temple after another by claiming there's no sin that separates, no eternal punishment, everyone's divine and reality is berries and cream. You insist that you're just like the rest of us and most of what's written of you is rot. You say your mom conceived you in the normal way and your death, as an atonement, was pointless. Next you'll be telling me you were happily married . . . with children, two dogs and a nanny.

J: I'm glad you raised the topic of marriage. As you know, in the gospels I'm often addressed as "Rabbi," which means "my master" or "my teacher." You may not know it, but the gospels never claim that I was celibate or single and it *was* fairly uncommon—and sometimes actually forbidden—for an unmarried Jewish man to *be* a teacher. In many circles, getting wed upon becoming an adult was viewed as one's foundational moral duty, an important part of the divine plan for procreation and growing the 'family of God.' But let's leave it there . . . you've trouble aplenty already.

DK: You're right, I'm not sure the world is ready for Jesus the family man.

J: Well, then, back to that spellbinding exposition on the Bible. Go ahead and grind away.

DK: Oh, c'mon—that painful?

J: One notch below circumcision, I'd say.

DK: I'll try to pick up the pace . . .
So, around the third century, the most popular Greek translation of the Old Testament was known as the Septuagint. Supposedly it took 70 scholars, spanning nearly a hundred years, to translate it from Hebrew between the 3rd and 2nd centuries BCE. One can just *imagine* the slip-ups in *that* logistical slog.

J: Unless, once again, you're okay with divine intervention . . . and some would say that's initially what took place. On the Five Books of Moses, the Jewish Talmud states that Ptolemy II Philadelphus—king of Ptolemaic Egypt from 283 BCE to 246 BCE—gathered 72 elders and placed each in a separate chamber, not telling them why they were there. The king then told each cloistered elder, "Write for me the Torah of Moshe our teacher."

DK: "Moshe" meaning Moses.

J: Right. The Talmud then declares that the king's experiment resulted in the miraculous: "God put it in the heart of each one to translate *identically* as all the others did." The loved philosopher Philo of Alexandria would later add that the process itself, ironically, took precisely 72 days.

DK: So the claim is that all 72 elders came up, independently, with the same, exact wording for the entire Torah?

J: That's what the Talmud says. They all even made the same *mistakes*.

DK: Hmmm . . . very peculiar, this Bible development stuff.

J: Tricky business, for sure—and especially when God *isn't* in charge. The creation of the famous Vulgate Bible illustrates perfectly the chaos that follows when the job is left up to men. When Jerome was commissioned by Pope Damasus to write a Bible in Vulgar Latin, the form spoken by the man on the street, he basically had to invent a new language. Even though Vulgar Latin was routinely spoken by the Roman middle class, nearly all writing was either Greek or Classical Latin. But the middle class couldn't *read* Classical Latin. Nor could they read Ecclesiastical Latin, the form invented by another big church influencer, Tertullian—a man who hoped, with true Christian benevolence, to gaze down from heaven on hell's tortured souls and take satisfaction at such. He also was the guy who claimed the Apostle John was thrown into a vat of boiling oil by the Romans and escaped unharmed . . . a certified, Kentucky fried miracle.

DK: So, to create a Bible in the language of the masses, the Pope's man Jerome had to jury-rig a *written* Vulgar Latin.

J: Yes, and the result was the Vulgate—a Bible composed in a kind of made-up language and based on prior versions filled with compromises, errors and concessions. So even the Vulgate itself was an untamed beast, and its masters were whipping it into submission for decades.

DK: It would seem that divine inspiration can't be rushed. As a writer, I'm solaced that even God could have so much trouble with *editors*.

J: And don't forget . . . until Herr Gutenberg showed up in the 15th century and cranked out the first *mass-produced* Bible on his newfangled printing press, creating a full-length Bible was highly labor-intensive and was tedious, time-consuming business, which left even *more* opportunity for distortion—accidental or not.

DK: So, here we had lengthy ancient documents reproduced by hand and changed from one language to the next by countless translators from different cultures over hundreds of years, none of whom ever laid eyes on the earliest texts—in other words, translations of translations and copies of copies. And if all the first manuscripts from Old and New Testaments are gone, no one knows for sure exactly *what* the books' authors might've said.

J: Not verbatim, at least.

DK: Well, it seems to me that we've all taken a helluva lot for granted. The church has led us to think that its scripture contains no significant errors and that every blesséd syllable is inspired. As a long-practicing Christian, I never suspected that certain groups or persons had altered or influenced scripture for their own theological ambitions. *Now* I learn that even church fathers were less than honorable in reporting the facts.

J: You're sounding like a rebel with a newfound cause.

DK: Hey, after giving so much of my life to Christianity, I've got a good *right* to feel hornswoggled—common courts of law wouldn't have that kind of fast-handed finagling on a small-time probate will. The church has built an empire on a layer of mud and with the very flimsiest of 'evidence.'

J: That's how it looks from here.

DK: Well, pardon me, then, if I'm more than a little *upset*. Devious scholars, power-mad dictators, and Councils with secret intent. You'd expect these kinds of things from a drugstore mystery thriller—not from a major religion. The whole nasty mess is like a huge game of politics and control.

J: To some degree, yes. But that hints at collusion, and you needn't stretch nearly so far. Sure, some of the key players in Christian history tried making the church into their image—but others were just over-zealous and badly ill-informed.

DK: So you don't have to be a conspiracy freak to question the accuracy —or even the authenticity—of the Bible.

J: No, because translation is terribly tough under even the *best* conditions. Take the famous Lamsa Bible, for instance. Dr. George Lamsa, the project's director, said there were enormous differences between the Aramaic manuscripts his team translated and the old Hebrew and Greek texts . . . between ten and twelve *thousand*, he guessed. In the New English Bible, British scholar Sir Godfrey Driver's intro to the Old Testament speaks directly to the challenges of Bible translation. He says that while the first five books, the Pentateuch, are translated fairly well, the Old Testament in general is dicey and many of its books contain what Driver called "sheer absurdities." So *that*, old pal, is the bumbling business of Bible-making.

DK: Not an exact science, it would seem.

J: No, I s'pose not . . .

[Jesus sounded suddenly detached. I looked up from scribbling my notes to catch him watching ducks paddling around in the river.]

DK: You seem distracted.

J: I'm trying to decide what's worse—a drawn-out discussion of Bible history or relatively quick crucifixion.

DK: Sorry, I'll try droning on a bit faster. Here's a few of my beefs . . .
   The Old Testament scriptures are the obvious roots on which the church's credibility relies. But clearly they aren't the inspired writings many believe they are. And it seems *Christian* factions did everything they could to make their newer writings match with those ancient scriptures of Israel. But the earlier works, by all evidence, had nothing to do with you or any part of your life. This is important, I think, because forcing an artificial Jewish/Christian connection gave the impression that Judaism was just a steppingstone to Christianity—a thought even the Lord himself never mentions. If I understand correctly, when Yahweh laid down the law there was no *subtle hint* that it might one day be repealed. And if *that's* true, then we're *really* living in Whacko World. How could He expect his people to renounce and abandon their sacred traditions, that He alone had established, without any warning that all of their legal and moral code —*their entire way of life*—was nothing but a starter faith for one that makes it void. It's grossly unfair Yahweh never informed his people that He had an 'only son' who would later be taking over the family business and who could, if the Jews weren't careful, inaugurate their postmortem pain!!

J: Is this a summary or a filibuster?

DK: C'mon, I've got a truckload of serious questions here. More than two billion people claim to follow at least some of the Bible's teachings, so I figure it's worth a few minutes covering its history when it's rarely taught in synagogue or church.

J: Objection sustained. But let's move on or you'll witness my Second *Going*. . .

CHAPTER FIFTY-ONE

DK: You seem a bit edgy of late. Patience is a virtue, you know.

J: I was just thinking the same about *brevity*.

DK: Don't worry, we've only one Testament left . . .

Now, as for the *New* Testament, it presently contains 27 books—13 of them generally credited to Paul. But the churches *I* attended never explained that these particular texts were not the only ones vetted for canonization.

J: No, in fact huge volumes of Christian writings were generated during the first few centuries after my death. Only a small fraction made its way to the Bible, however. And even today, the authors of the Old Testament, and many who contributed to the New, are still unknown and will likely stay anonymous forever—even for the books of the Old Testament prophets.

DK: I've read that even the authorship of the four New Testament gospels is still a mystery, since scholars now know that Apostles Matthew, Mark, Luke and John had nothing to do with the books that bear their names. Shockingly, some researchers contend that several of Saint Paul's epistles —*and* all the letters credited to Peter, James, and John—are outright fakes. They figure that since these documents were written by people claiming to be someone else, they aren't worth the papyrus they're forged on. And if their very *foundation* is a lie, then calling them holy or inspired is absurd.

J: Agreed . . . but it was pretty widely accepted that many Christian writings during the first two centuries or so were anonymous. Either that or they were pseudonymous, meaning the work was *credited* to someone important, such as an Apostle, but was actually scribed by someone behind the scenes.

DK: Sort of a hazy system, though—doesn't really justify the unscrupulous work of writing fraudulent letters and gospels and passing them off as divine.

J: No, but at least it provides some insight regarding the general methods of the time.

DK: Okay, but there's no proof you ever instructed to *establish* a formal written code or authority. And even if one argues that you started a new spiritual orientation, we've no cause to think you were founding another religion. So why the need for an official Christian holy book at all?

J: Some students wanted scripts of my life and thoughts to study and pass along. But as these new works began circulating, calling something 'scripture' nearly always caused big complications. So churches started shaping them to convenience—blessing some writings while flatly rejecting others. Lots of wrangling went on about the meaning and importance of the works that were spreading, and one cult's heresy was another's firm creed.

DK: The same kinds of fights we have now.

J: Not too much different at all, really. And that's why church authorities —always pros at taking control, of course—stepped in and established their preferred texts as 'holy' while banning all those that fell short.

DK: Defining 'holy scripture,' then, was far more human than divine.

J: Arbitrary and subjective from start to stop. No beatific visions or voices, no lightning and thunder—no proven divinity at all. It was solely the choices of various churchmen and politicians over the centuries that governed which books became scripture and which ones got tossed.

DK: It seems the New Testament was causing problems for Christians even long before it was final . . . in 367, I think. And really, they were offering a New Testament based not on divine revelation but on compromise and grudging adjustment.

J: Yes, and it was bound to occur, since scripture considered legitimate by one faction was often contested by others. Disputed works included Codex Sinaiticus, Letter of Barnabas, Codex Alexandrinus, Clement I, Clement II and many more. In the late second century—with dozens of gospels now public—church father Irenaeus argued only four should be allowed in the canon. His *logic* was a bit fuzzy, though. He said there should be only four sanctioned gospels, as the earth has just "four principal winds."

DK: Thank God he didn't base it on *lakes* . . .

J: This kind of random justification by powerful clergy caused many of these popular writings to be ditched, even though some were already sacred.

DK: Except for the relatively recent news on the Gospel of Judas, we don't hear much talk of other gospels.

J: Christians rarely know they exist . . . but plenty were floating around back then. Along with the Gospel of Judas there was the Gospel of Thomas, Gospel of Phillip, Gospel of Peter, Gospel of the Hebrews,

Gospel of the Egyptians, Gospel of James, Gospel of Truth, and even the Gospel of Mary. Many of these works were quite popular in their day, but choosing which to endorse was a scriptural joust. As an example, Irenaeus—a true hardliner allowing for no salvation outside the church—firmly denied the apostolic authority of 2 John, 3 John, James, and 2 Peter. And even though he fought to keep them out of the canon, all four were kept even so.

DK: Well, it's no big surprise if folks were confused. Scripture-picking might've been better handled by Larry, Curly and Moe.

J: Things did settle down in the early third century as formal works of scripture thinned out. Two especially popular books—Wisdom of Solomon and the Revelation of Peter—were finally scratched, as were the Secret Book of James and Dialogue of the Savior. At that time, Letter to the Hebrews was accepted in the East but spurned by the West, whereas the Revelation of John was embraced by the West but routinely snubbed by the East . . . and never the twain would meet.

In the fifth century, the Letters of Cyril—fully approved by official church chieftains in 431 CE—were nonetheless ultimately booted from the Bible. From then on, for a document to qualify as scripture it had to be penned by an original Apostle or at least personally sponsored by one. Saint Cyril's work met neither of these demands.

DK: Well, I guess if you're assembling an official Christian guidebook, those standards make as much sense as any.

J: Normally I'd agree. But each of the New Testament gospels was written by *several* authors—all of them still unknown—using data from a wide range of sources. In fact, not a single New Testament book was written or even sponsored by an original Apostle. And since Saint Paul really wasn't a true Apostle, having not known me 'in the flesh,' *his* stuff wouldn't have qualified either, even though several of the thirteen works ascribed to Paul are surely his.

DK: This mishmash of anonymous writers and their vastly different views might explain why the New Testament carries such a strange, uneasy mix of literalism and Gnosticism.

J: Sure. In the long years of New Testament revision, both groups added their own editorial slants.

DK: So if the church had known centuries ago what it knows today, most of the current New Testament wouldn't exist.

J: Right. Using the church's own 'Apostle-related' criterion to determine scripture, just *three* of the New Testament's 27 books might now make the cut: the two letters of Peter and the book of James. And, as you said, even those three are soundly rejected by some Bible scholars as forgeries. So the case can be made, depending on whom you consult, that nothing in the church's New Testament should be seen as legitimate scripture. Strangely, the Gospel of Thomas was excluded from the Bible, even while scholarship ascribes as many of my authentic sayings to *that* gospel as it does to any of the four deemed Bible-worthy. Thomas, after all, was indeed an original Apostle. Curiously, his writings never refer to either my birth, my death, or any resurrection post the fact. Thomas's gospel also claims I was married and had a young child—the Gospel of Phillip says the same. These awkward facts were enough for church bigwigs to strike both works from the canon.

DK: Were Thomas and Phillip the documents' true authors?

J: How does it matter? Either way, it shouldn't detract from their value. No one knows who wrote the four gospels of the Bible.

DK: So the church's scripture selection scheme caused a lot of quarreling and grief.

J: Yes, and the battle was never-ending. Fifteen hundred years past my death, some in the church were still feuding over which books should be in its Bible. Even as late as the Reformation, Martin Luther himself was disputing the scriptural worthiness of Hebrews, James, Jude, and Revelation. Finally, after many long centuries of hostile bickering, political gamesmanship, struggles over meanings and interpretations —and of course those pesky translation nightmares—the Roman Catholic Church fixed the Bible as it is during its three-phased Council of Trent, from 1545 to 1563.

DK: So even *that* consensus took nearly twenty years.

J: Yes, but even though the church gave in to the Bible's current structure, every Christian should know that the final product was never a collection of universally approved 'inspired' writings. Even now, various Christian sects around the world are using Bibles whose contents differ markedly from favored Western editions. Think of all the doctrinal shock waves of *that*.

DK: Christians most likely don't realize that their scripture affairs were so random. Using works from the Hebrew literature for the *Old* Testament was certainly sensible enough. But the church was purely discretional —and quite *divided*, it seems—on what the *New* Testament would be.

J: The means weren't always reasonable or fair. In truth, it was mostly church fathers—no church *mothers*, take note—who whimsically decided which writings they wanted as scripture and which ones they didn't. So if there's anything *divine* in that whole fire drill, I'm sorry I just cannot find it. But that is in fact the nutshell evolutionary adventure of what's often called the infallible, internally consistent, and spirit-filled word of the Lord.

DK: Strange, but in all my years in Bible study groups, no one ever taught us that none of the Christian scriptures were selected for their obvious 'divine inspiration.'

J: There's *reason* for that. To avoid controversy—or threat to its power— the church promotes the belief that the Bible's authority stems straight from the Holy Spirit . . . which keeps folks from asking too many questions. But the books of the Christian Bible were chosen firstly to satisfy the needs of a growing institution and were largely determined by forces *within* that institution. Unfortunately, some of the church's main players had motives that often weren't pretty. And in every case, deciding on a particular work's 'holiness' was really just a matter of opinion or even authoritarian force. There's no proof their 'God' ever knew it was happening.

DK: So the whole business of scripture-making was actually quite secular.

J: Well, lots of people *believed* that some of the sacred works were inspired. But the church certainly didn't use 'confirmed inspiration of Spirit' as the yardstick to choose Bible content—how *could* they!?? It's strictly a fact of history that, over a 1500-year period, various church influencers, mostly Catholic, decided that Christian scripture would consist of what they *said* it would be. Holiness by clerical decree.

DK: Quite a cartel they devised.

J: And it set a very dangerous precedent, which too many Christians have blindly accepted or willfully overlooked. Presuming the authority to determine all virtue and evil—to define what's holy and what *ain't*— the church has basically assumed the role of God, even taking on the job of its 'savior' as the more *relevant* arbiter in matters 'tween heaven and earth. In claiming its chosen sacred writings are divinely revealed, and therefore exempt from inspection, the church has positioned *itself*, not God, as the sole cosmic guardian of goodness.

DK: Pretty baffling when considering that definitions of goodness and evil can shift diametrically from one age or culture to the next— yet always based on readings of the very same scriptures.

J: The worst part might be that the church effectively institutionalized inspiration and revelation, teaching that one's own heart is not to be trusted. No more could Creation reveal Itself to *everyone*—only those favored by the church could henceforth claim heavenly touch. Anyone else would risk harassment, ridicule, ostracism . . . even brutal torture and death. One minute you're tending the herb garden and next you're burning as a witch in the local Town Square—just like Jesus would've wanted.

DK: So the church embarked on a real power trip.

J: In that light, however, Christianity is hardly alone—nor does this all lie peacefully in the past. In many parts of the world today, religious rebellion can be fatal, just as it was for me twenty centuries ago.

DK: Well, at least the Christians no longer burn heretics at the stake.

J: No, but some would surely do it if they could . . .

DK: Okay, so I think I'm ready to move on.

J: God in heaven be praised!!

DK: *Heh heh.* That grueling, eh?

J: It's just that all this Bible stuff leaves me dazed. In fact, here's some valuable free advice: If ever you're told that you've got only months to live, spend as much time as possible brushing up on your biblical history— you'll soon start to feel as if time is now dragging on forever . . .

CHAPTER FIFTY-TWO

DK: Our scripture evolution talk was enlightening . . . but I fear you've bled most of the power and mystique from your world's number one bestseller.

J: Hey, don't put the Bible off on *me*—I have no ties to the thing. And it didn't become "the Bible" until a thousand years after my death. Its title, by the way, derives from the Anglo-Latin word *biblia* and it basically just means "book."

DK: Hope the ad firm didn't charge much for *that* one.

J: And calling it the Holy Bible was largely *political*. Religions count on no one questioning things 'holy.'

DK: But even in *your* day you had your venerated texts.

J: All the books of the Hebrew Bible were sacred, of course, but its most revered scripture was the Torah: the first five books of what Christians call the 'Old Testament.' Remember, though, that these Five Books of Moses —Genesis, Exodus, Leviticus, Numbers, and Deuteronomy—were only best-effort attempts to describe a fabled 'history' passed down, mostly by mouth, from as many as fifteen hundred years back. And knowing how a story can grow wildly warped after only a few days of re-telling, even in a fairly small village, imagine the sweeping changes that surely take place as these tales are shared across drastically different cultures over centuries.

DK: So the Books of Moses quite obviously weren't written by heaven.

J: Bible scholars can tell you that they weren't even written by Moses. This should be obvious to anyone who's read Deuteronomy 34, where he writes of his own death and burial. The point is that our scriptures were based on *oral* histories, dating back hundreds of years. Naturally, many Jews believed these works were special . . . but they were no more consistent or free of error than the New Testament books that came later. Mostly they were the Israelites' colorful narratives of their favored-son status with this fickle 'protector' god Yahweh—told from their own sharply biased perspectives.

DK: I guess it's only logical that scriptures appointing Israelites as a specially chosen people were composed by those very same tribes.

J: Of course. The documents were written *by* the Israelites *for* the Israelites. Christians simply snatched some of the old Hebrew texts and then, quite retroactively, claimed partial ownership of them by interpreting vague passages as prophesies about me and my life. You can see, then, why the Jews and others thought it pretty outrageous for Christians to call their new religion relevant—and in fact *compulsory*—for every last soul on the globe. Even the Jews themselves never suggested something so audacious.

DK: So Jewish scriptures were meant only for them and their descendants, which of course included you.

J: But even from an early age, I clashed with *those* writings, too.

DK: How so?

J: Mainly I felt that very little scripture taught peace. Way too much space was given to stories of violence and strife. God is conveyed as a quick-triggered, brutal oppressor who's constantly stirring up conflict and mass-whacking humans like He's killing a mound of ants. I mean *hypocrisy* is the guy's middle name! He orders his tribes to live peacefully, respectfully and with compassion—but He himself will have none of it. These texts have Yahweh blessing slavery, murder—even torture and rape. A controlling Mafioso-like Godfather, He's ever out hunting for trouble— the man is a regular *magnet* for barbarous violence. And here's a good example of how it doesn't take much to make Yahweh go full genocidal . . .

In 1 Chronicles 21, Yahweh is furious with King David for ordering Joab to conduct a national census—don't ask me why. When the counting is done, Yahweh plays mind games with David in a grim kind of 'Deal or No Deal.' He sends down his morbid offer through Gad, one of David's prophets, who comes to bring David the news.

"Yo, Dave, thus saith the Lord: I'll have to punish you for that census— but I'm willing to let *you* pick your poison. You've now got three choices."

"Let's hear 'em," says Dave.

"First," Gad tells him, "Yahweh can curse your people with three years of heart-wrenching famine."

"That one's overdone," Dave balks. "What's next?"

"His second offer," Gad continues, "is to let your enemies butcher your people for three solid months while He renders them totally helpless."

Now, as you can probably imagine, King David is starting to sweat. Sensing that a plea bargain is likely not the final proposal—and knowing that *any* of the three is a PR disaster in the making—David remains skeptically cautious. He's thinking that *surely* the last will at least be a little less bonkers. "Two's not so very tempting, either," he objects. "What's left?"

"Well," Gad explains, "the Bossman says that *you* can spend three full days fighting with *Him*. But here's the catch: while *you're* busy fighting with Yahweh, He's going to slaughter your people like fruit flies and spread various plagues 'round the country, in addition to having his angels of destruction wreak ruin and social turmoil nationwide."

DK: I'm starting to see the charm of those other gods . . .

J: So Yahweh lets David choose not just the manner but also the *length* of his punitive suffering—three years, three months, or three days. The third pick has Yahweh testing David with a kind of god-and-mortal, hand-to-hand combat as He lays down every holocaustic, sociopathic scourge you can imagine onto his people.

DK: I'm tellin' ya, this guy is freakin' *nuts*. And what a lousy set of choices! Not one of them shows peaceful or wise resolution. The first two are downright demented and the third's just a heartless mix of the others. I'll guess that giving his sincerest apologies was never an option for Dave.

J: Nope. And don't forget that God declares elsewhere in the Bible that his love for King David will never end.

DK: *Sheesh*. After *Gad* showed up, David probably had his first doubts. So what happened next, pray tell?

J: Well, on pondering Yahweh's latest three offerings of love, David says to the prophet Gad, "Okay, pal, I've given it some thought and I'll take my chances with the Lord. After all, God is merciful and I'd rather fight with Him than suffer by foes—no telling *what* to expect from *those* thugs." And with this startling show of naïveté, David signs on to a freaky sort of grudge match with his so-called 'merciful' God, who quickly sends the recent head count diving by killing off 70,000 Israelites through one of his patented plagues. This, of course, left David's surviving subjects with a burning question: "When will Yahweh ever come to his census?"

DK: *Heh heh.* You never quit . . .

J: And just to stress the dumbfoundingly strange nature of the episode, the Lord—whose ways, as we all know by now, are *very* damned mysterious—feels that David and Joab, the culprits *behind* the fiasco, should be spared from his savage justice and must only watch their *victims* pay the price of his census-stirred wrath. Here again is the biblical theme of forcing the innocent to pay with their blood and their lives for the lawless behavior of the guilty, while the perps walk away untouched.

DK: Hmmph. Typical life under government . . .   So, having dodged death once again, David is feeling luckier than a guy whose executioner just came down with the flu.

J: Yes, and with great jubilation and relief, Dave does what *any* normal man would do on ducking divine bullets this way: he throws together an altar and burns some animals. And the guilt-wash pays off fast. Smelling the smoky perfume of David's ox roast, Yahweh is finally appeased and calls off the heavenly dogs, just before his angel of death wipes Jerusalem from the face of the earth.

DK: Pretty clever of David, though—saving the remainder of Israel just by charring an ox or two. That's what I'd call some seriously holy smoke.

J: But, c'mon . . . seventy thousand people starved for a mere uncertified *census*!??

DK: It does seem that a good, stiff fine of gold 'n silver would've sufficed— maybe some additional days of sackcloth and ashes to make the point. But you're right: the Lord's violent ways are bizarre. I guess we've gotta trust that He knows what He's doing and lean on his long-lauded grace.

J: If He's much like He was back in *those* days, better not *count* on it, if you know what I mean . . .

CHAPTER FIFTY-THREE

DK: I don't mind telling you, bro, that census drama's downright scary. With heavenly guardians like *that*, who the hell needs enemies?

J: This is why calling each scripture 'holy' rumples my robe. Divinity in the Bible is nothing short of insane. And scrap those ideas of the Bible's inspired inerrancy or its touted internal consistency. Even the story of David and the census is vastly different in 2 Samuel 24 than the one we just heard from 1 Chronicles. The two versions differ in most every way, including the results of the census and the terms of Yahweh's cruel punishment plans. Neither story, by the way, explains why *counting* people was a bad thing. The weirdest clash in these two records is that in 2 Samuel it's *the Lord* who "incited" David to perform the curséd count, even though He later starves seventy thousand people when it's done. In 1 Chronicles, though, it's now *Satan* who does the inciting—Yahweh on the one hand, his devil on the other.

DK: Bizarre discrepancy, for sure.

J: There is one fact, however, on which the two books agree: God's freaky, indiscriminate killing of the seventy thousand, who seemingly did nothing more harmful than stand to be counted for David's inexplicably dangerous and ill-fated census.

DK: That's gotta be one of the kookiest stories ever . . . you'd have to be on drugs to find meaning.

J: Hey, I'm not kidding when I say this Bible God makes Chairman Mao look like president of the Rotary Club. No wonder folks kept Him at arm's length.

DK: Whaddaya mean?

J: Well, even after Yahweh had allegedly led them from Egypt, opened a path of miraculous escape through the sea, 'liquidated' Pharaoh's troops, fed his disgruntled people with sweet heaven-sent manna while offering them hope of a land flowing with milk and honey . . . even despite all that, some of the Lord's 'chosen' chose to worship a metal bovine instead.

DK: And who could blame 'em? At least with a golden cow you don't have to sleep with an eye half-open.

J: The strangest part may be the story's ending: it makes the entire Exodus seem like a lesson in futility. After leading them safely from Egypt amidst loads of dramatics then testing them in the wild a couple of years —even though the promised land Canaan lay within easy walking distance— the mighty Lord Yahweh does finally bring his adopted offenders to the edge of their longed-for utopia.

DK: Wasn't that the goal?

J: Sure, but sadly it turned into a terrible human resources fail. In the end, Yahweh is able to make only *two men*—no women, of course—fit for entry to their promised new home. Apart from Caleb and Joshua, the Lord says, everyone else, Moses too, will be barred for their treacherous disloyalty.

DK: So Yahweh keeps his peeps sweating out in the Sinai sun.

J: Yes, and leaves them *wandering* there for the next forty years. No milk, no honey, no lovely parting gifts or discounts on future purchases.

DK: It appears the promised land was more like the land of broken promises. If I were one of the chosen, I think I'd be longing for the waters of Babylon or the good old days of servitude back in Egypt.

J: Some may see it as victory, I suppose. Eventually, with their forty-year tour of the desert behind them, the Israelites—the ones who hadn't died wandering, that is—finally take possession of their home. But not very much had changed. The people have barely unloaded their trailers when Yahweh promptly kicks off a reverse welcome wagon of merciless, wholesale death. He quickly orders his people to go murdering the land's longtime residents.

DK: Wow, and there goes the neighborhood!! But hey, look at the bright side. At least He finally delivered his people and kept his promise of protection.

J: But was it truly protection? Or had they unknowingly swapped one cruel overlord for another? I mean it's not like Yahweh took constant opinion polls. Much like many Pharaohs of Egypt, He usually just barked out orders— everything was on *his* terms. As Jonathan Swift observed, government without consent of the governed is the very *definition* of slavery.

DK: Any way you view it, the Middle East has never been the paradise that followers of Moses were pledged.

J: Hardly so. For nearly all involved, Yahweh's 'protection' would often result in a virtual landslide of pain. Despite his big-time assurances, what his dear ones actually *got*, according to scripture, was a long and miserable litany of disappointment, hardship and grief. Life in the nation of Israel often meant great suffering, starvation, or continuous war and death.

DK: I can see that being the Lord's chosen was never a joy.

J: Nor was it for many of the *non*-chosen people who crossed their path. All things weighed, Hebrew history has been largely one of chronic duress and never-ending all-in drama. No doubt Tevye speaks for *many* Jewish people in suggesting to the Lord in *Fiddler on the Roof* that perhaps He could choose *someone else* now and then.

DK: *Heh heh.* It's a fine line between devotion and resentment . . .

J: Let's move on to some other intriguing Old Testament stories . . . like the one found in the thirty-first chapter of Numbers. Here's another account of God's deeply mysterious nature. In this one He orders Moses—and again, heaven forbid Yahweh should ever make a simple *request*—to have twelve thousand troops murder all the citizens living under the five kingships of Midian. Incredibly, Moses finds this a perfectly good idea though it's based on the very last motives one expects of a wise, loving God: jealousy and revenge.

DK: And what was the problem this time?

J: It seems the Lord was bothered once again over some of his people out scouting about for new gods—even if there aren't supposed to *be* any others. Apparently, Midianites were having too much profane and 'other-godly' influence on the chosen. But lest He confront the question of why his people find those other gods so steadily appealing, Yahweh simply shoots the messenger and figures that resolving things with another quick ethnic purge should do the trick.

DK: So God directs Big Mo to start the latest round of heavenly slaughter and flush each living Midianite from the earth.

J: Yes, and with no further discussion Moses tells his army to wipe out the entire Midianite culture—posthaste.

DK: Five bucks says they celebrated by burning a few animals.

J: Oh, this affair went well beyond bar-b-que. Once their little genocide is done, the chosen people start doing some choosing of their own. First they steal everything in sight and then burn every Midianite camp and city to the ground. And the fun didn't stop with that early killing and looting.

Later, on the outskirts of his peoples' encampment, Moses learns that his soldiers have spared the lives of the Midianite women and children. Hearing this most troubling news, Moses puts his officers back to work: "Now therefore, kill every male among the little ones, and kill every woman who has known man by lying with him. But all the young girls who have not known man by lying with him, keep alive for yourselves."

DK: Geez, this is just way too much. A glorified prophet kills *thousands* and claims that his 'God' *told* him to? Could such a thing even be true? And did anyone ask him to prove the instructions were Yahweh's? How on earth would they know? In *civilized* nations we *lock down* a crank who kills on 'instructions from God.' And yet, with that same rationale, this biblical 'hero' exterminates *five major human populations*!!??

J: Except for young girls and virgin women, of course . . . Moses has *other* plans for *them*. But first he'll indulge in one final war zone delight. He'll ensure that all the remaining young boys and their mothers —having just been forced to watch the violent, blood-soaked murders and mutilations of their fathers and husbands hours before—must now watch *each other* being brutalized and killed at the hands of his cutthroat assassins.

DK: Holy Moses.

J: And once the godly atrocities are complete, Moses tells his army to keep and divide amongst themselves and their families all the young Midianite virgins—*thirty-two thousand*, we're told—just past the shock of seeing their loved ones killed in cold blood. The same kind of thing appears in Judges 21, where God's people massacre most everyone in the camp of the Benjamites, fellow members of Israel's original twelve tribes. When the terror strike is finished and most of the Benjamites are dead, the victors kidnap hundreds of Benjamite virgins for their personal pleasure.

DK: So in both stories the virgin girls and women are handed over to the brutal lusts of the savage soldiers and others, while Yahweh oversees it.

J: Yep, a kind of winner's war spoils. Most would become concubines— maidservants, sex servants, lower-tiered housewives . . . really just a useful commodity. We could go on if you want, but I think the unvarnished horror speaks for itself. And remember, Yahweh didn't just passively *observe* these things. With Moses and the Midianites, you'll recall, He was the one *demanding* the carnage and smiling as the savagery played out. Adding insult to butchery, Yahweh then *rewards* this demonic behavior by not stepping in when his soldiers divvy up their warring plunder, with virgin young girls being—dare I say it?—the battle's most coveted booty.

DK: Good grief, I'm not even sure what to think. These stories recall God's words to mankind in Matthew: "Inasmuch as ye have done it unto one of the least of my brethren, ye have done it unto *me*."

J: Consider also that the "fruit of the spirit" in Galatians 5 includes love, joy, peace, patience, kindness, goodness, faithfulness, gentleness, and self-control. Ironically, Christians believe this list was inspired and set forth by the very same deity who ordered the holocaust at Midian—and that was but one among many.

DK: I get a sick feeling just *hearing* that stuff . . . I now like the Bible God even *less*. As for Moses . . . well, *these* days guys like that are tried for war crimes. Strange how the most heinous acts of barbarism and hatred are often not by common criminals but by 'respected' leaders of nations. And we let them do it through the sanctioned murder called war.

J: But Moses and David weren't the only Bible big shots with penchants for bloodshed and death. Other Old Testament leaders were equally sadistic and vicious during their own merciless reigns. Even by scriptural accounts, many were reprehensible. In one of the more *infamous* stories of imperial impiety, Israel's King Jehu has the evil Jezebel—queen to former King Ahab, a pretty nasty fellow himself—thrown out an upper window to her death. Blood splashed 'cross hell-'n-creation, her body is then trampled by horses.

Now, in such a case, you might figure Jehu would show a bit of remorse—at least offer a prayer for the royally departed or fire up the barbie for an offering. Instead, Jehu's first move after sending Jezebel diving into the dirt is to sit down and take in a warm, hearty meal with a good jug of wine. By the time he thinks to have Jezebel buried, her gory corpse has been eaten by dogs—all the way down to her skull. Presumably the episode was very much pleasing to the Lord, who allegedly had predicted it. Sordid stuff, this majestic madness . . . but hey, long live the king.

DK: Pretty outrageous, alright. And religion has turned some of these shady scamps into saints.

J: Well, believe me, nary a soul is safe when the *saints* go marching in.

DK: But Judeo-Christian writings certainly don't corner the market on violence. Even the Vedic scriptures, probably the world's oldest, hold stories of warring saints.

J: True, and the gory stuff doesn't comprise the entire Bible. But the Bible does often leave the impression that barbarity is inherent to God's nature, if not his most impressive and predominant trait. He frequently orders his children to brutalize and kill. This stands in stark contradiction to many other Bible passages calling for the compassionate treatment of *everyone*— even including one's enemies. Now, admittedly, adhering to this directive was a problem for the Israelites and even Yahweh himself could rarely do it. And *because* of all this 'godly' violence in many of the world's popular scriptures, billions of modern believers have come to accept a creator who readily unloads lethal force upon those He dislikes. We've touched only a few examples, but hundreds of pages of divine insanity and God-ordained killing—mine included—are lurking in these honored 'holy' texts.

DK: Fun for the entire family, eh?

J: *Oh* yeah. For spiritual upliftment, the Bible's like a day at the morgue. The thing could easily have been titled *Divine Crimes Against Humanity.* Or what about *Murderously Funny Tales of Our God.* Or maybe they could call it *Inspirational Stories of Brutality and Death.*

DK: This Bible God is downright evil. Is malice truly part of his makeup?

J: Why don't we let *Him* answer the question . . .
  In Jeremiah 18, God declares: "If that nation, against whom I have pronounced, turn from their evil, I will repent of *the evil that I thought to do unto them.*" In verse eleven He reiterates his fondness for spite: "Thus saith the Lord: Behold, I frame *evil* against you, and devise a device against you."

DK: Hmmm, devising a device . . . sounds ominous. So Yahweh readily admits to having a mean streak.

J: Yes, and when issuing threats, He's not always vague and poetic. In the second chapter of Malachi, He rages against some disobedient priests for not sufficiently glorifying his name. I mean *what else*, right? He warns, "Behold, I will rebuke your offspring and spread *dung* upon your faces . . ."

DK: Oooh, nasty.

J: And again the poor *children* pay the price of their parents' mistakes. Another example of the Bible God's devotion to evil lies in 1 Samuel chapter 15. Here He directs King Saul, the first king of Israel, to take up arms and attack all the bad-guy Amalekites. As usual, the motive is simple revenge and no one is to be spared. Not the young, not the innocent— and no, not even the animals. The Lord tells Saul, "Now go and smite Amalek, and utterly destroy all that they have; do not spare them, but kill both man and woman, infant and suckling, ox and sheep, camel and ass."

DK: Geez, this tyrannical deity doesn't take pity on family, flora nor fauna.

J: He's not much of an animal lover, really. He once ordered Joshua to cruelly slice the hamstrings of his defeated enemy's horses—an excruciatingly painful procedure in which at least one of the animals' leg tendons is severed by a sharp knife to prevent it being used again in battle. King David does the same to *his* enemy's horses in 2 Samuel 8. Clearly, the crippled steeds—crying and screaming in pain and terror—would never be able to run again and often had to be immediately killed. Would you say that a deity who encourages or even *allows* this kind of thing might qualify as evil?

DK: I'm starting to be a believer . . .

J: And here's even *more* Bible proof of Yahweh's bent for devilry and gall. In Exodus 32 we read, "And the Lord repented of the *evil* which he thought to do to his people." First Samuel 18 is even clearer: *"an evil spirit from God* rushed upon Saul."

DK: So now we've read several passages in which the Lord harbors evil intent toward his children—and still others where He actually carries it out.

J: Yes, He constantly threatens and imposes ghastly horrors on his morally deficient creation. And even though his laws direct his people to be kind to their neighbors and such, He's certainly not leading by example.

DK: Well, maybe it's not true with his *promise* . . . but when Yahweh gives warning, He usually means what He says.

J: Oh, there's certainly no question of *that*. And for more confirmation, have a look at Numbers 11. The Lord again directs the flame of his eternal love toward his people by incinerating a large assembly of them.

DK: What!?? You mean He *burns* them to death?

J: Torches 'em like a cheese fondue . . . they may as well have moved to Sodom.

DK: Crikey, what'd they do *this* time—jack around while bringing in the sheaves?

J: They complained.

DK: Well, *of course* they complained. I complain, too, when I'm 'bout to be burned alive.

J: No, I mean that's the *reason* He scorched 'em. They were complaining.

DK: Huh?? You mean to say that Yahweh charred the chosen just for doing a little whining? About *what*!??

J: You're stumbling over a feather here, pilgrim. When the Christian 'Lord of mercy' sets his children on fire because they were bitching, does it really matter what they were bitching *about*?

DK: You're right, the man's completely over the edge—yet the church calls Him a God of great love.

J: Actually, on the Bible God's list of priorities, judging and vengeance rank considerably higher than love. But perhaps you could make the argument He's not always quite that *sadistic*. In Numbers 21 He kills another unlucky flock of his sheep in a way that—if you're willing to distinguish between *levels* of cruelty and spite—could possibly be considered more humane. He merely has them attacked and bitten by lethally poisonous snakes.

DK: *Sanctified serpents*!! Does He ever just garnish someone's wages??? You know, until now I thought I had a pretty good handle on the Bible's nuts and bolts—but I never knew it had so many *nuts*. Hearing one biblical barbarity after another, I have to say it's incredibly strange that religion uses books like the Bible to teach its followers how to behave.

J: Considering headlines, they seem to have caught on fast . . .

CHAPTER FIFTY-FOUR

DK: Well, you've proven *one* thing for sure: it's no great challenge trashing religion. There's so much to scorn, it's like being a political analyst. But some people say that we have to believe in *something*. I mean these gods of religion are fast on the trigger, true, but a flock still needs a shepherd, no?

J: People may sometimes claim that the Lord is their shepherd— but time and time again, the minute they enter the valley of the shadow, they're fighting with their rods and staffs. Viewing violence, revenge and aggression as viable 'Christian' behavior, they quickly attack first and pray later. They figure that any conduct acceptable for God will surely be good enough for them. And where did they *get* this historically dangerous idea? Why, straight from the pages of the 'Good Book,' of course.

DK: Many Christians likely aren't familiar with the Old Testament— or even with the Bible in whole. They prob'ly don't realize how much of it should be X-rated . . . or the death, hypocrisy and destruction it contains.

J: And the problem goes far past the violence. Apart from being *spiritually* jumbled, these scriptures test the intellect as well. Did Jonah really get swallowed, transported and coughed up by a giant fish onto the beach? Did Noah build an ark and bring in two of each species on the planet to ensure their survival? How would that happen? We're never told the answers.

DK: Various parts of the Bible have proven historically accurate, though.

J: Plenty have proven historically *in*accurate, too. The very worst of logic is to think that if *some* parts are true, then the *whole thing* is true. Ask any cop.

DK: Okay, I agree it's not smart to indulge every word of the Bible— especially given all that science, academics and researchers have learned in the thousands of years since all of its books were penned. Nevertheless, even if not the *literal* truth, some of it may be important *theologically*.

J: Sorry, pal, I fear that dike won't hold. Not if we're talking about torture, planned starvation and other forms of serial mass murder. Don't say that Yahweh killed *seventy thousand people* over a census and then preach of the "Word's hidden truth." Crazy is crazy, my friend. Defending mass murder because *God* thought it up . . . well, it just doesn't wash with me. Even the very concept is insulting. Shouldn't the deity be *preventing* this kind of thing?

DK: You're right, God is the *last* one to be making excuses for.

J: Look, I don't give a friar's frock what 'moral' or allusive significance these screwball scriptures may have. If I'm the average human and religion tells me that God dumped a murderous purge onto Israel because two guys took a citizen count—or burned his kids alive because they were *griping*—I don't want this scary dude within a mile of me or my clan. And you?

DK: Well, obviously a lot of that stuff is mere allegory or tribal mythology.

J: That's not what the church would say. It's only a problem for literalists, of course, but you can't claim the Bible is the flawless word of God and then call *some* of it mythological, mere legend, or symbolic. Creating an all-or-nothing proposition, the church has boxed itself in. But does it show integrity for a group to hide important information on its history —and keep members even from *knowing* it—if it might be bad for business? How loyal to the cause of human advancement is *that*?

DK: One philosopher said of religion that we *must* be critical when criticism is needed. He said if something can be destroyed by the truth, it *should* be.

J: Right, because every ideology that discourages self-inspection will decay into a dangerous, self-righteous hypocrisy. Claiming the Bible has no major defects and each line's an utterance from God, churches must suppress, obscure, denounce or ignore the vast mountain of proof that they're wrong.

DK: It does make for a good debate. For example—speaking of mountains— did Moses really come down from Sinai carrying tablets with writings from God? Or is the story merely good fiction? Either way, those words had serious impact on the planet.

J: You bring up the Ten Commandments, but you may be surprised to learn that the Torah contains not just ten, but *six hundred and thirteen* separate commandments. Many, however, were relevant only for certain groups. In Christian circles, the ones given Moses on Sinai got most of the notice. And they would better be called "statements," not "commandments."

DK: Well, *whatever* you call 'em, in the book of Exodus God supplies Moses with his now-world-famous Top Ten.

J: Actually, if you read 'em through, you'll find you've got some small ones mixed with the bigs. Technically, then, there's more like fifteen or twenty. One of the laws Moses brings back from Mount Sinai is "Thou shalt not kill." But this freshly made policy, which surely wouldn't have been a new insight to any *civilized* society, strangely doesn't catch on. The minute he returns from Sinai, Moses finds his people worshiping the infamous golden calf—worked up at their request by Moses' own brother, Aaron. Bull worship was common in those days and some of the Israelites had succumbed to its temptations. As you can well imagine, Moses is not much amused. And we already know that when Moses gets a bee in his bonnet, homicide lies very close indeed.

DK: I've forgotten most of the details, but I'm willing to wager that Moses zeroes Aaron on the spot.

J: Lucky for you I'm not a betting man—because Moses virtually ignores his brother's central role in the mess. He does conclude, of course, that severe punishment is required and wastes no time with his response. Brushing aside Yahweh's newly published mandate not to kill, Moses quickly summons those "on the side of the Lord" and orders these specially assembled ninjas to strap on their swords and go through the camp—"from gate to gate"—and carve up all their idol-worshiping brothers, neighbors and friends. Predictably, Moses claims this gruesome order came straight from the Lord himself. Later, with three thousand members of the tribe ferociously murdered at his decree, Moses tells his blood-soaked henchmen that their actions have "ordained" them "for the service of the Lord"—a divine rite of passage, it seems— and the Lord will now *bless* them for it.

DK: Wow. The Moses no Bible teacher will teach!! Moses may have been "slow of tongue" but he was damned quick to order up death.

J: And even aside from the vicious acts of Moses, Yahweh telling people not to kill was fairly shocking from the start when you think of his *own* long history of lethal deeds. And the biblical madness mounts. In two chapters *following* issuance of the new ethics policies in which killing has officially been outlawed, Yahweh pulls a strange and confusing turnabout by listing nearly a dozen offenses for which He clearly orders the Israelites to kill— even just for cursing one's parents.

DK: I'd have been dead by age five . . .

J: Next, upon giving blessing to slavery, Yahweh warns that the following crimes shall inevitably result in one's death: kidnapping; owning an ox that kills someone; engaging in sorcery; committing bestiality; and of course building altars to those never-seen-but-always-problematic "other gods."

DK: So, is that the end of Yahweh's capital offenses?

J: Actually, there is one more . . . and possibly the strangest of the bunch. The Lord lastly warns that *He personally* will kill *everyone* who dares to wrong widows, orphans or strangers. This too is a paradox since scripture says that Yahweh killed thousands and thousands of strangers in foreign tribes and armies, thereby filling vast regions with widows and orphans!!

DK: So Yahweh himself is swelling the ranks of the groups He's so intent on protecting.

J: Exactly. And here's additional Old Testament mystery worth mention . . .
   The book of Leviticus reports that insects have only four legs instead of the required six now known to science. Chapter 11 says *birds* have four legs as well. Second Kings 8 states that King Ahaziah was twenty-two when he started his reign as monarch, whereas 2 Chronicles says he was *forty*-two. Then we've got three *major* conflicts in the two books of Samuel regarding the death of King Saul. First Samuel 31 states that Saul committed suicide by falling onto his sword. *Second* Samuel has *two* accounts of Saul's death— and neither jibes with the suicide report. Chapter 1 says that Saul was killed by an Amalekite, while chapter 21 states that Saul was killed by Philistines. The Old Testament also has what might be called a 'giant' contradiction, as it leaves serious doubt about who really killed Goliath.

DK: What?! The fight between David and Goliath is one of the best-known tales of the Bible. Young David, future king of Israel, slays the supersize bully with nothing but precocious bravery and a sling.

J: Do the research and you'll find a peck of problems with the 1 Samuel story of David and Goliath. In the earliest text of 2 Samuel 21, a member of one of David's elite fighting units, a man named El-hanan, is clearly said to have killed the famous Philistine giant. First Chronicles 20 *expands* the confusion by stating that El-hanan killed Goliath's *brother*. In another story of David, 2 Samuel 8 states that when David defeated King Hadadezer, he captured seventeen hundred horsemen. But chapter 18 of 1 Chronicles says that David took *seven thousand* horsemen. One claim in the two versions is consistent, though: David had his soldiers sever the hamstrings of hundreds and hundreds of enemy horses post-battle.

DK: I can't even think about that . . .

J: Another Old Testament discrepancy involves the number of sons born to David's father Jesse. First Samuel 16 states that Jesse had eight sons, while First Chronicles 2 says he had seven.

DK: So, we've got some accounting snags.

J: But it's not just the Bible's *numbers* that don't add up: the very claims themselves are extreme. In 2 Kings, the writer states with certainty that Elijah was carried off to heaven by horses and chariots . . . made of *fire*—again a possible familiar reference of the period to an advanced alien craft and civilization. Exodus says the Nile River once turned to blood and that placing striped sticks in the presence of breeding sheep would somehow produce striped offspring.

DK: I wonder if placing an axe produced lamb chops . . .

J: Here's one that's always good for a laugh. Judges 1:19 reads, "And the Lord was with Judah, and he took possession of the hill country, but he could not drive out the inhabitants of the plain, because they had chariots of iron." So the all-powerful God of creation cannot rid the land of its rightful owners because their *chariots* are just too damned strong.

DK: Omigod, how funny! Any other oddities worth sharing?

J: This one might be of interest: in two separate Bible books and chapters, 2 Kings 19 and Isaiah 37, you've got Yahweh, as He did with the Torah, 'inspiring' different writers to say exactly the same thing—and at quite some length as well. And let's not overlook the biblical animals that *talk*. First, of course, is Eden's infamous serpent. Speaking perfectly fluent Hebrew, I suppose, he coaxes young Eve into eating the forbidden fruit, therein becoming the most influential reptile in history. In Numbers 22, Balaam's donkey lectures him sternly on animal cruelty.

DK: *Heh heh*, cute. But it wasn't the *last* time a sermon came out of an ass . . .

J: Here's a curiosity. According to Genesis, which actually has *two* creation accounts, an entire cosmos was created in only six days—a record that still stands, by the way. But are we asked to believe that a God of limitless brilliance used the revolution of a tiny orb called "Earth" to keep track of his schedule during creation? Did He *really* plan his work by its rotations, starting in each morning like a common hired hand? And why did He bother splitting the task into shifts? Did the Almighty Lord of creation need a periodic nap?!! And what about Eve? Was she truly created as only an afterthought because Adam was getting a bit lonely? In the natural world, the *female* is the starting point of creation: life begins in the womb. But Genesis has a *man* at the center of it all—he basically 'gives birth' to the woman.

DK: Well, as you've made note, that's the kind of thinking you'd *expect* from a patriarchal society.

J: Sure. I'm only saying that biblical writers—and therefore their *writings*—were products of their cultures. And why would you believe differently? Their works reflect the same scientific ignorance, social realities and myth-based theologies that heavily colored their worlds. Taking each word literally is absurd. Don't lean on the lazy belief that God whispers every word of scripture into the writer's waiting ears. Here's a couple of passages whose claims differ by an order of magnitude. Second Chronicles 9 says that Solomon had four thousand stalls for his horses. But First Kings 4 claims that Solomon had *forty* thousand stalls—apparently, God got his figures confused. And scholars have fought over this kind of stuff for years.

DK: Alright, so there's numbering brawls on Sol's stalls. Is that sort of thing a real problem?

J: Only for hard-headed literalists. They're cornered into using the most cockamamie, convoluted arguments conceivable as they fight all these scriptural feuds. This typically amounts to insisting that up is down and black is white—or that "cat" doesn't really *mean* "cat," but in fact should be taken to mean "grain silo." These obvious Bible discrepancies have always made the church squirm. Conceding *even one* biblical boo-boo would mean that it can't keep selling its scripture as inerrant or inspired 'words of God.'

DK: Because that would raise questions about every line in the Bible.

J: Right. Which means the church is faced with defending ideas even the average teenager should mock. And not only is the Bible unreliable as a history book, but it's packed with stories of a deity who's often violent, illogical and corrupt—casts Him in a pretty bad light, wouldn't you say?

DK: So, not a hero the average person can admire.

J: No, and this makes a terribly tough case for those who insist that *God* was the author of Jewish and Christian scripture. If the Bible is Yahweh's authorized biography, He surely didn't make himself shine.

DK: And scientifically speaking, scripture's full of intellectual challenges.

J: Yeah, like the story of Lot's wife turning into salt . . . the Bible's *peppered* with 'em.

DK: When you think about it, very few parts of the Bible would strike objective readers as inspired. I'd bet that not a single biblical writer ever imagined that his work would become holy scripture.

J: Old Testament authors would be especially shocked at the content of the Christian Bible. Never in their wildest dreams would they have envisioned their writings being used later on to link Judaism with an upstart religion that directly and theologically opposed it. The Bible's not without value, of course— not at all. The historical and spiritual implications of some of its more *cryptic* parts are paradigm-shattering for those who can properly interpret. But don't flush common sense down the drain because someone slaps old writings between two lovely, gold-embossed covers and calls 'em holy. I mean face it: The Bible was never meant to *be* a Bible. A thousand pages of mostly disconnected, meandering pseudo-history, much of it is nothing but silly or monotonous drivel.

DK: Speaking of silly, I remember a funny scripture from Sunday school— something about barring guys with groin problems from church.

J: The passage is from Deuteronomy. Yahweh declares that any man with crushed testicles is banned from the assembly of the Lord.

DK: Yeah, that's it. Who could've known that a thing like this would be such a serious problem? But maybe there was perfectly good *reason* for that rule. A fundamentalist would argue that no scripture lacks significance.

J: What about the Old Testament book of Esther? The text never once refers to God. For that matter, neither does Song of Solomon.

DK: Some say it refers to Him allegorically.

J: Oh, I see. Only *parts* of the Bible are the *literal* word of God, while other parts must be interpreted *figuratively*.

DK: I should've kept my mouth shut.

J: Better not to mount the horse if it won't getcha back to the barn . . .

DK: Alright, any last bits of Bible-bashing before we move on?

J: Well, one of my personal favorites comes from Genesis 21: "The Lord visited Sarah as he had said, and the Lord did to Sarah as he had promised. And Sarah conceived . . ."

DK: *Heh heh.* I can see how you'd get a good chuckle out of that one— like Sarah became pregnant directly by . . . well, let's just call it the 'hand' of God.

J: Right, and this would mean that her son Isaac's conception was every bit as wondrous as mine allegedly was. The common conclusion, of course, is that Sarah later conceived through her husband Abraham, just as Yahweh had promised in Genesis 18. We assume the Lord "unlocked" Sarah's womb in the same way He did with the women of the house of Abimelech in Genesis 20. But that's not what the passage *says*— it says the Lord *visited* Sarah. He didn't do that with Abimelech's women. You gotta wonder why Sarah rated this special visit from Yahweh and what exactly happened while He was there.

DK: Whatever it was, it clearly required a house call. One can only *imagine* the gossip *that* must've caused: "Guess who dropped by Sarah's place last week . . ."

CHAPTER FIFTY-FIVE

The warm, sunny day had been a long one and a cooling breeze kicked in as the late afternoon sun fell toward the skyline. To cover as much ground as possible in the time left, I sensed a need to move things along . . .

৩৩

DK: This talk of biblical madness could probably run on for days—but we've only got a few more hours of light. Anyway, I think you've made your point: we can't believe everything we're told.

J: Well, why take theology from those who thought the sun circled 'round a flat earth? Not that ancient cultures had nothing to teach later generations or that all of their wisdom is trash. But believing every word in their 'holy' works is really no smarter than believing all that religion, politics or education puts forth today. In a few hundred years, people will look back in shock at much of what was formerly held 'truth.'

DK: I just realized something ironic. In several churches I've attended, they conclude their scripture readings with "This is the word of the Lord." But now I'm thinkin' they should probably add on, "if you can possibly ever believe *that*." On the other hand, a few religious groups are starting to ask important questions. The United Synagogue of Conservative Judaism even came out with a modernized Torah called *Etz Hayim*.

J: Yeah, Hebrew for "Tree of Life."

DK: So, this newer look at the Torah finally accounted for some of the latest discoveries from anthropology, archaeology, and "ologies" I can't even pronounce. And these explosive academic writings in *Etz Hayim* created quite a stir at the time. For example, the scholars give pretty solid evidence that Abraham—the great biblical patriarch upon whose heritage Judaism, Christianity and Islam are based—never even existed!! Think of all the implications of *that*!! The same is true of Moses, too. Consensus among academics is that Moses was indeed a *legendary* figure and not a historical person—a pretty big deal since Moses is the Jews' most honored prophet. And some Jewish scholars now say they know for certain that the Exodus, among other Old Testament stories, was total fabrication from the start. So, which is it . . . provable fact, or fiction?

J: Frankly, I was never okay with that Israel-in-Egyptian-captivity thing. My biggest question was one that never gets asked: if the Lord was so vexed over his people becoming enslaved, why did He ever *allow* it? Scripture says He used one miraculous power after another in *extracting* the Israelites from their woe. Why not use those same unlimited powers to *prevent* it? The same could be asked of the captive years in Babylonia.

DK: Ah, c'mon, you danced around my question. Five percent of any publishing profits to your favorite charity if you'll give me an exclusive—a little something to hang my journalism degree on.

J: Fantastic!

DK: So you'll do it?

J: No, I mean it's fantastic how a journalist managed to dangle a proposition *and* a preposition all in one sentence.

DK: You really know how to hurt a guy . . .

J: Hey, I'm not here to rewrite any history—but only to discredit certain *versions* of it. I intend to free my name from the age-old clutches of religion; to squeeze through the prison bars of dangerous or limiting beliefs; to clarify that no one person or institution has control of the Christ and that every human being potentially *is* the Christ.

DK: Okay, good enough. But have a heart and toss me a morsel or two. These new Bible findings are bigger than a Hollywood divorce.

J: I'll give you this much: there's no evidence in Egyptian sources that a large population of Jews was ever held captive there. The monumental pyramids of Egypt—something even a casual passerby would surely make careful note of in his journals—are not once mentioned in the Old Testament. Nor is there a single archaeological trace of Moses in the Sinai desert. For all of his *biblical* glory, Moses never appears in any Egyptian records of the period—even though some will claim that Moses himself was Egyptian. Either way, the story of him and his captive tribesmen didn't seem to make it to the papers.

DK: Wait, that makes no sense. Unless I'm mistaken, the Israelites were, in theory, confined to Egypt for, what, three or four hundred years? You can't have an exiled nation enslaved to a string of monarchs on foreign soil for *centuries* without someone in those various regimes making a note of it. That's impossible.

J: But they didn't. The world will be stunned to learn that the tribes of Israel never set foot in Egypt, and there's no evidence to support the Bible story of the Exodus, just as there's no confirmation of the Nile turning suddenly to blood. You would think at least a handful of Egyptians living along the delta might've scratched a few lines on *that* major development, too. But no, not a peep. Same thing with Jacob's son Joseph. The Old Testament claims he was Pharaoh's right-hand man—the second most powerful guy in the government. Yet Egyptian annals say not a word of the biblical Joseph *nor* of his famous coat with many collars.

DK: I believe you mean coat of many *colors*.

J: *Whatever*. The point is that Egyptian writings never describe this stuff. If the Israelites *had* lived in large numbers under ancient Egyptian kings —who were never called Pharaohs, by the way—the Egyptians, apparently, didn't give an Aswan damn.

DK: Sounds like some time-honored Jewish 'history' is being wiped out. Researchers are even raising questions about King David. Some insist that if he existed at all, he probably was a Podunk leader at most. As I said, even major *Jewish* historians—Israeli professor Dr. Shlomo Sand and others—have solid evidence proving that some of these stories were strictly legendary or heavily hyped at best. It's not even debatable anymore.

J: This isn't the big problem it seems. Millions of Jews—and probably hundreds of millions of Christians—don't read their scriptures literally. Some ministers and rabbis are in fact proudly outspoken atheists. Honest academics know for certain that the Jews never existed as any kind of nation-race. The storied saga painting them as an ever-oppressed, earth-wandering people of exile, longing for 'home' in a land biblically granted by God, was actually the 19-century product of Zionist fanatics, and no plot of Jewish land in the Middle East was ever divinely foretold. Even the popular "Diaspora" legend, a claim that Rome banished all the Jews from Judea following destruction of the great Second Temple, is now a scholastically confirmed myth.

DK: How'd the story take root?

J: Interestingly, this part of the Jews' 'history' was spread by Christians. They sold it to the world as a story of divine retribution for the Jews' rejection of the gospel. But it never happened.

DK: Then the Jews weren't 'scattered to the corners of the earth' as we've always been told.

J: Nope. Most *non-Israeli* Jews are heirs of those *converted* to the religion through evangelists within their native lands. Not only is the Zionist myth untrue, but the vast majority of Jews on the planet don't closely relate to Israel and they feel no special kinship to a separate Jewish state. They simply identify as citizens of their homelands—just as you'd expect. The average Zionist Christian will be shocked to learn that 99 percent of present-day Jews, either in Israel or abroad, have no historical or genetic ties at all to the original twelve tribes of Israel or the biblical kingdom of Judah.

DK: Yeah, these maverick Jewish scholars have even shown that many *Palestinians* are much more likely than the average Jew to have ancient Semitic roots—all the more compelling with the Jews themselves spreading the new knowledge.

J: It shows courage. It proves that *real* spirituality doesn't need old myths to keep it breathing. Religions the world over need this same kind of honest debate and should ask what they're really achieving. If pledging to save your soul is the best they've got, they may as well shut the doors and give refunds—maybe do some remodeling and make the joints something of use. Homeless shelters, hospitals . . . all-night taco stands. When religion teaches that you're anything less than a sovereign, immortal and universal being, you may be wasting time with that religion. What truth would you be hoping to learn if not the truth about your *Self*?

DK: I think it's mainly an issue of authority. When told by people we trust that something's straight from the mouth of God, we tend not to question it—especially if we're young. The people we love and respect take it seriously, so we think they must know what they're doing, as we carry on the tradition.

J: Well, let's be honest: most of religion's radical claims would never survive past the 'sacred' books that contain them.

DK: True. Religion gives weight to ideas and beliefs that on *reasonable* grounds are absurd. Yet there we sit—in synagogues, churches, temples, and mosques—nodding our heads in accord.

J: But what exempts one's faith from critical thought? Why use your brain in all walks of life but religion? Even ignoring its fantastical stories, you've still got problems to face. Take the accounts of Genesis, for instance. Creationists will argue that Adam and Eve showed up in the Garden about

4,000 BCE. But how could that be? By then, humankind was using the plow and the wheel . . . even sailing the seven seas. It's scientific fact that people have existed for hundreds of thousands of years. So Christians have *another* big Gordian knot. If mythical Adam and Eve were not the world's first humans—and science knows for certain that they weren't—then 'original sin' has no meaning, and never was there any need fo—

DK: For *you*! Now I get it!

J: Well, I was going to say no need for the Christian Atonement—no need to pay for the famous 'first sin' in the Garden. Don't negate me entirely, though, I still played a critical role . . . but certainly not what Christians have come to presume.

DK: You've sliced about six full notches off the Bible Belt. Where do we land after this scriptural scrubbing and scrapping?

J: We're right back at the beginning. You now know the Bible is a collection of subjective documents written by people with colored viewpoints and whose aims were all over the map. Often they were simply retelling ancestral legends or reconstructing old myths from earlier cultures. Finally, the Catholic Church with a good bit of sway from the Protestants and their powerful Reformation—gave blessing to the works that supported its narrative while purging all those that didn't.

DK: So the stark reality is this: the Bible is based entirely on third-hand copies of works all done in isolation from the others and in vastly different cultures—*centuries apart*—by writers we mostly don't know. And since the original texts are gone and can't be matched with the ones we're using today, we'll have to trust the church to be honest with us, even though the church itself selected, interpreted, edited, assembled, and canonized these writings, ultimately calling them the inspired words of God. This is the truth of the Bible . . . is that pretty much the gist?

J: Yes, and all down the line its books were scribed, translated, copied, altered, doctored or even fabricated by people with vested interests—just like tyrant Constantine, all had an axe to grind. The hoax wore on for centuries with a cast of thousands. Popes, patsies, thugs and theologians. Scholars, schemers, fools 'n fanatics . . . frontmen, friars and frauds. Entire texts were changed or rejected at the whims of those with Christian influence or power.

DK: You know, in some ways your timing really stinks. You should've come 'round within a century after your death—before things got so crazy. *Now* the church is dug in and won't "go gentle into that good night." And not only that, but Christianity continues to splinter like rotten wood. Protestants are constantly fighting and some have even filed for divorce. Catholicism is holding up mostly okay, I guess, but it's always plagued by those nonstop felony filings and haunted by its violent, abusive past. Now *you* show up and make da Vinci's code into a five-buck theft from petty cash.

J: It's true. If religion's in turmoil *now*, wait until *this* hits the wire.

DK: Not to spoil the party . . . but if you're hoping for another Reformation, you probably shouldn't hold your breath. Even if Christian leaders are learning the *real* Bible story, they certainly aren't eager to spread it. So I see two possibilities. Either they *want* us to know the facts but they aren't telling us. Or they *don't* want us to know and they *won't* tell us. Either way makes me wonder who's guiding the ship.

J: Just like the early days of old. Never was it *God* guarding the enlightening Tree of Knowledge, but rather just purveyors of *religion* . . .

CHAPTER FIFTY-SIX

DK: I can't speak for other religions, but I know that Christianity is *intended* to establish an environment of harmony and peace. In spite of its faults, the Bible is, theoretically, a book of redemption and hope.

J: Hope of what? Appeasing a deity who'd otherwise slit your throat? A pretty unnerving 'redemption,' my friend. Your spirit isn't in danger and your line to 'God' is *built-in*—it's yours in a cathedral or jail. So the Bible may or may not be useful, but it certainly isn't needed for your growth or for any kind of meaningful salvation. And how could the Bible be seen as a helpful 'spiritual' text? It's one scary thing after another.

DK: You've walked on thin ice for a good period now—but you just busted through to the chilling waters below.

J: But have a good look at the world. The Bible and other revered writings have been spiritually counter-productive and led to some blood-spilling brands of religion.

DK: Hey, I'm the first to admit that, with the Bible, one *has* to conclude that its God isn't often too loving. He's a violent, self-serving bully who's never content until everyone else is dismal and atoning for his chronic dismay— we're always bowing prostrate in dust. I mean when *Yahweh's* not happy, ain't *nobody* happy.

J: Scripture says salvation is a gift of grace, offered by God in mercy and in love. It also says to work out your own salvation "with fear and trembling." Now, aside from the fact that your Self can never be darkened and doesn't need saving, everyone knows that grace and love do not cause "fear and trembling." That phrase, directly from the holy New Testament, is a good example of the dread that often poisons religion.

DK: Well, I have to say that I'm sick of hearing that God is hovering over my shoulder, watching my every impure thought and noting every moral infraction. I guess it only proves your point: the God of the Bible is often just a control freak with a bad case of OCD. He rules with a grudge and a fist.

J: He's a God of immense contradiction, as well. Yahweh forms a universe in only six days yet needs *thousands of years* to deploy his convoluted plan of salvation—a bizarre scheme which teaches that only injustice and a barbarous murder could finally bring love to its full.

297

And since no one bothers to ask it, where has this Bible God *gone*? First He's hawking his peoples' every move and meddling in their stuff like nosy neighbors. He lays down mountains of laws for the Israelites, watching over even the most mundane parts of their lives. But suddenly the man goes missing. Without so much as "Amen" or "Goodbye," this 'God' goes into hiding and then rules two thousand years *in absentia*. He births Christianity but then, like so many millions of his followers, doesn't even show at Christmas or Easter . . . although, in his defense, He's likely not too keen on pagan holidays.

DK: It seems He's lost all semblance of presence and power. He can't even get his *preachers* to behave. But maybe it's just as well He's so withdrawn. Considering how things are going, He'd likely start another big flood. Bible God is something of a crackpot uncle Irv. It's true that He's crotchety, antisocial and weird—but we cut Him slack 'cause he's *family*.

J: If "perfect love casts out fear," as the New Testament says, it also must cast out a *God* of fear. In your letter, you questioned the honesty of those who need the life scared out of them before they're compelled to convert. And you're right: that's not faith, it's just a wary precautionary measure. Salvation through slavery is an absolute sham and isn't worth the name— true salvation is freedom *from* enslavement.

DK: I'm shocked we've been so patient with religion's fearsome God who sends his stubborn, sassy children off to hell. The notion would seem beyond any smart person's will to believe it—yet *I* bought into it for *years*.

J: Ironically it's the very *threat* of damnation that keeps most believers from daring to doubt its truth—they're sure God wants them believing crazy ideas. Fearing for their souls, they give themselves over to the concept of hell and then buy costly insurance plans from the same institutions that scared them with hell at the start! I mean is this a cunning business model or what!!?

DK: But *Christians*, at least, have darned good *reason* to play safe, with hints of hellfire from Matthew to Revelation. The church claims its scripture is *sacred* and its creeds are the one path to life . . . so folks take the tale as it's given, even if it doesn't make sense. Still, I guess it wouldn't seem right to burn the whole cornfield just because it has a few bugs. Even *I've* found comfort in various scriptures, and some truly do inspire.

J: Of course, but we're not talking of mere inspiration—we're speaking of *salvation of the soul*. Trust me, I'm all for getting inspired. But when these writings cause self-loathing, conflict, hatred or fear, please heed the call of peace and walk away.

DK: Is all scripture ultimately unneeded?

J: Technically, yes . . . because Truth is your very nature. Some scriptures can certainly be helpful and even spiritually enlightening—it's strictly a personal thing. You're none the worse, however, if you find no value there. So snuff out the fires of your sacrificial offerings and rise from the dust of repentance. While you're at it, throw out the sackcloth and rinse off the ash.

DK: Hey, martyrs just wanna have fun.

J: Look, if God is the character so many imagine and He's set on saving all from a dreadful fate, He'd easily show up for a chat this evening with each suffering soul on the globe. In one night's work He'd remove all doubt about himself and his eternal intentions. You'd think that sparing his children from hell would be worth the additional stab. If all the *written* orders don't do it, a one-on-one counseling session might.

DK: A bit unworkable, perhaps.

J: Why so? It's *God* we're talking of here! By the story of Sarah's miraculous conception, He's seemingly good with putting in private appearances. He could do it all at once on a worldwide scale. Does He figure it's not worth the trouble? Or is He too perturbed about oversexed schoolboys lusting for the pep squad girls?

DK: Alright, I give up. It's time to rethink my beliefs about God.

J: A better start, I'd say, would be rethinking your beliefs about *you.* Once you understand *yourself,* you'll misconstrue God no more.

DK: That recalls an old spiritual proverb. "At first I had a hundred questions about God—but then when I *met* Him, all of my questions dissolved."

J: Right, because once you know for yourself, the questions fall away and beliefs lose their punch—you see them for the fakers they are. Not by chance does "belief" contain the word "belie." Open your dictionary and read.

DK: Okay . . . "belie: to lie or give false or misleading ideas about something; to disguise maliciously or misrepresent; to prove false."

J: Now do you see the tie? Beliefs tend to "belie" your reality. They're false gods made of thought-forms. Conceptual graven images. Subtler versions of the infamous golden calf. At the feet of these idols you sometimes slay all reason and spiritual discernment. Never believe anything you forever have to *believe* in. I taught a spiritual path that eclipses all doctrines and ideas and puts you in touch with the One. Obsessing over words leads to dangerous devotion to beliefs—the root of the world's great suffering. Instead of pointing to something external, I constantly urged those seeking answers to go inward to the place of discovery. The kingdom lies always within.

DK: You're quoted telling your disciples just before your capture, "These things have I spoken to you, while I am still here with you. But the Counselor, the Holy Spirit . . . will teach you all things . . ." Now, I notice you didn't say that Spirit would teach them *some* things, and the rest they would learn from specially blessed 'Apostolic' writings.

J: No, I said that Spirit would teach them *everything*. This is revelation, not learning . . . spiritual *experience*, and not mere mental acquisition. Political and religious creeds and doctrines are ultimately self-defeating—they always hold you back. They keep you stuck in the mind and cause judgment, conflict and guilt.

DK: So what do you advise, kind sir?

J: Release all concepts and be still. Be open. Accept *confusion* for a while, if necessary—because it's fine not to have all the answers, right?—and move toward the Great Unknown. Have a good look at religion's grouchy God who's so obsessed with human behavior He has no life of his own. What really *is* this force in back of creation? There's not much about it you know for sure, fair enough? So, better to stay present, take time to be quiet, and patiently wait for some guidance.

DK: And what if we ask for guidance but can't hear a thing?

J: Then follow Bucky Fuller's rule of thumb: When in doubt . . . *don't*.

CHAPTER FIFTY-SEVEN

DK: Talking of seeking universal assistance, let's spend some time on one of religion's absolute basics: prayer. Now, it's obvious that prayer is how most of us make contact with whatever we conceive to be God. But often I wonder what's happening at the *other* end, you know?

J: Prayer may be the most misconstrued part of spiritual life. Lots of people view it as a way to get things they want—a way to prod the Almighty into doing what He doesn't *want* to do or hasn't yet thought of on his own. Some even try making deals: You give me this and I'll give you that. Their God is a kind of cosmic flea market merchant, an outside force with whom they must carefully negotiate or petition with utmost regard.

Prayers are often based on belief in separation . . . in other words, based on *fear*. The supplicant feels he's split off from God and he's lacking something God has either failed to give or consciously wants to withhold. You can see, then, that the nature of your prayer is a pretty good measure of how you view relationship with the All. The highest prayers are songs of praise and reflect the awareness that *everything has been given and received*.

DK: You and your philosophical nirvana!

J: Don't get me wrong: living in the world, it's apparent that you do *need* things. Instead of *confirming* this world's reality, though, your sense of lack is an excellent reason to *question* it. If God created his children as *bodies*, shouldn't He give them that which they need to be comfortable and safe in a dangerously unstable world? I mean they're already scrambling for their souls from the moment they land. Is it asking too much for an all-wise deity to attend to the obvious and bless them with life's bare essentials? Should prayer for these things even be needed? Would you want *your* children begging or gushing with gratitude before giving even the basics of human survival? A God like this would be the ultimate megalomaniac— the dude could be president, no problem.

DK: Maybe God figures that we have all we need if we share with compassion and love. He's taking the hands-off approach while He sits back and observes.

J: That would make Earth basically God's little ant farm—a novel experiment for his passing amusement, while the fates of a hundred billion spirits hang in the scale. In that case, what would be the practical point of prayer? A God of *laissez faire* policy is as good as dead . . . more useless than a freshly re-elected politician.

DK: Perhaps He truly cares but wants to see how we manage on our own.

J: You're proposing that God is *able* to ease the world's suffering—but won't.

DK: Hey, if I've learned *anything* today, I've learned that—with the scary, mysterious God of religion—*all* things are possible.

J: Wouldn't that make Him heartless and wicked for sure?

DK: Maybe He *wants* to help but somehow He can't.

J: Then clearly He's weak and He's impotent, starkly opposing religion's claims on the almighty nature of God.

DK: Well, that leaves only one way forward if this God of religion exists. He doesn't *want* to help the world nor *could* He, even if He tried.

J: Making Him cruel *and* powerless—again refuting all biblical and clerical thought. In *those* conditions, why bother calling Him God?

DK: I've painted my back to the wall, it seems. I'll stand while the latex dries.

J: You're not stuck at all, old boy. There's one choice you didn't address: your life as a body-mind isn't your ultimate reality. You're not the 'person' you take yourself to be, and God is probably not what you take *Him* to be.

DK: Still, no wrong in casting prayers to heaven now and then.

J: Many prayers are real-time shows of distrust. To claim great faith and then make appeals or demands is to verify the weakness of the faith— it sometimes shows your doubts about the benevolent nature of the divine and whether you can trust it unadvised. What if an experience quite difficult or painful is all in keeping with the plan of your 'higher' Self? What if it's actually a *gift*? Can you trust that Life sees the bigger plot and that things do finally work together for the good? Anything less is believing that Life can't be left on its own—that it definitely shouldn't be as it is. And you always suffer when resisting that which *is*.

DK: Hold it, I've got a hitch. We've talked of how the world is a horrible mess and it has to change quickly or we're all going down in flames. Yet *now* you tell me that nothing is wrong, that everything's dandy, and all things are 'in divine order.' But that doesn't seem to make sense. Our problems are the *reason* we pray ... when no divine order's *apparent*.

J: But remember, we're looking at things from *your* standpoint, not mine. So it's tricky. The same words can be true or *not* true, depending on one's perspective. The view *I'm* suggesting at least shows the mind a new way. The best prayer takes you from *wanting* to *knowing* and brings the understanding that the Universe knows what it's doing and that you and 'the Father' are one.

DK: But prayer isn't always about *getting*. Life can be painful, and sometimes we pray when we suffer.

J: Of course. But I address the *root* of the suffering, which usually begins in the mind. Suffering brings into awareness the need for correction, peace, and the restoration of oneness. It's needed until you see that it's *un*-needed. Yet suffering is often what it takes to drive one deep enough to see it's a choice. This is all that *could* bring any peace or lasting content— otherwise you're victim of grief and affliction for as long as they might persist.

DK: So it's possible to end suffering completely.

J: Yes, and nothing else is any real success—what sort of redemption leaves you stuck in the occasional hell? But you must learn to stop *choosing* the suffering and to choose peace and harmony instead. Earlier you quoted the Buddha's statement that life itself *is* suffering. He also proclaimed, "Behold, I show you suffering, and the *end* of suffering."

And *that*, my dear friend, is what some people call 'enlightenment' . . .

Chapter Fifty-eight

DK: I've got a confession to make. You've said repeatedly that God and I are one and that our will is therefore the same. In my current state, however, *mine* is the one will I'm certain of, while God's isn't often so clear. And I'm not even sure that I *want* God's will . . . I worry what He might be planning.

J: That's partly what keeps a lot of folks from wanting to know the truth—they fear what it might turn out to *be*. They think it's going to *cost* them and that God will ask them to sacrifice or give what they'd rather *not* give.

DK: So we'll always have a problem in accepting 'God's will' if we think it's somehow different from our own.

J: True . . . and religions' scary scriptures give their readers every right to fear the so-called will of God. For sheer scare value, nothing beats the story of my crucifixion and the church's claim it was all part of 'God's holy will.' But the idea that God actually *planned* my murder is the craziest thing ever conceived. God gives only life—and He gives it forever. It isn't taken back upon death for later review. With Love, there is no loss but only gain. It's the main lesson of the Resurrection: nothing real can be threatened and nothing that's *unreal* exists. Take comfort in this understanding, for herein lies the peace—and holy will—of God.

DK: So, now it's plain: if God would ask symbolic 'crucifixion' before some promised resurrection, then *my* will and *his* will would never be the same. And sacrificing something to an almighty *God* is beginning to sound absurd.

J: And yet, sacrifice of one kind or another is the keystone of many religions. But God isn't *asking* for anything. *Ever.* Many believers have wrongly connected God's will with sacrifice—a notion that arises from their own fearful thinking and from living in a world where "there's no free lunch" and "you can't just get somethin' for nothin'."

DK: So, no crucifixion required, is that what you're sayin'?

J: Actually, if you think about it, you've already crucified yourself if you believe that God is somehow pleasured by your grief. But those who understand reality will scoff at the notion of sacrifice. You and God are one—and God doesn't martyr himself. He who is, has and *gives* everything isn't seeking to take something *from* you. His one will for you is endless joy through eternal, creative expansion. Could *your* will possibly conflict?

DK: You say that God and I are one—that we share the same will and He's got my best welfare at heart. So if He *is* to be trusted and needs no recommendations or reminders, what good is prayer in the end?

J: The basest form of prayer is fairly pointless. You really don't need to be heard as much as you need to *hear*. To truly expand, let this one prayer encompass all others: "Father, into thy hands I commend my spirit." You're essentially saying, I *trust*. You join the cosmic 'flow' and stop fretting so much about outcome.

DK: Oh, believe me, brother, I'm not near as worried about *out*come as I am about *in*come. It's hard to stay peaceful and trusting if you're constantly under the gun.

J: It's true. And you don't tell someone hanging from a cliff to "detach from results." But remember: courage isn't mustered or even *needed* when fear is *absent*. When fear is rising up like a monster and telling you to panic . . . *that's* when you've gotta show faith.

DK: Then prayers for specifics can sometimes be signals of doubt.

J: Or simple good intentions stemming from lack of information or likely not getting the big picture. My own prayers were generally focused on the spiritual side of things. I never doubted I would be cared for and knew that each thing needed would come in its time.

DK: Easy for *you* to say. In the seventeenth chapter of Matthew, when the government boys came looking to collect your taxes, you quickly sent Peter off fishing. You told him that the first fish he caught would have a shekel in its mouth to pay the half-shekel tax for you both. Sure enough, the fish coughs up the cash exactly as promised. What do you say about *that*?

J: The first time in history a fish got a man off the hook.

DK: You really should be in TV . . .

J: The lesson of the shekel-bearing fish tale is that life provides in surprising ways. Often the best you can do when facing a problem is to 'go fishing.' You stay calm and do what you can, then try to let go and relax. Instead of *worrying* about the condition, you can *affect* the condition by *not* worrying about it. This shifts the energy dramatically and is miracle-mindedness in action—it allows for things not possible in pessimism or despair. Realize that if a problem can be fixed, there's no sense stressing about it.

305

If it *can't* be fixed, then stressing will do no good. So you try to stay grounded in trust, knowing that fear and anxiety make things worse. Just as the body tends to heal a wound—even minus conscious involvement—stressful conditions will generally go better without all the meddling and fret. In light of reclaiming their birthright, people's ideas of what they need can sometimes be pitifully small. They very often ask not for too much but for far, far too little.

DK: Ideally, then, how should one live?

J: First and above all, peacefully in harmony with the whole. Calmly do what needs doing but be ever aware of the life-force within—the Energy that's 'doing' your life. Devote some thought periodically to the notion of union, to knowing your oneness with 'God' and that nothing can injure the Self. Don't confuse the body with the one using it. Whatever befalls a body, nothing of eternal worth is lost since Spirit knows of neither loss nor harm. So surrender as much resistance as you can and keep trusting that help will come . . . though rarely does it come in the way you *planned*.

Also, develop the habit of forgiving all grievances—especially those you may hold against *yourself*. Releasing your grievances is essential for joy and there can't be a single exception. Forgiveness is the only savior from the tragedies and limits of time. It leads to internal peace, the charm that releases the heart to love and gently preps the mind for revelation. A mind in conflict cannot see its reality—another reason you must question the mind and its commentary, judgments and assumptions. Determine if you know for certain your conclusions are true; very often the answer is no. And always be as kind and loving to yourself as you would be to a child.

DK: Alright, what else?

J: Stop finding reasons to be offended. Being offended is a *choice* you make and not something that happens as if you were victim of some intrusive, unchosen decision—you 'take' offense, it doesn't take you. Taking offense is a subtle kind of self-righteousness . . . a socially more acceptable way of judging. But even if it gives you a sense of moral supremacy, your rancor doesn't serve either you or anyone lectured from atop your sniping tower of snobbery. When you're offended, you're viewing others' behavior as a *personal* thing, even though it's never actually personal. It has nothing to do with you, even if you think it does—it's all about what's going on with *them*. So take a stand if you need to, but try to be kind as you do it.

DK: They say that our biggest messages in life come not from what's happening in the world, but from what's happening in *us* as we experience it.

J: Right. It's how you *respond* to life that shows where you are in awareness. Once you've lost your own harmony, you ruin others' harmony too. This brings even more discord and adds only darkness to life by lowering people's energy to strife. How would this vicious circle of 'taking offense' lead to any kind of genuine "peace on earth and good will toward men"? More specifically, how would it lead to yours?

DK: So, choosing to be offended is also choosing to be *upset*.

J: Of course, because peace is total—you have it or you don't. There's really no difference between a twinge of annoyance and maniacal rage. In either case you've lost your peace completely. Acknowledge the truth of what *is*, but strive to bring more neutrality to life . . . especially when ego demands judgment. This doesn't mean liking, enabling, condoning, or tolerating. It only means *not judging*. Not viewing things from the limited scope of a 'person'—not taking things *perso*nally. This one simple decision can free you beyond belief.

DK: One writer I'm fond of said that not taking things personally is so powerful that it's basically like immunity from poison in the midst of hell.

J: Exactly. No matter what ego may tell you, you're never obliged to be angry. How people behave is all about what's happening in *their* consciousness, not yours. And this is true even if they're responding to something *you* have said or done. It's like if you accidentally cut a guy off in traffic. Suddenly there's this fellow you've never seen, losing all composure and screaming at you from his car while making frenetic hand gestures that seemingly have some tie-in to your sex life.

DK: But that's really not about *me*.

J: No, because the guy is just reacting to his *perception* of 'reality'—to a world that exists in his mind and has little to do with things as they really are. You're rarely upset for the reason you think, and neither is anyone else. The root of your disturbance lies far beyond the realm where it unfolds. So why take anything personally or be offended when it's so much more empowering not to do it? Compassion is understanding that, at *their* level of awareness, everyone is doing the best they can . . . even if that means thinking they're doing substantially better than they are.

DK: Well, it all seems fairly straightforward.

J: It's pretty simple, in fact. Become the impartial observer while watching what's happening within. If the mind has a stressful thought, question it from a view of neutrality, if you can, and look at the assumptions behind it—see if you can tell where they came from or what might make you see things in this way. The practice of neutral observance and not reacting brings fast results. And finally, maintain a commitment to peace. For without peace you can never know God, who I would call the 'Author' of peace. But keep in mind that *praying* for peace is not nearly as powerful as *choosing* it.

DK: Evidently, true prayer makes specific requests irrelevant.

J: Well, who doesn't want to feel joyful and complete? But reaching the top of the prayer ladder is a process—so start where you are. Asking for specifics may seem important, but don't conclude your prayer isn't heard or respected when not met according to specs. Life could well be guarding or helping you in ways you could never foresee.

DK: Yeah, I remember hearing stories from 9/11 of folks who didn't make it to work that day. Some were running late, others missed their trains, some had sick children—random stuff like that. Early that morning they were all bemoaning their luck. But soon they found their misfortunes remarkable boons, and their seeming 'bad luck' had saved their lives.

J: People curse heaven for things they'd be cheering if only they knew all the facts. Keep that in mind the next time you're stuck in slow traffic . . .

CHAPTER FIFTY-NINE

DK: Alright, I can maybe see the selfishness that plagues the average *personal* prayer. But surely there's meaningful difference between praying for myself and praying for someone else.

J: All prayers are ultimately for the One Divine Self. Still, in praying for people, you acknowledge the spiritual connection and 'send' them that prayerful, uplifting energy—and of course *you* profit by it as well.

DK: In praying for others, then, we actually bring healing to ourselves.

J: Of course, because giving and receiving are one.

DK: Meaning what?

J: Well, in this world you've been taught that to give something away will always leave you with less. It's typical egoic thinking, which is always upside-down and backwards. In the world of Spirit, the way to *keep* something is to *give* it—whatever you keep for yourself is what you lose. Do you want to experience love? Extend your love to the world. Do you want peace? Offer only peace to others. The giving and receiving are simultaneous and one.

DK: So, spiritually speaking, sharing *multiplies*.

J: Exactly. Giver and receiver both end up with *more*. This is why sincerely praying for others creates more healing for all—you consciously extend your love to those 'beyond' you. Creation *is* the ongoing extension of love, and it's the same reason Cosmos created *you* . . . ya follow? Everything of worth is your nature, so anything you would ask for—if you see what has real value—is yours with no prayer at all. Knowing this for certain, your cup flows over with gratitude and joy, and your ongoing prayer to Creation will be, *"Thank You."*

DK: As a Christian, I often viewed prayer almost like placing an order with room service. But I never knew if anyone would deliver . . . or even if the message arrived.

J: Every prayer is heard and answered appropriately. You often don't *hear* the answer since it's not what you're *expecting*. Universe works continually for your expansion and addresses the need *behind* the prayer and not just the prayer itself. You may not be aware of this unknown need, so when you're driven to pray for something specific, try to conclude with the trust that says, "not as *I* will, but as *Thou* wilt." In other words, *this* . . . or something better. Your current understanding is limited—what's truly helpful or apt to bring joy may be something far different from your plea. When operating from ego, your view of what's needed is usually mistaken, and if Spirit's answers seem to be irrelevant, the wrong 'judge' is doing the evaluating.

DK: So, with prayer, there's no cosmic puppeteer, pulling strings and handing out prizes.

J: Well, if there *were*, the only thing you could fairly say is that the puppeteer is cruel, weak-minded or inept.

DK: Goodbye, Rock of Ages.

J: Look, you have more than enough experience to know that the God of your religion does not exist as advertised and never did . . . and this should be the happiest realization of your life. You can change your mind on this today or stall your advancement awhile. Either way, only the truth is true— and nothing else ever was. Your task is to start the conceptual demolition. You've got to learn that the great Life-force is not somewhere outside you: you're a brilliant incarnation of it. *Communing* with this force makes a lot more sense than *praying* to it as though it's somewhere you're not.

DK: I guess I fault my religion. It made the force external by calling it God— being raised in the Christian church, I took the bait. I believed this force was elsewhere and somehow not quite part of me . . . and clearly not always kind-hearted. They've got Him living in another dimension where He's sitting on a throne surrounded by a bunch of seraphim, cherubim, and other imported furnishings, waiting for all of us to die while He makes careful notes in our permanent files and readies for his biblical 'last days'— the big Pink Slip Session in the sky. Sounds pretty much like an outsider God to *me*.

J: 'God' is just a convenient term for something your intellect can't grasp. Even in *naming* this power, it takes on the feel of something that isn't us. We make this cosmic energy into just another *thing*—the biggest and most *powerful* thing, perhaps, but a *separate* thing nevertheless.

DK: Then you sympathize with our confusion.

J: How could I help you if I didn't? I was raised with the same illusions that have plagued men and women from the start. Even as a child, though, I dared to question it all. Finally I discovered that I was part of all creation; or, to be more precise, that all creation was part of *me*. I and the Father —the light and connective Energy of the Cosmos—are *one*. The ancient Vedic writings say it thusly: "*I* am that; *you* are that; and *all this* is that." Understand?

DK: Perhaps a bit baffled about this and that . . .   But if unity *is* a fact, your stance on prayer makes total sense and there's no need to ask for a thing.

J: Well, I certainly wouldn't tell you not to pray. But have a look at the *kinds* of prayers you're sending and see what thoughts and beliefs may lie beneath. When you read the prayers of saints and mystics—like Paramahansa Yogananda, for instance—they aren't asking for mountains of money or a house in the hills. They're asking for more wisdom and understanding. More *light*.

DK: Okay, but again you have to be *practical*.

J: Aligning the mind with immutable Laws of Nature is impractical?

DK: Well, I mean sometimes we pray because things need serious changing.

J: Sure, but trying to change circumstance before changing your mind is like taking the long way home. The inner changes the outer, not the other way around. Whatever state you experience *within* will roughly reflect back in your 'outer' world. Surely you've noticed this, yes?

DK: So we'd be wise to stop 'moving the furniture' and blasting requests toward heaven, and instead to seek understanding and simply have faith in 'the Force.'

J: True enough—but hardly would I call it simple. Rare is the person who lives by unquestioning faith. O, for a small child's trust! A mere mustard seed's worth can be scarcer than a humble celebrity.

DK: Personally, I find it's easier to trust when I've got more of what I *want*.

J: Faith when things are good is nothing special. Let me share an old story about the challenge of keeping faith when it counts . . .

A large ocean liner is sailing from New York to England. The ship is half across the Atlantic when a fierce storm blows in and starts the great vessel tossing violently in its waves. Passengers are naturally quite concerned. One of them, a woman nearly hysterical with fret, insists on speaking directly with the captain. A crewman reluctantly agrees and leads her to the big ship's bridge where she quickly starts pounding on the door. The captain himself answers and invites the woman in.

"What may I do for you, madam?" the old mariner inquires.

"*Captain*," the woman says in an unreasonable tone, "I demand to know how you intend to ensure the safety of this ship's passengers!"

The skipper maintains his composure and replies calmly, "Madam, I assure you that my crew and I have done everything possible to keep you and the other voyagers from harm. All we can do is place trust in the almighty God."

"*Good heavens*," the woman squeals in panic, "has it come down to *that*!!!??"

DK: *Heh heh*. A bit of us all in that story.

J: What I'm telling you, I guess, is that your faith hasn't really been tested until circumstances come down to *that* . . .

CHAPTER SIXTY

DK: Well, twilight's closing in and I still have loads of material.

J: Better whittle it down to the vitals . . . got prayers pouring in by the *millions*.

DK: Alright, let's talk about the name Jesus. It's neither Aramaic nor Hebrew.

J: Some of the earliest Christian authors employed what's now called gematria—from GEOMETRIA, the Greek word for geometry. It's an old system of encoding certain words with meaning by assigning numeric values to each of the word's individual letters and then adding the numbers together to give the word a particular total. In addition to the one in Greek, similar systems were used in other early languages too, such as Arabic, Hebrew and Sanskrit.

My original Hebrew name was Yeshua, a common alternative form of Yehoshua. The name means 'to save, rescue or deliver'—essentially 'to bring salvation'—and clearly it should've been translated to English as "Joshua," as it is many times in Western versions of the Christian Old Testament. Indeed, some gospel writings do in fact portray me as the new Joshua. The name Jesus has no intrinsic meaning and was just a rough translation of IESOUS, meaning "healer" in Greek mythology. IESOUS contains high mathematical and symbolic significance and in gematria IESOUS computes to exactly 888. The fact that Christians began using this specific name and number in reference to *me* is no fluke.

DK: Sounds similar to the book of Revelation, where John gives the number 666 to what he calls "the beast." How did scripture writers come up with numbers like 666 and 888?

J: Before we get into it, let me say that some of this stuff is a bit involved, and it's not even slightly important to understand it. But it *is* important to know that it was quite relevant to the authors of the New Testament gospels and the growth of Christianity itself—so we'll spend a few minutes discussing it. But focus on the bigger picture and don't sweat the details . . .

As with several ancient cultures, the Greeks placed big emphasis on the arts and sciences. In Pythagorean music theory, 666 is the string ratio of the perfect fifth—the interval of C to G. It's one of the two most powerful harmonic intervals, the other being the perfect fourth—the interval of C to F. Recalling the prominence of the sun in early cultures, 666 was an esteemed solar number and was important even in the mystical Hebrew Kabbalah, where it represents "the Spirit of the Sun."

DK: So it wasn't mere coincidence that Revelation's wretch had a name that totaled 666.

J: Well, John clearly didn't mean to *glorify* "the beast" by using a sacred solar number. But the chance numerology allowed him to finger the villain in a way far safer than giving an actual name. A pretty weird strategy, though, if the dream was truly divine and was directed not to the world of John and his comrades but to one twenty centuries down the road. If Yahweh found it urgent to reveal the beast's identity to his church, why would He encode the name in a way near-impossible to decrypt? Was the Lord unaware of the trouble this tactic might cause? And why was this critical info given only to a lonely guy living in bitter exile on a small, remote island in the Aegean Sea? The other side of it is this: if anyone did crack the code on John's beast, it had to be someone of *his* day and therefore the mystery was never meant for the modern-day world.

DK: Which casts big doubt on the soundness of a final-days Rapture, no?

J: It kills the entire prophecy since it clearly never unfolded as foreseen. And even now—two thousand years on—the church *still* doesn't know the identity of Saint John's "beast." Or if it does, it isn't 'fessing up to anyone else.

DK: Okay, so that explains the importance of 666. But why were *you* tied to the Greek word *iesous* and the number 888?

J: Because it, too, was a valued solar number. For many Christians of the time, I was the new "*Solar* LOGOS." Like certain 'pagan' divinities, I was often known as "the Spiritual Sun" which, in ancient cosmology, was symbolized by 888. And don't assume my naming as the newborn sun god was something put forth by a few sects of misguided kooks. Some of the early Christian factions openly gave me titles of the Sun— "the only True Helios," "Sun of the Resurrection," "the true Apollo," "the Sun of Righteousness" and others.

DK: Well, Sun of the Biggest Gun—now you've *really* got me going! But don't stop here . . . this stuff *alone's* worth at least a few talk show gigs.

J: So as I just explained, my unusually transliterated Greek name, *iesous*, was deliberately manufactured to total 888, symbolizing the *Solar* LOGOS. If we examine the Greek word for Christ, CHRISTOS, we find that its gematria value is 1480, representing *Illuminating Knowledge* on the Greeks' spiritual hierarchy scale of the multiples of 74. Just like 666, the numbers 888 and 1480 are both evenly divisible by 74. Adding together the two numbers for the words *iesous* CHRISTOS—888 plus 1480—results in 2368, the highest, or pinnacle, number on that scale of 74s. For those with the secret knowledge, combining the two ideas completed the powerful revelation: *The Illuminating Knowledge of the Solar* LOGOS. This refers directly back to me. New Testament authors knew all this, of course, and in Second Philippians Paul cryptically states that mine is "a name which is above every name."

DK: My childhood pastor is turning in his grave.

J: Ah, but there's more. In music, 888 is the string ratio of the whole tone— the step from C to D. Musically, the ratio of 666 and 888 constitutes the relationship of the perfect fourth, one of those two dominant harmonic intervals I mentioned.

DK: Music was never a strength, I confess. It all sounds impressive, though, that much I'll grant.

J: The special numbers 666 and 888 also have a major *mathematical* relation. Their geometric mean is 769, the gematria value of the word PYTHIOS, one of the many surnames for the Olympian sun god Apollo.

DK: Why is that important?

J: Because it was Apollo who preceded me as the *Solar* LOGOS. His mythology served as the inspiration for some specially encrypted stories that were later reworked by Christian scripture writers and added to the gospels as 'Christ' episodes. Incidentally, the 8-8-8 pattern will also be recognized by those familiar with the Ionic Greek alphabet, which has three numerical levels—monads, decads, and hecatads—each containing eight elements. Taken together, they symbolize the comprehensive nature of totality, or 'the All.'

888 was also the number of the bard Olen who, according to legend, helped establish the oracle of Apollo at Delphi. The magical three eights —which could also be looked upon as three upright symbols of 'infinity'— were revered and thought to symbolize completeness, power, harmony, light and perfection. 888 was *packed* with meaning and Christian Gnostics sometimes called me "the Plenitude of Ogdoads," or "the Fullness of Eights." Others referred to me directly as "the Ogdoad."

DK: Well, it doesn't take a genius to see that Christian use of these special 'pagan' numbers can't possibly be a coincidence.

J: Geometry and math were among the sacred sciences of the Greeks, and they're used throughout the gospels to reveal secret teachings to initiates. In John 1:42, Simon Peter is given the name Cephas which, in gematria, computes to 729—a solar number representing the 365 days and 364 nights in a year. This was reminiscent of the solar god Mithras, whose name computes to 365. Mithras' mythology has him born from a rock and therefore called PETROGENES, the "rock-born" god. And note that his name contains the Greek word for Peter, PETRO[S], which literally means "rock." Peter, of course, is the "rock" on which the Roman Catholic Church was said to birth.

DK: So Peter's reflection of these hidden 'pagan' themes was carefully engineered by early Christians.

J: And with quite some precision indeed. Peter was also assigned some of the features formerly ascribed to yet another of the old solar deities: the Roman god Janus, for whom the month of January is named. Like Mithras and Peter, Janus is connected with the solar earth year and is sometimes shown in statues symbolically forming the number 365 with his hands. As a worshiped sun god, Janus was considered the heavenly gatekeeper whose primary emblem was a key. In Christianity, these two symbols are incorporated through Peter, who holds the famous 'key' to heaven's 'gates.'

DK: This gospelated pagan stuff is cool.

J: You like that? Here's more . . . The familiar account of the feeding of the five thousand—cited in all four gospels—is actually a mathematical 'story problem,' similar to one you'd see in a high school textbook. The tale hides schemes of encoded wisdom using various numbers in the reading: two fishes, five loaves, five thousand men seated in groups of hundreds and fifties and so on. When properly understood and applied, these figures produce a beautiful geometric pattern where I'm drawn as a twelve-petaled 'flower' design. The number twelve, as you might guess, denotes the twelve baskets of leftovers in the story, symbolizing one for each disciple. Furthermore, each arc in this geometric 'flower' measures exactly 74 units. Multiply 12 times 74 and—*Presto!*—again you wind up with precisely 888. *Now* are you getting the picture?

DK: This is downright stunning. I never dreamed the gospels contained so many ties to paganism. Can Christians call anything their own?

J: The Inquisition, perhaps. Even the religion's cherished fish motif had well-established pagan origins, and not through chance did it come to be adopted by the church. During *my* era, the fish symbol denoted the approaching "new age" of Pisces.

DK: And *you* were deputized as the god who would usher it in.

J: Yes, and on top of all the other pagan influence, I was made to be just a newer version of Orpheus the Fisher—the ancient Greek god who inspired the Orphic cults. Another part of the Christian fish-related trope involves the famous 'Star of Bethlehem' said to have heralded my coming. As you may know, scholars have placed my birth between the years 8 and 6 BCE— just near the close of the astrological age of Aries the ram. So the timing of my birth with the 'dying' ram was perfectly in sync with the Christian 'slaying of the Lamb.' The astrological age of Pisces was approaching, a time when various spiritual groups were expecting the emergence of a new world teacher—a messenger to lead them to the happy 'Golden Age.'

Finally, in the year 7 BCE, they got the clear 'sign' they all wanted . . . something so rare it happens once every nine hundred years. Jupiter and Saturn came into conjunction in the constellation Pisces three times in the same year—in May, October, and December. Each time, the two planets sat about one degree from each other—brightly shining and almost appearing to touch—beaming down a beautiful ray of light upon the earth. Astrologers and others were excited and took it as an auspicious celestial omen.

DK: Why was that considered good luck?

J: In the symbolism of ancient astrology, the fish sign Pisces—the final sign of the zodiac—was said to represent the 'last days' and the end of all earthly suffering. For Jews, Jupiter and Saturn were both astrologically powerful, so the 'joining' of these two was important. The hope was that this rare string of astro-events was the sign a great messiah would soon rise up. The stage was set for fireworks—and it all came together like a puzzle with the dawning of the Age of the Fish.

DK: You're a walking, talking search engine. I love it.

J: And now that you're hooked, there's a few more fish on the stringer. Early Christians used the Greek word for fish—ICTHYS—as a code word for my name and an acronym meaning, "Jesus Christ, Son of God, Savior." But these devotees, and the gospel writers themselves, were all well aware that, for many centuries prior, ICTHYS was the Greek name for the quasi-godman Adonis, who wasn't actually a god but a demigod—a mortal.

DK: Hmmm . . . seems there's quite a netful of Christian-pagan fishiness.

J: Let me school you just a bit more on this fish thing, because it's pretty important to basic Christian symbology. When two equal circles overlap so that each intersects the exact center of the other, they produce a fish shape known in pagan sacred geometry as *vesica piscis*—Latin for "bladder of a fish." It's that simple line drawing you see plastered on possessions of the world's most in-your-face Christians. But it wasn't a Christian creation. More than two hundred years before me, the great Archimedes was already calling this geometric ratio "the measure of the fish," and the Greek mathematician Euclid, often called the father of geometry, was using it decades before that.

DK: What's the big deal behind *vesica piscis*?

J: When a rhombus shape is drawn inside this 'fish' figure, it's found to have a height-to-width ratio of approximately 153-to-265. Dividing 265 by 153 yields a result of roughly 1.732, which is mathematically key since it's the approximate square root of three and the controlling ratio of the perfect equilateral triangle. This is one of the ratios at the core of the natural world. Like many ancient Greeks and others, early Christian writers understood that the cosmos is based and deployed in *number*— ratios, proportions and such. The popular Fibonacci spiral is an example.

Gospel writers purposely constructed their stories to reflect these rudiments of ancient wisdom, and in fact the Orphic canon of number —part of what's basically the Orphic Bible—would later provide material for a few of the so-called 'miracle' stories found in the Christian gospels.

In John 21, the *vesica piscis* number 153 is exactly the number of fishes in the unbroken net. This story, explained by those "with ears to hear," reveals still another detailed geometric figure with several meaningful elements taken *directly* from confirmed pre-Christian cosmological science. The resulting diagram prominently features what mathematicians call "Root 2" and "Root 3"—that is, the square roots of the numbers 2 and 3— both of them key numbers in pagan sacred science. This wisdom long precedes Christianity, of course, and its gospel use was hardly accidental.

DK: This is nothing less than Christianized paganism.

J: Yes, and academics have written entire books on the subject. When you run across these 'hidden' New Testament mysteries, you can know it was all by design. Root 3 was especially important to the Greeks because it's the foundational link in a precise geometric and algebraic relationship —also reflected in the 'Christian' fish symbol—between the fully engineered gematria values of Olympian deities Hermes, Zeus, and Apollo.

DK: Well, gods above . . . I never knew that Christianity was so strongly colored by the Greeks. I thought it was mostly a spin-off from the Jews.

J: A common misconception. The Greeks had at least as much to do with the construction of Christianity as the Jews did—after all, the New Testament was *composed* in Greek. And really, it does make sense that Jews wouldn't be the main cheerleaders for a new religion that canceled their own and focused on a man *they* considered nothing but a miserably fallen failure. For most of my Jewish peers, I wasn't even a legitimate martyr. To them I was just an over-hyped 'holy' man who didn't show very good sense.

DK: Which is probably why Paul had so little success among Jews.

J: Yes, but the Greeks, by contrast, were thoroughly ripe for the picking. The long-known Orphic mystery teachings of the slain-and-resurrected Dionysus had paved the way. And while Jewish and Greek thought both left clear markings on Christianity—Matthew, for instance, depicts me as a reinvented Moses while John launches me as the LOGOS—at its core, Christianity is actually a *Hellenistic* religion. Greek thinking and cosmology appear throughout the New Testament, and in fact ancient Greece deserves most of the credit for the birth of spirituality in the West. So Yahweh, in many respects, had far less impact on Christianity than did the long-revered gods of Olympus.

DK: Well, I couldn't help but notice that Apollo keeps popping up.

J. And with good reason. For Greeks, Apollo was among the most powerful of the twelve Olympians, and the gematria values of Apollo and his 'little brother' Hermes are directly involved in the gospel story of the 153 fishes in the unbroken net. Even the net itself symbolizes Apollo's net-wrapped OMPHALOS stone at Delphi—the starting point, or center, of the Cosmos. As I said earlier, Christians later gave this well-known rock symbology to Peter, or Cephas, the central "rock" upon which I'm said to have started my church. And not only is he the 'foundation stone' of the Christian church and the holder of the 'key' to heavenly abode, but Peter himself is the key to some pretty compelling esoterica . . .

As the Christian OMPHALOS—Greek for "navel," thus indicating a birth or beginning—Peter is literarily laden, as *I* was, with symbols added to his character by gospel writers quite learnéd in Greek mythology. Just as the OMPHALOS stone at Delphi marked the center point of the Grecian KOSMOS, so too does Peter represent the center of the Christian EKKLESIA, the assembly of Christ. And Peter's position as the bedrock of Rome's new state-sponsored Christian religion wasn't merely superficial—gospel writers made sure it was 'solid as a stone.' The Greek name for Peter, remember, is PETROS, meaning "rock," just as the name Cephas derives from the word for rock in Aramaic. As I explained, Cephas in gematria computes to exactly 729, a solar number that was meaningful even to the likes of Plato and Socrates centuries before.

It also was the number of DELPHINION, a temple of Apollo Delphinios, and in one of his writings the Apollonic priest Plutarch states that 729 specifically represents the sun. So if you thought you knew Peter before, now you've *really* got the man's number.

DK: This Christian solar connection is startling. These things can't possibly be meaningless or random.

J: Oh, not in the least. Peter's gematrial gospel grooming directly mirrors his cosmological stature among various groups of early Christian sects, people well-schooled in these old 'pagan' themes.

DK: Wow. Pagan mysteries right there in the Christian gospels. Who knew?

J: Church father Bishop Irenaeus, for one. And scholars have known for decades that these unknown gospel authors quite intently wrote secret cosmology and numeric coding into their work, and that all of it came from very much older lore. But don't expect any *churches* to make it known. Widespread knowledge of these pagan-based gospel myths might lead the world to wonder what *other* parts of the Christian story are contrived . . .

Chapter Sixty-One

DK: As long as we're covering the *occult* side of the New Testament, let's study the Rapture a bit more. We already know that in the book of Revelation, Saint John assigns 666 to "the beast." And it seems that every era tries to dump this 'devil's number' onto someone living. Yet no one has proven conclusively who John was revealing. Some believe it was the first-century ruler Caesar Nero.

J: It's true that Nero's name in Greek is an exact numerological match for 666. And he was indeed widely despised by the Jews. He also was especially cruel toward Christians, so John would've certainly shared the overall rancor toward Rome.

DK: But again, if John was cleverly fingering one of his contemporaries —in this case, Nero—that kills the premise for any forthcoming Rapture.

J: True, but Nero couldn't have been "the beast" since he had already killed himself when John was exiled to the island of Patmos by the new emperor, Domitian. John wasn't pointing to a dead man.

DK: A lot of Christians think the beast is on earth *today*.

J: Revelation's riddle has had people pinning those three feared sixes onto presidents, popes and other political or religious heads for nearly two thousand years—but I'll admit there's been plenty of qualified candidates.

DK: Some *Protestants* claim 666 could even be the Catholic Church itself— but most conservatives say the beast is someone specific. They point to the King James Version of John's statement in Revelation 13 that reads, " . . . it is the number of a man." On the other hand, the Revised Standard Version is even less precise and says only that "it is a *human* number." So, definitely some ambiguity—and that's just the start of it. In addition to the beast, Revelation also talks of a great "false prophet," and it doesn't make clear that either one of these characters is the antichrist.

J: The writer of John considered all who rejected the gospel as antichrists, or basically enemies of Christ. You can make the case scripturally that the antichrist isn't one person. In the first letter of John we're told that *"many* antichrists have come"—that's twenty centuries back, don't forget— and that "antichrist" is *anyone* "who denies the Father and the Son." This would seemingly mean all who reject Christianity. The text states quite forcefully that the spirit of antichrist "is in the world *already*" and sternly declares, "Children, it is the last hour." This resonates well with Revelation 3, where God tells his many churches, "I am coming *soon*." What He was waiting around for is never made clear—and why He hasn't come *yet* remains a real puzzle. I mean, how bad do things have to get!!?

DK: So these letters were clearly meant for readers of *that* era, not this one.

J: Sure, the writers were addressing their peers and spoke of redemption expected to occur *promptly*. John and his fellow Christians would've found no service in apocalyptic tales of trepidation for the ages centuries ahead. A lot of Christians don't realize that the Bible never uses the word "Rapture," and the basic idea, taken from a painfully literal reading of Revelation, was never part of traditional Christianity after Rome began quashing the religion's end-of-the-world dramatics. The literalist vision of the Rapture didn't even enter popular consciousness until the 1800s, when a couple of extremist preachers gave it life—and they were thinking it could happen any minute. The difference from the *Apostolic* vision of the Second Coming, it seems, was that literalists would be looking for the demons and dragons.

DK: Still, the Rapture does seem to have a solid biblical foundation.

J: So does killing psychics and gays. Leviticus 25 even gives a godly thumbs up to purchasing male and female slaves, or even children, from foreigners. "Treat them as your property," it says. So, just because something appears 'blessed by the Bible' doesn't necessarily make it okay. Besides, the Rapture and Tribulation are problematic from the start. Spirit is *one*—it's *everything*. And everything has no opposite and therefore has nothing to oppose it and nothing to oppose. How can *nothing* be in conflict with that which encompasses all? Anyway, why can Yahweh predict a time of Tribulation more than two thousand years in advance when, in certain Old Testament stories, He's not even sure what's happening *now*. But the Rapture has far more serious implications. For if this bleak foreboding is truly inspired and biblically bound to occur, wouldn't it mean God knew right away that my suicide mission to redeem everyone would eventually be a terrible fail?

DK: Now, *there's* another angle I hadn't seen. He clearly didn't have much faith in your odds of success . . .

CHAPTER SIXTY-TWO

J: So you're starting to see that you've got big challenges taking Revelation literally, as you'd *have* to do if the Rapture has any meaning. For instance, why would God wait six thousand years past the storied 'Fall of man' to incarcerate his great archenemy Satan? Doesn't He know that by the time He responds, billions of his children will be doomed to perdition through the devil and his fellow nonconformists?

DK: Yeah, very strange behavior from the man. I've often asked since leaving the church why all this stuff is believed.

J: The answer, O ye of vanished faith, is both simple and impossible to refute: *"It's the inscrutable mystery of God!!"*

DK: *Heh heh.* Yes, I've certainly heard *that* a few times.

J: And here's more food for thought . . .
For those who manage to survive Armageddon, the earth, according to John's vision, will be a smoking badland of rubble. Yet John says he sees "a new earth." So how will God fix the place? How will He make it livable again for my thousand-year, no-term-limits reign of peace? Can He quickly make Nirvana from a war-torn planet of death? How will He beautify his ugly, plague-ridden wasteland from hell?

DK: I guess if He built the cosmos in under a week, He'd quickly clean a small planet in between hymns. For God it's just a side remodeling job.

J: But if He has that kind of power, why won't He get busy *using* it? Instead of waiting 'til the very last minute to *destroy* the world in a devilish onslaught of war and deadly plagues, He could show up tomorrow and direct all that pent-up energy to *healing* it. And again, why has God so long delayed victory over Satan? Why does He let billions suffer hell here on earth, only to live it *perpetually* after they die? And all due entirely to the devil's deceit and God's own curious willingness to stand back and watch.

DK: So why not simply *axe* this low-life bastard, is that what you're sayin'? The Lord puts out a contract and it's done.

J: Well, it isn't like He's got no experience. I mean He's made a bloody *career* out of his *killing*—why can't He take this devil *down*? Has God spared Satan so his end-of-days timeline matches up with ancient scribbles of an angry man living in a cave off the coast of Turkey? Quick! For a chance to win a lovely, white Ascension robe, tell me how we justify this puzzling show of madness by the Lord.

DK: Okay, I'll play along . . . *It's the inscrutable mystery of God!!*

J: And if, as Revelation claims, there will be no spiritual corruption found in heaven, what becomes of humanity's precious free will? Who says that no one behind the gates will misbehave? Living in celestial paradise didn't stop *Satan* from starting a grassroots-level revolt. So why should God's Golden Age earthly heaven be any better than his *first* one back in the Garden? And speaking of Eden . . . if the snake in the Garden was Lucifer, as many Christians believe, then who the hell placed him there? And *why??* How could Yahweh call everything fine—and in fact "very good"—with a slick-tongued, soul-corrupting *devil* sliding around!!? There's only the one explanation, thou solemn seeker of truth! *Shout it with the choir from the pews*!

DK: *It's the inscrutable mystery of God!!*

J: And further, if God is the one creator, then who made all the strange and evil life forms in John's horrific vision? Who made the human-faced locusts, the six-wingéd monsters, and the scary seven-headed red dragon? Does Satan have the same creative powers as God? And why have they not been *revoked*!!?

Also, in unleashing these various plagues upon the planet, how does God warrant still *more* needless drama by turning a third of Earth's oceans into blood? And lastly, if He wants the world thoroughly prepped for his Great Tribulation, why won't He give 'em the precise bloody time and date!!??

But never mind rhetorical questions, O trusting devotee. Praise to the power of religious demagoguery, and glory to the *Gawwwd* of the Christian church-centered cosmos!!!

[Laughing hysterically, I applauded with gusto as Southern Preacher Jesus, now beaming from ear to ear, stood to give an exaggerated stage bow.]

DK: Bravo! Bravo!

J: [Impersonating W.C. Fields to perfection] Thank you, one and all, for that most enthusiastic ovation . . .

DK: *Heh heh.* Just when we're winding down, *you* go and get all wound up. But I think I've got the picture. When Revelation's read literally, God becomes a psychotic demon on crack. But it makes me wonder if *any* of it is credible— this vision of shooting stars and fiery dragons, four mysterious Horsemen, fist-fighting angels and The Devil's Last Stand. You sayin' it's not inspired?

J: Oh, don't take me wrong. If that's not truly inspired writing, I'm not sure what else you would call it. But should it be taken *literally*? Did it come by the Lord himself? Well, that's another talk altogether.

DK: I see why some church honchos didn't want John's vision in the Bible.

J: Personally, my biggest problem with Revelation is not its *psychedelic* stuff, but the parts that are clearly spelled out. For starters, Revelation's focus is strictly on the future, missing the only moment that ever counts: the *now*. Revelation's airtight predictions ignore all hope of ingenuity, social progress or overall human advance. The book's gruesome forecast could rightly be viewed as God's very own prediction of his miserable failure to overcome Satan before all the damage is done. These writings are the Lord's personal admission of his staggering inability to save his fallen world with any success—and a curious testament of his strange resignation to it all.

DK: But the literalist remains unfazed. To him, any thought of world peace before apocalyptic catastrophe is heretical.

J: It's true. Peaceful, pre-Rapturous resolutions to earthly problems are out of the question, and Revelation's literalists use the present but as means to make fearful predictions of an ominous, doom-filled future. Not to worry, though. The only ones suffering, they assure the world, will be those who don't see things as they do. But ask anyone who won't swallow this bunk and they'll say that's a pretty dim view of 'salvation.'

DK: Not for the literalists it isn't. When I was running with the bulls, they didn't take this dismal prophecy with any dejection or grief. Perfectly fine with the prospect of world destruction, they're eager for the games to begin. In *my* days of Bible toting and quoting, we used to tell people that, for those who have their spiritual houses in shape, Revelation gives hope of redemption and a never-ending heavenly joy.

J: Boy, when life gives lemons to a literalist, he doesn't just make lemonade— he starts a full-blown orchard!! There's nothing hopeful in a scheme that brings salvation to the few, while everyone else burns alive. Of course it's only natural that a literalist wouldn't fear the Tribulation. He thinks that he's *special* and will therefore go soaring off-planet before meeting harm. The only ones shaking in shock, it would seem, are the short-sighted dolts who *rejected* his rantings regarding God's favored 'elect.'

DK: So the literalist figures that the very first trumpet will surely give *him* the last laugh.

J: But, verily I'll tell ya this: one who would revel in the sufferings of another is as far from the spirit of Christ as you could wander. He wouldn't even know me if I came to his house with a six-pack and three chubby cherubs.

DK: Apparently, Saint John's vision of vengeance mocks every moral principle we've held. By the time Revelation comes around, the Lord's done a total U-turn from his views in the first part of Genesis: "And God saw everything that He had made, and behold . . . it sucked."

J: Unfortunately so. The God of John's vision quickly ditches the forgiveness so firmly preached in the gospels and—mysteriously, of course—reverts to his roots, once again solving his problems through bloodshed and strife. Aside from making a sociopathic goon of creation's Uber-Genius, the Tribulation is also a problem *metaphysically*—that is, if you put any faith in 1 John 2:16. "For all that is in the world . . . is not of the Father . . . And the world passes away." Here, scripture states clearly that the world has no ultimate reality. As presently perceived, it's not a Universal creation.

DK: Just what you've been telling me all day! I've read the New Testament maybe twenty times over but I never stopped to give that verse thought. Instead of asking questions, I probably kept right on reading.

J: So now Christianity hits *another* rock wall. If the world is indeed a passing illusion—as scripture asserts and as science is now confirming—how would the Lord wage battle there? And why would He need to *fight* something? Can't He just make it disappear? But that's not the end of it all. A further snag with this dark 'holy' vision is its shredding of my *own* moral fiber. Through writings of John the Divine, I'm now history's greatest impostor.

DK: By what view?

J: Well, all throughout Christendom I'm seen as a guiding paragon of light. For centuries the church has sold me as the blesséd Prince of Peace, the gentle Lamb of God . . . the savior and redeemer of the race. In the Bible, I urge people to love, to forgive, to show compassion and such. How is it, then, that in the 'last days' I morph into a death-crazed cosmic samurai, striking the earth as a vengeful, bloodthirsty thug. No longer set on *saving* the world, I come back to utterly ruin it. I drop in from heaven to inflict on humanity a strange and perverse kind of 'justice'—the nightmare described in Revelation. In short, Hebrews 13:8 apparently has it wrong: Jesus Christ may be the same yesterday and today . . . but not necessarily forever.

DK: *Phew!* Thank heaven—at least now I know I'm not crazy. For quite a long time I questioned myself for not joining Christians who had what I call 'apocalypsy' . . . they almost seemed to *want* the world's demise. I felt that if the nukes weren't launching pretty quickly, they'd be bummed.

J: One of the Laws of Mind is that whatever you focus on *expands*— you tend to create what you visualize, think and believe. So the most ironic part of this 'end times' schlock is that John's grim foreboding could well become self-fulfilling. All thoughts are energy, so there are no neutral thoughts. Thoughts are *things*—and when millions hold fast to an image, helpful or not, they drastically boost its chances of occurring.

DK: I imagine we could go hours picking Revelation to pieces.

J: Only its literal side. Because if ever there was a sacred text *not* to be taken literally, it's clearly the book of Revelation. But the literalist just can't resist, even when every part of his reasoning mind is rebelling. Taking this text as the literal truth is a gross intellectual treason.

DK: Frankly, even in my most fanatical days—even when I believed in a hell of eternal damnation—I never took John's vision as literal fact. For me it was embarrassing even to *say* it. In lie-detector tests, how many smart, educated people would pass if answering yes to the question, "Do you *really* believe Revelation to be literal?" I mean it's ridiculous. The words were never meant to be read that way, and John of Patmos himself would've probably confirmed it.

J: For those with the knowledge to decipher it, however, Revelation, like many other parts of the Bible, is layered with hidden wisdom— and some with profound implications. If bent on making it literal, though, what you *should* be asking of Saint John's Apocalypse is this: Could God truly be so brainless, warped and sadistic . . . or did John get his island mushrooms confused?

CHAPTER SIXTY-THREE

DK: Now that we're near the home stretch, I don't think this talk would be complete without a short discussion of miracles—the great crown jewels of religion and the ones that get most of the notice.

J: I said before that Spirit is focused on *content*, not on form. Miracles are cosmic expressions of love, so they too are centered in content . . . the *meaning* of life and not just its passing appearance. And which would a wise, loving Universe likely stress?

DK: Well, we hear these miracle tales so often of the avatars and saints, some would almost *have* to be true. So we're curious.

J: There's no doubt that when the *mind* is changed, circumstances will respond—that's how it works. Form takes the shape of consciousness because form *is* the shape of consciousness. You're always 'forming' your life, by intention or by default, and using the powers of Mind with love and wisdom can indeed alter your life and those around you. People with this 'hidden' knowledge will sometimes use it to great effect. But miracles aren't meant to *impress* anyone—they're intended only to *heal*.

DK: Heal what?

J: The only thing that's ever truly sick: the separated mind. The mind that views reality as splintered and chaotic and sees things only as parts of a random heap. Miracles bring wholeness where disease and separation seemed real; knowledge where before was only doubt; peace where there was conflict, fear and guilt. The move from separation to wholeness occurs not in the world but in *mind*—that's where real healing is needed. This one shift in thinking, the miracle itself, sets everything 'outside' in motion.

DK: Is anything beyond a miracle's power?

J: Nothing is beyond the impact of love—the energetic basis of life. Miracles work by reminding—literally *re-minding*—those who experience them that reality is far beyond constraints of the body or limits in the world of form. The miracle comforts with the knowledge that Life knows you exist and is working for your growth and expansion. So miracles bring healing by helping you learn who you are: an immortal and universal Spirit-being choosing to have a human experience. But miracles don't alter the laws of physics—they merely *reflect* them in ways you don't understand.

DK: Speaking of miraculous healings, many years back I watched a pair of popular evangelists on the late-night tube. They'd 'lay hands' on some trusting soul who'd come to the stage, moaning of some terrible malady, disability or whatever. The poor schlep stands there pathetic, of course, while the overacting preacher spouts a prayer "in the name of JAY-sus" and open-handedly smacks the guy on the noggin. Next thing you know, the dude's fainting back into four waiting arms as he's healed, while the ushers then pass the collection. Would that be considered a miracle?

J: I guess it would if no one's arrested.

DK: No, seriously.

J: Maybe it's a miracle, maybe not. Healing and bodily changes aren't always the same . . . they occur on two different levels. The *real* miracle is the shifting from ego to spirit. Either way, if faith's brought to bear, healing *can* take place in an instant—and sometimes it does. The mind-body-spirit link is powerful and faith's driving force is robust. Physical healing is no gauge of health, however, if sickness persists in the mind. You could say true healing is nothing more than genuine inner peace . . . and nothing *less*.

DK: So healing, really, comes only from knowing the truth of our existence.

J: Yes, and from meaningful, serendipitous events that raise your vibration and expand your views of Self and your potential. Healing is the removal of all that stands in the way of this knowledge. A miracle's *form*, therefore, isn't more important than its *effects*—the clearing away of illusion and a liberating lift of awareness. The miracle gives you all of this and more.
Miracles bring more love and strength to all and are proof of something those who want to be happy should quickly grasp: *Giving and receiving are always simultaneous and one.* Whatever you're giving out is what comes back —multiplied—even if on levels you can't see. Miracles collapse time, speed your learning and defy 3D restraints. But miracles don't 'break' any laws— they're laws not yet understood. If ever they learn how miracles work, even scientists will hold them in awe.

DK: Well, like all of us, science hates anything that screws up its paradigms. When someone claims to have experienced a genuine miracle, science just explains it away. But even the genius scientist Terrence McKenna said that science itself gets at least one "freebie miracle," as he called it, with its popular Big Bang theory. He said it's one of the nuttier things science ever conceived—that in a big fat Nothing, *something existed*, and, on top of that, *something happened*!! It all took place in a moment, the scientists tell us, and *from* this potent pop within the void, everything that now exists arose.

J: Bloody hell . . . and science balks at the story of a burning bush!?! In other words, no one knows how it happened, but something somehow came from nothing—and then all at once there was everything.

DK: You got it. Or to say it more concisely, a miracle put the cosmos in play.

J: Sounds scientific, alright.

DK: So the universal origins of religion *and* science seem essentially magic at heart.

J: The difference, though, between science's all-time-prize-winning miracle, the Big Bang, and religion's first miracle—that, in the beginning, *God*— is that science's miracle logically couldn't happen in the first place and was always just a ludicrous idea, nor does it even *help* you at all. Whereas *religion's* primary miracle, referred to by many as 'God' —at least if seen as a powerfully smart, interrelating and creative field of energy buzzing through Universe—can indeed be experienced and known.

DK: That's certainly been true for *me* through the years, even though it's all been pretty mysterious and I still can't begin to explain it.

J: You needn't know *how* this force works, nor even how it first came to be —which could've been *after* the cosmos began—to know for sure what it *does*. Your experience of it proves it exists, and that's enough to keep you moving forward . . . you come to see that you're so much more than you thought. So *that's* a miracle you at least can make practical use of, is it not? The Big Bang miracle, conversely, is nothing but theoretical hogwash and has all of life—*and consciousness!*—aimlessly rising from spiritless molecules of carbon. And even if this theory brings your *body* into being, it denies your most important realities.

DK: I wonder that so many scientists swear there's no possible cosmic intelligence. I mean what keeps these folks so convinced? If you'll swallow the Big Bang theory, you'll easily choke down *nails* after *that*. From my view, there's far more grounds for a living multiverse than ever existed for the crazy, 'scientific' Big Bang. For backers of the magical Big Bang tale, believing in a God-force, in miracles—or even in *leprechauns*, for godsake—should be a cerebral slam-dunk.

J: But if science gets one free miracle—easily the biggest miracle of all, by the way, and the biggest that could ever be *claimed*—how can it mock those with far less preposterous, and much more relevant, miracle stories of their own? Healing a terminal cancer is a quick snap of the finger to a stunning, unthinkably vast universe that somehow burst forth from nothing. Compared to this most miraculous of all occurrences, raising the dead is vanilla cake, and calming the sea is for kids.

DK: And that's *another* point I'd like to discuss: what *about* those so-called miracles of yours? Many clearly came from old legends and myths—I get it. But some of the gospels' miracle stories speak directly of you and your culture. Even if just a handful are true, your healings and conjurings must've had 'em rushing the stage. And what a way to muzzle your critics!

J: I never used miracles as spectacles to prove I was special. Miracles aren't meant to boost beliefs about *me*, but to shatter old paradigms of *you*. They smash through barriers and free you from your narrow ideas of who you are and what's 'real' on the physical plane—they broaden your views of reality.

DK: So we've gotta learn to 'think outside the box.'

J: But you can't think outside the box until first realizing you're *in* it. And very often, thinking *is* the box . . . the root of all delusion and dogma. This miracle of changing your mind has no constraints: It topples regimes and sends the phoenix rising up from the ash.

DK: Then you don't have to be a saint to manifest miracles.

J: Miracles are all around you and they happen without your effort. They're Life's way of getting your attention and earning your trust. Watch for synchronicities and where they seem to be leading you. In a miraculous universe, miracles are your natural reality. When they don't seem to be happening, you've just lost awareness of *love*.

Here's a thought to keep you on track . . .

Live your life in mystery and love and then be realistic. Expect miracles.

CHAPTER SIXTY-FOUR

DK: You've talked about the value of stillness. Should we meditate?

J: That or at least be still for a while. Maybe start with fifteen minutes a day.

DK: And if we're too pressed to find even those fifteen minutes?

J: Then you'd best make it a full half-hour.

DK: I get the point.

J: Chosen silence is so much more important than most of the world's cultures understand. Stillness isn't just a dearth of activity and noise— it's where answers and inspirations reside. If you're too busy to give a few minutes each day sitting calmly in the center of the Self, you're probably way too busy. If it seems like great inconvenience, discomfort or 'work' when pausing to be still and quiet the mind, then you, of all people, should probably sit down and do it. At least make some time to go silent when you can and 'tune in' to the peace at your core. And remember, a hundred times a day if need be, to bring your attention back to the *Self* and to the now—it's all about present awareness.

DK: What's the importance in awareness?

J: Awareness is crucial because most thoughts aren't worth thinking, and many are quite self-destructive. Thoughts, if you let them, form an endless, expanding spiral downward—each one clamoring for attention, selling you on its own importance and why you must think and believe it. Rapt by these voices and pictures in the head, you're clueless to what's happening around you, or even within . . . you don't even know you *exist*. Entranced by the mind and its musings, you've lost control of the ship— the *mind* is now using *you*. The proper relation, of course, is the other way around. Awareness allows you to *consciously direct* your attention and to stand apart from your thoughts as you observe them. Inquiry then allows you to know if they're even true and to see how they affect you when you believe them. So if you're wanting things you can 'do' for your spiritual progress, this is the doctor's prescription. And remember to *laugh*, for heaven's sake. Humor is an underloved asset these days.

DK: Anything more?

J: One of the keys to joy in life is sharing your talents and passions with the world. The gift on both sides of this sharing is the perfect proof that giving and receiving are one—meaning giver and receiver are one as well. This is how you learn that taking and getting isn't nearly as rewarding as sharing and receiving. Also, start practicing patience and acceptance—especially when you don't really *want* to. When stubbornly insisting or trying to control, remember that ego does want control, yes . . . but *you* primarily want *peace*. Very often a bulldozed result will cause you pain. Don't confuse manifesting, a state of gentle moves and allowance, with force.

DK: It would seem, in the end, that spirituality is the most vital part of our nature.

J: Hmmm, let's talk about that . . .

Sometime when you've got a few minutes and things are quiet, close your eyes and focus on your own 'internal' energy. Not the mind or its thoughts, but the very essence of youself—the *being* for whom the mind is functioning. Ignoring all the old ideas and beliefs, ponder awhile on this essence—this *is-ness*—within. What is it, exactly? What is it made of? How does it work? Does it ask you to believe anything? Is it spiritual, non-spiritual, or something else altogether? Is it evil? Is it goodness? Do such ideas even apply? Is it religious, non-religious . . . or nothing remotely of the sort? Is it human or something you can't even name? Is it dead, is it alive, or neither? Can this energy force be insulted, or somehow attacked and destroyed? Is it ever afraid of anything? Can you make it disappear? Where did it come from and where is it going? Can it even be said to be moving? Does it seem at all connected to religions, ideologies or gods?

DK: And so, what's the point?

J: If you're honest, you'll find that no description applies to this infinite, indefinable Self. You know it's real because you're aware of it and you experience it. But can it be seen as a Democrat or Republican or proven to be this, that or the other? Even calling it 'spiritual' is only an acquired idea. You are what you are. Why label it?

DK: So, what's the best 'next step' that someone can make?

J: Simply start right where you stand with whatever you're facing. Trust the emotional signals of your body and your spiritual intuition, and gently move to the light—that which in your heart *feels* best.

For lots of people, even the least *glimmer* of light is better than absolute darkness, and with greater wisdom comes strength to keep going and trust in the Ancient Unknown. You'll always move forward faster if you move without too much fear. So, walk your way through the world in peace—patient, poised and alert. When troubled or discouraged, ask for help and then remain quietly open.

DK: Open to what?

J: The power of the unexpected . . .

CONCLUSION

DK: Wow, what a day. Considering the longtime layoff, I'd say you've done pretty well.

J: So, time for the big closing speech?

DK: Yep, the floor . . . uh, that is, the ground's all yours. You talk and I'll write. But try to finish strong if ya can—the publishing business is *brutal*.

J: Don't worry, I'm known for my dramatic endings.

DK: I've got the ears to hear . . .

J: Well, the very first thing to know, whenever making serious changes to established thought systems, is that ego has a paranoid *resistance* to change. Ego is critically interested in keeping things known and 'predictable' and is even quite pleased with your seeking—as long as you don't actually *find*. And religion can be one of its most effective tools. Religion often keeps you gazing *outward*, directing attention to a God hanging out in the ethers and telling you that nothing good can ever come from examining a sinful 'self.'

So, to know any meaningful change in the way you experience the world, you'll have to start by re-evaluating what you think you already know. To realize anything new, of course, you must release the old—the familiar and the 'known'—and become more comfortable with the *un*known. Does your current thought system really tell you all you need to know about the complex nature of reality? You must learn with clarity that the world of beliefs and perception isn't nearly the world as it is . . . thoughts and opinions about something will often have little to do with the thing itself, and perception colors every experience.

In the case of Christianity, it's good to start discerning between a religion *about* a Christ and the renewing, mystical teachings *of* the Christ. The *religion* was precisely manufactured and is all about the world of *effects*— what's happening within the illusion of the earthly plane. Like many others, the Christian religion is a fully egoic perspective on life, so its creeds would naturally hold themes of separation: judgment, guilt, punishment, and costly atonements or amends—a thoroughly bridled view of reality.

The Christ *teachings*, conversely, are specifically centered on *cause*. That means *you* as an incarnate child of Spirit. Begin to see yourself as a cosmic creator . . . a *partner* with the divine and no longer one of its subjects, servants or pawns. See how your unquestioned thoughts and beliefs about reality can often limit and control how you experience the world each day.

And how did it all come about? Could you have had a say in the thing? If you can't or won't engage this line of thinking, then once again you're stuck. You have to accept at least *some* responsibility for your experience. So, have the courage to ask how faith fits in—because taking your religion seriously means it's apt to influence a pretty big part of your life. And even if you simply 'inherited' your religion as a child, at some point you continued to choose it. This means you've now got to *own* it.

But has it really served you? Has your religion ever once encouraged you to question your beliefs about it all? Even your beliefs about God? Does it ever suggest that your soul was never endangered and you carry the same potential as any 'savior' who ever walked Earth? Not likely. It's not a sustainable business plan for growth.

Religions typically focus on some major deity figure while stressing your own mortal weakness and the insurmountable distance between the two of you. Within Christianity, of course, most of the church's energy is spent expounding upon *my* name, *my* experiences—*my* great significance to the world. You, on the other hand, are the bumbling, guilty bystander, says the church, and you're never quite enough as you are. But not to fret, say the clerics: *you* keep making the messes, and *I'll* keep cleaning 'em up.

Not only have they missed the point completely, but their views were never valid from the start. Selling someone as a heaven-sent savior means you'd better have rock-like proof of two things: that the soul is actually in peril and that the allegedly divine godman is somehow able to save it. You can't just create a new line of dogma, call it religion, then threaten or criticize those who don't bow in fear. While religion has for centuries put its skeptics on the defensive, the skeptics are under no obligation whatsoever to debunk its outlandish avowals.

Just as with science, responsibility for establishing the truth of one's position must always fall to the claimant himself. To say there's a colony of purple aliens in one of Jupiter's moons and then challenge *you* to prove me wrong is clearly absurd. For a theory is not true until proven false— but it *does* remain theoretical until proven true, and anyone making bold assertions must ultimately bear the burden of backing them up.

With Christianity, we've already seen that the religion can't survive its careful dissection, and the church plainly cannot confirm what it preaches. Churches the world over have built empires made of fumes . . . *and they know it*. Most of Christianity's major claims were stolen from traditions far older, as those who've done their homework can attest.

So the church's case is flat-out indefensible and groundless from the start. Every part of its worn-out godman story, with its ages-old theme of soul corruption and potential everlasting damnation, can be fully dismantled —completely and forever demolished—by way of just two simple words: *Prove* it.

Now, some will no doubt argue that it just takes faith. But faith in *what*, I would ask. Faith in a God who sits ready to torture billions of his kids for all eternity, just because they were *human*? Faith that the God of the Bible—the nutcase behind all those savage acts of insanity—is somehow deserving of your lifelong love and devotion? Faith that He might show mercy and benevolence if only you'll take *me* as your Lord and savior? Well, I guess if you'll be roped into all *that* madness, you sure as hell *do* have a limitless ocean of faith.

Still, a gaping-wide gulf lies 'twixt childlike faith and childish naïveté. As an educated, rational being, wouldn't you want to know if your faith is intelligent? Can it bear the light of rationale and reason? Or do you fear *using* any reason to weigh your religious beliefs? In not vetting thoughts about God by subjecting them to reason, you must be afraid that your God is, quite literally, *un*reasonable. And if *that's* true . . . well, you've *really* got something to fear.

As you've discovered today, very little of religion withstands inspection. But why do so many of them continue to belittle and attack their critics —sometimes threatening harm to body and soul—despite their sorry 'evidence' and the thoroughly senseless nature of their claims?

Consider this: how much confidence would you have in a scientist who announced some colossal but unverified discovery, and yet became angry and resentful—even hostile and aggressive—whenever his claims were questioned? What if he insisted that everyone should take him at his word? What would be your thinking if he threatened or disparaged any soul who disputed his assertions, even though, when pressed, he couldn't actually prove them?

With the clear exception of politics, and maybe the imminent prospect of sex, where outside of religion does the world so quickly embrace the scrapping of critical thought?

Perhaps we can agree, then, that religion, like *any* subject of importance, requires some honest review. Let's take as an example one of Christianity's basics: the Crucifixion. Unlike the Resurrection, whose acceptance demands the highest levels of faith, the Crucifixion is something even a hardened atheist can consider as at least an historical possibility. That is, no one could deny that a little-known religious reformer in ancient Palestine may well have been betrayed and wrongly killed.

The problem lies in the church's explanation of these things: God drew up plans several thousand years back to take part in a suicide mission wherein He himself will be crucified out in the desert, through a stated 'only son,' at last permitting Him to forgive his errant children—more than 99 percent of whom had not yet even been born. Now, to any fair, reasoning mind, this thinking is patently insane. And let us not forget that humanity's 'sinful' nature was an option built in to their design by this very same deity.

But even if you manage to ignore the scores of challenges presented by this remarkable saga—and even if it *had* happened as told—who in the story did it help? Certainly not the murdered man himself. Nor can we make a sound argument that the Crucifixion somehow served the Lord, who surely can forgive you without spilling blood. So the only answer that *might* make sense is that it theoretically helped humanity. But here you've got to ask, *how*? How did my needless death *profit* the world in ways the average person would find sensible and needn't take anyone's word for?

So Christianity clearly asks too much. It plays to emotion while ignoring the heart and seducing the intellect. I mean it's one thing to talk about a whale that swallows a man. But now, to qualify for heaven, a man is suddenly asked to swallow a whale!!

And not only does the religion fail to pass all scientific standards of historical and intellectual analysis—but neither does it meet the simple benchmark of common sense. The killing of an innocent man for curiosity over Adam's apple is not intuitive or intelligent to *anyone*, and how it would dawn on a *god* is only a guess. Christianity teaches that the cosmic energy called 'God' is a force so insane that, to fully love its very own creations, the torture and murder of a virtuous human being was required, and no other fix would suffice.

But again, the question that Christians never ask of this depressing 'salvation' story is, "What was in it for God?" And the answer should now be obvious: nothing. So why should the *Christian* view of God be given more weight than those of the Hindus, Daoists, Jains, Sikhs, Confucianists . . . or even the hippies? After all, no stated claim of the biblical Christ is proven.

At the end, of course, it doesn't really matter what arguments you wield, what facts you dig up, or what you might verify in scripture. Your scholarly research, your archaeology, your syllogisms and highbrow theories will all prove equally vain. At some point you've got to face one question: do you honestly believe in the violent, irrational and intolerant God of the Bible? Is this truly the deity you worship? If so, then you're likely acting solely out of fear—conservatively covering the bases. No way on earth could you actually *love* this frightening character since nothing's remotely lovable *about* Him. If minding your Ps and Qs and doing all the right things is done only to sidestep his post-mortem torture, how free or joyful could your 'worship' possibly be?

But even if Bible literalists opt to challenge all errors and conflicts —with carefully chosen scripture, long-winded arguments, and plenty of smoke and mirrors—they still have the hopeless task of explaining how a 'God of love' could also be a sadistic, mass-murdering maniac who'll be torturing his belovéd sons and daughters for the rest of time and beyond. But literalists are forced to defend the indefensible, and if you're taken in by their nonsense, you're doomed. You'll never move past the old, stale beliefs to empowering states of knowing.

And that's where literalist religion is a problem. Not piercing its surface to find the wisdom, you're left with a paradigm for living that's both spiritually and intellectually repressive, and with a God who's very often hypocritical, sadistic . . . and sometimes just plain dumb.

But, okay. Maybe you insist on labeling yourself, on calling yourself this thing or another and layering *personal* qualities onto the limitless, immortal expression of Infinity that's 'you'—it's a freely chosen decision. But if you *are* going to be religious, at least do some internal digging. Find out exactly *why* you're committed and what you're committed *to*. Don't be like Saint Augustine, who admitted outright that he would never have believed the Christian story had not the "authority" of the Roman Catholic Church *compelled* him to.

Far too many faithful have never bothered probing their convictions. Perhaps they fear they'll wind up like Mother Teresa, who spent the last fifty years of her life secretly anguished and fighting off waves of depression for her faltering faith. Her experience didn't match up with the church's claims on the nature of God and reality. While millions looked on in admiration, Teresa was filled with despair. "If only they knew," she wrote in her diary. Her beliefs had collapsed and she questioned God's very existence. "Heaven means nothing," she cried in existential distress.

Other Christian leaders have fought the same kinds of lingering doubts. Even church apologist Tertullian—a stickler for the rules who condemned remarriage for widows and even fleeing from persecution!—recognized the absurd nature of the Christian gospel and justified his faith in it by resorting to a kind of desperate reverse rationalization: "I believe it *because* it is absurd."

Absurd indeed. With *that* kind of logic, why rule out an Easter Bunny? This automatic faith among followers is a hallmark of most major religions. The only way to make most of them work is to start with angry statements 'from God' that no one can ever prove, and then hope that people sign on.

At this point in earthly human history, many believers haven't yet questioned their religion—but they should. For Christians, their faith has given them a God-sent 'savior' who shows with some really bad news:

The Lord of creation is angry with them because two kids punked him six thousand years ago—and now He's come to pay his wrath forward. To save themselves from their God's post-Judgment abuse for this crime of their earliest ascendants, they'll have to accept a few strikingly bizarre, empirically unprovable, philosophically nonsensical proposals.

But how could any sane man or woman possibly view this alarming message as any kind of upliftingly 'good' news!?? I mean, seriously . . . what sort of comfortless Christ *is* this stern Christ of Christian literalism? Why would anyone want, welcome or submit to this threatening doomsday pessimist? And how does the church's telling of this man's story really *help* the world in ways that a balanced agnostic, for instance, would find useful, intelligent, inspirational, beneficial or kind?

But let's suppose for the moment that you bear it all without blinking. Like evangelist Billy Graham, you can always decide that, since you can't actually prove it, you'll just take the Bible as inspired words of God—on *faith*. Graham said his agonizing choice to finally just *believe* and move on with establishing his ministry allowed him to "go beyond" his "intellectual questions and doubts." Billions of other believers do the same.

Still, if you happen to call yourself Christian, you've got to know that all meaningful practice of your religion would have to move you beyond mere belief to some heart-level, Christ-like understanding—to spiritual maturity, tolerance, forgiveness, insight, humility, and heartfelt general goodwill. In short, your *thinking* must blossom into *wisdom*. But there is no wisdom in a set of beliefs that pits you or God against any of your brothers and sisters. Faith like that never helped *anyone* . . . and never will.

My call to my followers was to seek for the kingdom within. This has no connection to changing the world or even changing anyone in it. Telling them what to think, believe or experience dishonors their unique paths to knowledge and robs the human spirit of its natural tendency for creative, independent Self-expression.

I urged my disciples to let their light shine—a *passive* thing that requires no persuading or converting. Other people's beliefs are not the problem . . . *your own thinking* could well be the problem. Teaching or believing that God kills as a means to save, punishes because He has to, and tortures because He loves, you'll overshoot devotion and grow spiritually toxic and blind.

The thing most needed in the world is peace. That peace is waiting *now*, and the one thing required to have it—the trailhead of the golden path back to heaven—is knowing that *peace is a choice* and one that you do want to make. So, *choose* it, every instant you can. Each choice for peace is a conscious decision to heal and brings miracles, new options . . . new *life*.

And life, as should be obvious, is *change*. One thought I leave with you is that *creation, by its nature, is ongoing and continuous*. Never was it a static, motionless state addressed once and forever in books. You are an ongoing creation *and* a creator—and this you can know. But first you must see there is a way to know without having *learned*. No document holds the fluid information welling up inside you each day. What happened thousands of years ago is not as important as what's happening now in this breath.

Open your mind and heart to the fresh, ever-new revelations always 'broadcasting' from Source. These epiphanies, along with the surprising, delightful discoveries that a peaceful mind and loving heart inevitably encounter, are meant specifically for you. No one else's answers, no matter how wise, are *your* answers . . . so reclaim your trust in *yourself*.

Your 'higher' Self's guidance is directed to *you* and is needed for your life *now*. No book—no matter how sacred—can ever impart this special blessing or the timeless knowing that forever lies within.

The gift of true freedom that humans have long desired can indeed be claimed and accepted . . . but only when heart and mind are joined in union. A heart and mind in conflict cannot hear God's revelations nor fully feel the comfort of his love—they cannot know the happy state of Oneness. Hence the importance of recalling once again the invaluable blessing of peace, which opens the door to reclaiming all the treasures that it sometimes seems are lost within the challenging earthly experience.

But whatever trials you may face, remember well that *you are not the body* and all worldly suffering, as with all worldly pleasure, will pass. Never were you limited by the body or the mind, and *knowing* this truth is salvation.

Lastly . . . dare to be yourself. Your *authentic* Self. Don't be enslaved by dysfunctional cultures that never truly encourage authenticity and wouldn't survive if they did. Walk in the knowledge that you are free—a sovereign, immortal being—for only simple ignorance would keep this veiled. If you don't already do it, bring your natural divinity to the flow of your daily life, and savor the many fruits of living in the glory of this heavenly power. Always respect the paths of others, but never stop following your own. In learning to live joyfully as your truest Self, you will change the world with miracles, alter the course of history, and sway a constellation of realities far greater, far more dazzling and brilliant, than anything of which you ever dreamed . . .

Epilogue

I awoke that evening to a million chirping crickets and the constant rattle of cicadas throughout the woods. I was sitting alone in my chair by the river—the second chair now empty, as it was in my pre-visit dreams. Still groggy, I checked my watch. A little after ten. A wondrous sense of expansion left me eerily free of the usual limits of the earthly space-time continuum . . . I felt I was something quite new.

Marveling at what was happening, I was confused, to be sure. I recalled quite clearly, however, that I *seemed* to have spent the entire day talking with Jesus. In our last few minutes together I had asked him to guide me in a short meditation. He agreed and suggested that I close my eyes and focus easily and gently on breathing. As I did, he spoke softly of the "energy dynamics" of the breath and how it does much more in its function than science at present can grasp. He explained that breathing deeply "with awareness" can be life-changing all by itself. This was the last thing I registered, and some time into the process I must've dozed off.

As more normal consciousness returned, a still-rising, nearly-full moon would gracefully beam enough light for me to gather my stuff, load up the truck and head back to town, where I'd rented a cheap motel room the prior evening. The day's demands had caught up with me and I was dead tired. Despite my enormous fatigue, however, I did not sleep well that night.

☙

I arrived home two days later, on Tuesday, around 8 pm. Road weary and mentally exhausted, I had struggled on the long drive back to understand what happened that day at the river. Was I delusional? Could I *possibly* have had an all-day conversation with *Jesus*!? Reaching no firm conclusion, I chose to forget it and focus instead on unpacking the truck and taking a long, hot bath before bed. Hauling things inside, I grabbed the small duffel that held the few hundred pages of scribbled transcript from that mystical day in the woods. If nothing else, I thought, at least I had the notes for some small reassurance that the meeting did in fact bear truth.

I pulled out the ream-size box into which I'd hastily thrown the thick stack of handwritten pages on waking by the river that night. Until this moment I hadn't really given them much thought. But now I was forced to have a quick, soothing look, hoping to glean some comfort from them just before hitting the sack. The notes, after all, were the one piece of proof I was sane.

Placing the box on the dining table, I removed its cover.

Suddenly I froze, barely able to move or think. There before me was the full conversation, word for word, but gone was the entire shorthand transcription of the day's dialogue—no scratch of penmanship remained. Instead, the pages were fully typed-out in my favorite font . . . as if they'd been just freshly coughed from my printer minutes before. The kicker? The pages weren't even wrinkled.

I stood there staring and stunned. So shocking was this sight that what vigor remained in my bone-tired body seemed to drain from the soles of my feet—like someone pulled the plug on my electrical grid. Helpless with disbelief, I shuffled, near-stupefied, over to the calling sofa, practically fainting as I sat.

The rest of that night is a blank and I did not stir from the couch until Wednesday mid-afternoon, having slept more soundly—and awoken more peacefully—than I had in many years.

Over the following months, as my story began making the rounds, I often was asked by Christians, and sometimes with anger, how I could *warrant* these claims. Wondering if they ever voiced that same kind of doubt at their religion, I would dive into lengthy specifics of the meeting, desperately telling skeptics of my honor and my earnest recording of facts. Most of them left unimpressed. Finally I gave up and began offering a *simpler* response and the one I should've used all along.

"It's the *inscrutable* mystery of God!" I would tell them with a smile.

And who can possibly argue with that?

Resource Materials & Acknowledgments

"There is nothing new under the sun," says the writer of Ecclesiastes. Likewise, some material in this book has been spoken of or written about by others across the last two millennia, and after more than thirty years of Christian study I cannot always recollect the source for a given line or concept. On top of having plenty of 'cosmic' assistance and insight in this regard, countless books and other writings were utilized in creating this complex manuscript, and the following ones have been quite influential:

- *The Jesus Mysteries* by Timothy Freke and Peter Gandy. This was *The Daily Telegraph's* Book of the Year in 1999. The footnotes section alone is an education in itself.

- *Jesus Christ, Sun of God* by David Fideler. An academic masterpiece. Packed with fascinating, in-depth information on the symbol-rich 'paganism' that came to form so much of the Christian religion. This work is especially recommended for those intrigued by the information in Chapter 61 of *Wrestling.*

- *I AM THAT* (Talks with Sri Nisargadatta Maharaj). This Indian saint, like Sri Ramana Maharshi and others, is considered by many of his devotees to have been a pure embodiment of the enlightened soul. In these marvelously transcribed interviews, the words of the Maharaj are as powerful, cutting and transformative as any I have encountered. A worldwide spiritual classic for the serious seeker.

- *The Power of Now* by Eckhart Tolle. This book is no secret among the metaphysical crowd, having now sold millions of copies in several languages across the globe. Helped by his many appearances on "Oprah," Tolle has become a true world teacher and has led countless humans to their first real understanding and experience of the liberating power of "presence." A beautiful, long-needed blending of East and West, this is, at last, accessible spirituality for everyone, and my heartfelt love and thanks go out to this man.

- *A Course in Miracles*, published by the Foundation For Inner Peace. The first truly life-altering book I ever read. Especially useful—and challenging—for those who operate primarily from the intellect. As a brilliant scholar once declared upon first encountering this astonishing work, "Only someone like Jesus *could* have written it."

- *A Course of Love,* by Mari Perron. Thought by some to be a kind of 'secular sequel' to *A Course in Miracles,* Perron's inspired work is every bit as powerful as *ACIM* and even more directly addresses the critical issues of our modern-day world and our spiritual relationship to it.

- *The Invention of the Jewish People* by Schlomo Sand and Yael Lotan. From the Amazon product page: "A historical tour de force that demolishes the myths and taboos that have surrounded Jewish and Israeli history, [the book] offers a new account of both that demands to be read and reckoned with."

- *The Naked Bible: The Truth about the most famous book in history* by Giorgio Cattaneo. I have chosen to list this book last because it is nothing short of paradigm-shattering, especially for those who have grown up in or around Judaism or Christianity. My own book, *Wrestling with Jesus,* was written from the perspective of the *surface* forms of the Jewish and Christian traditions as most of us were given them by the two religions. Sadly, nearly all of it is distorted or, frankly, downright false. In *The Naked Bible,* author Cattaneo interviews Mauro Biglino, one of the premier Bible and ancient language scholars of our time (and a man the Catholic Church itself has long officially consulted for clarification of the earliest scriptural writings) as he breaks down various parts of the Bible into the rawest, most accurate —and most shockingly compelling—presentation that I am aware of. Without this information, the average Bible reader really knows almost nothing about the actual truth of its contents, and one must conclude that Biglino's work is indisputably world-changing.

Thanks are due as well to authors Anthony De Mello, Malachi Martin, and to the Truth Seeker Company for their generous allowance of the use (and ruthless mangling) of the original "Open Letter to Jesus Christ" by D.M. Bennet, founder and first editor of Truth Seeker. Through their books, lectures and writings, many others have unknowingly contributed to the development of *Wrestling with Jesus,* and if I have failed to credit where due, please write us at the publishing group's e-address on the copyright page in the front of the book and we will try to fix legitimate oversights or errors in future printings. Lastly, I am deeply grateful to the Universal Divine for always filling my needs over 22 difficult, doubt-filled years during which this book evolved. Perhaps I am living proof of these famous old words:

"Whatever you can do or dream you can, begin it.
Boldness has genius, power and magic in it."

Made in the USA
Las Vegas, NV
27 June 2023